The Cruelty of Magic

Shawn Amick

CONQUEST PUBLISHING

A Conquest Publishing Original

Conquest Publishing

https://conquest-publishing.com

Copyright © 2024 Shawn Amick

Cover Design: Abigail Baia

Map: Victoria Diaz

Edited by: Brittany McMunn

Paperback ISBN: 978-1-962739-26-9

Hardcover ISBN: 978-1-962739-25-2

eBook ISBN: 978-1-962739-24-5

Dragon's spine

Ansei Mountains

The Lost Woods

Cravenwood

Anseilia Forrest

Field of Bones

The Woodland Sea

Dwaharim

Kaiya

Magic Folk & Characters of Kaiya

Acolytes of the Deep – Agually priests

Agualyte – Water wielders

Airwei (Wind Rider) – General to Harigamun

Ansei – Silver-skinned elf

Arimeus Santar – Runefall's Chief Runic & Runic Councilman

Asmodeus (Pyrosi) – Stolen child of Runefall

Balooffi (Dwarf) – Grunffi's father

Bancala the Scaled – Kaiya's largest dragon ever known

Barigund – Head of the Runic Council and Commander of Runefall

Barklo (Dwarf) – Member of Grunffi's company & Saroria's brother

Belia (Agualyte) – Stolen child of Runefall

Beror (Dwarf) – Member of Grunffi's company & Bulroar's son

Bulroar (Dwarf) – Member of Grunffi's company & Beror's father

Crytungr – Frosted fowl of the Northern lava caves

Dagora – Dragon titan & son to Dremhirra

Dalias Lanis – Commander of the Runic Vanguard

Dhamri (Dwarf) – Member of Grunffi's company

Dire wolves - Beasts who roamed the North, reaching upward of ten and twelve feet high, if spotted upright

Dremhirra – Dragon titan & father to Dagora

Dwiddli (Dwarf) – Dwarf of the Northern lava caves

Draguar - Descendants of the High Wyvern

Elias Harkor – Commander of Runefall

Flaurin (Ansei) – Grendalla's brother

Furin – Chair of Commerce of the Runic Council

Galantis – Master General of the Runic Army

Gaiara – Earth wielders

Gayllen – Titan, the Final Son

General Toak – General, leader of the Woodland Army & Protector Among the Trees

Gnomes of Dragon's Deep

Golem – A being created entirely from inanimate matter, usually clay or mud

Gremanhas Silverskin (Ansei) – Kyra's mentor & teacher

Grendalla (Ansei) – Leader of the Exiles of Raknar

Groff (Golem) – Groffrick Heilimdower, Champion of Beliria, Steward of Unhoused Souls, & The First and Final Golem

Grunffi – Dwarven King

Gwalli (Dwarf) – Dhamri's second in command

Haffi – Dwarven Prince

Halorin (Mystic) – General to Harigamun

Harigamun (Pyrosi) – Warlord of Kaiya

High Wyvern

Hirkar (Gaiara) – Stolen child of Runefall

Ikba (Dwarf) – Member of Grunffi's company

Krabella (Dwarf) – Member of Grunffi's company & Skolgrim's wife

Kyra (Ragi) – Runic magician

Litree – Small, bronze-skinned elves who live in the South

Melro – Gnome of Dragon's Deep

Mystics – Telepathic magic wielders

Litree – Small, bronze elves who live in the south

Ograas – Dwarves from the South

Premus Hydik – Historic Librarian and Spell Keep of Runefall & Runic Councilman

Psions – Mystics who can perform mind control

Pyrosi – Fire wielders

Ragi – Rune magic wielder

Rocco Frapor – Commander of Runefall

Roki – Reaper of the Lost Garden

Samiel (Litree) – Companion to Kyra

Saroria (Dwarf) – Dwarven Queen & Barklo's sister

SeaHorse – Stags of the Agualytes

Shade – Conjurer from the dark elven tribes to the far East

Shalix – Chair of Agriculture of Runefall & Runic Councilman

Sheiba – Grendalla's jungle cat

Singher (Pyrosi) – General to Harigamun & Second in Command

Skolgrim (Dwarf) – Member of Grunffi's company & Krabella's husband

Sodsheim (Gaiara) – General to Harigamun

Thorns – The garden's army, those loyal to Roki, and the life he seeks to protect

Tir Vari – Scribe of Salaril the Rune God & Runic Councilwoman

Titan – First beasts ever created and bent to the voice of Baylar

Turmin – Architect of Runefall and one who constructed the Wall of Turmin, Runic Councilman

Varelia – Daughter of Varus

Varin – Runefall's Lord of Summons & Runic Councilman

Varus – Father to Variela

Whaleback (Agualyte) – General to Harigamun

Wind Riders – Air wielders

Gods of Kaiya

Ada – Wife of Dwarahir

Baylar – Beliria's husband & God of Summons

Beliria – Baylar's wife & The Shackled Maiden

Dwarahir – Creator of dwarves, called Dreadsmith by Baylar

Harei – Matriarch of creation

Ishmail – Brother to Salaril, Lord of Dreams, Prophet to Kaiyar

Krishalla – God of Lightning, King of the Gods

Larina – God worshiped by the Mystics

Raknar – Blood Lord and Beliria's lover. Leads two tribes: Exiles and Nomads, who both practice blood magic

Salaril – Brother of Ishmael, Lord of Runes & Creator of Runefall

Salarilias – Priestess of Salaril

Uvanion – Lord of Water

Locations & Landmarks

Cravenswood – Woodland area outside of Nightfall

Court of Flowers

Dragon's Spine – Birthplace of the Dragons

Dragon's Deep - location within Dragon Spine

Dwarahir's Forge - In the depths of Dragon's Deep where Dwarahir carves his dwarven creations

Dwirehall - The entry cavern within Dragon's Deep

Dwaharim – Home of the dwarves

Dwalham - A great dwarven city in the South

Fields of Dagora – Land outside of Runefall

Larina's Veil

Nightfall - Home of Varus and Varelia

Northern Lava Mountains – New home to Grunffi's company

Pyra – Birthplace of the Pyrosi

Riverbed – Home of the Agualytes

Runefall – Hidden city created by Salaril

Stained Temple - Temple of Beliria, otherwise known as the House of Summons

The Lost Garden – A separate realm for summoned creatures

Unda'Hearth – Home to the Crypt of Kaiya & House of Demons

Vari – Birthplace of Varus

Dedication

To Mamaw Sandy,
Three books in, and she's still the only one in the family to read them.
Thanks for loving my stories, but mostly, for loving me.

CONTENTS

1. Before the Storm   1

2. The Return of the Ogre Dwarf   16

3. The Mad Scientist   32

4. The Cruelty of Magic   50

5. The Warlord of Kaiya   66

6. Baylar in the North   85

7. Kyra's Chance Meeting   106

8. The Mad Sculptor's Death   124

9. A Divided Council   146

10. The Slaying of Gods   168

11. Kyra's Burning   188

12. The Golem's March   208

13. The Call for Giants   227

14. Dwarahir's Burden   248

15. The Lost Garden   270

16. Breaking the Seal   290

17. The Clay Dragon   307

18. Smelting the Ogre   330

19. A New Age   337

20. My Final Thoughts of War   348

About the Author   351

CHAPTER ONE

BEFORE THE STORM

A message from a god is quite like a message in a bottle. The message could be important, but you never know who it's coming from. If the message from Runefall proves false, I'll be sure to kill its messenger.

— Harigamun, *Thoughts of War*

Two young guards, hardly men, stood gazing with nearly picturesque tranquility into the luscious plains of a field seemingly untrodden, and they knew that picture to be a lie.

As the silence around them lingered, crickets sang into the fading darkness while flowers dreamt of the sunlit morning, the drowning night's breeze growing stronger, turning to a bellowing gust.

"There's a storm brewing," the Agualyte said, looking at rain clouds not far off in the approaching darkness.

"You're no sorcerer," growled the Pyrosi, who was also not a sorcerer. "You can't commune with water any more than I can whisper to fire. Don't speak to me like them clouds tell ya their plans!" he spat and turned away.

Neither of the two guards were capable of such magical acts—for most people of Kaiya were not capable of wielding magic, nor were the vast majority in both of their respective armies.

"I'll not speak for the other cities," replied the Agualyte, "but we all have an affinity to water in the Riverbed. Though you are correct, I cannot bend it to my will. I still hear the streams, though, and tides are turning."

But the Agualyte wasn't being truthful. He couldn't hear the streams any more than the Pyrosi could translate embers from a flame.

The Pyrosi scolded his counterpart with a smirked groan of mockery while gazing into the night sky. An unusual amount of starlight had descended upon the open plains before him, enough to curiously study the harrowing clouds above.

"A bit odd, yea? Don't ya think?" the Pyrosi asked.

"What's that?"

"Such power," the Pyrosi continued. "Harigamun. To have such power, all the power in one army. It's not just the—"

"Yes," the Agualyte answered, "I suppose it is. One man ought not be able to conquer so much…"

The Pyrosi guard shot a glance toward the Agualyte with the intention to cause cowardice, for his counterpart's words bordered the lines of treacherous conversation.

"And when the city falls?" the Pyrosi asked, trying to probe but not necessarily expecting to be given the delicious information he sought. Indeed, such a revelation into the ever-frustrating mind of the Agualyte army would be something *war-changing*.

"Yes?" the Agualyte pressed, intending to force the Pyrosi into asking something more direct.

"Will you and yours still follow? Will ya remain loyal to Harigamun?"

"Ah," the Agualyte quipped. "Will the Agualytes of the deep continue to bow to the Warlord of Kaiya—our sworn enemy?" He sighed, wanting to say a great many words, all of which were too meaningless for the ears of a Pyrosi. Instead, the Agualyte turned back to his companion and simply asked a question in return. "Will you?"

"Perhaps you're right, ya little barnacle," the Pyrosi chuckled while crossing his arms and avoiding the question. "Them clouds are behavin' awfully strange."

"It's the bones," the Pyrosi said, changing the subject. "They call out queer portents wrought for that damned city!"

"The bones?" the Agualyte asked, unsure of the Pyrosi's meaning. "I'm a long way from Riverbed. What bones do you speak of?"

"This," the Pyrosi outstretched his arms toward the plains before them and gleamed a taunting grin, "it's the Field of Bones, it is. We've marched here for more reasons than one, boy. Varin, Lord of Summons, has brought us here for great calamity! It'll be fire and death when we find that city," the Pyrosi looked up to the sky, "and it seems as though we've found it–Runefall's time has come. Harigamun will take more than just his army by the end."

The Agualyte knew the monster of which his condescending companion spoke, yet, said nothing. Rather, the Agualyte turned toward the clouds, the Pyrosi's incessant words drowned out by a growing breeze, and he pondered what the end of this conflict would be...and if he would see its end.

The peculiar clouds gathered—quite intentionally—circling the untouched field of splendor before the bandying boys playing men at war. The plains separated two large forests from one another. Unbeknownst to the two soldiers, the storm gathered directly over the hidden city of Runefall.

Arimeus rushed through the streets of Runefall and toward the council meeting meant to determine Kyra's fate. As Arimeus passed scrambling merchants, each of them in a state of panic, he wondered whether or not the city's ruling council had the right to decide this young woman's fate, especially with Harigamun's army surrounding the hidden city.

The thought of the Warlord surrounding the city hadn't been enough to stagger Arimeus's hopes, however, the Warlord had recently laid a watchful eye on the fixed position of the city. Arimeus knew the city could stay safe behind its great Runewall, hidden from the prying eyes of the Warlord through rune magic. But Arimeus found himself wondering, *are we truly hidden if eyes sit upon us?*

As he ascended the steps of the grand stone halls of the Council Chamber, Arimeus gave deep thought and regret to the choices made of late, and of many years ago on behalf of the city. In particular, considering the Warlord's army at the gate, Arimeus doubted whether or not Runefall should have taken those children all of those years ago—even if it were a god who told them to do so.

"To prevent war," the god told Tir, who had shared details with each of the council members over nineteen years ago.

Arimeus's doubt had only grown over the years, but he could not stop the city from following the order of a god. But it was not Arimeus alone, on the day of The Gathering, challenging the kidnappings. Not a single council member agreed then, and likely, not a single one backed the decision now—Arimeus knew he did not.

Perhaps we should have given people more of a choice, he thought. *Was it a mistake to centralize the power of magic? Did we need to trick the rest of the cities and towns into allowing us to keep all of the books and scrolls? Did we have the authority to make these decisions for the rest of Kaiya?*

Years of searching by Harigamun, the Warlord of Kaiya, led a fearsome army to Runefall by the leaked word of one of the few merchants allowed to enter and leave the city. Arimeus had heard of the merchant's discovery by the Warlord, but there was nothing to be done. The merchant was likely dead or perhaps worse by the time the news had reached the city. Arimeus considered whether or not it was folly to think they could remain hidden from the rest of the world. Or at the very least, remain safe.

Was this inevitable? Arimeus thought as he ascended the last of the many stairs before him, dreading the upcoming council meeting.

Arimeus entered the chamber and took his seat, finding all the other members of the council had already arrived. His gaze trailed slowly across the stone slab which had been carved into a table by great dwarven smiths decades ago. It served as a remnant of time passed; before the city and all its men turned against dwarves, before Runefall cut itself off from the rest of the world at the word of a god, and long before Arimeus knew where his own surprising role in the war facing them would be.

As he sat, he breathed long before speaking at length. "I am beset with the memories of failure, condemnation, expulsion, segregation, and in the worst of my moments, adulation. You all, myself included, are here to decide the fate of a young woman, Kyra, who wields runes in ways this city has long dreamed. We are to cast her out into the world, have her chase shadows and hope, and to do this at the beckoning of long-silent gods. Hearken to me as I say, we have cast out the dwarves, condemned the silver-skinned, neglected the long lost halflings, and betrayed a far greater many more peoples than I have known. It is with this moment, this opening of the court of a once great city, that I hope to dissuade you from sending her out, for our armies will follow. We must keep to our walls, keep to our ways, and await divine punishment, should it ever even truly come."

Arimeus's words were met with silent stares for a few moments before the Chief Runic spoke once more. "Time has taught us the absence of gods." He closed his statement with, "We cannot allow the girl to leave."

Arimeus often exuded confidence, much as he did in the gesture. He could have wanted more in physical stature, for he was smaller than most his counterparts, but his reputation within the city commanded order when he spoke, and thus, the council listened.

Well-fit and worn from battle-hardened experience, the Chief Runic lacked neither the capability nor the will required to act with a forceful hand, but his words were often his sharpest tool.

"Forces have gathered their full purpose to march upon the city, and you would have us risk complete discovery?" Arimeus asked the council, racked with uneasiness. "Speak!! Lay claim to your words as I have done on mine and bear witness to the havoc they may cause, the lives they may surrender!"

"You would risk the end of an age, then?" Barigund retorted.

The stoic Barigund served as head of the Runic Council and Commander of Runefall, as made evident by the crest of a great and unknown rune sewn into his garb. His raised voice bellowed as if commanding the great alabaster hall before him. His voice seemed to grip the very stone from the foundations of the city, causing weakness and worry to those who might hear him.

"The girl's name appeared upon the carved stone. She must answer the call," Barigund said. "An age, our lives, and the lives of those who call Runefall home; they depend on us heeding this call and yet you stand cowering behind the Wall of Turmin."

Barigund Half-Hammer, who sat at the head of the Council Chamber, solemnly flapped his darkened garb which stood against the white, shimmering cloth of his counterparts. A pronounced beard dragged against the stone of a table, his hair ebbing as his gaze looked to the gathered lord, each of them silently stalling.

"Perhaps the walls have been too kind to us over the years, Arimeus Santar," said Premus Hydik, the Historic Librarian and Spell Keep of Runefall.

Premus had long cautioned the headwinds to befall their great city from hiding in the shadow of Turmin's Wall and always made sure to stand against Arimeus, no different than the current moment. The Head Librarian always had a scroll, a book, or a journal. Sometimes Premus would carry all three, such as this day.

"Perhaps, we put these spells to use and meet them openly." Premus's long lashes flashed his silver eye, accompanied by a coy smile meant to dismiss the fears of his opponent. "You Easterners, always so coy, so wry and so patient." Premus rose and leaned over the table. "In the West, we hunt! Perhaps you ought to return to where your wanton woes inspire the cowardice you seek."

"Perhaps you've spent too long in the study," Arimeus rejected. "Perhaps, in your studies, you've forgotten the toll we must pay for the practice of magic. Berate me if you must but generalize not. The East is no more the East than the West is the West. A direction nor the shape of your eyes gives no special circumstance to life."

Arimeus knew the cost of magic well, and the predisposition his counterpart had toward his heritage. The Chief Runic had paid magic's price time after time and felt a stinging loss each time that could never be repaired. Not with all the spells in Premus's library could the wounds of Arimeus be healed, nor Premus's hateful heart.

"I train them. I see them. The fear in the hearts of soldiers who loathe the thought of having to exact a true price to continue breathing. PERHAPS YOU'VE—" Arimeus rose from his seat with a growing roar quickly silenced by the Commander.

"Enough!" The Council Chamber echoed with the voice of Barigund. "It will be put to a vote. If needed, I will cast my ballot, unless you lot settle it amongst yourselves."

The chamber grew silent.

"The young woman, Kyra, has been called forth. Her name appeared upon the stone." Barigund stood to address the council with his mane flowing over the chest of his garb.

The council members grew restless. Eight of them sat tightly bound between fear and fury as they awaited the results of the vote.

"This moment only happens once in an age," Barigund addressed the chamber. "So, the stories say...The story upon the stone tells of a pilgrimage to the far east of the Stained Cathedral. This is where Kyra must go, though we know not to what end."

Barigund sighed and reclaimed his, gazing out to his fellow council members who sat below him around the rune-carved circle of adamantite. For a brief moment, staring at the table, he felt regret for the treatment of the dwarves. He knew he'd made the wrong choice then and hoped he wasn't making the wrong choice now.

"We know not what fell deeds await the woman's journey, as we no longer know a great many things due to our isolation. But we do know we risk all of the world if we ignore the prophecy," the Commander explained with a disheartened breath. "Tribes of magic have launched their offensive as rumors of our location have spread. The Wall of Turmin hides us from sight, but not fully from discovery. The choice is laid before you, the Council of Runefall."

Barigund looked to the host of lords before him with a cracked hope, yearning for the right choice to be made. Though, he was unsure what the right choice was.

"Open the gates for Kyra to leave and risk open war, or keep the seals of our wall closed tight," Barigund posited. "Choose to share nothing with the young woman and she will remain here as we all watch our age diminish and fade into yet another unwritten legend of the past. Let her out with an army at her back and we will surely all walk into a fiery chasm."

Arimeus jolted from his seat, nearly smashing his legs against the adamantite stone table. "There is still yet time, time enough to find another way to appease the foretelling of a doomed age," Arimeus said, his fingers tightly latched onto the table.

Arimeus Santar cast his vote to stay hidden, eyeing a smiling Premus as he walked to the ballot box placed before Barigund.

Next, Turmin, immovable and stoic, peered from his seat at his fellow council members. With short, gray hair and muscles abound from a lifetime of builder works, the architect trudged to the head of the table near Barigund and cast his vote into the oaken ballot hold. As he did, the old half-dwarf said, "We cannot beat them, brother."

Turmin also voted to remain behind his thick walls built all those years ago. His faith in its capacity to protect the city was as immovable as he was. All of the children capable of using rune magic, along with Arimeus and Turmin, toiled away for months sealing the city of Runefall behind his invisible force.

Arimeus and Turmin added other forms of protection against siege and allotted for hidden exits. Alas, to the regret of both the Architect of Runefall and its Chief Runic, the exits had a limited capability. Kyra would not be able to stay unseen by the Warlord for long, but she and the army at her back would have a head start.

Premus smirked at the Chief Runic and turned to the Commander. Making no move to stand from his seat, Premus cast his vote to open the gates by sending his ballot through the air with the use of a rune written onto the ballet. His inability to move for mere seconds was a small surrender to float a piece of paper. It seemed an unnecessary and childish option to Arimeus but seemed all too appropriate for Premus.

"What is the cost for such a lowly spell then, Premus?" Arimeus snarled at the careless use of magic. "I see you have no mind for consequence."

"I see you have no mind for risk! Fear not for my safety, my friend," returned Premus. "Such a small spell commands but a small price to use. Much like the decision to do a grander good rather than clinging to one's own thoughts of safekeeping behind bonds of stone. Nay, we need not stay here, much like we needn't fear the use of rune magic against those who mean to rid the world of our culture, our knowledge...our skill," he hissed at the last words.

As Premus finished his retort toward his counterpart, the Chief Runic noticed a small cut, no larger than a thin paper cut, slightly beneath the librarian's fingernail.

"Had that cut been there?" Arimeus said, recounting his past struggles with Premus.

"Who knows," Premus said. "I'm a withered man with old spells, much like yourself. Perhaps I gave up more than a moment of movement for the ballot. Perhaps there are always unforeseen circumstances and costs to our actions. What do you think the cost of hiding will be?"

Arimeus considered the words of his opponent, recalling their many years in competition. Was he merely standing in opposition, as the Head Librarian often did–out of principle to defy Arimeus–or was Premus truly convinced of his position?

"Perhaps, if you followed my guidance in the past as we rose through the ranks, you wouldn't have fallen as you did in your practice." Arimeus grinned then, knowing his effect landed.

"Fallen you say?" Premus turned to the Commander, but no movement nor sound came as he seemed resolved to let the course play out and, certainly, the rest of the council was ready and willing to watch a show. "Among the few as we were, gifted as some are with the touch of magic, I rose to Keeper of Spells in the grandest city of all known magic, and you say I've fallen? Surely when matched against the Chief Runic we all must be so low. I focused on being proficient for war and you learned to teleport! It would be the acme of ignorance to question that decision... surely." He looked to the commander.

"When one wins battle after battle by closing gaps impossible for others, it's hard not to reward that which brings victory," Arimeus answered. "You fought, I led. When you were focused on glory and name, I saved, healed, and infiltrated. I cared for our own! You cared, and continue to do so, for yourself. Disagree with me if you must but do it for something beyond petty hate."

Premus did hate and he hated well, so well in fact, he was prepared to watch the city fall to stand against Arimeus; but it was not purely out of hatred for Arimeus, indeed, nor was it the majority of the librarian's reasoning.

"I stand against you and the wrong doings of this city, Arimeus. I vote against you because we are, continue to be, and were wrong. We had no place to do what we did, and now the city must pay. I'm done cowering. Either the army of Runefall marches against this threat, or Premus Hydik does so alone!"

Next, Furin, the Chair of Commerce, pushed his chair backward and allowed enough space for his large torso to rise from the table.

"Commerce is a difficult thing to manage...without trade," Furin said. "These walls have kept us long enough, I say," he spat. "The city of Runefall grows crops from within Turmin's walls and what cannot be grown is supplemented with the aid of magic, which is rarely accomplished by me. The crop capacity of all Runefall never seems to be enough for growing. It causes much resentment in the city for myself, as I'm not quite the magic wielder the rest of you seem to be. And when trade fails, as it has of late, I'm left to take the stinging hatred of the crowds. I do this, gladly, and at the behest of your lead, dear council." He bowed. "Although this is not the life of prosperity Runefall once knew, I take refuge knowing at least the city and its people survive."

Furin, being of large stature, overabundance, and a want for the unnecessary, long missed the days of trade and of want over need.

"However," Furin continued with his gruff voice. "I do not think we can continue to survive."

The broad-bellied trader announced his vote prior to depositing his ballot.

"Be damned with hiding! Let us feast once more!" Furin was heard throughout the hall as he came crashing back onto his hand-carved, stone seat and eyed Shalix across the table.

Shalix served as Runefall's Chair of Agriculture and allowed Runefall to survive without trade, though not in a glorious lifestyle. She was a woman of refined fashion, preferring efficiency over adornment. She stood shorter than all of the council and relied on a not entirely subtle form of intimidation as her position was too well understood as absolutely necessary. Thus, her title carried her in most circumstances.

Her cold eyes glared at Arimeus. "We have long passed the dying usefulness of my basic herbology fused with Agualyte magic. We are running low, dangerously so." She turned to Barigund. "Everything about this place, from what we claimed to be to what we claim to have becomes a larger lie by the day. There is no hope in this place. We have become targets for underground markets and shadow trades by those who prey on our weaknesses—the same predators who likely sold information to Harigamun!"

Shalix's darkened lips, with eyes molded by a forest of hazel warmth, commanded captivation upon the slightest glimpse, allowing her underhanded forms of intimidation.

"On rare occasions, the pressures I place on some of those underground markets are enough to slow them down, or in some instances, stop them altogether. But another always returns, and mercenaries don't come cheap. Our safety is lost, and our livelihood is false. I've thought better of you, Arimeus," Shalix said with condescension as she cast her vote to open the gates and release Kyra.

Arimeus tried to ignore the comment. The Chief Runic was not absent-minded, nor was he feckless with his vote, for he suffered more than any on the council by the unknowable consequences of magic. He felt the sting and stare of the council before him.

"Look into my blind eye!" Arimeus shouted. "For the sake of advantage in battle I was given this wound, a day I'm sure you all remember..." his voice calmed as the council beheld his white eye. "Rise Shalix and shake the cold hand of death." He outstretched his arm, offering to shake her hand. "For the mighty blow, I did conjure that day, I am now left with an unfeeling stub, the dying trunk of an old tree."

Then, Arimeus scratched a rune on some parchment and whispered some unheard words. Suddenly, the rune carved into his skull to hide frightful burn marks from seared skin as a result of stolen spells he took from his father's study as a child seemed to stop working—his burns were visible once more and he was a pitiful sight.

As the scars faded into view, the spell which wrought fire upon the house of his parents and their servants, and even scorched much of the wildlife surrounding his family's once great hall, became a living and felt memory for Arimeus. The Chief Runic's mother did not survive, and his father would carry the burden of guilt unto death.

Typically, the rune carved into Arimeus did not allow the growth of hair, leaving a long white mane on the right side of his head, with the facade of only slightly scarred tissue on the other. But now, those slight scars from only moments ago were a viscous and ugly warning.

"If you must call me a coward then do so!" Arimeus's fist slammed onto the stone. "But do not idly walk into the fires of war..."

Arimeus knew the risks of keeping the gates sealed, but what would be the risks of fighting? How many would suffer from the cruelty of war? Arimeus, however, was not the only one to recoil at the notion.

Galantis, Master General of the Runic Army, was not the typical military leader, and he did not plan on giving a typical vote for his position.

"I stand by the lives of my people," Galantis said as he voted to keep the gates closed. The Master General knew it was likely the vote would see the gates open, but he wanted to make sure his voice was against the decision. To Galantis, the world might end if the prophecy was unfulfilled, but Runefall would surely fall if the gates were opened. "The Blood Wars, the Stone Crusade, the Silver Death. We've had no wars with just cause in the hindsight of mortal eyes. This would be no different. This would be no better. My army may say I'm strong and battle-hardened as the dwarves we slaughtered for fairy tale stone, but I have no wish to use those strengths, nor those skills, for the rest of my days. I have scarce few moments of sleep in the night, thus, I will not risk the small comforts in life that remain to me for this petty prophecy."

Beside Galantis, the markings of a dampened quill could be heard

beside the Master General as the chamber's scribe kept record of the
hearing.

Tir Vari—Scribe of Salaril the Rune God—was a woman of silence
and highly valued when she took the time to speak, if she took the time
to speak. Small, she kept to herself mostly by hiding her beauty beneath
the cloak given to her by the council.

As Tir raised her head, her small sanguine eyes flashed by torchlight,
captivating her audience as her incandescent and rubicund gaze always
did. Out from her cloak sat the showings of great white hair, not as
beaten and worn such as Arimeus, but vibrant with youth. Each member
of the council, as well as all who saw her, be they man or woman, found
her features irresistible.

Even still, Tir considered herself an abomination. Both for her
appearance and for her decisions, the Scribe of Salaril felt little more
than shame. A brush with exiles years ago left her eyes permanently
afflicted—distorting the colors--with the presence of blood magic after
peeking into the mind of a blood mage.

Tir had served as the vessel to the divine for Runefall, but their
tellings had gone silent in recent years, as had Tir. She rarely spoke except
where conviction was involved and conviction fled her those nineteen
years ago, the night of The Gathering. Tir was the only one among
the ruling council who still truly believed in Salaril's messages, even if
those messages hadn't been heard for years, and even if she doubted that
day. For his voice always seemed so resplendent, calming, and altogether
arousing for her. In fact, none knew Salaril's divine voice, in a way, held
her heart.

"Salaril's silence leaves many questions," Tir warned. "Namely, what
could cause his silence?" Tir rose from her chair as a battered child bereft
of companionship. "This...uncertainty, gives me concern this may not be
the only fight to come. The risk is too great."

Tir voted to keep the gates sealed.

"I miss my lord and his words. I miss much that was given to us for a time. There is little to know in this life and, I fear. I am beyond meaningful learning without a teacher." Tir looked at each council member. "Forgive my isolationism, forgive my ignorance."

As the scribe cast down her ballot, she felt an unfamiliar dread, as if she'd done something wrong. Or maybe the feeling wasn't wrong at all, but as though Salaril disagreed. Not having heard from him in quite some time, she ignored the feeling as all of his previous communication was intentional and direct. Tir turned back to her seat, giving her eyes to Barigund, awaiting the final decision.

Barigund sighed deeply as he peered at his ballot. He knew why the vote had fallen thus, but the circumstances did not make it easier to accept the weight clearly falling onto his shoulders.

"So," Barigund let loose a weighted breath, "we have decided."

The Commander thought about challenging the vote, as he held the power to do so, but it would just allow for more discussion, more arguments, and more pointed malcontent between those he cared about as they voraciously defended their positions. The decision had been made, and he would not contend against the will of the council...no matter how much he wanted to. "We shall keep locked the doors and pray the walls of Turmin continue to serve us as they have in days past," he said with a sorrowful look. "None shall tell the young woman."

Murmurs covered the chamber in a shroud of doubt and suddenly Arimeus rose from the table with a swiftness unlike any other council member had ever seen of him before.

Where might he go, I wonder, thought Premus as the others bickered. *Surely, he intends to stay hidden, as his cowardly vote suggests. Where does someone so failed run to but for the halls of cowardice?*

Chapter Two

The Return of the Ogre Dwarf

"The Ogre Dwarves of old would have served me well in this war. The weapon of all weapons, the destructive hammer against creation, the blade that cuts divinity. Now all that is left of them is a tale. Even the Ograas which drove the dwarves from the south hold no resemblance to the true meaning of the word–Ogre."
— Harigamun, *Thoughts of War*

Grunffi's father told tales of lava mountains, though not many of them spoke to the mountains of the north. In fact, armed with so little, he did not know of the northern mountains, the dwarf prince had made an error. Rather, a grievous, guilt-stricken decision laden with death, discomfort, and pain; yes, that was the decision Grunffi had made for he was horribly unaware.

The tales Grunffi recalled spoke of long-dormant mountains–sleeping hot rock. As the mountains in his father's tales never bled with lava. And those mountains *certainly* held no scarlet hue above them...

A cloud of blood, it, Grunffi thought as he first set eyes on the mount. *And so, doom has followed.*

No, the mountains Grunffi recalled were quiet mounds of earth, warm with the dampness of a tropical forest to its south, and often surrounded by wild and unmanaged vegetation.

That range of childish tales was not the one which greeted Grunffi. Nor did he find a forest of warmth waiting far off into the depths of the south. There was a new barrenness to the land down there. Slightly out of reach from the entrance of the cave, a warmth could be felt on the ground which kept the blizzard at bay.

"No. There's no warmth here, no hearth. This be something strange, foul even," Grunffi said, stepping one foot onto the barren land. However, the heat did not stretch very far from the cavern entrance. "We'll not survive this relentless tempest," he shouted, turning to the rest of his kin, "we make camp in the heat of the mountain!"

"Damp and hot caverns, or an unforgiving blizzard. My, oh my," a scathing voice said, "the leadership of the dwarves surely knows none better!"

Grunffi knew the voice. It was the same voice that always scolded him, haunted him, degraded him–*Dhamri*.

From the wide earthen roots holding the great mountain before him at the base of his new home, Grunffi gazed upon the erubescent peak of the lava mountain, ignoring the chastising comment from Dhamri. A cathartic beauty merging with a primal fear rose within Grunffi as the mountain groaned.

After a few hours, Grunffi organized scouting parties to seek out the deeper holds of their new home whilst those renowned for their hunting skills gathered near him. Additionally, the builder dwarves made the best of the resources left to them to scrummage together something resembling a home within the cavern.

"Aye, friends," Grunffi said to the surrounding hunters. "It'd be quite the sight for us to find some juicy meat taking refuge near this blasted hot rock hole, wouldn't it?"

The dozens of dwarven hunters released deep-bellied laughs before their dwarven king.

"Yes!" Grunffi continued with a great breath. Let's find us a Grand Hide! Surely one of them fat-bellied bastards lurk in the snow." He laughed, as did the other hunters.

Great-maned with wide tusks, the Grand Hides stood higher than ten of the shortest dwarves stacked on top of one another. The beasts could move at frightening speeds quite surprising for their sheer size. Yet, their bellies were soft and low hanging, swinging like that of a loose sack covered in thin hair.

"I'm taking one for meself!" another dwarf shouted. "I like the balls!" He licked his lips sarcastically, bringing forth more laughter.

"Yes, Barklo," Grunffi said, "we know your appetite."

The dwarves had grown accustomed to the taste of Grand Hide over the last few weeks of journeying. Leading to the mount, they were something plentiful in the right spots. Indeed, those belly-filling behemoths were the only thing Grunffi found comfort in since their expulsion from Dwaharim—the invasion of the Ograas—for the Grand Hides were thicker and tougher in the South, though these were mere scraggly reflections of the fatty beasts he once loved.

"Long-axes at the ready!" Grunffi looked at one of the dwarves holding a stout little bow. "Come on, lad. You know the arrows aren't of much use."

The Grand Hides forced the dwarves into a new form of weaponry, a great long ax. These new weapons were quite low in number as the unending gale surrounding them these past weeks prevented most attempts at crafting, though a good dozen of them were circulating among the fighting groups.

Grunffi's own axe was in his hand. He stared at it and simply called it by name under his breath. "Bari."

The long axes varied in length, some held reach beyond four or more typical dwarven arm lengths while others were much larger. Grunffi, being a fright larger than his kin, bore his monstrous long axe which seemed almost unnatural to his brethren.

Grunffi held his axe with him while addressing the hunters and dug the blade's hilt into the ground beneath the weight of his bearing. His hand rested upon its unique bladecraft which consisted of a double-sided battle-axe, straight, pointed edges stretching from three points–both sides and the middle.

With a great growl, Grunffi ripped his ax from the ground and pierced the air above him, shouting "Let's hunt!"

The dwarf exuded a confidence comforting to his hunting cohort but feared the worst of what was to come. *Too many have fallen to the cold...the ice doesn't belong here. We need furs, we need Grand Hides. We need—*

The dwarf's last thought was interrupted by the latest condemnations of Dhamri.

"Of course!" yelled Dhamri. "Let us hunt together! In fact," the dwarf cast down his long axe, "let us die together in the frozen wastelands of our fearless leader's false promises!"

Grunffi kept his lips tight. *One day... soon.*

"How many might you lead to death this time, King?" Dhamri bowed as only a thespian could.

Indeed, the dwarven party's dozens of members fell far below what used to be hundreds when the dwarves originally headed north.

"You cast no guilt left uncarried," Grunffi answered with a low voice. "If you're offering anything beyond contempt, such as guidance, we are here to listen."

Dhamri grunted but mostly remained silent, almost intentionally stoic.

"Those we have will continue to have my heart." Grunffi continued. "If mine beats," he turned to the hunters, "then you have companionship. Beyond that, there will surely be darkness. Just know you will not walk into it alone."

The dwarven hunters hoisted their weapons and followed their King into the storm, Dhamri last. It was a strong party, numbering just thirteen.

As Grunffi walked out into the maelstrom, he started to see something, though he knew, or thought it to be untrue–for how could it be true? As it was a haunt of his past, albeit a recent past. He saw Silver. A glimmering silver just beyond the veil of endless snow with pointed ears and the deadly sirenic voice of death.

The sight haunted him, robbing him of rest far too often. The deaths of his kin clung to his ankles like shackles, weighing down each decision and each moment of silence, and those shackles were tied to that silver glimmer. *The Silver Shadow follows me.*

"So that's it then?" asked Dhamri as if he were asking a question rather than questioning Grunffi's judgment. "Near to nothing more than a day in the warmth of a cavern and–" Dhamri shivered and called to his surrounding guild with pervasive eyes and a crooked smile, "suddenly all is well enough to return to a forsaken frost and hunt a beast which may not even show itself?"

The challenging dwarf stepped to Grunffi, nearly standing equal to his opponent's head, but not nearly enough. For, in his rashness, Dhamri found his eyes set on the chest of a dwarf a fright larger than himself with boulder-like shoulders. Still, the opposing Dhamri's features gave no sign of fear or impunity.

"You're not short of wit, lad," Grunffi said. "But by the Builder, you sure do act like you are."

The leader of the dwarven company looked down at Dhamri, as down as he could at least for they stood near equal in height, and Grunffi beamed with disgust and rage. The two had shared words on more than one occasion as Dhamri fancied himself the wittier of the two. Possessing wit with formidable strength not easily matched by the other dwarves,

Dhamri considered himself the rightful leader.

Dhamri glared at his King. *Nothing more than the winner of a blood lottery*.

In Dhamri's mind, and his heart, his king was nothing more than a strong arm holding a sharp blade. He thought his people deserved better. *It's not enough to hold a sharp blade, a leader needs to also have a sharp mind.*

"Death to Ograas in the South and frost to the North. Death to Silver Shadow in the West and the hatred of men in the East. You hold the blame of our folly! Your own grave will be marked as the bringer of the end for dwarves..." Dhamri spat.

"You'd take nothing more than a sharp ax and hope into this ferocious storm which has already taken more than enough of us at your hand," Dhamri called out. "And now, whilst we've managed to find a warm hole, you'd throw us back into the squall! What've ya got planned after that Grunffi?"

The hunting party chattered amongst themselves so loudly that words could not be discerned. However, it was clear to Grunffi that discontent was in the air, and it was felt by more than just his opponent.

There was little food left in the cave. Scraps of frozen meat from a bounty captured near a fortnight ago were still available, but it would be a while before they could be thawed. The scraps would hardly be enough to ration the small army of dwarves which still numbered near thirty in the mountain.

"I'll not force the lot of ya back into the cold," Grunffi said, turning toward the gale alone. "Stay near the warmth." His words ended as he felt no need to continue the discussion. It was right for them to want to stay, to be warm, to feel their blood pump as it should. Grunffi wanted those things too, but he wanted to be assured his people would be fed even more.

"I'll go," Grunffi said lightly, walking away. "There's not enough food to feed us all, and I'll not watch younglings go hungry this night if I have a say in it. Should you lot wish to cower in a hot cave with Dhamri, then do so! But leave me out of it as I have mouths to feed and hope to foster."

Grunffi sighed with deep pain as he placed his hand in front of his face and realized how difficult it was to see. It would be nearly impossible to find a Grand Hide and certainly, it would prove impossible without the help of a hunting party.

I won't beg.

"Not alone, you won't," rose a low voice.

Grunffi turned to see his old friend.

"Barklo, I might have known you'd still come," Grunffi said with a slight grin, speaking louder as he was outside of the warm entrance of the cave, only barely stepping into the squall.

Barklo was more than just a friend to Grunffi. In fact, Barklo was the closest dwarf to Grunffi outside of his wife, Saroria. Barklo's connection to the dwarven royals was in part due to Barklo introducing them two decades ago, though when Barklo introduced Grunffi to Saroria, Barklo did not expect his oldest friend would wind up marrying his sister.

Barklo was a well-fashioned dwarf, though to his own kind he had a queer look about him. Whilst most dwarves kept a rather unkempt appearance, Barklo preferred to use a short blade he crafted to routinely cut his hair and beard. Grunffi, in contrast, had an almost straight mane running from chin to chest, deeply braided and laden with stone, but Barklo wore a trimmer cut on his face that seemed too well sculpted for a dwarf.

"Can't have you coming by with fables to my sister about cowardice now, can I?" asked Barklo. "And she'd never let me sleep if I let her Grumpy die in the snow."

They shared a laugh.

Four others from the hunting party stepped forward to join the hunt; Bulroar and Beror—a father and son—along with a dwarven couple by the names of Skalgrim and Krabella. The rest of the hunting guild walked back into the mountain as the hunting party marched their way into the glacial hailstorm. Those who returned to the caverns found Saroria's scouting and building parties hard at work.

"There's a scent of fire in the air," grumbled Haffi. "Embers spark against the darkness of the tunnels further in. Somethin's here."

"It seems we were not the first to seek refuge in the hot mountains," Saroria muttered with a low voice, trying to remain unheard by those who might already be dwelling in the mountain.

"Mother, we ought to turn back," Haffi said.

"I've always joked that your father is named Grumpy. You seem far too in likeness that I should have named you Happy, instead of Haffi, though his be true while yours is…well. For that might have been the only way you'd be happy considering you carry the same foreboding weight of judgment and grief that burdens your father," Saroria said.

"Those who chase escape to the darkened places of the cavern and fire, so beyond the reach of normal dwarves and men alike, much as this blackness, should not be trusted," Haffi said.

"My son." Saroria reached a hand to his shoulder and met his flashing yellow eyes. "We chose to escape here, too."

"And we should not be trusted by the likes of others," Haffi said with regret, rising from his crouched position within the shadows. "For I have not but death and judgment left for the world."

Saroria fought back tears, not recognizing the man before her who was once so filled with passion. *I am sorry you lost her*, she thought, and wanted to scream out, but knew it would do her no good.

In fact, in the moments Haffi caught his mother offering him silent sympathies, he often did the same for her. Neither of them bothered to share unnecessary words, for the hurtful darkness swallowing their hearts was beyond the reach of condolences. Instead, Haffi often repeated the same line over and over when he caught her broken gaze looking for help—*I should have been there. I should have saved him.*

The two turned behind them to see a great gathering of dwarves shuffling in the darkness awaiting command and doing all but holding their breath to remain quiet. Saroria and her son routinely led scouting parties as they had a quick, light-footed traversability about them mostly unknown to dwarven people—a gift of hunting in the wilds while others toiled in mines.

Furthermore, Saroria was nowhere near in size to her husband, but she was thick and brawn with a wide bearing. She could battle with some of the strongest and out-think the most cunning. Even still, no living dwarves considered Saroria to be less capable of battle than any other, not after her darkest day in Dwaharim.

The dwarven matriarch of the company wielded two normal battle axes, one for each hand. She fought like a berserker with a ferocity few could contend. In standard fashion, Saroria kept a clean-shaven face by the use of small blades each day, and long hair shaved down to the skin on the sides and often accompanied by oils to hold it in place. She liked to prepare her hair in a variation of patterns depending on her expectations of battle for the day. For instance, exploring the darkness of the lava mountains, Saroria's hair was braided and bunned.

Haffi, however, was almost diametrically opposed to his mother in every way and resembled much of his father. He was one of the few bald dwarves. He took the time each morning to shave, but he was rash and impatient, and so he boasted many cuts on his hairless head for a lack of care in the process. He rarely felt the pain due to the calluses formed from mistreatment of his already hardened skin, a trait common to dwarves. His beard, beaded by his mother many years ago, still held.

Haffi made routine weekly attempts to dissuade stray hairs from diluting his beard, and for the most part, it did look far more well-kept than the vast majority of his kin. Additionally, one other attribute, aside from his garment which had far less coverage than the typical male dwarf in order to show his muscular build, were the weapons he bore—one long-spear, and one short-spear, which he made. There were no others in Grunffi's dwarven company, over its many years of existence, who used those sorts of weapons.

"A dwarf needs an axe," some would tell Haffi. "Or a sword at least. Spears are for dancers, merry folk!"

Haffi hadn't felt merry in a long time.

"Must we wait for the hunting party?" Saroria asked.

"Too many dwarves make too much noise," Haffi answered. "We go forward and do what we must before they come... and make this mountain ours."

"Do what needs to be done." Saroria repeated the words in her head and her thoughts became haunted with fear for who he'd become. *He's so willing to take from others. Can I condemn him? He takes for us...*

Would this path allow Haffi to become a great leader, one who uses his unquenchable thirst for force as a means of authority against those who would take from those he loves? Or might he wield force and strength as a means of control toward the purpose of subjugation? Saroria had never seen behavior that would suggest the latter, though Haffi's capability to do so could not be argued, and who Haffi *was* seemed to be fading away.

Haffi turned back to his company and stood resolute like a blood-lustful Bahnin, something his father had taken to calling him of late. He turned slowly and slightly to his front, where the notice of embers reflected off the obsidian lining of the cavern wall. With a controlled and light thrust, Haffi pointed his long spear toward the light.

"Let us see who our neighbors are," he whispered with a grimace as the dim light from behind him revealed only a portion of his weathered face. *Give me reason to die! Send me where I belong.*

Slowly, the dwarven company approached the fire deeper in the bowels of the mountain. The company had scarcely traveled less than a day within the mountains so far and found no signs of life within. The food the dwarven company brought with them dwindled as the rations from the last Grand Hide proved to be scant, as the beast was only a calf.

"Meat," whispered a dwarf behind Saroria. And the dwarf was right. Meat hoisted onto a pike laid across a ripe fire, though it brewed an incorrigible smell. Saroria's instinct was to turn, to run, to grab all of her people with her and head back to the mountain's mouth—but she heard the sounds of her kin, the need for comfort.

Perhaps it was the scent of warmth resting on the cavern stone mixed with the swirling dust of the place. The stone was something altogether new to the dwarves as they preferred their grander stones of fashion, such as; diamonds, amethysts, sapphire, emeralds, and others. This stone was black, and though dwarves knew the obsidian well embedded into the walls, the small mining already started by hobbyists within the dwarven company revealed some new stone below the black rock which seemed to be the largest material lining the cavern.

"They've gone and left the meat! Perhaps they heard us and ran off, m'lady," said a muttering dwarf behind Saroria.

Haffi's eyes glinted as embers filled his bright-yellow eyes and a loathsome frown overtook him as his brow folded into itself with anger. He was looking for a fight, and the cowards had run. While others wetted their lips for meat, Haffi was altogether consumed with a wanton calling for savagery—a need to die bloody and for the right reason.

"I am quite starved, m'lady," groaned the talkative dwarf once more. "May hap I could try the meat, just to make sure nothing is amiss. Can't have anything happening to you now, can we?"

Saroria looked to Haffi who was already holding a scowl toward the muttering dwarf. The weak thing continued to make a mockery of himself with his small mouth chattering about his appetite.

"Let the weak one go," grumbled Haffi. "I'll not eat anything smelling like that. Ikba's death would hardly be a loss." The words were said loudly, proudly, and outright with harmful intent, and the weak dwarf clearly heard them.

Ikba skulked his way into the empty chamber. He passed the edges of the wall blocking the view of the broader dwarven company, taking notice of many, many fires roasting meat. The damp heat of the cavern made approaching the fires even worse for Ikba. He felt a stream of sweat swell from brow to toe and removed the pikes from the fire. Desperate for food, he gave no thought to its temperature and sank his yellowed teeth into its char. Struggling at first to chew the meat, Ikba cringed slightly at the ore-like taste of the distasteful meal. After a short moment, the weak dwarf raised the pike to his company and pointed it, and the meat, toward the large, open room of meat-covered fires signaling for the other dwarves to join him in his feast.

"It tastes like veal!" cheered Ikba with celebration, which he quickly muffled. Suddenly, the company of dwarves shuffled as quietly as dwarves could and hastily made their way inside the chamber.

Saroria and Haffi stayed back taking small steps to the front of the chamber where the other dwarves speedily entered. Just under two dozen dwarves spread across eight fires viciously pulling and prodding to take meat from the pikes. The distinct lack of sustenance the past few days had made the dwarves overtly appreciative, though many sat wondering who it belonged to as they feasted. However, none thought more of the meat's origin than Haffi... who grew restless.

"Eat light," he warned, "for honor fled these shadows long ago. Desperation lingers, and we shall meet it."

But they did not listen. The dwarves ate, and they ate, as dwarves do—heartedly.

Some eight hours or so passed and many of the dwarves slept on the ground after their meal while some spoke of unpleasant feelings in their stomachs. Haffi and Saroria did not eat and were left to wonder if the meat wasn't fully cooked through.

"It shouldn't matter," Saroria said.

"Dwarves and their stomachs," Haffi agreed. But he couldn't think of anything else that would cause such an ailment.

Then, out of the far side of the chamber leading further back into the mountain, a creature emerged from the shadows. It stood the height of a shorter-than-average dwarf but lacked the fortitude. Once fully into the light, the unkempt hair, long but thin beard, and stature allowed the surrounding dwarven company to reach their conclusion before the creature spoke–it was a dwarf.

With his teeth chattering, the grim and garish dwarf from the mountain's belly spoke to the scouting party with a raspy voice.

"So, you've come to take my home, then?" the gangrenous dwarf asked.

"No, sir," answered Saroria who stepped forward to meet the dwarf. "We simply seek shelter and a place to call home. We have suffered much on the road getting here and fear we have no place to return. Other races of Kaiya have unfairly judged us and there is nowhere else to go." She turned to Haffi, looking for support.

"This is why we came to the northern lava mountains," Saroria continued. "We do not wish to take part in the coming wars of man and elf-kind, nor do we wish to continue to be tormented by the growing Ograas in the South."

Haffi peered around the mountain chamber and looked for signs of dwarven presence as his mother spoke with the shambles of a dwarf in front of her. He stepped closer to the wall to study the rock and he confirmed a sneaking suspicion he made not an hour into the start of the scouting expedition—the caves were carved. Haffi didn't want to startle anyone at first because he wasn't sure, but now he knew the suspicion to be correct.

"Where are your people?" shouted Haffi as he turned to meet the dwindling dwarf. "I dare say a dwarf as frail as you could scarcely have carved this mountain hall yourself. So, tell, friend." Haffi scowled with a half-hearted smile. "Where is the rest of your kin?"

The frail dwarf laughed. "Yes," he giggled. "You'd be right to say I could hardly have accomplished this great hall," chittering flowed out of him with indiscernible words, "myself."

Haffi walked to the side of the mysterious dwarf, placing a hand on his shoulder. "What is your name, and where have you come from?"

"Well, those I've called kin through the years have always called me Dwiddli," he answered.

"And where might we find those kin of yours?" Haffi asked with a forced smile.

Saroria noticed a growing frustration in Haffi's eyes. *He's going to kill him.*

"Those left sit further back in the caverns," replied Dwiddli. "It saddens me to say few are left in better shape than I."

"Aye," answered Haffi. "I dare say you might be one of the smallest dwarves I've seen in a great many years." His grip tightened on the frail dwarf, forcing a frail whimper.

"It was not always so, sir," Dwiddli said with a soft sadness, trying to pull away from the tight grip. "I was once one of the largest of my company. I was great and strong and could wield an ax better than the best! I was taller, too." Babbling followed by an odd laughter. "I was bigger in many ways!" He winked at Saroria.

"Taller?" Haffi scoffed with a scowled laugh, tightening his grip so hard he felt the little weakling's bones. "How've you shrunk then?"

"Ahh," Dwiddli filled with a dry laughter once more, trying not to squeal. "You think dwarves are like other creatures then? We should just grow until we're grown and then never adapt? Never change?"

Saroria and Haffi both seemed utterly confused as they looked at one another. Saroria turned to view the rest of her company, most of which had lain down for rest, assuredly due to a reaction from the meat.

"We grow and shrink to meet the needs of our nature," explained

Dwiddli with a smile. "Dwarves are the most adaptable race on Kaiya."

This statement shocked Haffi and he let his grip go. Could he shrink if his circumstances demanded it? Better yet, could he grow if nature allowed it? *How might one grow to fight death? There is more to this.* "Speak!" Haffi yelled. "Speak not of riddles and chittering! Be useful or begone, and I do not mean back to whence you came..."

"You've a great number of dwarves with you," Dwiddli said. "So, think for just a short moment. Consider who is the tallest, the largest among you, and then consider the shortest. Where do they spend their time?"

Haffi thought to himself for a moment and considered both his father and Dhamri. Grunffi spent most of his days exploring the woodland areas when he could, which was quite different from the typical dwarf. In the same vein, Dhamri had spent the last thirty years or so stoneworking for Dwalham, a great dwarven city in the South. At least, it would have been a great dwarven city had it not been sacked by Ograas.

Then, Haffi thought, he often accompanied his father and also was known to do stonework within Dwalham. He spent a little time in the darkness of the mines but not often.

Saroria mirrored the same behaviors as her husband and son. The tallest among them spent a larger amount of time outside of the mines with quicker access to food and drink, and in the same fashion, were typically among the strongest. Though many of the hardworking miners were also incredibly strong from the hard labor of the mines, they were just smaller in stature with an unwavering stoutness.

"And what circumstances might we need to adapt to live in the lava mountains?" asked Saroria as her son worked through a new understanding of his people.

"Well, I'd suggest not relying on the hunting of those great beasts with furs that are known in the North," Dwiddli answered. "Perhaps, best be open to a new kind of diet." He laughed as a manic might.

"Why's that?" asked Saroria, thinking of her husband in the cold, distrusting of the nasty Dwiddli in front of her.

He's done something foul...

"Once you've gotten yourself too close to the mountains, you're in the domain of Crytungr," warned Dwiddli with a grim haunt about him. "Best not to wander round his part of the mountain."

"And who is... Crytungr?" Saroria asked with a confused look. "What part of the mountain belongs to him?"

"The Frosted Fowl, a winged beast thought lost to the ages," Dwiddli looked to the roof of the cave. He spoke as if the great beast might break through the mountain. "If a great bird such as an eagle or phoenix were to ever armor itself with the scales of a dragon, it would still not be as menacing as this beast. Crytungr is all of those things and more, for he is hardened by a pure crystallized skin that looks like metallic ice! Many dwarfs have died wanting to touch the bird and craft from its skin. But its wings measure in meters, its talons are beyond the reach of axes, and its great shrieking call deafens those of weak heart. The mountain belongs to Crytungr. All of it! That is why we are here."

Saroria looked at her son with immense fear. "Go, get your father!"

Haffi took hold of Dwiddli with one fist grabbing the tattered cloth remains on his chest. "If anything happens to my mother, you'll not need to fear the bird any longer. I need no reason to kill you. I only need reason to let you live." And with that, Haffi raced off to save his father.

I'm coming, father. The North was a mistake!

Chapter Three

The Mad Scientist

"With the Lord of Summons at my command, I will have the power to bring life back to that beast's sacred old bones. It will be mine to control, like the mindless golems of legend."
— Harigamun, *Thoughts of War*

The city of Nightfall, which once represented the vibrant artistry from each corner of Kaiya, was left destitute and in darkness. Painted black it was, with most dwellings nailed shut, hiding away some of the most vile creatures and people across the continent. Varelia knew each fine, corrupt cranny of the place, but she knew the sewers best of all.

A petty and corrupt City Watch trolled the streets taking advantage of the unfortunate and few innocents still scraping by whilst the majority lived a low life of miscreant skullduggery and mischievous moral ambiguity in gray shadows–and the gray shadows are where Varelia called home. The city had become a prison where it once represented the finest expressions of freedom and life, but even in such darkness, fear kept her from fleeing; fear for herself, but mostly, the fear of losing her father kept her trapped.

In the sewers of Nightfall, Varelia's father scratched away at a parchment by candlelight muttering to himself, hoping to finally give life to creation–meaningful, lasting life.

"Dragons are gone they say? Ha," he grumbled. "Dragons and dark beasts, the gobby women and hard folk of yore. No, no they can't be. They won't be. I won't let that happen, no!" He coughed from a breath taken too quickly, as those with madness often might.

"They don't have the scrolls," he continued muttering to himself. "But I do. I have the scrolls!" he continued chittering about in the darkness. "Well, *a* scroll. My scroll. But this one will work this time. I *know* it will."

A loud crash alerted Varus as broken glass shattered behind him.

"Who goes there?" he yelled. "Stray yourself from my darkness, intruder, and I may yet let you leave!"

Nothing from the darkness returned his call, although he did notice a leg from his dilapidated table missing. The broken glass lay in shambles.

"Reveal thyself from my shadows or feel my wrath!" Varus leaped with fury into the air, crashing his ink-soaked quill onto the sewer floor.

Without warning, a rat dumbfounded Varus as it streaked from behind the table to his quill, packing up the writing utensil and running away leaving Varus stunned. "Be damned with you, fool! There is no story of worth nor turn of phrase desirable by that which comes from a rat!"

Immediately Varus thrashed about, tossing the tattered table aside and breaking its remnants searching for the hairy thief. "The scroll is almost complete, you farce of a vermin!"

He then noticed a small hole in the wall toward the direction the rat escaped in. "You've done it in for yourself now, my lad! Hah!" Varus towered over the stone slit in the wall cackling at his imminent victory over the petty thief.

He fell to his knees and shoved the scroll into a pile of mud before starting a prayer–a prayer of beggary for a scroll of desperation, a last attempt before succumbing to unexplainable failure. At least, Varus couldn't explain it, and therefore, the failure seemed beyond unjust. So, here he would conquer this small beast of burden with his own creation, or he would abandon the goal with admittance that he would never attain even enough skill to defeat a thief... a rat.

Thus, spoke Varus.

"To the chained goddess, I pray

Look upon your child this day

I pray for you to break your chain

Form this clay for mine own pain."

A pile of clay, looking nothing more than a puddle of mud, formed into a boxy creature which seemed to melt, die, or some mixture therewithin. Madness and obsession joined to create life. This life, this ancient something of grim ways, had come by the hands of Varus! He was a sculptor of old, a maker of clay men!

Varus shouted to the creature, "Bring down this wall! Cripple the thief of my night!"

Promptly, the clay beast moved toward the wall, splashing its degrading form upon the floor with each step as it groaned, seemingly, with intolerable pain. Its voice whirred in the dark as a creature born of no purpose. It moaned as its steps grew ever closer to the wall housing Varus's great thief of the sewer. Seeing the foulness of his own making, Varus knew the beast would die, and die soon, but life was necessary for death, and he had made it that far.

Varus took a deep breath and released a final command, "Break down his walls!"

Forthwith, the creature burst upon the walls, splashing clay onto Varus's tattered linen trench coat, spilling onto the floor, and into the thief's hideaway. After a moment, the clay receded from the rat's treasury and brought both a drowned rat and the treasured quill with it. But the creature was gone, after so short a time—nothing more than the puddle of its initial becoming. Death had come for Varus's new life. His heart had longed for more and now panged with loss.

Varus studied the puddled clay with contempt and misunderstanding. "Why can't you live?" Varus would often shout following his failure to keep the creatures alive for more than a few seconds, but this one was different—this one moved; it spoke of a sort.

"What must I do to create a true and powerful golem? You give me no sign! No such word from God nor devil dares lead poor Varus to meaningful purpose!" He was convulsing again, breaking anything, he could find, and lighting up the darkness with his tirade. "Take, take, take from Varus! Yes, take from a withering man again! My wife? No! Not enough! You must also try to steal my daughter!" He spat and was in tears, frustrated at his own failure. "Lo, the damnation of Varus is the condemnation of one, the suffrage of all who might wish to call forth a great and terrible golem! Alas, for nothing!" Remaining table parts, still partially put together, went flying. "Be damned with the ugliness of divinity then, Baylar!" He cast his recently recovered quill to the side of the chamber. "I'll consign myself to the failure of it all then. I'll call forth no golems and hold no faith. Be damned with you!"

After a final look upon the quill thief, Varus took a restless seat on the ground. Abruptly, Varus's howls had scoured the sewer walls by this point, but even still, a new terror rang through the sewers when the madman accidentally scraped his finger on broke wood, giving him a splinter.

It was not a mere splinter which broke him, but his constant inability to bring forth a golem paired with the stupid splinter, and his inability to escape the sewers. It was the unknowable circumstances awaiting him if he did manage to escape once again paired with the safety of his daughter... The circumstances and possibilities were too many. Thus, there in the tiring gloom of forgotten sewers, Varus let out a final pious roar. "Set me free from these chains, Beliria!"

"Baba," cried out a voice from the darkened tunnels. "Baba, who do you call for? Have they come for us?"

Upon that moment, Varus glimpsed toward his daughter. She wore similar tattered cloth to her father, though her garb was much more worn with dirt and wetness. White eyes glistened contrasting brown skin layered under darkness; her black hair pulled back as it always was when she journeyed to the surface.

Varelia's eyes were a light blue, matching her mother's...as Varus would rarely say. Perhaps it was the darkness that kept Varus from seeing her eyes unless the moonlight was prominent—as it was in this moment—prompting the memory, or perhaps it was the prompting of memory causing the man pain. Whatever the case, Varus would seldom revisit the haunts of his past, nor his daughter's.

Just talk about her, Varelia thought. *Just be honest with me about her and feel something!*

She knew why her father was set on summoning a golem. Both of them knew it would likely be the only way they could escape Nightfall alive. It mattered little, however, because Varelia never truly held onto hope for long that her father would openly have a meaningful conversation with her. No, he would keep them trapped down in the sewers and refuse to speak of her mother. Darkness and suppression, to Varelia, seemed to be her father's chosen path over the risks of the world.

"I've stolen some bread and a quite plump chicken. The merchants never give me a second look these days," his daughter explained. "I think they're well past hunting thieves in Nightfall."

"Many things are well past Nightfall, Ibna," Varus replied with disheartening sorrow. "If there's one thing to be appreciated this night, it's that I have a thief next to me in the sewers." He winked.

Varus looked painfully at his daughter, ashamed of the circumstances of their living and their absence of a true home. Then, Varus turned his eyes to the drowned rat, taking a light snicker at the comment of being close to a thief—he often considered himself humorous and made it known when Varelia wasn't acknowledging his quips.

Still, Varus couldn't risk the dastardly authorities of Nightfall catching onto their thievery.

"Blood brings blood," said the City Watch, and Varus would hear it when they walked overhead as he wandered the sewers. Indeed, they'd do much worse than drown Varus in his own clay if he were found out, and he tried never to imagine what they'd do to his daughter.

But it has to be done, Varus would often reassure himself, for he had to talk himself into the idea of trying to leave daily. *This is no life for one such as she.*

Varus had drifted off for a moment, contemplating his consistent failure with the golem, the consistent pain he knew he forced his daughter to endure.

"Will you tell me about her?" Varelia asked. "You never tell me about her." She had asked many times before, but her father always managed to dissuade her from the conversation.

This night was different. Whether it was the chasing of the rat, the endless failed attempts of creating a golem, or simply life in the sewers becoming too much...Varus knew he was running out of time with his daughter in the sewers. She deserved a better life and her constant wanderings to the surface to steal food were no longer enough. In truth, he knew it was never enough, and that eventually the air up there would taste too fine.

She's right, Varus thought. He couldn't remember the last time he spoke about his wife. While most wanted to preserve the memories of those they'd lost, Varus would only feel hate when his wife's name entered his thoughts. He grew hateful of the city for falling to Raknar's brood. He felt hate for Runefall for all they'd taken from him. But most of all, he rued the day of The Gathering and all who were responsible for it.

"Yes," Varus whispered to himself before looking into his daughter's wet eyes. "I—I suppose it has been some time since we've spoken of her.

Come, sit with me."

Varus turned and realized his earlier thrashings would make it difficult to enjoy dinner, so he quickly constructed a makeshift of what he served as a dinner table and then pulled a chair from the dank corner of their abode for each of them, which was in a separate chamber. "Ahem," Varus cleared his throat after hurriedly crafting the laughable dinner table. "Now, sit with me."

Varelia had learned to pay no mind to her father's outbursts, as they were never directed at her. Though, she always pitied her father when she knew a fit had come about. Most would see madness if they saw her father desperately trying to create life from clay, but Varelia only saw the desperation that brought her pity for her father—her baba. He was calmer when she was around, but she'd hear the clamoring madness welling within him when her father thought he was alone.

Varus sat for a moment and looked into his daughter's eyes as he struggled to find a deserving description for her mother. "Varelia, would you like to know the greatest crime ever committed in the lands of Kaiya?"

Varelia cocked her head slightly to the side, unsure of her father's intention.

"The theft of your Madar's love," Varus answered his own question softly. "You were robbed of the most perfect experience of love I've ever known, and I'd dare say that anyone has ever known."

Varelia was saddened and inched her chair closer to the table. She outstretched her arms to the center, or what was left of it, in hopes her father would reach for her hands. In that moment, Varelia longed for an embrace, even one so small as a holding of her hands. However, her father had already become lost in his thoughts. *Let me in. Let her out! She deserves to be spoken of...* Varelia would not hold her need to speak of her mother, not today, not again.

"I'd have done anything to save her, truly, I would have. This was never meant to be the life you'd live. Scrounging upon the darkened, hollow sewers of Nightfall is no such way for a girl to have a living." Varus drifted off and rose from the chair, muttering into the darkness.

Varelia couldn't make out the words, but she honestly didn't need to. The feelings of her father were obvious—regret, fear.

"Why do we stay in the sewers, Father?"

Varus snapped his neck back toward his daughter as he regathered himself, realizing he'd wandered off into the darkness of his mind. "For the secrets your mother bore," Varus replied, a heavy weight in his voice. "A heartless, hasteful hate clawed at her ankles in silence and shadow."

Varus's entire body shivered and chilled as if his spine had split in two. Aches took hold of his chest and suddenly he fell to the damp ground beneath him, crashing in a pool of sewer water.

Varelia watched as her father fought to breathe, but he could speak no words. Seconds felt like hours as she watched unknowingly if her father would die in the darkness. She made attempts to lift him from the ground, even patted him on the back as if to break something free of his passageways and enable him to breathe. But it was all for naught...Varelia watched her father struggle in the filth of the sewer and felt the proximity of death with its irreverent gelidity.

However, Varus raised his head and saw tears bubbling in his daughter's eyes. Air rushed into his lungs as the panic subsided and in a moment, he stood once more.

"Are you alright, Baba?" Her breath trembled, still full of fright. "I won't ask again. I promise!"

Yes, I—" *It's been a while since I let that happen*, he thought, shaking off his dizziness. His chest had seized within a moment and dark thoughts took hold of his mind. He'd returned now, with his daughter in front of him, of sound mind and stable heart; but there was a foreboding nature surrounding them. His willingness to live could fade away in an instant if she was not near to distract him, to remind him, to bring him back.

"I sometimes forget, or try to forget. The remembering, you see—" Varus searched for a cup of water while his hands shook, and a cough rose. "Remembering your Madar—" he coughed "—causes me great pain, Varelia. Not because—not because I do not, or did not, love her. No, that—*that* could never be true, nor will be true. For that, I fear, will always be part of me. The knowing and remembering what she did, and why she did it... That pain will never cease to follow me."

"What did she do?" Varelia's eyes widened as tears dropped, shimmering in the fractured light of the sewer. "Why have you never spoken of this? You told me she was taken to prison for fighting the City Watch when they tried to take me in The Gathering. Is there more? Speak, Baba, please. I need to know her."

Varus pondered for a moment, losing sight of the fact he stared at Varelia, making her feel greatly uncomfortable. He lost sight of her in order to see his wife—they were so similar to him, nearly identical in the bright light. "Forgive me. You know how sometimes I stray off." Varus turned back to the darkness, focusing his ears on the droplets falling onto the conduits around the bend.

"She saved you, Ibna." With a turn, Varus gripped the back of her hair, and pushed their foreheads against one another. "She would have always saved you. And I know she demands the same from me...I know she deserves the same from me. *YOU* deserve the same from me." His speech became muffled by tears and sobs as he trudged through a thickness of words. "It makes it hard to leave, Ibna. Here we can stay safe. We stay alive."

Frustrated with the answer, Varelia pulled away from her father with a hard push that almost landed him in the muck beneath their feet.

"What will you tell me?" Varelia grew angry. "How many years must I endure darkness and filth without truly knowing why we hide? Perhaps I should announce to the City Watch my name and see what they have to tell me? Perhaps then I might know the true fate of my Madar and why I am forced to live in the shadows with you! Survival isn't living! You have us waiting to die in darkness!"

Varus bent both of his knees and squatted low to the floor, placing his hand over his sweating and furrowed brow. A gap from the sewer's stones above allowed a beam of moonlight to escape, providing Varus a reflection within a murky puddle on the floor. With brown skin, far darker than his daughter's, Varus grew weary and fraught with tremors As he stared into a reflection of himself in a puddle by the moonlight peering into the hollows of the sewers through a gap in the stones above them–brown skin far darker than his daughter's–Varus grew weary and fraught with tremors. The chittering madness of a failing father overtook him. How could he do both, tell the truth and keep Varelia safe? Especially when Varus himself didn't feel as if he knew the full truth to tell.

Varelia tried and tried to pull him out of the fit to no avail. She knew a broken mind could not be mended by hands, and she once more watched her father's convulsions, knowing full well she'd been the cause this time. His screeching and aches of inner turmoil bled from his mouth like lava from a volcano, slow and dangerous. Syllables formed without meaning as a language unknown to her spilled off her father's tongue, a language he'd only uttered once before, and even then didn't know he'd spoken in a strange tongue when his mind came back to her.

When Varelia saw his eyes return to color and sanity, she tried to tell him not to speak, not to worry; continuing down this horrible path did nothing good for either of them. But he did speak, he did so loudly, and fast with pain.

"Alarms broke the night's silence, the last night of peace in Nightfall. In a single day, we went from the comfort of beds, lively fairs and parades of unparalleled art to fire igniting the darkness as the city became wrought with flame. The news came late from Runefall. They wanted every child born on a certain day, the day you were born. Your Madar wouldn't have it though. We heard the crier echo through the streets and knew we couldn't let them take you. It was the demand of some Kaiyan lord who wrote commands on a stone. *'And why should we be beholden to that?'* Is what your Madar had asked me. She didn't pay heed to those Kaiyans. None save Beliria, and she refused to answer us."

Varus watched her mouth form to ask the question as he interjected before the words came out. "Beliria, the Shackled Maiden."

"So, we ran away?" Varelia became more intrigued by the story, and she wanted to know everything. This was her father's first real speech regarding her mother, and she was not about to waste the opportunity. *I need to know.*

"No, Varelia. We fought."

Varelia's eyes lit with surprise. "Who did you fight?"

"The City Watch. They came knocking on all doors that night and had records from the town's library of who was born on what day. I was scared and cowering. but your Madar, she was strong, formidable, brave. She was ready to fight and break them. They knew about you, and they were coming to take you away and send you to Runefall!"

"So–" Varelia's voice shook. "What then?"

"Even then, I was no better than I am now with these damned golems. But your Madar commanded me to do what I could. And what I could, I did do, not because your Madar demanded it... but because she was right."

"You fought the City Watch?" Varelia yelled in shock, leaving an echo through the tunnels.

"Shhh—" Varus looked around and listened for movement in the gutters. "Yes, Ibna, but it wasn't—"

"It wasn't what?" Varelia grew impatient. She was getting closer and closer to the answer that had eluded her for years. "Please, tell me! You know I should know!"

"I didn't fight with my hands, Varelia..." his trailing voice signaled something sad. "I fought with your Madar's blood."

Grief, pain, shock, and a myriad of emotions stopped Varelia in her line of questions. She became stoic and sat still trying to understand what she heard, though the stoicism was short-lived.

"You—" Varelia whimpered.

"NO!" Varus's fist slamming against a rickety table shot through the entire sewer system and ruined what small hope of stability the tablet had left. "The most powerful form of blood magic can only be achieved through a mother's blood. I used magic to conjure one of my many failed golems, but this time, it did not fail! Your Madar wasn't cut enough to die, but it left her weak. I commanded the golem and left her hidden in the home. We thrashed about outside, destroying what seemed to be legions of guards from the city. It was unending and I became more and more convinced we could not hold them. I rushed inside to grab you while—" he coughed; his speech became tighter, more frantic. "The golem continued to dismantle battalions of guards which gave me enough time to hide you in the sewers. I returned to the battle with the golem to see—" a pause, a sigh "—absolute desolation! The golem had taken a mind of its own and became lustful for more blood. Violence raged within it as it ripped apart the guards and ate their remains, drinking what it could of their blood. Its savagery grew beyond my control." Varus took a deep breath and looked his daughter in the eyes. "Their fear of the golem became immense, and it was likely the captain of the guard knew how to counter blood magic, for Blood Rogues and all of Raknar's brood grew their presence in the city at that time, thus, they had good reason to know how to fight–we were desperate and damned."

Varus's eyes ran like a busted dam. Unending torrents of regret spewed from behind his eyes. His speech became stuttered, and guttural. "Suddenly, fire bit our home. Flames seared across all of our memories, our happiness, our love, and our life." Varus wept at this, taking a moment to come back to coherent speech. "With your Madar weakened from the immense blood loss, she could not run…but she could scream." Varelia sobbed and her speech became more difficult. "As she screamed, the cries became quieter, and the flames were beyond approach. There was nothing I could do. Upon the last of her breaths, I saw the golem begin to die. That's when I knew I needed to run. That's when I knew I had to get to the sewers—*we* had to get to the sewers."

Many moments of silence passed as Varus struggled in his poor attempt at repairing the table while his daughter wandered the tunnels near their home in the sewers. More formidable was she, thus, she often kept watch for them; being of quicker foot and sharper mind, she could survive… thrive even. "You didn't need to go after the chittering rat, you fool," he'd said to himself. "All these years, all this pain, and all you can do is conjure a ferocious puddle of mud." His furious speech turned to making noises more akin to the forceful chattering of the teeth than words until his relentless inane babbling and lip-swinging caused him to bite his tongue.

"Damn you, rat!" Varus heard a faint splash of water from the tunnels that grew ever closer with each second. "And behold, there comes shallow minds guided without their own thought—a soldier is a thoughtless tool."

"I'm sorry, Baba," Varelia struggled, trying to catch her breath, disturbing the water with footsteps as she came closer to Varus. "They must have heard me earlier. I'm sorry!" Her eyes were thick with redness and the weight of fear.

"It wasn't you," Varus regretfully sighed. "It was me who squabbled about over that damn quill. So much trouble over a quill, but then, a quill is never just a quill. I just wanted to get the contract right!" The shout was muffled but no less frustrated. "But that matters not for now. How far behind are they?"

"I heard voices, so it can't be too far. They'd have to be lucky to guess the right path to find us." Varelia felt a slight relief as it became clear to her, she understood the sewer while the City Watch was foreign to the intricate system. "We can make it out, Baba. We can run..."

"Brigands and thieves are all who hide about in these tunnels, might as well string 'em up right soon as we catch 'em," a fell voice grumbled in the distant air.

Varus turned to his daughter and his in a low whisper. "Gather your things, we must breach the wall."

Varelia's eyes bubbled with shock. "We've lived here so long because we didn't know how to get past the walls. We can't!"

"The release valve," Varus responded with a sternness, and what sounded like apprehension to his daughter.

Abruptly, fearing what her father had said, Varelia turned to gather her few belongings. So did he who once again searched frantically for his quill. In those short but rushed moments, the two collected themselves and once they made eye contact both knew it was time to run. They took off through the sewers moving their feet from one side of the curved wall to the next to avoid stepping in the water resting within the tunnels—they called it Sewer Stepping.

Unexpectedly, Varelia dropped her diary. It was one of the only items she cared to take with her and thankfully it did not fall into the water. The book caught itself against the sewer piping and slid down to the edge of the water.

However, Varus thought it might have been better had the diary fallen into the water. The metal clasp of the leather-bound book clanged against the piping walls and rang through the tunnels. All of a sudden, water trembled in the surrounding tunnels and voices filled the air as the City Watch came ever closer to Varus and Varelia.

"I want the credit for this one boys," yelled a low-pitched and raspy voice. "If they got a bounty on 'em, I'll be gettin' a promotion for hanging 'em."

The sound of a great waterfall filled the air as Varus and Varelia continued dancing through the sewers. Varus swerved through unnecessary tunnel paths while intentionally splashing the water where the chambers would split into multiple directions trying to misdirect the guards.

As the waterfall grew closer, Varelia tried to whisper to her father over their sewer stepping, trying not to alarm the guards. "Baba, you can't," but her voice fell on empty air beneath the continued trouncing of the guards and her own footfall.

Varus heard the waterfall's crashing grow closer and closer as they approached the valve, but then he started to slow. He stepped toward a wide opening with piercing light hammering down onto the basin before him. The great height of the sewer valve bled into Uvanion's Bed—named after the Lord of Water.

As Varus gazed into the rising sun that slashed the sky with shades of red, he pondered the height of the drop. *Must be over a hundred feet,* he thought to himself as his daughter caught up. A moment before the incoming reckoning gave only a slight respite at the deathly view of splendor. Trees far out and away were being overtaken by a rising sun as the river below flowed out toward the distance. The fall could be their end, but staying surely would be, and in this fearful thought Varus stepped slightly closer to the edge, a there he saw the deepest of all fears he'd ever felt. This was beyond a cliff and the scale seemed like that of a mountain, and his heart stuck with terror knowing his ibna was about to jump...

"You can't swim!" Varelia tried to whisper but her anger grew during the sprint from the City Watch, turning the whisper into a volumed condemnation. "How many have we heard of surviving this fall?"

Varus grinned at his daughter. "Those who'd make this jump don't do it to come back telling stories, now do they?"

Varelia became increasingly frustrated. "Is there no other passage? Is there no other way out from this?"

Her father turned back to the mystifying sunset and inched closer to the edge of the fall. Varus peered into the depths of the riverbed and could see pointed rocks pierce the river, awaiting the misstep of escapees hoping to make a safe landing.

The clamoring grew louder once more, and it became clear the guards were on their heels. "We've nowhere else to go. Look at the rocks below and do your best to avoid them. If you take a quick look, you'll see there are less of them there." He pointed to their left.

"How do I save you if you can't swim? What if I'm hurt and it's too hard to pull you to shore?" Varelia's voice was panicked and riddled with anxiety.

Then, a guard's voice rose from the edge of their tunnel; they'd been found. "Go on then, lads. Jump," the raspy voice laughed. "I'll just collect your bodies from the pool below. Your bounty probably doesn't care much if you're livin' or dead."

Varus grew impatient with his daughter. "I need you to jump!" The guards rounded the corner and met eyes with Varus. Immediately, he grabbed hold of his daughter and threw her as far to the left as he could toward the water.

"Jump then," the guard roared behind Varus as he struggled to gather his footing after barreling his daughter into the river. "I said jump!"

But then, Varus felt something pierce his left leg in an instant. A small jolt went through his skin as he fell to the ground, his hands and knees falling to the sewer's floor. His leg had a short spear that went clean through. He could not stand as the pain grew intolerable and fear overtook him. His daughter was at the bottom of the riverbed and now he could not make the jump—at best, he could crawl to the ledge.

"Go on then," the group of three guards cackled at Varus. "Jump!"

The three men walked over to Varus and kicked him toward the edge.

Varus took one last look over the ledge before he heard one final assault from the raspy guard. "I'd rather carry 'em back dead from the water. At least then we won't be carryin' his big ass through these sewers."

Finally, a great kick to the ribs sent Varus flying into the depths below.

In Uvanion's Bed, Varelia fought to climb to the surface of the river after launching her diary as far off to the shore as she could. While it hurt to swim from the deep cut on her side from an unseen sharp rock, she managed to get to shore. She turned and looked for her father at the edge of the release valve...and it was then she saw Varus fall into the depths of the riverbed.

Varelia could tell he did not jump of his own free will and knew something horrible had happened to her father. She rushed back into the riverbed as the pain from her side all but disappeared. She voraciously swam to the edge of the basin where she thought her father would have fallen. Into the water she searched for him but found nothing more than a snapped spear shaft.

"Baba!' Varelia cried in her search. She dove once more into Uvanion's depths, and this time swam all the way to the bottom of the riverbed. She held herself there and searched in all of the dark directions she could. With each fighting breath she mustered, Varelia lingered in the depths only to then race back to the surface of the river taking a large gulp of breath before returning to the dark.

Varelia's fear overtook her as her breaths became more strained. She cried out in search of her father. It became harder to hold herself afloat, her swimming strength long gone, and her cries forcing water into her lungs.

In that moment, Varelia knew she had to get out of the water before she either drowned or lingered too long for the guards to come. Exhaustion was taking over and her strength to paddle became difficult. The fall from the valve hurt and the possible loss of her father was unbearable. She painfully swam until she reached the shore of the river and cast herself upon the sharp, rocky ground. She coughed a bloody cough filled with water and struggled to regain enough strength to stand. Once she did, Varelia took a final look at the river and realized she still could not see her father.

But then, Varelia looked down shore and saw a body beating against the edge of calmer waters. The body wasn't moving.

"His mind languishes in my absence, falling prey to his haunts of the past–our past. His madness is staved when we are together, but I spend so much of my hatred on these sewers. Some days I pang with a mean dread—if I scare away his madness for him, will my own come for me when he is gone?"

— Varelia, *A Mad Diary*

CHAPTER FOUR

THE CRUELTY OF MAGIC

"If the Runic fails to bring her to me, I'll tear down the city without her. His treachery is a path, an option, not a necessity. His death will be determined by his viability."

— Harigamun, *Thoughts of War*

In the city, the Chief Runic--Arimeus Santar--broke from the council chamber in pursuit of a young woman. He meant to tell her a decision made by the ruling council...on her behalf.

The two had never met until that moment—Arimeus and the young woman—but being one of the members of the ruling council who would decide the young woman's fate, Arimeus had learned much about Kyra over the past few weeks. He had no choice, for everyone on the council had studied the young woman from the moment her name appeared on the stone at the order of Barigund.

The council watched as Kyra proved herself quite adept in the mastery of rune magic, surpassing all others who trained with her in their capabilities. Supposedly, the girl could cast spells without incurring the same costs others encountered when doing the same, and to Arimeus's eyes those past few weeks, it was true.

Alas, that was not all the old runic had learned of Kyra. He saw peace and serenity in the fair woman. She was disciplined in her meditations, calm where others stressed, kind when others shined bright with ego. She was all the best of her teacher, and to the eyes of the Chief Runic, none of the worst. *There is a coldness to her*, he thought, which he could not detail, nor would he ask of her teacher, for such words would surely bring fire and spite to the old silver-skinned elf. Thus, he continued to see her from the shadows as she studied, practiced, and kept to a clean regimen. She was the ideal student and were her empathy left to be unconsidered, she could be taken as... dangerous.

This was Arimeus's belief, that the Ragi was not entirely focused on her studies for the sake of Runefall, but for her own want of power.

The Chief Runic took to watching from afar to see how she managed to perform such power, but her secrets always remained just that... secrets. The young woman simply performed magic as if it were a natural expression of her physiology, like an additional limb no others possessed. She was gifted, and Arimeus was about to disturb her training.

Kyra sat in a meditative state across from Gremanhas Silverskin, her teacher.

While most outside of Runefall had lost the idea of houses and surnames decades before, few behind the Wall of Turmin, in Runefall, still held onto them. Gremanhas's surname, however, was more an open acknowledgment of his skin, and what he was, rather than respect to a familial name. Though, most didn't know what he was even though they treated him as one of the cursed, Ansei elves.

"One comes," the silver-skinned elder said to Kyra, disturbing her peace. "Be ready." He smiled as the last word left his raspy throat. His speech may have seemed weak to most, which served immeasurably effective as a deterrent to those without knowledge of the silver-skinned mentor. He was often regarded as unthreatening, someone to be protected. Adding to his feeble persona to a stray onlooker, Gremanhas was a man ripe with age. In fact, the teacher was among the eldest members of Runefall.

Kyra's eyes opened, the rumble of heavy steps approaching the double wooden doors of the temple gave her warning. She turned to see the cause of the footfall, and there he was. A sweat-stricken Arimeus burst through the door with a tinted brow beneath a uniquely scarred head and white mane.

Kyra rose in preparation for battle. Her hands were formed together in a defensive rune meant to create a forcefield. Arimeus recognized the hand motions and stood aghast.

While Kyra's spell could protect against the standard weapon bearer, the cost came, or should come, with near guarantee of the loss of the caster's own life. For Arimeus knew, if magic, a blade, or some other weapon were to penetrate the shield under the proper enchantment...once the spell came into contact with the blood of its caster, the spell would spread like poison throughout the body. But could the spell be less or more effective without calling to a written rune, as Arimeus would need to do if he were to try and use this spell?

Kyra clearly did not use a written rune.

The hand motions were obvious and visible, but even still, the old man knew Kyra was aware of something he was not. She had something bound to her, unknown whispers of the very magic Arimeus claimed to be an expert in.

Once Arimeus met Kyra's eyes, the Chief Runic looked down to the ground, laid his two swords out, and bowed in a gesture of both reverence and peace. The act of respect gave Kyra calm as Gremanhas often attacked her with the same level of surprise to test her mettle.

"Battle does not frighten you," Arimeus said with a muffled voice as his face pointed at the ground.

At Arimeus's bow, Kyra too lowered herself to a more respectful stature. But her sidelong glance at Gremenhas gave the intruding Arimeus pause.

"Training has that effect on some," she answered.

Arimeus's blades lay before Kyra with faded arms the color of rust, but rust had not taken them. Age was embedded into the blades which once flowed with spells from a great number of runes carved into them.

Arimeus saw fit many years ago to tamper with the runes of his weapons in a meticulous effort that took many weeks to accomplish. Truly, it had been one of few moments requiring his great, arcane knowledge and use of his runes which did not cause him great peril, except the loss of time. His reward—the look of aged blades, unmatched defensive maneuvers, and an ever-sharp steel.

"So, it is time?" Gremanhas asked with sorrow and relief.

Kyra shot a glare at her mentor who clearly had made plans without her knowledge. It was unlike him, and unfair. She was furious and without concern about what decisions had been made for they were made without her.

"Time for what?" Kyra asked her weathered teacher with a touch of disdain.

"You've heard tell of the prophecy, yes girl?" Arimeus asked in return, rising from his bow.

"Hardly a girl, though she is quite young, not quite through her nineteenth year," Gremanhas said with a slight smirk. "You'd do best to watch how you speak. She bites."

"Yes," Kyra said with a tightening brow as she glanced back and forth between Arimeus and her teacher. "As most do..."

"Speak it then, girl. You have a role to play," Arimeus said, pressing toward her with a controlled intention.

"As it is written on the stone, I cannot recall," answered Kyra. "But I'll play no role that is commanded of me. Ask, *sir*, and perhaps I'll feign interest."

"Speak as you know, Kyra," responded Gremanhas, trying to hide his smile. "Ignore the plights of patriarchal surety, including my own, if you can find the forgiveness to do so."

She was always forgiving of Gremenhas. There was no other way to be with the old elf, if he were indeed an elf. Thus, she spoke, hoping to get to the bottom of things. "The end of an age will befall all of Kaiya unless the name upon the stone meets the challenge of the Kaiyar," Kyra answered.

Arimeus continued his line of questioning, "And, pray tell, what is the end of an age?"

With great annoyance and a frustrated look toward Gremanhas, Kyra answered the question, which she would clearly now bear the burden.

"Was it...my name?" Kyra asked.

"Answer the damn question, girl!" Arimeus picked his blades up and thrust them into his scabbards. "You've not had the time for fear, now answer the question!"

Kyra's eyes began to wet before she answered. She was ready to hit him, but not with her fist. All of Kyra's rage bent toward making the old man understand how little of an expert he truly was in the ways of rune magic.

But she stalled her indignation, held back her metaphorical swing, and continued to play the game. "The ground will open, cities **will be lost**, magic will vanish from the world, and all that was thought great in this world, all of our stories and warmth will fade to unending cold as the spirits who haunt the Unda'Hearth as a wicked punishment for failing to honor the Lords of Kaiya."

Kyra stared into the broken eyes of Arimeus. Something hid behind the Chief Runic's scornful look as he seemed to be holding anger, or resentment, toward her.

The mentor thoughtfully watched the old runic, attempting to discern his intentions, and more importantly, understand the thrashing just laid upon his student.

"What scratches your walls at night?" she asked, eyes narrowing upon Arimeus.

Instantly, the Chief Runic remembered the day Tir had spoken with one of the Kaiyar, though which one he could not tell. But Tir was told the birthing day of the one who would be chosen to honor the Kaiyan Lords. For good reason, all of the council remembered that day–their worst day.

Arimeus remembered what came next, too, for he took part in it. Six children were born on the day named by Tir, and six children were taken from their homes across all the lands of Kaiya. They had to be taken, Arimeus was told. Who would dare risk the end of an age? It was up to Runefall to hone the skills of those children and prepare them for prophecy.

Prepare them for war.

Arimeus pretended as though Kyra didn't call out his obvious discontent and instead spoke to Gremenhas. "It seems you've made a strong one over the years."

Being children taken from the love they might have known, Gremanhas could only show his pupils kindness. Still, circumstances never slowed his intense teaching methods, which often caused great pain to his students.

After a moment of pondering, Gremanhas asked, "How do you know?"

"You hear how she speaks to me, yes?" Arimeus growled.

"No," Gremenhas corrected. "How do you know it's her?"

"The strongest among you will travel to the Stained Temple," Arimeus said with a low-hanging head.

Indeed, Kyra proved to be the most capable student in the runic arts and developed a keen intellect for its practical use while avoiding much of the pain others consistently endured. Still, her abilities had yet to be truly tested in any real battle, and books and teachings could only do so much while being hidden behind the Wall of Turmin.

Suddenly, Kyra burst out in defense, "But I'm not the strongest!" Her fear overtook her. Skill with rune magic aside, this was bigger than a training ground. A new pressure started to burrow into her.

Many spoke of the prophecies, especially since the rise of war around the hidden city, and Kyra heard all those rumors, least not of the warlord surrounding the city. The young woman was clueless to what the outside world had become over the many years. Now, all of a sudden, the responsibility of Near'Hearth and its people was placed upon her? It was unfair, it was ridiculous, and she felt betrayed.

With a long sigh, Gremanhas replied to her, "Kyra, when the Lords of Kaiya, our gods, speak of strength, they care not for the weight of stone which you can carry. No. The gods speak of their own image and their own gifts they have bestowed to our lands. There is no question here; you are the strongest Ragi among your fellow students."

"But, but I—," Kyra was intentionally cut off by Arimeus.

"You're frightened, Kyra," Arimeus's eyes slowed and the anger within them faded. "We know you are lost in this. We could not be certain, and for that lack of knowledge, we could not be preemptive."

Kyra looked at her teacher and quickly back to Arimeus. There were no changing things, no altering the words etched in stone. There was no going back. With fear or with courage, she was being called to this task, and she would answer with a strong showing.

"If I have no choice—," the young mage said before being interrupted again.

"You do not," Arimeus jumped back in with a boom in his voice.

"I understand," Kyra responded with a stiff neck and hard eyes. "I understand you believe I do not have a choice, that you and the council have decided my fate for me. I understand it is your belief I will accept these words… " Kyra's words trailed away as she bowed and gave a quick eye to her teacher before her gaze returned to the floor.

In the depth of Kyra's bow, she studied the cracks of wood beneath her. Against the grooves, she rested herself on all four limbs with a continued false reverence to Arimeus and his demands.

"If I should go, my Lord. I would ask that I not go alone."

The quick look told Gremenhas all he needed to know. Kyra wouldn't bandy words with the Chief Runic any longer for he'd lost her respect. That being said, the old mentor understood his pupil knew the cost even if she chose not to hear the words of prophecy.

"I'll not condemn a world for the actions of one man," Kyra's accusation rang clear, "but I'll also not face an army outside of the gates alone."

"No," Gremanhas replied with a smile. "You shall not go alone."

"I'm afraid you'll be staying within the city walls, Gremanhas," Arimeus said with authority. "The girl needs—"

Without warning, Gremanhas exploded with an anger Kyra had never witnessed from her seasoned teacher, her typically well-spoken and mild-mannered teacher.

"You tell me to raise these children as my own? I've done so! You tell me to weaponize these youth for a battle beyond any of us? I've done so! I've dedicated my life to these children, and as the moment of calling finally arrives you would tell me to stand aside and hope for their safe return?"

Arimeus watched his old friend writhe with fury. The Chief Runic's stomach gave way to dark and hollow pits.

"I will not stand idly as I watch the closest thing I have to a daughter walk these lands alone to be scorched by the fires of war!"

Arimeus lowered himself to one knee and bowed his head to Gremanhas.

"You may command legions, Arimeus. But you do not command me."

Slowly, Arimeus raised his head to his old friend, still resting on one knee.

"Gremanhas, my long friend—," Arimeus started to explain.

Kyra's mentor continued to erupt. "I'll not be patronized by you or your damned council!"

Arimeus rose from his knee. "This ought not to be said in front of the girl, Gremanhas. Give me a quiet room, and I'll explain."

Gremanhas glared with fury into Arimeus' silver eyes. "You'd send her to the ends of the world to fulfill your prophecy, but a look into the politics of the realm is too much for her? Share what you must if all of our fate so clearly hangs by her hands."

Arimeus recognized there was no turning back from this point of conflict, and in truth, he recognized Gremenhas was right. If Kyra could be thrown into the wilderness without the safekeeping of her teacher, perhaps further knowledge of Runefall might hasten her steps, or at the very least give her cause to keep moving forward.

"We need you to fight. A battle is coming, and I know you see it," Arimeus's voice changed to a tone reminiscent of disparity. "Chieftains of all sorts gather, and alliances have been made between sworn enemies to bring down this city. We've remained hidden from sight by the protection of runes, and should they fail, all that separates us from wanton death is the wall of Turmin—great as it may stand, the wall has never been tested."

"You doubt your fellow lord's wall?" Gremanhas grinned with a touch of sarcasm.

"I do not doubt that should this city fall under siege it will need one of the greatest mages we have ever known to defend it," Arimeus answered with impunity.

Once more Kyra stood in dismay. Talk had filled the city with fears of the surmounting armies rising against Runefall, and the few who could leave the hidden city spoke of powerful forces gathering for the purpose of Runefall's doom. Yet, those living in the city were always reassured the barriers would hold, Turmin's wall was impenetrable, and the runes hiding the city from sight could not be shaken. Why then was this concern, which stood contrary to the reassurances offered by

Runefall's ruling council; why then should they be so afraid they could not send the most able mage within the city walls to help Kyra?

Gremanhas, trying to understand, abruptly asked, "What could have caused such fear in you to doubt what hides this city? The runes were carved by Salaril, Lord of Runes, were they not? Our lord protected this city with his own designs which remain untouched and incorruptible."

Arimeus became smothered with deep-seated dereliction. "Yes, Gremanhas. We hold Salaril's favor," the Chief Runic explained, "but he no longer holds favor with the Kaiyar."

With a hard discomfort, Gremanhas burst once more. "How? How could this happen? How can you know? How long have you known?"

"The depth of knowing matters little. Tir spoke with Ishmail in Unda'Hearth," Arimeus explained. "It has been many years in the making, but a deep reckoning has befallen us. Salaril and his brother Ishmail hide in Unda'Hearth."

"And of Raknar, the Unda'Lord?" Gremanhas demanded as panic filled his words. "Where has the blood lord gone?"

"This, we do not know," Arimeus answered with regret. "He offered safekeeping to Salaril and his brother, the Lord of Dreams. But after that, it is said Raknar meant to question the pantheon of lords and has not been heard from since."

No, Gremenhas thought, *no this cannot be. If Salaril has been abandoned by the Kaiyar . . . then his followers must be—*. He dared not think it. The old elf cast thoughts aside of him being punished for the choices of his deity. For a moment, Gremenhas considered the possibility of the Kaiyar being wrong in their chastisement of Salaril, but even those thoughts seemed to border betrayal for one so obviously pious. Thus, in a moment of discomfort, while trying to cast all of his thoughts away, he realized a new, dark tiding. *If Ishmail, Lord of Dreams and Prophet to Kaiyar, has been punished for nothing more than kinship... we are doomed.*

It was then Gremanhas heard the world break against a crash of thunder. Within a second, the entire city fell to the point chaos became encased by fearsome screams which vibrated the temple. All of a sudden, a bulky and somewhat tall Litree broke through the door with a sweaty brow and shiny, bronze skin.

"My lords," the Litree fought as he tried to catch his breath. "Lightning struck the city. Our barriers hold, but the energy from the strike courses with each moment, pulsating across our borders. I've no doubt this can be seen from miles and miles away, my lords." He stopped once more and hunched to catch his breath. "What should we do?"

Gremanhas looked to Arimeus as the Chief Runic became wracked with disbelief. "This was no accident, then," the teacher said to Arimeus as the crackling of electricity surged around the city. "Thank you, Samiel," he said, looking at his student—the Litree.

"No, old friend. This was Krishalla." The words left Arimeus' mouth with a lingering horror behind them.

"The council bade Kyra hide behind the walls, but that has clearly gone to folly," Arimeus sighed. "Gremanhas, I would ask that you join Galantis as he no doubt gathers the full force of Runefall. The city needs its best mage. In your stead, I will travel with Kyra to the Stained Temple, but we must move with haste as the eyes of Harigamun fall on our fair city for the first time, and should our enemies witness our leave, I fear what may become of us."

Gremanhas stood in disbelief. He found himself questioning why that prophetic rune ever fell from the heavens to begin with. *Why should my city carry the burden of this land just for it all to come crashing down?*

Then, Gremanhas thought deep within himself, and his piety became flooded with doubt in an instant. *What if the prophecy is wrong?*

For just a short interlude of silence, no more than seconds, Gremanhas regained his piety, or he tried. Rather, even if he did not regain his piety, he chose to voice it for others—not trusting in his own confusion.

"I know not the correct path. In fact, I know not even what I believe on this day," Gremanhas responded, "but... I have followed my lord's will, and it's all I know to do. Salaril has said Kyra should make haste to the Stained Temple, and so she shall, so says Tir."

Gremanhas looked to his right out of a grand window of stained glass depicting the fall of the first rune to the city. It was beheld as a glorious moment of thrashing colors striking the air, like a rainbow of lightning. The earth shook and quaked and the stars stepped beneath the clouds and shone with a beauty most thought was within reach if they could just jump high enough.

That day was the deliverance of not only rune magic, but magic as Kaiya knew it.

Outside of the window, Gremanhas saw the crackling of Runefall. Lightning surged across the city, and he knew this would be the beginning of a horrible war. The teacher pondered whether the decision on that day of the city, the council, and himself, was worth it.

"Take Samiel," Gremanhas said with a quickness to his breath. "Physically, I've no stronger fighter out of those I've trained. He's brutish in combat but never lacking in compassion for Kyra. You'll need him." The teacher looked at the Litree. "He will be instrumental to her success."

Samiel looked shocked at the suggestion as he was still trying to piece together the conversation. "I'm going to the Stained Temple with Kyra?" He excitedly thought to himself, *I'll be the first Litree to ever see it!*

Samiel was a spectacle to behold, and until this moment, Arimeus hadn't paid him any mind. Now, the Chief Runic noticed the obvious–Samiel was significantly larger than those of his kind in more ways than one. Being of Litree, his kin were most usually among the smallest beings of Kaiya, but he'd grown far beyond what was normal for his kind. This Litree stood around the same height as Kyra, which would doubtless be near two feet taller than his average kindred. Furthermore, beyond any of the other children taken in by Gremanhas, Samiel worked at his strength daily, and his body showed that fact. Samiel placed little value in being able to practice magic for himself but insisted on being able to protect his friends who did.

Thus, to Arimeus, Samiel boasted the muscle of a battle-hardened warrior with the innocent features of a child. His brown hair atop his almost bronze-yellow skin made sure he stood out, as Litree were not often seen in the city of Runefall, and travel had been restricted for many years which prevented any newcomers. He wore fighting leathers with light-skinned boots, as he preferred to maintain his mobility at the sacrifice of greater protection.

Although, no matter how much it got in his way when he was fighting, the Litree refused to cut his shoulder-length hair.

Kyra, however, dressed in traditional garments laid out by the highest practitioners of rune magic and kept shorter hair–hair Samiel stared at frequently. He also frequented her stones lining her robe. He thought it was interesting that her runes were sapphire, he found them beautiful.

The Ragi told him long ago that her stones represented her expertise in defensive spells, but Samiel liked to tell her "it's because you can be as calm and treacherous as the sea."

In contrast, Kyra desperately tried to have a ruby embroidery made for Samiel–she greatly admired his strength. Though her order would not allow it then, in part because they could not do so even if they wanted to.

Now, Kyra knew the dwarves of the south crafted the robes on behalf of the Ragi many years ago and the city had not seen a new robe for well over a decade.

A pulse of energy came again.

"Called for prophecy and you aren't even in shoes," Gremenhas said with a rushed tone, "Ready yourself, Kyra."

The young Ragi more often wore shoes for court, rather than battle, and often removed them to meditate. In fact, she so often removed them that she would leave training and completely forget that she had worn shoes, which then required Gremanhas to deliver them back to her.

The old elf always smiled when he returned her shoes.

Kyra's weapon of choice, however, was her double-sided, perfectly symmetrical staff, and she always had that on her. Dreadfall, she called it. The staff was intricately woven as if two oak trees were entwined to perfection, root after root crossing over each other in the most intentional design. Kyra frequently referred to the root pattern as a song– a song of dread for those who would oppose her, for it had something hidden about it that none could tell.

"Gather what is needed and let's go," Arimeus rushed the two untested fighters. "We've a long road ahead and the city is not safe. We must go before Harigamun attempts to breach the walls."

Kyra became fixated on Arimeus. *This is all too...organized*, she thought.

"What of the others?" Samiel always had a heart thicker than his muscles. "Where are my brothers and sisters meant to be in all of this? Do they have a role to play?"

"They will aid me, Sam," his teacher explained. "You will go with Arimeus and Kyra. Keep her safe and deliver her to the Stained Temple," Gremanhas continued as he glanced at a closet in the corner of the room. Samiel didn't have a clue where the temple was, as no one did. But such as the good soldier he was, Samiel nodded and looked to Kyra with dedication.

"I don't understand what you were saying about the lords and gods of Kaiya," Kyra said to her teacher. "I've always felt Salaril was alive, and the others I just assumed were part of the story. But you speak of them as if you know them." Kyra's brow raised as her confusion grew.

"We don't have time!" Arimeus' voice thrashed about the oaken frame of the temple with a boom. "You'll learn what you need to know on the damn road! We don't have time for childish questions or history lessons.

We need to get out of this gods' forsaken city!"

Have the gods forsaken the city? Gremanhas asked himself. Was he about to fight in a war that he was already determined to lose? The weary teacher did not know and could not know. He could only hope his actions were serving the correct idea.

With that, Kyra sprinted to the closet Gremanhas was looking at to grab some common linens and change out of her robe. It would be best, she thought, not to be recognized as being from Runefall, let alone a Ragi, in the open world.

With a loose gray tunic, worn leather shoes, and bottoms of a fading, red-stained leather, Kyra latched onto Dreadfall and walked over to Arimeus—who stared her down with ripe annoyance.

But suddenly, the feeling faded, and a smile breached the Chief Runic's scowl.

"I am sorry, Kyra. This should not have been placed on you," the Arimeus said. "I'll do what I can along the way to keep you safe."

Samiel also ran to the closet and grabbed a bag of dirks along with a long-sword and its scabbard. Whilst Arimeus spoke with Kyra, Samiel fastened the scabbard and tied the bag of dirks to his belt while his teacher watched.

As the old elf watched Samiel grab his weapons, the teacher had a small chuckle. *He'd have grabbed a pike if that's what was in there.*

"Do not lose yourself in this journey, Sam. We will need you yet," Gremanhas said softly with a hand squeezing the back of his students' necks as he pushed their heads together. "Go with haste, but not with hate."

Without delay, a second crash of lightning battered the city, and the world shook beneath their feet.

"Gremanhas, get to Galantis as soon as possible," Arimeus shouted over the continued crackling around them. "The pulses are growing closer. Harigamun's move will fast come. We must be prepared!"

Arimeus, hastily and without compassion from his companions, launched forward into a sprint indicating the other two students were meant to follow him. The three of them charged off with speed driven by fear as Gremanhas turned back to the closet where Samiel grabbed his weapons, and Kyra her attire.

The teacher opened the door and pressed his hand against the back wall where a rune suddenly appeared shining with a clear-blue sheen in the shadows. The back wall shuttered and then opened revealing a suit of armor and swords behind flawless cobwebs. After adorning himself, Gremenhas lowered himself, for a final time, at the altar of Salaril. *I've forgotten more than others have lived. Let this be my last battle, lest I wander the scorched remains of a dying land. If my last memories are to be of fire, and if we have been forsaken by the foul divinities of Kaiya, then give me the courage to die well.*

Chapter Five

The Warlord of Kaiya

"A decade of battle has bent the mystic, elemental, and summoning armies to my will. Years of searching have brought me near the gates of Runefall. A lifetime of suffering will come crashing down on this city in an instant, as my world was crushed not so long ago. Get ready, brother."
— Harigamun, *Thoughts of War*

The Warlord of Kaiya closed the pages of his journal and gently wrapped it shut with a loose leather string latched to a golden clasp. As the final twist knotted, one of the seven members of his War Council burst through the flaps of the tent.

"My lord, my sight is clear, and Krishalla has joined our fight," the voice excitedly announced.

Harigamun turned to see Halorin, his chosen council member for the Mystics.

"I take it you've spoken with Krishalla, then?" The warlord rose from his seat, putting out the small flame illuminating his desk.

"My lord," Halorin stammered at the question, knowing full well the answer would displease the warlord. "None have spoken to Krishalla this age. None from Kaiya I've known have spoken to him... but you know this already."

Harigamun grunted, cleared his throat, and spat into a jar on the floor as he ground his teeth for a short moment, glaring at Halorin. "I've no patience for you Psions trying to tell me of these so-called gods and their messages. Be out with it, coward," he growled. "How come you by this information?"

Halorin shivered at the warlord's voice. Harigamun's towering figure overshadowed the small cleric. He stood as a colossus among men, staunchly larger than even the most feared warriors with a predisposition for heavy, blunt objects and armor made of stone.

On the battlefield, the warlord's adamantite armor was painted as red as his Pyrosi flames, and his helm bore the horns of a demon from the Unda'Hearth. At least, those were the stories told by his legions since none had ever set eyes on such a benevolent being. Stories say the warlord forced a great dwarven smith to forge the armor long ago, but there had been other stories.

"The beast wears stone for armor," his soldiers would say. "What man among us wears stone?"

"My lord," Halorin gulped. "Lightning has struck the city of Runefall. Who could this be...other that Krishalla? We were told to come, and told he would strike, just now how. It's clear as the next dawn...he has cast his mighty fury down onto this city so that we might take it. The city is lit! We need look no longer; it is time to set Runefall afire."

So, the gods do still look down now and then, Harigamun thought to himself. A joyous smile overtook his face, he grabbed hold of Halorin, and jerked him under his arm to feign friendship.

"Take me to the fireworks," said the warlord with satisfaction. Harigamun wondered if the many scouts he had stationed all around the Field of Bones were watching the reveal of this horrible city. His came was vast, decorated with a multitude of cultures with vastly different armies. The scale of his camp spread like a ring around a fearsome mountain, ready to volley into the depths of a sleeping volcano just to start a war. After a lengthy walk to the edge of his camp, passing through tapestries, pottery, embroidery and all the smells in the world from gods knows how many different kinds of food, the warlord saw it...

Death has come.

The hidden city of Runefall appeared before Harigamun as lightning surged all around it. The great wall of Turmin went on for miles and miles to encircle the grand city.

"Tonight, this city will fall, and our hearts will begin to mend, Halorin, son of Halor," Harigamun said to the council member. "Those walls which have kept them from my sight shall become little more than a tomb, a ruin marking the time of mortals for all of Kaiya to remember."

"There are so few great houses left, my liege. It will be good for us to rebuild, as in the days before—" Halorin was interrupted in his resplendent recollection.

"The days before what, may I ask?" The warlord's voice grew angry, quickly. "What days would you harken me to as if we have known them ourselves, my little lordling?"

Halorin's knees began to feel weak, but he could not show it. "I meant nothing by it, my lord. I only meant—" Halorin was once more interrupted.

"Go on, then. Tell me what it is you meant."

The Warlord's eyes grew red. He could do that—bring fire to his eyes—and do that he did, often. To the Warlord, it was a small price to pay, but the fear arising in a man's heart when he summoned flames to his glare was well worth the raised heat within him, requiring little more than a drink of water to recover. Though he did prefer the drink to be cold.

"I—," Halorin, again, was stopped from speaking.

"The houses we've claimed these many centuries have turned to dust, betrayal, and blood more often than they've ever built anything of lasting fashion!" Harigamun preached, degrading the welp before him." In fact, most houses are *claims* to a name, rather than the name itself. Much of this land has given up on the idea of it altogether, save the elemental tribes who live nomadic lifestyles and cling to a luxury they've never known. The damned Mystics—such as yourself—like to tell stories of lordship and lordliness we'll never have! Houses are gone and faded," he spat. "The only records of civilized life and past houses of political miscreants are held behind the walls of that damn city! There're no true houses left, only the primitive use of magic and control weaponized by those who wield it. My house is nothing more than a fable, like yours and any other. You've no house name, just the recognition of those who birthed you. There is no recognition of the power of man under the degrading rule of gods..." He turned his back to the Mystic general.

"I apologize, my lord," Halorin sank to a bent knee. "How should we understand the mending of our hearts and the life we used to know?"

"Through those who lived it," Harigamun said with regret. "Nothing will bring us to an age of political niceties and civilized living. The world fell to chaos the day Runefall kidnapped my child, killed my wife, and took what was left of the great houses at the behest of that pretentious rune god."

Odd, Halorin thought to himself. *Odd that most of the great houses birthed a child on that day.*

Harigamun thrust the Mystic forward, releasing his grasp on his general. "Gather the War Council. We will march on the city come the morrow."

In the following hours, Halorin sent messengers to the far reaches of Warband's camp, bidding their leaders gather at the War Table in the center of the settlement which spanned miles in each direction.

Later on, early the following morn before the sun rose, Harigamun sat in his tent writing and awaiting the arrival of his chieftains . He wrote of many things: loss, love, vengeance, but most of all, he contemplated—as only one of philosophical resentment can—his inevitable end.

"My wife is gone. My sons are gone. My city is gone. My heart still burns.

My day has come."

— Harigamun, *Thoughts of War*

As the sun rose, Harigamun joined the War Table. The place was a monumental tent fashioned from many hides. They hung by the light of candle wicks crafted by the war wives of each tribe and lit by Pyrosi fire.

Six chieftains were seated at the opulent table: Whaleback of the Agualytes, Singher for the Pyrosi, Airwei for the Wind Riders, Sodsheim for the Gaiara, Halorin for the Mystics, and the Lord of Summons, Varin.

By Harigamun's order, the true names of the elemental lords were abandoned. They had all taken their own chieftain names in recognition their houses would never return, thereby making their past lives irretrievable. They commanded no surnames nor banners under Harigamun, only their titles so long as the Warlord was willing to give them. The Warlord glowered at each of them as they awaited orders, signs their servitude might come to an end.

"I take it, my lords, you've all spent ample time with your war wives these past days, enough to satiate yourselves for the coming battle?" The warlord roared with false laughter, though his surrounding chieftains bought it...for the warlord hated this custom.

"Aye," Whaleback grunted. "I've had me three since yesterday, and me back ain't the only thing the size of a whale!" The enormously wide man's belly brushed against the table as he laughed.

"Not all of us take the unwilling to bed, your Lordship," Varin, Lord of Summons, spoke from the far end of the table.

He was a man of nobility—Varin—and next to the scholars of Runefall, the summoners of Varin had established an impressive system of education. Even still, he would explain how the School of Summons was far more impressive than anything in Runefall, be it true or not.

"We take from them who choose not to fight with us," Sodsheim responded with a guttural disposition. "If their men won't fight the likes of Runefall, then they don't be deservin' of no wives, now do they?"

Harigamun took no war wives, and in truth, had a disdain for those who did, showing in the false tone he carried each time war wives were mentioned. Though, the taking of men and women to bed quelled the urges of many of his chieftains. Such caused him to think it a necessary price to pay for peace, or at the very least, pushed him to tolerate it. His greatest gripe was the need to refer to them as that...war wives. Many of them who were taken from past conquests were men, especially for Whaleback—all of the Agualyte's war wives were men.

"The winds have changed," Airwei said with an ethereal voice. "Perhaps we should discuss battle strategy, my Lord."

Harigamun looked to the Master of Winds with respect. His people, the Wind Riders, were always well-behaved and polite, though their sharpness and betrayal could come at a moment's notice, as surprising as a foul breeze upon the air.

The Warlord looked to Singher who seemed to have been staring at Whaleback; the Lord of Waters had not seemed to notice the glaring discontent.

"It takes a man to take a man," Whaleback growled. "You can't even handle more than one woman!" He laughed, coughed, or some elated combination of the two. "If I can hold down three men, boy, imagine what I can do with you!" The last words were intentionally foul and littered with malcontent, as he hated Singher, Host of Flames.

Singher looked to his Warlord, his leader, and waited patiently. The Host of Flames, second in command behind only Harigamun, was well placed with his niceties, always looking to his King for permission. And permission was granted.

"Our people are of a loyal kind," Singher answered. "We bed as we die—once. We love as we live—forever in flames. Take what you must to fill your foul gut, Whaleback. I have yearning hearts waiting for me while you have rooms which sigh as you enter. There is no likeness between us, thus I burn with joy as you prove such a point. Continue speaking for yourself, as all who have worth stopped listening to you long ago."

"Why you fu—" Whaleback was interrupted by the Warlord, and instantly, the Lord of Waters hushed.

"Airwei is right, dear council," Harigamun rose from his seat to address the table.

Singher also rose but quickly sat once more after a quick and disapproving glance from the Warlord. The Host of Flames knew better than to suggest equal footing and instantly corrected himself.

"We know where the city is, and based on the reports we've received, also know the weaknesses of Turmin's Wall," Harigamun's voice rose to a stoic command. "Singher, you'll cycle your casters. They will ready the trebuchets with the Gaiara who will craft large objects of metal and stone from the earth to be wrapped in flame by the Pyrosi and shot into the city. Not at the wall!"

"Yes, my Liege," Singher responded with a courteous bow, even from his sitting position.

Then, Harigamun challenged the idea, his own idea. "How will we keep the casters from becoming weary? The fire will drain the warmth from the bodies of your men and women. The pulling from the crust of the earth to craft objects will lead to the Gaiara absorbing its materials into their blood if they aren't careful."

"Once their fingertips burn, mine know to step aside and let another fulfill the role until their warmth returns," Singher replied.

"The taste of metal is something all too familiar for us, my Lord," Sodsheim replied. "We know when to step back."

"There will be no stepping back!" Harigamun yelled, booming for miles outside the War Table. "We will continue to march forward, and you will properly manage your arsenals, or I will have not only your titles, nor your luxuries, but your lives and those of your cities! Need I counsel the rest of you on the management of your armies?" The Warlord's impatience grew as the surmounting battle enveloped his mind. "Alright then," Harigamun closed off his council from answering the question, which he intended not to be answered.

"Halorin," Harigamun's voice grew hasty. "You'll enter the weaker minds of the city and be our eyes and ears. Those of your ilk who cannot manage this task will—" the Warlord was interrupted.

"I know what to do, my Lord," Halorin responded with an intentionally abrasive tone.

Harigamun looked at the Psion with disgust and anger. He hated the fool but quickly decided it was not the time to scorn one of his chieftains, at least, not to the extreme he wished to. He had other intentions for the Mystic.

Then, Harigamun looked at Varin. "What can we count from your forces, Lord Varin?"

"Quite a many golems, my Liege," Varin said with a smirking grin. "And one surprise I'll leave for the battlefield." Varin, Lord of Summons, bowed. "Though you know of what I speak..."

"Once the city is breached, I expect you know your abilities better than I. Respond effectively in the specified flanks designated to you." Harigamun gestured to the map covering the length of the table before them.

Each of their armies were represented on the marked battlefield hurriedly put together in the past few nights by a number of cartographers from the Mystics.

"Kaiya has not known a siege of this breadth in our living age," Harigamun said as he eyed his generals. "I understand the majority of your generals are also the few who can use your spell craft, thus leadership in the field will be sparse. Our attack must be ineffable, unflinching, and relentless! Do any among you doubt the foot soldiers of your armies in the absence of a general?"

Halorin smirked. "The Mystic generals need not be physically present to command an army, my Lord."

Harigamun glared at the Psion, imagining how long Halorin would be able to stand a slow rising heat coming from the Warlord's hands if he were to grab ahold of Halorin's throat if nothing more than to watch his body boil.

"As we did this past night to make the map, we can Soul Break to communicate with those willing to listen," Halorin said as he walked around the War Table. "In fact, we could also lead each of your armies should they be willing to submit for a short time." Halorin's grimace disgusted the other generals.

An eerie feeling fell upon the surrounding generals as they had all heard tales of the practice, but none wanted to take part in it. Then, Harigamun's rage broke for a moment.

"No, Halorin. I've a better use of your skills. You will station Soul Breakers near each of the commanding forces for each army. Can the strongest among you create a bridge between myself and each of the generals?"

Halorin stepped back in confusion at the request. "Wait, you want one of us to enter your mind, and create a connection between you and every general on the field, whom we will also need to convince to let one of us into their heads?"

"There's no convincing needed," the Warlord answered. "Generals follow their general, and their generals follow their Warlord, and I won't be asking. How long would we need?"

Harigamun's confidence in the idea gave Halorin a sinking presence of fear, or anxiety, as he could not tell which. But then, Halorin saw an opportunity.

"It can be done," the Mystic answered. "However, it will have to be me who bridges the connection. No others among us will be strong enough to hold the bridge." His words seemed a small hiss to those present.

Harigamun thought for just a split moment. "Done. Now, how long? Our window is closing."

"I wouldn't worry about that, my Lord," Sodsheim interjected. "My men have been marking the terrain surrounding the city this night. Should the lightning stop, there's no hiding from us now."

"Gather the generals," Harigamun ordered Halorin.

Within two hours, all sixty generals from each of the six armies gathered. Each brought with them their second in command. Their Warlord stood above them on a small hill looking down upon his gathered forces with pride and indignation wrapped together like a violent wind fanning an ember.

"Each of you will open your minds to Halorin tonight," the Warlord ordered.

Murmurs among the generals started and doubt filled the air.

"I will be the first among you to do so. Halorin will create a bridge between myself and each of you, ensuring there will be no confusion on the battlefield."

The Warlord saw the discontentment of the generals in front of him and it made him uneasy, though he masked it well.

"Unless, unless you would rather send your men and women into battle without direction, but then... I wouldn't think to call you a general. I also doubt your men would want to follow if you were so willing to leave them alone on the battlefield."

Harigamun knew this battle would have been no different than any other of his recent years were it not for the sheer scale of it. The city was wide, the army deep, and sixty generals could not keep accurate track of over 30,000 soldiers. Even though the Warlord knew this, and he knew typical battle practices would see many of these soldiers not having a general near them. Harigamun still saw a moment to sell the need to his armies. The Warlord needed them to know this mental bridge, this psionic connection between him and all the other generals... he needed them to know it was the only way they could win.

The murmurs of the crowd thickened.

"Raised hands for those who oppose me!" Harigamun's voice boomed above the generals, and then, one hand shot up from the crowd. The hand belonged to one of Whaleback's men, of the Agualytes.

"You'd have us not just open our minds to these damned Mystics," the Agualyte general said, "but you'd have us give our minds over to you as well?"

The murmurs rose to gasping shocks.

The Agualyte's condemnations proudly continued. "We've already bowed to your war crimes. We've already signed on to fight your wars because we have no choice in your *united front*. Now, we must give our minds to our oppressor?" The general cast off his armor, approaching Harigamun.

Met with silence, the opposing general continued as he marched toward the Warlord. "Some may support your cause, and truly, all oppose the city of Runefall!" A grand gesture followed. "But you've forced us into more than enough for a lifetime and I'll not sit idly by as you commandeer not only the lives of my people, but their minds as well," the general spat at Harigamun's feet. "If my choices are freedom of heart and mind, or death, then step down and let me be finished with this life once and for all. Let loose your armor of stone and prove your worth as a Warlord one last time... before *ALL* those who would cower before you."

Harigamun turned his skulking gaze to Whaleback who sat silent and nervous. It was one of the Agualyte's generals after all. The leader of the Agualyte army felt a great sense of dread crash upon him as if the waves of a raging sea berated a feeble stone, chiseling away at its outer shell, and giving way to its core.

The Warlord leaped from his peak atop the hill, from which he was addressing the generals, and dirt puffed into a small dust beneath the weight of Harigamun as he landed. He tossed his heavy stone chest piece to the side, its weight digging into the ground. His chest was as refined as the stone armor he adorned with no cloth covering his striated muscles. To the surprise of many, the Warlord wore no tunic beneath his adamantite chest piece. Markings from the raw rubbing of stone to skin covered his body with callous scar tissue creating its own layer of skin.

Next, unstrapping his stone grieves, the weight of the armor fell first with a loud thump, revealing tattered linen pants worn with time and ripped from knee to ankle with a long slit. Stepping out of his boots, callous blisters rimmed his monstrously huge and raw-rubbed feet. And there he stood, with nothing but tattered linen cloth pants and no weapon. He gave a low grumble and a sudden stretch of his jaw before reaching both hands onto his own head and forcing his neck to crack. He looked upon the Agualyte general, who he recognized now, and spat on the ground before replying to him, as his opponent did, out of respect.

"Glorfin," Harigamun said with anguished laughter. "Your bravery will be missed on the battlefield!"

Within a short moment, Glorfin turned to one of the Pyrosi generals and jolted his body into a stance, facing him. He quickly joined his hands together. Like a punch, Glorfin thrust his hands toward the Pyrosi who stood twelve feet away, as if he would be able to hit him, but then the Agualyte pulled the thrust back toward himself which pulled the Pyrosi's blood from his body and sent it flying like a liquid spear toward Harigamun. Before it reached the Warlord, Glorfin threw his joined hands once more toward the Warlord before separating his hands and gesturing a clenching fist which froze the blood into a hardened spear, heading straight for the Warlord's face.

Faster than Glorfin cast the spell, Harigamun simply raised his hand catching the spear. The Warlord shifted in a cyclical motion and launched the spear back into Glorfin's skull, leaving the Agualyte general with a head split in half and a pool of blood surrounding him. Those standing closest to Glorfin at the time noticed his skin was almost ashen and seemed cold, almost frozen.

The Warlord turned to face Whaleback.

"You've lost a general, and my respect," said Harigamun. "Is this how your army regards our efforts? Do you not stand with me? Do you not seek the return of your daughter?"

The Agualyte general approached Harigamun and took notice of the blood dripping from the Warlord's hand which was cut from the spear. The Warlord showed no sign of pain, nor acknowledgement of the wound.

"My Lord, you conquered us one by one, and united us under a single banner. For better, or for worse, I and mine follow you to the end of Runefall, and likely to the end of this age," Whaleback lowered himself to one knee, barely able to keep his obese body balanced. "I cannot justify the actions of my general, my Lord. But I can—," the oversized man lost his balance and fell as he spoke.

Surrounding generals of the other armies laughed as Whaleback tried to reclaim his balance on his knee.

"Ahem," Whaleback cleared his throat. "Lord Harigamun, Warlord of Kaiya, and King of Elements, you cannot expect there not to be bad blood where conquering is concerned. But I would assure you, I harbor none of this ill will, and neither do my remaining men."

Whaleback struggled to lift himself from his position, but once he did, turned to his remaining generals.

"Speak now, lest you suffer the same consequences for betrayal as Glorfin has." All of the remaining Agualyte generals fell to their knees and bent their heads to the ground in silence.

Harigamun turned to the crackling city of Runefall beneath a storm of lightning as it faded into the distance. The lightning was dwindling.

"Halorin," the Warlord ordered. "Ready yourself and your men. We march within the hour.

Harigamun gathered himself and a few of his most trusted guards to rest upon the highest peak of the impending battlefield amidst a plethora of candles lined into a cross at the peak's center. At the base of the cross lay a fabric fashioned into the likeness of a golden seal with an eye at its center, rimmed with embroidery and amethysts. On the horizon, the lightning began to fade from the cityscape, and six immense armies sat nestled behind a towering mountain just outside of the view.

"Have you any questions, my Lord?" Halorin asked.

Harigamun felt an uneasy notion concerning the Mystic. But he also felt relief. Not present relief, but something forthcoming.

"I need not fear the unknown, and I need not fear what you might reveal from the unknown chambers of my mind," Harigamun scolded. "For, if you pry too far, there is no realm in which you are safe from me."

Halorin, sensing he was losing the safety he once thought came with his position, tried to hide his trepidation from the Warlord and could not tell if he was successful. "My Lord, I would never—"

"Because you know better," Harigamun interrupted. "Now, whilst bridging a connection between me and my generals, you will also be able to split your body allowing us a greater view of the battlefield, yes?"

"Soul Breaking, my Lord. And no. Though, half of my generals will be doing so, your connection with them will make sure you have a complete view of the battle at all times."

"Hmph," the Warlord grumbled. "I see you've managed to keep yourself focused on me then."

Halorin grimaced. "Of course, my Lord. I wouldn't imagine another path for myself."

Harigamun lowered himself to the golden seal below the menacing eye. The Warlord had never experienced a mental connection with one of the Mystics, though he had read heavily on the matter, especially of late, from the scrolls he'd taken from the Psions when he invaded.

"What must I do?" Harigamun barked, getting himself comfortable in a leg-crossed position atop the fabric. "Get it done."

"Close your eyes and repeat after me."

Harigamun's waited for a moment, knowing what he was about to do. He had no practice in this kind of attack, but he took comfort in knowing any battle was in his favor.

As quick as the fire lights, I will break him . . .

The Warlord's mind wandered into a dream-like stasis, and he felt his mouth move to say words, likely the words Halorin spoke to him, but he could not hear nor feel them brush past his lips. There was only movement and a white void.

As Harigamun moved to stand, he felt a tug against both of his arms. Chains clutched his wrists, great chains the likes of which the Warlord had never seen. A piercing pain shot through his feet; the fracturing of bone unmistakable. As he looked, stakes protruded from his feet.

A cold stone clasp, the size of his enormous waist, wrapped around his stomach, buried into something immovable. The ground shook and the Warlord rose higher and higher into the air, incapable of discerning the sky from the floor below as it stretched on forever and froze his skin. War-torn skin pulled away from bone and muscle against the feel of the tree's bark. He felt bark scratch against his back, as if he were pinned to a tree, a great and large tree the size of which Kaiya had never known. And then, a fell voice filled the air.

"Does the tree feel familiar to you, Harigamun?"

Harigamun struggled to turn his head, hoping to catch a glimpse of the tree behind him. All he saw was pure white bark and it felt as if roots were breaking against and penetrating his skin.

Bound to the tree, Harigamun recalled the Siege of Wizard's Staff in a vision more clear than memory.

Fire broke against the poor stone walls built by the Mystics and their home crumbled with ease. Many of Harigamun's generals were taken by Soul Breakers who turned his army against one another, leaving ash and burnt skin next to the flayed victims of wanton disaster perpetrated by the leagues of Raknar's Exiles—which the Warlord had recruited at the time. The Pyrosi generals were empowered with blood magic from the exiles, allowing them to smash the barriers the Mystics had created through a connection of trees used to worship their god. It was a disastrous raid causing the fall of the white trees and all of the living Mystics then bowed to Harigamun.

In the last moment of the siege, Harigamun ordered a blaze of fire upon the exiles for their horrendous treatment of the people who did not fight. He burned them beneath the ashes of the white trees and sat in revelry, listening to their screams amid a blaze of his own making, surrounded by darkness and littered with burning snow.

The vision went black, and the white void choked his senses once more as the Warlord returned to consciousness, or what form of consciousness he could claim in the strange prison of Halorin's making.

"Larina's love shielded us from you and your evil. She gave us power over our own minds and lives and gave us abilities the rest of you can't even begin to imagine," the voice returned.

"Seems she didn't protect you enough, did she, Halorin?"

The Mystic general materialized before Harigamun's eyes as the Warlord struggled to break from his shackles. Halorin's size was measured in a greatness Harigamun had never seen. He was beyond the giants of old stories, and he outstretched the ever-growing tree imprisoning the Pyrosi Warlord.

Halorin leaned in and whispered in Harigamun's ear.

"Your trust in me has brought your folly, and now I will command your legions! Once I take this city and scorch the earth beneath it, I will turn your army against itself one final time. Your penance for treason against Larina, your redemption for the corruption of our land, both shall be paid with the final spark of fire in your heart as you pay for every sorry sin!"

Harigamun smiled and seemed unmoved by the pain he felt moments before from his bindings.

"Remind me, Halorin. What was it about my sacking of your city that hurt the most?"

Halorin's eyes glazed over with the yellow fire of hatred as he grew in size once more, ripping Harigamun from his bindings. The Mystic's hand wrapped around the Warlord like a mountain holds a rock, a towering behemoth in an endless void, and, somehow, the Warlord appeared without fear.

"The defilement of my city!"

The Warlord smirked once more.

"No, Halorin. What did I take from your city?"

Halorin's blazing eyes dimmed and whitened as he cast them open wider in realization of what the Pyrosi meant. A ringing terror tried to slither up from the Mystic's heart and wrap around his throat as a harsh anxiety, and dreadful abandonment, scratched behind his eyes.

No, he couldn't.

"Larina's tablet," Halorin gasped. "But it is of no use to you. What have you done with it?"

"No, my friend. It is of no use to you."

Harigamun's body burst into a wicked flame within the Mystic's hand, forcing the giant to drop the Warlord into the white void below. The void conformed itself into the heart of a volcano. Molten rock ran like a river between them, and the heat became unbearable... for the Mystic.

Lava bubbled and the mountain roared as if it were about to explode as the stench of charred rock distorted the Psion's senses. Halorin's size had fallen to his normal, less-than-impressive statue in front of the Warlord.

"You cannot control this realm," Halorin quivered. "Only a Mystic can alter this place and you are Pyrosi. None can hold the powers of more than one magic. All who have tried have failed!"

"All others were weak, much like yourself." The words came cold and callous with certainty.

Harigamun raised his closed fist into the air and brought it crashing down into the river of lava before him. An eruption shot upward from the river and toward his opponent.

Halorin ripped the mountain from its roots and blocked the lava with the mountain itself. "I can play here too, savage! You are no king, no lord of merit! You are a child with fire burning anyone who gets in your way!"

The Mystic looked to the gaping top of the volcano and outstretched both his arms, grabbing the top of the mountain to bring it crashing down onto both of them.

Harigamun leaped into the stream of fire and rock and launched a scorching breath into the air, raining molten rock down onto both of them. The rubble stayed still, and nothing moved for a moment as the dust settled and the mountain roared.

In an instant, Harigamun broke free from the molten rock in a shaken furry and cast lava across the debris trying to find the Mystic.

Then, a massive boulder barreled down and crushed Harigamun, leaving almost all of his bones broken.

"You may have learned something of being a Mystic, but you're still no master," Halorin hissed, floating above the Warlord. Halorin lowered himself closer and glared at the Warlord with joy. "You don't get to conquer the world, Harigamun. Now, your reign ends."

Without warning, a crushing weight fell on Halorin and pinned him to the ground, smashing his face upon the remaining molten rock, and burning his skin. A heavy force to the back of the Mystic's skull smashed his face into the mountain once more.

Harigamun's immense hands turned the Psion's body over to face the Warlord, who stood over top of the Mystic. In that moment, the Mystic knew he'd been tricked. The Warlord had created a double of himself, and Halorin fell for it.

"Call yourself the master of anything you'd like, Halorin, but this army, and your magic, are mine."

Harigamun breathed deeply as if gathering a storm in his lungs and his chest radiated a deep amber sheen. Following the great breath, the Warlord let loose a wind of great fire and lava which seared the skin from the Mystic's bones.

With a bright flash of fire, Harigamun was back on his knees atop the mountain's peak with his guards, and beside him were the broiled remains of the Mystic as the Warlord's company looked upon their leader in terror.

"Fear not," Harigamun gathered his strength and rose to his feet. "This battle is won, and now I control this army entirely. Runefall is about to witness a firestorm unlike any other. And I shall see the blaze from many eyes."

The warlord returned to his tent following the killing of Halorin, knowing he'd accomplished the final task needed to take Runefall. He washed his wounds from the bindings Halorin used on him and then grabbed his journal as one final thought entered his mind before he marched on the once hidden city.

"There is no one magic, nor strategy, nor army that will reclaim what was stolen from me. If I am to burn this world to its roots and rebuild anew, I will need to take that which has been too loosely given. I will rid the world of magic by conquering all of it."

—Harigamun, *Thoughts of War*

Chapter Six

Baylar in the North

"What would be the purpose of godliness if not for immortality? Of immortality if not for divinity? I fear divinity is weak, false, a lie. All we have is time and death; a god has neither, nor both. It is meaningless."
— Harigamun, *Thoughts of War*

Haffi sped through the deep caverns taking a moment to catch his breath. The thought of the frosted fowl of which Dwiddli spoke tormented the ill-tempered dwarf, giving him greater speed in pursuit of his father.

It had taken hours for Haffi's party to reach the depths of the cavern where the mysterious Dwiddli had his feast, which his party enjoyed in hearty gratitude. The time seemed nothing more than moments now as he hurried with breakneck haste.

The time it had initially taken for Haffi and Saroria's party to reach Dwiddli's hearth was stretched due to the studying of the labyrinthian caverns and strange stones winding like spirals of a tree's trunk, arguing about each secluded hole and how many it could sleep. It all faded in an instant as Haffi climbed back to the entrance.

At full tilt, Haffi's head smashed against something hard from hurriedly cutting a sharp corner, and he fell to the ground. Regathering his composure, the dizziness from the hit dissipated and Haffi realized in that moment what, or who, he had run into.

"Haffi!" Dhamri shouted. "What madness has you without your mother at these uncertain depths? Can neither you nor your father be trusted with your duties to family?"

Haffi, less interested in patient niceties than the opposing Dhamri who clearly and *loudly* had eyes toward his mother, rose to his feet and met his opposition nose-to-nose.

"I'll not hear your continued peacocking for my mother, you wretched rat," Haffi shoved his opponent into the wall behind him. "Play your games of unrequited lust if you must, but our hunting party faces death! Turn and face the frosted fowl with me or chase my mother into the cavernous bowels of this lava mountain. But be not in my way lest you no longer value your life!"

Dhamri was dumbfounded, both by the outright accusations and the plea for urgency. He lifted himself from the collapsed position against the cavern wall and leaned in to speak. "I know not what this frosted fowl is you speak of but tell me this, dwarf prince, who faces the greater danger, your mother or father?"

Haffi noted sincerity which seemed to override the emotional grudges the devious dwarf held against his father.

"I know not, Dhamri," Haffi freed a small breath. "Mother stands alone as the scouting party has all but passed into a trance of sleepiness from some unkind meal found deep in the mountain. But my father faces a titan of old, a gargantuan bird of ages lost—skin like crystals that likely commands the cold surrounding this mountain."

Within a second, Dhamri gave his response. "We go to your father. I will send what remains of my party to aid your mother."

Dhamri turned to his remaining company and spoke to his second-in-command, Gwalli. "You will give no quarter to anything that looks to oppose our calling of this mountain our home," Dhamri said, "and you will make sure nothing, not a finger, is lain upon Saroria! Should something happen to her, you'd best run far from this mountain before I return! I go to save a fool," he turned and gave a glance to Haffi before looking back at his lieutenant, "but I return for something far greater."

With that, Gwalli and his men sped off into the darkness of the tunnels.

Dhamri joined Haffi in sprinting toward the entrance of the mountain. The two dwarves made no effort to speak and often turned to see who had gained more footing on the other. They were not competing in sport nor were they enjoying each other's company. No, their interest was purely one of strength and vigor, most importantly, which of them possessed more.

As Haffi's numbers had dwindled within dark caves and food had become more and more scarce, the slow whispers of death crept about in the shadows of every dwarven mind. He knew the only way forward was made of bloody choices.

Eventually, Dhamri and Haffi breached the threshold of the cavern and were hauled into the freezing abyss surrounding the mountain. The shock of the cold from the cocoon of warmth wracked Dhamri's skin and made it crawl while Haffi, through Dhamri's eyes, seemed unaffected.

"Where were they heading?" Haffi demanded.

"Likely beyond the mountain's base. We came from below and thus we'd not seen any Grand Hides from that way. Would have made more sense for your father to go where we had not yet gone," Dhamri grinned. "We will climb!"

Dhamri is right, Haffi thought to himself. They would chase beyond the threshold of the mountain and go to what lay beyond, or above. With that, Haffi broke into a sprint and hurled himself into the white squall as Dhamri tried to keep up.

It seemed an eternity for the dwarves as their strength waned under the unfathomable cold of the intensifying gale of ice and snow. But then, Dhamri saw something that looked like a nest as they approached the hillside of ice leading up the mountain's peak. He called out to Haffi . . . who could not hear him.

"Haffi!" Dhamri shouted. "Haffi, we've entered its home! Haffi! Turn back for a moment and hear my calls! Haffi!"

Dhamri's shouts were useless amid the growing squeals of the blinding storm before them. It was then Dhamri felt his foot scrape against a hard piece of the mountain. He reached below the depths of snow and ripped the rock from the mountainside with a frozen hand, barely holding onto it. He aimed the projectile at his companion and let loose, hitting its mark in the dwarf's back and nearly knocking him down. Haffi turned to see his attacker pointing his long axe toward a glacial structure.

As they moved in closer, the two dwarves realized the nest before them was fashioned from crystal feathers in a mesmerizing design and was larger than any cave dwelling they'd ever seen. Both of the dwarves were privy to the grace of grand emeralds and other fine stones lining caverns in the deepest parts of the south and recognized the similarities immediately. It was something profound and gratifying while also being a horrid sight of strength by which small dwarves could never know. They shrunk under the sheer size of an egg, thus, infecting them with terror of the thing that laid it.

"This must be its home," Dhamri said as he looked at Haffi with fear in his voice.

At the far edge of the nest, beneath the quelling snowstorm, ten or more black eggs were revealed.

"They're oozing," Dhamri said as he approached one of the eggs. "The eggs seem to be bleeding some thick, green...something of a nasty sort."

Haffi looked at each of the eggs and noticed they were in fact releasing a green substance and had been horribly cracked as if trying to hatch.

With a surprise crash of Dhamri's axes against one of the eggs, the green substance splashed around the snow, and the top of one of the eggs crumbled. Haffi lifted himself to the edge of the broken egg by hanging his spear on the edge and pulling himself up.

"What do you see?" Dhamri's voice called from behind the screeching storm.

"Crystals and death," Haffi answered.

Dhamri's mind became racked with confusion. "What do you mean?"

"A frosted fowl, still yet a fledgling. I'd venture to say it never lived."

Dhamri's curiosity took hold and he began cracking eggs and climbing them the same way Haffi had done. He found the same—death and crystals. These things didn't die well. It was a sorrowful sight to see something of such crystalline magnificence smothered in the likeness of black tar and steaming death which smelled like a lost forge trying to garner fire–pointless and dark.

"Why did they die?" Dhamri asked, as if his companion had more information than he.

The two sat amid the green-covered snow and thought for a moment, trying to understand their circumstances in the raucous silence of the blizzard. Then, out of the white came a scream so painful the dwarves had to cover their ears.

A great flapping from tremendous shadows formed into wings which changed the direction of the snowstorm's turbulence. The fluttering wings of the frosted fowl caused an immense shadow beyond the gale until its crystal body glimmered inside a frozen tempest.

"Go, now!" Haffi sprang from the ground and raced toward the crystalline creature. "Bow down, Crytungr!"

Dhamri followed the dwarven prince with speed as he approached the icy vortex surrounding the great bird. A monstrous combination of unnatural circumstance and myth it was, the freezing unforgiveness of the worst of the world weaponized by a predator of mostly forgotten legends in which dwarves thought only lived in the stories of drunkards who sat darkness with handfuls of ale and meat.

"We must break through!" Dhamri shouted as the two dwarves stood outside the maelstrom.

Haffi reached his hand forward to touch the gale and within a split second, the tip of his finger was either frozen and knocked off or cut away. The cold left him feeling nothing.

"We cannot break through, not like this!" Haffi shouted back to his companion.

"Go now, Bulroar! Launch your spear and spread that crack of its skin," a voice within the vortex yelled. "Break its hold on this frozen hurricane!'

For a moment the vortex broke away and the two dwarves saw Grunffi and his hunting party. The party was trapped by the threshold of the vortex made by Crytungr but upon a weapon being flung toward the godly bird, a small break in the storm appeared.

Before Grunffi noticed them coming, Haffi slid into his father, knocking him into the snow, unable to stop his speedy approach after stepping onto the ice.

"Son, why have you come?" Grunffi rose from the ground and saw his son's companion approaching. "Why have you both come?"

"There's no time, not now," Dhamri answered. "We were told of the bird, and now we must escape!"

"There is no escape," Grunffi said with a grunt as he pulled his long axe from the snow. "The bird has killed Beror, son of Bulroar, and this is our home now. We kill the bird! Slay the fowl and honor Beror!"

Grunffi turned and sprinted toward the rest of the party who stood before the fowl as it wretched in pain from Bulroar's long axe.

Grunffi approached the enraged father of a fallen son. "Bulroar, do ya still have your other axe?"

"Aye, M'lord, and I'll bury it in the damnable bird," Bulroar quelled his grief, lips twitching, speech flinching.

"Krabella, you're the smallest of us all," Grunffi began as he garnered an unhappy look from her husband, Skolgrim. "If I can get close enough to the bird, I'll throw ya to its stomach where Bulroar's long axe pierces its crystal skin. If ya can further break its armor, or better, deepen the blade, we may yet have a chance of killing it!"

Skolgrim knew there was no time to argue, so he gave a dissatisfied grunt.

"Skolgrim, we need to lower the bird once more to the ground, and you're the fastest here. Is your blade sharp?"

Skolgrim, the bladesmith, looked at his leader but gave no more answer than before.

"I think I saw another crack in its skin just above its talons on the right leg. If you can bear your weight down enough, it may be all we need!" Grunffi knew his kindred was furious with him for suggesting his wife should be thrown to the talons of ancient myth, but Grunffi also knew his kin would follow.

The vortex began anew, and the hunters realized they had wasted too much time in the moments trying to devise a plan. Consequently, the vortex cast away all of the snow on the ground below the dwarves and left a bare mountain floor, shocking them all with a great gust. Within a second, Skolgrim took off toward Crytungr and bolted toward its leg.

The frosted fowl lowered its head to release another blow as it took in a deep breath. It was then Haffi launched one of his spears into the fowl's eye, staggering the monstrous beast.

Following Haffi's attack, Skolgrim reached the base of the bird but could not find a crack. Skolgrim was torn from thigh to neck by Crytungr's talons as the beast retaliated and the quickest of the dwarves was left bleeding on the mountainside.

Krabella cried out "Skol! No, not my Skol!" She turned to the beast and took off on her own, but to the bird's other leg.

The fowl lifted its limb and looked to stomp the newfound widow, but her quickness allowed her to dodge the heavy stomping. Krabella rolled back toward the leg and jumped onto one of its talons, and it was there she saw the crack! With a hard thrust, she broke the skin on Crytungr's foot, and the bird came crashing down onto its belly.

Krabella jumped off the foot of the bird and ran after Grunffi who raced toward her. Grunffi grabbed hold of her and launched her like a stone toward the axe lodged into the powerful bird, and she grabbed hold of it. Her weight bent the blade in such a way that it ripped open a larger portion of the fowl's belly, sending her onto the mountain with Crytungr.

Bulroar pounced as soon as he saw the opening that had been left. "I'll see you soon, Belror!" Bulroar rushed the fowl and launched his body at the cracked skin of the bird with his full weight into piercing its heart.

Crytungr let out a deafening screech of pain which knocked the attacking dwarf unconscious and sent him hurtling toward the ground. As the tyrannous fowl tried to regain its standing, Haffi let loose his last spear, and further impaled the beast.

Crytungr tilted back and forth as it struggled to breathe, and then came down... crushing Bulroar. The frosted fowl of forgotten fables was slain, and so too was Bulroar, son of Belrackum, father of Belror.

But then, the fowl's body faded into ice leaving a broken Bulroar below, as if the bird's body was never there; while snow reclaimed the mountain and the vortex disappeared, some life crawled from the dying dwarf's lungs. "I go to halls of ancestral stone," he coughed with a smile, reaching around as he clearly looked for his weapon.

Haffi handed Bulroar his blade and he instantly pulled it to his chest weakly. "I yield to the undying death and on to the forever forges to stand with he who crafts creation." Blood followed the cough. "I will be in the hardiest of company, with beer and axe as companions, as I face the Long Forges with my," more blood forced its way up from his lungs, "my worthy son."

Haffi closed the eyes of his brother, sad and broken by his death, but with a small happiness as he did. *I hope I may die the same, beside my father.*

"How badly are ya hurt?" Dhamri asked Skolgrim as he rushed to his side.

Skolgrim, with a gash running from his thigh to his neck, struggled to speak. "The ice f-f-f-eels like it's f-f-freezing my blood," he said as his teeth chittered.

Dhamri looked over his wounds and deemed he could live, but not easily. "Can ya walk?"

"Not alone," the wounded dwarf answered.

"Grunffi, come and help me take Skolgrim back to the caves!" Dhamri shouted.

Krabella had already rushed over and was holding Skolgrim from falling into the snow. "Will he live?" she asked with a heavy weight on her heart and frozen tears on her cheeks.

"If we act quickly," Grunffi said, lifting Skolgrim by wrapping his arms around Grunffi and Dhamri.

"What of Bulroar and Belror?" Skolgrim asked as he coughed blood.

"We save the living, then we honor the dead," Grunffi answered.

"No, Grunffi, we still have to save the wife you chose to leave in the dark places of this mountain," Dhamri said with a scowl as they carried Skolgrim.

Before the group could take more than a few steps, the mountain began to quake, and a new hurricane of ice formed from the white storm approaching. As quick as their legs could pivot, they turned back and ran with all the strength their lungs mustered whilst Grunffi and Dhamri dragged Skolgrim.

Grunffi took a misstep and launched the three dwarves into a frozen pillar. His son, hearing their thunderous clap against the mountain despite the whirling frost, turned and stopped them from falling to even greater depths as he rushed to grab each of them, stopping their momentum just enough before jumping to the next.

As they recovered, Dhamri and Grunffi took less than seconds to regain their balance, but once they did, saw Grunffi's son racing down the mountain with the wounded dwarf hoisted onto his back while his wife followed, hoping, praying she was not fast becoming a widow.

Then, the icy sting of the storm stiffened their muscles. Howling from beyond, a voice ran down each of their spines and seemed to cast a spell of numbness upon their bodies, though the freezing cold stayed. Each of them stood idle amid the storm as the voice echoed around them.

"*That was more than just a bird, greedy dwarves,*" the voice chilled an already unbearable cold. "*What you call* Crytungr *was more than a myth. I have more than one titan of old at my call.*" The voice cackled, deeply. "*Return to your cavern, deal with the flesh-eaters, and then come deeper than those sickly abominations dare to delve. Come know a god and see how others have paid the price bestowed unto me. Come see how one can place suffering on another!*"

The words cracked harder against Grunffi and Haffi than any whip. *Flesh-eater.* The feeling rushed back into their legs, warmth returned to their heart just to be smacked with frost, blood returned to their hands and the dwarves dashed back to the cavern without speaking a word. Haffi breached the mouth of the mountain first, dropping the wounded dwarf mid-pace as he rushed into the depths of the mountain.

Grunffi slid, bashing into a stalagmite trying to slow his momentum as he broke through the cavern entrance followed by Krabella heading to her husband's side.

As she looked at her love, Krabella noticed a different paleness had overtaken him beyond the cold of the mountaintop. His eyes held the sheen of frozen snow, glinting with a coral glimmer from the fire struggling to keep its embers going in the harsh cold. She grabbed his hands and held back her tears as she felt the absence of her husband for the first time in two decades. Even in the unforgiving winds that could steal a stray finger under the mountain chill, Skolgrim's hands could still bring her warmth…but no more. *Grunffi was wrong.* The ice had in fact worsened the wounds in the short time the wounded dwarf was exposed to the foul winds. He was bitten with the worst of frost.

Krabella twisted to face her King with a quickness that left her stumbling to regain her footing and launched a rock she'd picked up from beside Skolgrim's head.

"You knew damn well we wouldn't find one of those damned beasts out there! You knew it and you still took us out there! Why? So you could feel as if you were leading us? So you could pretend you didn't lead us all to our deaths? We could have stayed in the South and fought!"

Grunffi blocked the stone with his forearm covered in a Grand Hide bracer. The rock left no mark on him, though his stomach felt unnatural, and his head turned sour. *She's right.*

"You ran from the death of your son and the fear in your heart!" Krabella marched toward him. "Why would you lead us into this if you knew the peril?"

"I didn't…" he whispered as his lips quivered. "I—I—"

"What do you mean you didn't?" Krabella stood inches in front of him with her weapon drawn on his neck.

"Cold. I knew it was c-c-cold." He began to feel it. The treacherous and frigid winds wiped out what remained of the flame and Grunffi's stomach formed into a black pit. No feeling could be felt, and tears formed, though he knew not why. "I can't…"

"You can't what? You brought us here, damn you! And now you say you didn't know? What didn't you know?"

Krabella slammed her blade against the wall beside Grunffi and he fell to his knees. She looked at her former King—for a King required a kingdom, a people, and he had none—as he fell, collapsing on the floor in broken speech. She realized the futility of questioning further for a forlornness had overtaken him; bereft of purpose, he kneeled as a weeping weakling in the eyes of the scorned widow.

"We don't have time for this, your wife is still down there!" Krabella turned and bolted down the bowels of the mountain leaving Grunffi in the dirt with nothing but the cold of the mountain and the carcass of a fallen warrior to accompany him.

Moments passed, and Grunffi had not kept track of time. His thoughts wandered into darkness. He was no longer aware of the passing events around him as he was locked in a dark psyche meant to deliberately tear him down—for he deserved to be stricken down. *I wouldn't have brought them If I'd known.*

Grunffi's mind was overcome with grief for those of his people he'd lost. The cold stinging in his heart reminded him of the dwarves who died to get to the mountain: Skolgrim, Beror, Bulroar, and many others paid an undeserving price for his decisions. But how could he turn back? How could he have known at the first sight of snowfall in the North it would have been so bad? It was never this way, not in his father's travels—least not in the stories.

No, something made the conditions of the North unbearable. This was not how it had always been, but he could not figure out how something so drastic could have happened and each step he took forward brought him further from the option of return. Once suffering commenced, turning back would mean surrender. It would mean choosing to fight in one direction or another, be it Ograas or men or elves. They had to push forward, and they had pushed too far. *They're all in danger, and I—*

He snapped back into himself. A black cold surrounded him in the silence of the cave as it was frosted by the outer icy winds. *Saroria,* he remembered. And with that, Grunffi rose from his crouched seat of pity and headed into the depths of the cavern, hoping he was not too late.

Grunffi's labored and exhausted sprint delving into the mountain seemed longer than his journey to the mountain. His heart ached and his stomach collapsed as tears blotted his vision in the dismal mountain cavities. Breathing became difficult and anguish overtook his mind as images flashed showing the death of his remaining company and his family. *Flesh-eater,* Grunffi recalled right before he tripped over an unseen mountain vein peeking from the ground. The dwarf's face crashed against the jagged wall, cutting him. As he lay there for a mere moment, he saw Saroria in his mind being roasted like a boar... and Haffi, how could he have let him run off alone?

With a great heave and blood dripping from his face, Grunffi launched himself back into the air. "Not now," he said aloud with a grunt. "Not until I know my failings are beyond repair."

A short sprint after his fall, a small and whimpered speech echoed against the cavern's odd stone. The crack of flames welded themselves against the cavern's deep and shadows pranced along the wall—small shadows, smaller than he could recognize. He crept to the edge of the fire's chamber and peered his head around the bend. There he saw a great number of scraggly, feeble fighters with chattering teeth, as if they were cold. But he felt a great warmth from the depths of the mountain, yet they still appeared cold, and the few faces he could see were pale and sickly. *What are they?* Then he saw a line of dwarves laid upon the wall. They were his company, and they were bound in rope.

"No, Dhamri!" a voice shouted.

No...Grunffi realized it wasn't just any voice. It was his wife's voice, and his son sat beside her. His head peeked farther around the corner, and Grunffi saw four wretched creatures hoist Dhamri onto his feet before dragging him, fighting, to a spit above a billowing fire as Saroria continued to scream his name.

For a moment, Grunffi considered the pains Dhamri caused him and the relentless questioning of his leadership. Perhaps, if he arrived too late, none could blame him for Dhamri's fate. Perhaps he could not affect his fate in the first place. *Such weakness. I was never fit to rule . . .*

But he heard the cries of his wife once more as she called Dhamri's name and pleaded with the mountain-dwellers to let him go while the other dwarves sat silently and watched. Their faces dripped from the deep cavern's heat and their stomachs racked like beaten drums dismayed from the foul meal they had stolen.

In that moment, Grunffi noticed a large, moveable rock. It was large enough to hide his body if only for a short time. He turned back the way he came and quickly shuffled down the tunnel as he heard Dhamri calling for help. But the cries changed. The dwarf no longer struggled to escape. Something was touching him, and he was pushing away.

Thereupon, Grunffi let loose a wild roar that echoed throughout the cavern, likely heard all the way back to the entrance at the base of the mountain if any were there to hear it.

The flesh-eaters shrunk beneath their small statures. Voices whispered to one another as they considered what the cause of the great howling might have been. Then, Saroria watched as Dwiddli—leader of the flesh eaters—ordered a large number of his company to explore the tunnels.

Dhamri was immediately dropped to the floor as his carriers were among those selected. As he lay beside the fire, Saroria smiled, realizing time was bought, for she knew the monster in the shadows.

Some fifteen or so of the flesh-eating dwarves headed into the tunnels against their own craven misgivings. One of them, in the back of the company, whispered to another who also made sure to be at the back of the company.

"I—I don't want to see what that did," the craven whispered.

"Better than being dinner," the other flesh-eating dwarf mumbled.

Grunffi could no longer hear the cries of Dhamri. *He's safe, for now.*

The dwarven leader watched from behind a large obsidian stone as those who dwelt in the lava mountain passed. Their faces were shallow and long with age of years written across them. They seemed sickly and unkind, likely brittle to a hardened touch. Grunffi quickly realized he could contend with many of these pathetic dwarves though there were still at least twenty which could still prove to be a threat.

Thus, Grunffi waited until grumblings began anew, and Dhamri's voice struggled once more. Clearly, the frightened group would not let fear stand in the way of dinner.

Grunffi stepped out into the cavern tunnel and turned toward the direction the flesh-eaters went and let out one more thunderous roar. The scouting party heard the wild noise behind them and immediately turned with a full sprint.

"If we passed them, there can't have been that many," the leader at the front of the group said.

However, those still in the chamber heard not just the menacing bellow through the tunnels, but now the tumultuous footfall of the flesh-eating, dwarven company rushing backward.

Dwiddli needed to take decisive action. "We're being attacked! Go now and claim the mountain deeps!"

At Dwiddli's command, the sickly dwarves jumped forth with tremors and drove into the darkness chasing the approaching threat. None of the dwarves from either side of the tunnel held a torch and the tunnel was thick with shadow. They were, each of them, beset with fear and hunger.

As the first scouting party came trampling down the cavern path, Grunffi launched his axe from behind the obsidian stone. The blade split one of the dwarves' skulls down the middle while the sharp edge at the top of its shaft pierced another in the eye. Their bodies crashed against the dust-covered ground releasing clouds of dirt as the surrounding company tried to stop and see what had happened.

The scouting party's investigation ended abruptly as the second party of dwarves rushed from the central chamber of the mountain and sprinted toward the scouting party—unbeknownst to either side—in the blind darkness. The scouting party from each side started to throw axes at the opposing, indiscernible group approaching them resulting in the deaths of two more dwarves, and suddenly, an eruption of war broke out amongst the flesh-eaters in the darkness of the lava mountain.

Amid the mayhem, Grunffi broke from behind the large stone, leaving his axe in the shadows. He darted into the main chamber where seven more dwarves and their leader remained, as the flesh-eaters fought amongst themselves in the darkness.

Dhamri yelled at Grunffi upon sight. "Get me untied so I can stick your face to the fire!"

Next, all remaining flesh-eating dwarves dashed toward an unarmed Grunffi.

The dwarven King took off sprinting toward his opposition and grabbed one of the fire-cooked cauldrons roasting above one of the smaller firepits. The blaze of the cauldron meant nothing to the enraged dwarf as he cast its boiling contents on the flesh-eaters approaching him, causing them to flail screaming on the ground as their faces began to peel. Grunffi cracked one of the dwarves with the now empty cauldron, still in hand, so hard it rang throughout the chamber and left the sickly dwarf's head smashed and utterly unrecognizable in the dirt, his lifeblood oozing onto the floor. Another two dwarves immediately stopped upon seeing their comrades' heads crushed, threw their weapons down, and fell to their knees with frantic, unrecognizable speech pleading for their lives.

The colossal dwarf—in the eyes of his enemies—walked toward them with slow steps, crunching the rocks beneath his feet. Once in front of them, he picked up both of their weapons, and without thought, stabbed their rusted blades through the caps of their heads so fiercely their spears, from top to chin, broke through their skulls causing the blades to hold their bodies upright. He slowly raised his face and eyes to Dwiddli who stood beside a bonded and cooking Dhamri, still alive, but unsure for how much longer against the unbearable heat.

Grunffi heard footsteps approach the threshold of the feasting chamber and he hurried to release the bindings of his captured company.

He untied his wife and son first, then a few more, before giving them blades to cut the bindings themselves.

He figured Dhamri would be fine for another few moments.

Haffi, with stiff red eyes, strained breathing, and a tightly clenched jaw, slowly walked to the three dwarves still screeching in pain from the boiling water cast on them.

"Fast, or slow?" he asked with a measured voice.

The three struggled to keep their faces up, stuttering as their bodies quaked.

"Last time. Fast... or slow?" he repeated.

"Please, sir," one of them began. "It wasn't for us. We didn't want to—"

Haffi shoved his spear from the dwarf's chin through the top of his head and quickly ripped it back out, leaving the sickly dwarf in a pool of his own making as the other two started to wail, snot running down their faces.

As the stampeding footsteps of the remaining flesh-eating dwarves approached the open chamber, Haffi had a brief look of sadness.

"Looks like someone else is making your decisions for you," Haffi said, and quickly slashed their throats before turning to see his fellow dwarves now all unbound with their weapons in hand.

Next, Dwiddli watched in horror as the innards of his company were strewn about the cavern walls—those of Grunffi's party had recovered from their sickness, and were, understandably, furious.

It was a slaughter. The few remaining flesh-eating dwarves, which had not killed one another within the shadows of panic, were stricken down by Grunffi's company. The leader of the flesh-eaters merely watched, continuing to stand near Dhamri who had not yet been set free.

"Speak," Grunffi said to their leader as his wife bent to free Dhamri. "What sickness drove you to the eating of your own kind?"

Dwiddli gave a raspy snicker. "Where do you think we come from,

Ogre?"

"*Ogre?*" Grunffi's left dimple rose as one of his eyes squinted. "I'm a dwarf, not a foul beast from the South!"

Another smile from Dwiddli. "Like me? Your hands seem fine." The pale dwarf looked down at Grunffi's hands which should have been scolded by the cauldron. "I speak of no such southern ugliness. I speak of the stone in your heart." He laughed.

"I am nothing like you!" Grunffi grabbed a hold of the frail dwarf's tunic and lifted him in the air.

"That much is clear," the shrunken dwarf responded.

Grunffi released his grip and the raspy dwarf fell with a loud yelp.

Dwiddli rose and dusted himself off as he met the dwarven King's eyes. "You have his bearing, you know."

Grunffi became bewildered. "Whose?"

The dwarven company behind him had started grumbling to one another.

"Balooffi, or Baloo, as we called him."

Grunffi stepped backward into his wife as he tried to reclaim his breath. In his moment of silence, she was the only other dwarf to recognize the name.

"How did you know his father?" Saroria asked.

"You've some nerve coming back to this mountain, Grunffi," the pale dwarf scoffed. "Fifty some-odd years since your lot abandoned us. You left the mountain!" He spat at Grunffi's feet. "You left your people! You left our god!"

"Our god?" Grunffi asked.

"Baylar, word-smithy!" Dwiddli fell to his knees and clapped his hands together. "God-forger and Lord of Summoners, he who gives life to all dwarves!"

"God-forger?" whispered the crowd of dwarves.

"Baylar gave power to the other Lords of Kaiya with nothing more than words! He is the smithy of all smiths, he who needs no fire nor heat nor stone to smith that which is strongest in this land!"

The surrounding company stood in shock as they witnessed Dwiddli continue to deliver praise for a god whom none had ever heard of. The flesh-eating coward spoke of bringing mythical beasts back to life, commanding legions of terrifying creatures the world would quake in fear of, and the single-handed destruction of an entire pantheon of gods... all at the hands of this, Baylar.

"Ya know of my lineage and speak of a god I know nothing of." Grunffi snorted in frustration. "You'd eat your own kind and yet expect me to trust your words. I say you might have known my father. But what of this god means anything to me?"

Dwiddli rose from his pious position on the ground and began to show his sharp and mangled teeth trimmed with a wicked yellow. "You and yours left this mountain upon Baylar's arrival. Your father had rested upon the same seat of judgment as you do now."

Grunffi couldn't recall his childhood as it was over fifteen decades ago. His memories of the North were nothing, oral traditions laid down by his father as all others from that age had withered. He had nearly refused to speak of it and left Dwaharim or died.

"What about Baylar made my father leave?" Grunffi asked.

In a rush of impatience and fuming with rage, Haffi surprised his father by leaping forward and jumping on top of the flesh-eater, beating him into the dirt. Grunffi acted just as quickly, pulling his son off the mangled dwarf, but the face of Dwiddli was bloody and his speech foggy.

"I need to know!" Grunffi threw his son to the side. "Stay yourself lest ya earn yourself a fate akin to the one you just brought upon this disheveled dwarf! You will have your way once I know what I need to know!"

Grunffi turned back to the beaten craven who was spitting out blood. His son stepped back in respect, not anger.

"Why did my father leave?" Grunffi's voice grew less patient and his tone spelled worse for the beaten menace than what his son had already given the vile dwarf.

"Your father was too scared of feeding him," the weak dwarf spat.

Grunffi's pupils went wide and a coldness swept underneath his skin. "What have you eaten these past years?" Grunffi's teeth grit against one another as he awaited a response.

"Whatever Baylar gives us after we feed him," Dwiddli answered as his eyes rolled black and his head smacked against the floor.

"And what did you feed Baylar?" Grunffi asked, a squinted brow and lowered tone held hostage by an inquisitive nature driving the dwarven King, for now, more than anger.

"Meat. Only meat," the sickly dwarf answered.

"And when you found no beasts to feed your god?"

Dwiddli cracked a final smile. "We became the beasts."

Grunffi turned to his scorned son and gave him a nod, a nod which became instantly understood as approving of something wicked—his son's violent satiation.

Haffi jumped onto the mongrel with his bare fists and continued beating him into the ground until all movement stopped and gashes painted his knuckles red.

"So, your father learned of this god who wanted to be fed by the dwarves, who supposedly created the dwarves, and he fled to the South?" Saroria asked with a contorted facial expression.

"He spoke of a long rivalry between Northern and Southern dwarves, though he never explained it as being more than a grudge against us for not living under a mountain, at least, not like those of the North. I knew they took hold in the deep mountains to avoid the harshest moments of winter, but Baloo never once spoke of winds nor snow quite this strong, and I cannot recall for myself." Grunffi scratched at his head.

"That's why he called you, *Ogre*," Haffi said. "They resented us for having a more fulfilling life as we grew larger, both in stature and life, more than they could hiding in these icy lava mountains." He wiped the remains of the bloody dwarf onto his leather.

"Ogre dwarves!" Grunffi said loudly as he looked over his entire company. "Perhaps it is time we create our own myth, eh?"

"What of the voice in the winds?" Haffi asked as he wrapped his hands in bandages.

Saroria, once again, turned to Grunffi looking for answers, and he gave them. "A voice on the mountain spoke to us after we felled a great beast. It called on us to delve deeper into the mountains. Now we know who the voice belonged to."

Grunffi walked around his remaining dwarven company, of less than twenty, checking their reignment, and pricking his finger against the sharpness of their blades. "Let's go meet a god, lads!"

CHAPTER SEVEN

KYRA'S CHANCE MEETING

"At what point does it stop being a crime to steal someone's blood, if it's for the right reasons? If my task is done and the lands of Kaiya are set loose from the bondage of religion, if I have given free will back to the world, would I be judged so harshly for taking the blood of one woman? Here be my confession, then. I did that and far more to end tyranny, and I would do far worse. See how your metal bars hold a man captive in death, for that is where you will find me . . . in the bleak after of which we do not know is where you will have the time to judge me."

— Harigamun, *Thoughts of War*

B uzzes and the whipping snaps of thunder filled the air as the sky cracked beneath the surge of Krishalla's lightning as it smothered Runefall. Hands holding swords—with the promise of final and everlasting glory—ached to clash against shields. But the hearts fueling those hands feared their final days. Women, men, and fighters of many races from different corners of the world gathered to spread like a foul torrent of revenge meant to wither old stone, and this knowledge haunted Arimeus

"Where does he mean to take us?" Samiel asked.

"To the Stained Temple, *as was prophesied*," Kyra jested, breathing heavily and struggling to keep up with the old man.

"Kyra," Samiel swung his hand out as if to grab her attention, "the temple lies to the East."

"And?" Her voice was nearly careless.

She wasn't careless, though, and Samiel knew that. Her limbs jerked with each step she took with the old man guiding them. She was angry; justifiably angry that a bunch of old men decided her fate, and that one of those insignificant men, who couldn't claim mastery of his magic, was leading her.

"We're heading Northwest of the city," said Samiel. He stopped running and leaned against the walls of a temple made by a large and archaic structure of ornate style detailing within marble stone, both to catch his breath and challenge their direction. The knotty and elaborate city proudly complicated its daedal architecture, but Samiel still knew where he was at all times.

"Where do you mean to take us? The Eastern gate lies not this way, Arimeus," Samiel said.

Kyra looked at her friend and saw a distorted, uncomfortable look on his face. She hung her head low, waiting for a moment, and preparing herself for Arimeus's outburst—for he would have one, that much was predictable. He had a plan but clearly did not want to tell them. *Why?*

"Would you have me deliver you to a scouting party, boy? Tell me, how often is it you've ventured beyond the wall? How often that you've parlayed with your enemy?"

Kyra watched as Samiel's face turned a pinkish tan as he straightened his back and stared at the old man.

When redness touched Samiel's brown skin, she always thought it was cute. Her favorite were the moments when he was frightened or embarrassed. For all his strength, Samiel was never quick to force. In fact, one might consider the oversized Litree feared his own strength with how little he wielded it—at least, that's what Kyra thought.

Arimeus barked, clearly growing tired of the insufferable questions. "Or, perhaps, you'd rather try explaining to me why it is that Harigamun and his brood wish to tear down this city? Go on then. You seem to have your strategy all figured out as the haunts of *war* knock at our doorstep! Enlighten me, and if not on your battle plans, then as to why would the battle even take place?"

"I—" Samiel cleared his throat and stretched his back as if to seem larger. "My friends spoke of the warlord. He bends all to his will, and when Runefall resisted his tyranny, he vowed to destroy the city. That's why Kyra and me, and the others... that's why we were all taken from our homes. Tir looked to the gods, and they told her we were the only chance Kaiya had to survive his war because we were the strongest."

Arimeus laughed, and Kyra quickly saw the Chief Runic's smile wane and his face crinkle into some broken feeling or loneliness of some kind. She could not make out the expression, but it did not seem happy.

"I do wish that were the case, boy." Arimeus reached to Samiel and pulled him close for a deep embrace.

The Chief Runic turned to Kyra, motioning her to join in the embrace. She did and felt warm for a moment, though she also felt incredible contempt as, just moments ago, Arimeus held back none of his harshest words in front of her teacher. It seemed out of character for him to be so compassionate now, the small amount of character she had known.

"War looms and I've not the time to tell you both," Arimeus said as he lowered himself to one knee. "I promise you; I will tell you the truth of the matter, but as of now, I need you both to trust me so I can get us out of this city. Though, I doubt we will escape without a fight," he gave a deep sigh. "Do not engage unless I tell you to and understand that all you deserve to know will come to be known. But for now, we must flee."

Kyra looked at Samiel who had a look of disillusionment which pained her as she could not understand the true meaning written on his face. He always tried so hard not to be scared. Was that what he was doing? Trying not to be scared? She could not tell, but Samiel did not resist the commands of Arimeus, so the two of them silently agreed to continue forward.

Tremendous flaming boulders battered against the city's barriers as they moved. The assault had started. Fiery masses shattered on impact creating a roaring ringing sound as if metal banged against a horrendous gong. Each flaming attack rang through the ears of those in Runefall and caused piercing pains to any who could hear. As three monstrous hunks of mass came clambering down upon the city, the pain dragged Samiel and Kyra to the ground, leaving Arimeus frightened enough to take cover behind a bronze statue of Barigund.

Kyra looked toward the other two gesticulating for them to gather around her. As they approached, Arimeus watched as she spat on the ground and formed a rune, he was familiar with using the small amount of liquid.

"What good will mind speak do for us amid this racket? I can't hear myself think!"

Kyra gave no attention to the old man. *How does nobody understand this magic?* She broke the rune symbol and crossed it with another. This sent Arimeus winching backwards with a mixture of fear, or sacrilege.

"If you break your seal and anything goes wrong you do not understand the cost of this magic! Look upon me for a moment so you might see what you risk!"

Kyra gave no heed to his words. She slashed the symbol and embedded it with another. Now, Arimeus recognized the second rune. "Not only would you have us speak through minds that cannot think, but you'd take away the wagging of our tongues in the same instance?"

Arimeus thrust forward to push Kyra away from the rune she crafted but knocked himself backward instead. In a state of confusion and laden on his back, Arimeus briefly met eyes with her, and he saw the glint of something flash against the thrashing lightning above.

"Perhaps you've more to learn of this magic than you think, old man,"

Kyra said as she cut the rune a third time. The spit faded, but she didn't care. She didn't need it. The shape was drawn in her mind. She didn't need something physical to enable a rune's power, she just preferred the visual element.

Samiel watched in bewilderment as his affinity to magic was close to nil. He gave up the practice years ago and held only a basic understanding. However, the young brute thought he noticed the third rune as one often used by Kyra in their youth.

"The sleep spell?" Samiel asked.

"What sleep spell?" Arimeus jumped up from the ground and looked upon the third rune she drew.

"This is no sleep spell." Arimeus stepped backward and glared at her. "This rune will deafen us. She would take away our ability to speak and hear."

A barrage of debris coated in flame came bashing against the barriers of the city once more and Arimeus fell to his knees as his hands reached to cover his ears. "I cannot see straight. We cannot travel like this!" Arimeus muttered as the young Litree struggled to hold his composure beside the old man.

Kyra though, she had gone away. Her mind was elsewhere, as were her ears and eyes, or that is what the Chief Runic assumed as she seemed unphased.

"Give me your hand!' Kyra took the young Litree's hand, pushing it against the thrice broken rune, and with a burst of energy, the two could no longer hear with their ears or speak with their mouths.

A larger barrage than before beat against the top of the city and Arimeus crumbled. He was supposed to have more time and now he would need to fight to get her out of the city. *Makes it seem more convincing, I guess,* Arimeus thought, trying to keep calm.

Kyra called over to the Chief Runic and placed his hands on the rune as well. She could not speak to him, and the sounds seemed not to affect her. The Chief Runic, for only a moment, wondered if he understood what she was doing, what she had been doing this entire time.

Samiel stood as if nothing had happened, showing no signs of pain from the bangs of war surrounding them. He and she and the old man too were in a stasis of silence. Their speech turned into a dialogue of the mind as thought became their wagging tongues.

"It won't last forever," Kyra assured the other two. "Just long enough for us to escape, I hope."

"Perhaps you are the one," Arimeus thought, and consequently said, rising from the ground before heading toward the edge of the city once more.

"The one what?" Kyra asked.

"Nothing," Arimeus answered, realizing all of his thoughts were being shared. "I just meant it's quite obvious why your name was the one chosen to go to the Stained Temple. You've a gift unlike that of others, and I see why—"

"La la la la la la," came wringing into their ears through the voice of Samiel.

"Sam," Kyra said. "We can hear you."

"I just don't want to think something stupid," he said.

However long it took them to get close to the edge of the city's walls, each of them only heard Arimeus focus on his breathing as Samiel tried his best to focus on songs. Neither of the two heard Kyra thinking anything until they nearly reached the wall of Turmin—the grand barrier etched in glowing runes which protected the city for decades.

A colossal flash of lightning swallowed the city and Arimeus turned to the other two. "A second strike," he said. "Run!"

The emblazoned masses being catapulted toward the city broke through the barrier, marking the first hit against the city's infrastructure, and the sacking of Runefall truly began. Immense buildings stretching far toward the heavens were seen at a distance by the Warlord's army, crumbling upon impact while citizens flooded out of their homes in panic.

"Break for the gate!" Arimeus sped, heading closer to the wall, casting his hand toward something next to the gate. Once more a flash of energy, though this time with a verdant shimmer, burst from a previously unseen rune, and the wall swirled and collapsed, forming a new door. The very air bent into itself and spun like a whirlpool of color and darkness, but it was silent.

"But it isn't just a door," Kyra said, forgetting her thoughts would be heard.

"No, Kyra. This is a doorway to another realm, now come with me," Arimeus said approaching the door, but he was intercepted by a band of Pyrosi. At that moment, Kyra's spell wore off, allowing her companions and herself to speak and hear once more.

Six Pyrosi men and two women now stood in front of the trio after coming through the newly formed portal. Two women, wreathed in flame, stood idly with their hands placed together as if in prayer. Fire scorched the stone beneath their feet and wrapped around them to create a cocoon of fire. Each of the men's hands was also blacked with blaze.

"Kill the women first," Kyra said with a low and menacing growl.

Samiel's eyes grew wide upon hearing the words, as did the Chief Runic's. She was cold often, as Samiel knew, but her demand was ruthless and without emotion. There was a shift, a violent one, taking place in her heart that raised a mean fear in the young brute's mind.

Kyra looked and saw a stream of water running down the crags of the city as it broke around her, aqueducts spouting from many angles, soaking the road in front of her. Kyra readied Dreadstaff and used it as a bracing with one hand placed in the rushing water.

Within moments, Samiel felt a flush breeze submerge him as if sinking into a gratifying fountain. The feeling of immersion overtook his entire body, and suddenly the magic she gave became obvious.

"Make sure to hit them with your fists," Kyra said to him with a proud grin. "Drown their fire."

Samiel leaped forward with such speed the Pyrosi men saw nothing but a streak following his long, dark hair until a strong flush of wind met their faces. The streak instantly disappeared over the Pyrosis's heads, and they shuttered. As the group of attackers tried to follow him, the Chief Runic crushed both of his hands upon the debris in front of him which left a split between each of the opponents. Two men stood on each side of the rock face which now had water rising from its crevice.

The Pyrosi rushed Arimeus, who felt a dripping of energy surrounding his body, almost as if he were profusely sweating.

Runes haven't controlled the elements in my lifetime...the words lost. Has she found them?

He turned his head and saw Kyra in a similar stance as the Pyrosi women. She glowed with eager violence, ready to fight, to show the field of battle something it lacked—skill.

"I see," Arimeus whispered to himself, and he changed his stance to a defensive one. He grinned slightly as he noticed the stream flowing under his feet. "Come on then! Have at thee!"

All four of the Pyrosi men jumped upon Arimeus in unison and all four of them were blown backward as the old runic threw his arms outward, a great torrent of water exploding from his hands. One of the Pyrosi landed impaled upon a statue of Tir and another fell to the bottom of the crag. The other two turned, seeing the two dead bodies of their women as if they had been drowned, flushed faces with shining features and a hollow coldness only fit for one in the ground

Arimeus's feet were increasingly soaked as he noticed the stream of water gathering under him. He turned to Kyra who stood stoically in the same stance, Dreadstaff in between her connected palms. He walked to the two remaining members of the company and noticed the flames from their hands were gone. He gripped each one by their crimson tunics and dragged them, screaming, to the edge of the crevice.

One of them pleaded, "Harigamun will not like—" and within an instant, they were both plummeting to craggy depths.

"What were they going to say?" Samiel asked.

"Whatever they could say to live, I imagine," Arimeus answered, dismissively.

Kyra walked toward them both as they looked at her. Samiel glowed with adrenaline and his face rested peacefully. Arimeus's brow beaded with sweat and his hands slightly shook.

"I thought I understood, for a moment," Arimeus said to her.

"Most think they do. But what specifically are we talking about?" Kyra's enjoyment was well-written on her face.

"There is a cost to what we do," he answered. "I understood before what the cost was. But this time, there was no price to be paid," but he wasn't being entirely honest. He learned something from this fight.

Kyra chuckled and held one of her small hands up to her mouth as she cleared her throat. "Perhaps, you just didn't get the chance to see the price."

Perhaps she's right, thought Arimeus. He could not understand what price was paid, and maybe that was the point. Thus far, she was the only Ragi to practice rune magic without cost, and yet, she could routinely out-demonstrate any before her. Now, he was forced to understand she could outperform even himself, and that she knew secrets forgotten, perhaps even the ones intentionally lost.

"We need to go. We can discuss this later," Arimeus said as he moved toward the glistening whirlpool leading to…somewhere.

"The enemy just came through there," Kyra interjected with a clearly annoyed tone. "This way was secret, so someone has betrayed us, and you are likely to walk us into a trap."

"Shall we walk out the front gate then? I'm growing tired of being questioned at each decision. Follow me or not, the choice is yours." The old runic walked into the doorway, leaving the other two surrounded by the leaking and breaking city next to the remains of the Pyrosi.

Kyra looked at her closest friend who waited for her decision. "Go, we don't have a better option," she said.

She felt as if she'd opened the door of her home to step outside. In one step, she went from the collapsing city of Runefall, shrouded in the contempt of war, to a gloomy, dank cavern ripe with damp smells.

"Where are we?" she asked, whirling around to find her companions; but she found no one.

Her emboldened voice caused a small echo through the tunnels, so she dared not try shouting again out of fear of finding foes, rather than friends.

Where am I? Kyra thought to herself, trying to understand what was happening. *My name is put on a stone, which none are allowed to see, except the council of Runefall. I'm stripped away from my mentor, the person who has raised me to become a Ragi. I was told to follow a member of the council, and brought here,* she paused at that last thought. *Arimeus was confident in the doorway and where it would lead. So, someone must have tampered with the doorway.*

Kyra considered the many ways a doorway could be tampered with, remembering what Gremanhas—her mentor—had told her about runic doorways many years ago. *I know every spell in the library and more. Why wasn't this among them? I gave up too much to not know this...*

"They are one of the few spells written on the very stones that fell from the heavens many years ago," he had told her. "One of the most basic of spells, though its simplicity allows for too much to go wrong should the wrong people learn of its existence."

That's right! She got excited once more and realized she'd grown too loud. Taking shelter behind a rock, she awaited any signs of movement in the dark as she continued moving forward.

"One cannot change where the doorway leads," Gremanhas had

told her. "Though it is possible to add more than one place to enter the doorway, should others know about it. It is also possible to set different exits for different people. But this requires the use of something forbidden."

"But what?" she whispered to herself. She could not recall the means by which one could set different places for different people to exit the portals, though one thing was clear; *someone meant for me to come here,* she thought, realizing there was no scroll in Premus's library for tampering with these doorways. *What other magic was not held in that library, or for that matter, in the other library—the one Premus keeps sealed*

Once more, Kyra hurriedly drew a rune, this time with nothing more than her fingers in the air. At once she succumbed to unseen shadows and her ability to speak was once again gone.

This won't last long. Immediately, her pace quickened, and she started through the darkness, taking care with each step not to make unnecessary noise. As she approached a sharp turn in the tunnels, she heard two ghastly voices sharing words with one another.

"The Dreaming Haunts went from a home to a prison," a gruff voice laughed. "Old boy should have kept his dreams to hisself if you ask me."

Another voice snarled with agreeing laughter. "He ought to think twice then about telling lies on his brother."

The first voice inhaled the air around him, deeply. "I taste something that don't belong here, Dhaga."

"Nothing willingly comes to the Unda'Hearth that doesn't belong," the snarling voice replied. "But I do hope you're right, Brotha."

The Unda'Hearth? Kyra's breath grew heavier as a striking pain in her chest burrowed like a sharp arrow. She slid her right hand through the buttons of her tunic, clenching the top of her breast to slow her increased panting. After a short moment, she reclaimed her breath, and the panting subsided as the conversation between the two Unda'Kin grew farther away from her. Her spell had worn off—the forced silence worked, and for now, she was safe.

"I'm in the Crypt of Kaiya, the House of Demons," she whispered to herself. "Why would someone send me here?"

She approached where the two demons spoke and noticed a doorway. Wooden, large steel bolts dug into the cavern to hold it in place, though the crooked frame was clearly ill-managed. A hole with four metal bars serving as a window looked like the door to a cell. She crept to the door, trying not to make any unnecessary noise. Slowly lifting herself to look within, she listened for any signs of movement.

The door was stone. "Just stone," she whispered. She stared at the stone for only a short moment before releasing her grip on the door and stepping away. *Why is this here?*

Kyra pulled on the door, and nothing happened, it didn't even shake. It was like the wood had melded into the rock. She took a deep breath and pulled as hard as she could once more...and nothing. The door did not move.

I don't understand.

In her anger, she lightly punched the wooden door, and it swung inward through the stone, as if nothing stood in its way the entire time. Now, she laughed. *No amount of force could open this door from the inside, but to go in...*

It was another rune door, and Kyra had a strong feeling she knew where this one led.

Stepping through, Kyra found herself on a cliff under a night sky littered with more stars than she had ever seen. A pass wound down from the cliff's ledge over a grand ravine flush with two waterfalls flowing into a barely visible river beyond the darkened crevice. Water thrashed about below and the smell of lavender caressed the air while the smell of salt seemed to operate in contrast—a sweet and salty conflict. Looking further into the sky, some of the stars shone more like floating lanterns than stars. At the bottom of the pass sat a black temple, though she could hardly make out any details beyond its blackness from afar. Thus, she headed downward, not feeling the need to conceal herself any longer.

Upon closer inspection, the temple was guarded by menacing gargoyle statues lining the upper rim. They were many, and small, all save for the monstrous statue seated near the door of the temple's entrance. Its teeth protruded outward like the wolves of the old stories Gremanhas would tell. They were larger than horses with fangs which could not fit into their mouths. Indeed, this statue held those fangs of old tales, along with an enormous wingspan on its backside covering much of the beast's body.

"This would have been such a beast to behold," Kyra said with no attempt to quiet her voice. "I wish I could have seen it."

The architecture of the temple was intricate and rigid. *Nothing quite like this stood in Runefall, and likely*, Kyra thought, *in the rest of the world*. Each black stone was placed in a way that seemed to show an entirely different design based on where you looked. "Indescribable," she said as she walked through the front door of the temple.

The doors panned open at her fingers' touch and Kyra beheld a monumental cell with metal bars spaced so far between one another it seemed as though she could walk right through. As she tried, some unseeable force prevented her entry. But once the force knocked her back, the clambering of gears and pendulums whirred as if a tremendous machine had been awoken. The cell spun, and the temple began to move as the floor trembled beneath her feet.

The entire structure quaked as if the temple's roots were ripped from the ground. "The temple is...moving?" she asked nervously to herself while trying to find something to grab ahold of. But then, in a moment, it all stopped. The temple turned, but the turning was sluggish.

Now, a person stood in the cell, and they walked toward Kyra, to the edge of the cell where she had tried to enter. The shadowy figure stood in silence.

"Who are you?" she asked.

He simpered. "Ishmael, lord of the Dreaming Haunts."

"I've not heard that name before."

She looked at Ishmael and studied him. He wore ragged and tattered cloth, though the clothing looked to had been of a fine making long ago. A deep blue mirroring the dark waters outside of the temple stained his tunic. His leggings, ripped or slitted as they were, prompted the imaginative mind and drew in wandering eyes. Kyra looked upon his dark and ashen skin. His hair had been braided some time ago and seemed to have collected a lot of dust.

He's beautiful, she thought to herself.

His eyes shimmered white yellow. In the darkness, his white teeth teased a gloriously glinting smile that ended with dimples on both ends, housing on a pristine chin.

"Your beaten rags do not become you, Lord Ishmael." She grinned.

Kyra hurried to shut her mouth and placed her finger over her lips as if it would take back the words. *Why do I feel embarrassed?*

"Thank you, my lady. Might I ask, what is your name?"

"Kyra," she answered, with a high-pitched tone. *Why did my voice do that? What is happening and why is it happening in front of him?* "And I was hoping you might be able to provide some answers for me. Namely, why are you in this cell, and why have I been brought to you?"

"To me?" he questioned. "As you can see, Kyra. I've been in this cell for quite some time. I'd hardly say you were brought to me as I was in no position to bring you here."

"That may be true, Ishmael." She was reclaiming her mindfulness now. Her voice was stern, "But it remains. I cannot imagine I've been brought to see the demons of the Unda'Hearth."

"Demons!" he laughed. "I take it you come from that city of my brother then?"

"Runefall?" Kyra's eyes squinted for a moment.

"Yes," he laughed. "Aptly named. Runes fall from the sky and suddenly your people name it Runefall. I guess it was fitting for the moment."

"Your–your brother is Salaril?" Kyra gasped.

"Ah, yes. I imagine you and yours have never heard the likes of my name before. I'm considered the old guard to these new Lords of Kaiya. And they have no kindness nor want where prophesy is concerned."

"New lords? Old guard? And what prophecy?" Kyra came closer to the cell and gripped its bars, bringing herself face-to-face with Ishmael.

His eyes shone and his smile comforted her. He shocked Kyra by quickly moving to the edge of the cell, wrapping his hand around hers. It was a soft and tatted hand, though she could not make out the depiction. "Yes, you have many questions, girl, of that, I am sure. Though, something tells me I have not the time to answer all of them." His grip tightened on her and she did not want to pull away. His mouth moved closer, as close as it could behind the cell. "But I'll get more time with you." He winked.

Kyra felt a desire to be offended, but she wasn't. He was immaculate in her eyes. His features were compelling and his scent—ethereal. He released her hand, took a step back, and rolled up the tattered sleeves of his linen, buttoned shirt.

More tattoos, she thought, staring at his forearms, wanting to know what the pictures were. She saw muscles in his forearms pushing from under his skin. It was no wonder the grip was so hard and so...secure.

"How much time do we have?" she asked.

Ishmael took a long look at her, grinned, and then stepped back toward her, closer to the bars with his face as close to hers as the cell could allow. "If you are right and you were sent here by someone, I imagine I'll have time for...three questions, possibly four. It depends on how much he used. But, as I said, don't worry, I'll make sure you see me again."

That last comment confused Kyra even further, but she had other pressing matters to resolve. *How much who used of what?*

"What is this place?"

"The Dreaming Haunts," he replied. "There is no life after death, my dear girl. The lanterns you see are vigils held by the dreamers of your world. They provide light in the darkness for all of you. When one meets their end on Kaiya, there is a choice to make. Live in an eternal dream where nothing is real, but happiness can still be found, or... take up arms and join the Unda'Kin in a resurrected body which will not age but can most certainly die."

No afterlife. No heavens. No hells. The Unda'Hearth wasn't a place for condemnation or punishment. It was a resurrection for a war. Kyra realized now that all of those tales of demons told by Salarilias—priestesses of Salaril--were untrue. There was no such thing as a demon, just soldiers.

"What are they fighting?"

"That, Kyra. Well, that depends on who they serve. For instance, when I led the armies of Unda'Hearth, our fight was meant to be had against Salaril."

"Why would you turn on your own brother? Wouldn't that mean you'd have attacked Runefall as well?"

Ishmael laughed. "No, unlike the other lords, I do not place any blame upon an ignorant city of men. And as for why, he meant to destroy all other forms of magic, save rune magic. He believed that if he could somehow rid Kaiya of other magic then the wars would cease, and the world would know peace."

That's three, she thought.

"Go on then," Ishmael said to her. "It seems we have time for one more. Though, I would suggest you use the opportunity more wisely than you have thus far. Perhaps," he grinned, reaching with his hand and revealing a pure white smile, "you want to join me?"

It was odd. She felt a compulsion, as if she wanted to. He was dark and refined, the cloth, the tattered cloth he wore, well it barely covered anything. He was strong, that was obvious. But, Kyra had never been with anyone, never felt this sort of pull. It felt unnatural, but she recognized it as an intense craving she wanted to act on regardless. But she wouldn't, she was still in control.

"Why was my name written on the stone?"

Ishmael's face contorted for a moment and then returned to a sly grin, far wider than before.

"I had a feeling it was you, it's the only thing that makes sense," he said. "Sadly, your name was not written on the stone."

Kyra fell backward as her breath was stolen from her.

"When the realms meet, the seal shall be broken by the strongest among you. The end of an age will come unless the seal is broken."

"What seal? Am I the strongest? Who demands this?" Kyra became consumed with questions.

"These were the correct questions to ask, Kyra. I will see you again," he chuckled with his deep voice. It was a voice that made her want to touch him, be touched by him. It was a frightening laugh, but she wanted to be near it. "Next time I see you, I'll be able to use my hands better," he winked.

A new doorway appeared behind Kyra but this time it sucked her in against her will. She reached for anything she could, fighting to stay and speak with the Lord of the Dreaming Haunts, but she could not resist the pull. All surrendered to black as she fell from consciousness and into a peaceful, empty void.

When Kyra awoke, she found herself in a tent surrounded by many people she could not recognize, and two whom she did. As her vision cleared from the stupor the doorway had caused, she looked to her right and saw Samiel next to her, and so was Arimeus.

Arimeus rose from the ground and stood next to a gigantic man dressed in armor who looked to be made of stone. The Chief Runic then looked down at her. "Kyra, I'd like you to meet Harigamun."

CHAPTER EIGHT

THE MAD SCULPTOR'S DEATH

"Varin takes the title of Lord in vanity, establishing superiority over those he sees as lesser. He does this in the absence of Lords, for I have ended such politics of this realm. That's how titles work . . . they are taken. Though, it does make me wonder. Who will take the title of warlord from me? What war will they wage?"

— Harigamun, *Thoughts of War*

The clapping of the waterfall flowing from the sewer banged against the brook below, leaving a walloping, deafening torrent.

"Father!" Varelia cried out from under the ear-splitting waterfall.

"Give me mud!" Varus outstretched his hands, reaching for the bank. "Let me have the mud!"

Varelia looked at her father's wounds. A spear stuck straight through his bone leaving the leg unusable and likely unhealable. She deemed it most certainly beyond any skill to heal Varelia possessed.

He's going to die. My father is going to die.

"Give me the mud, and where's my–" Varus wretched as pain ran through his leg and up his spine, locking him in position. "I—I—," he stuttered with a clenched jaw, trying to speak to his daughter. "The pen!"

Varelia immediately scanned for her journal and pen. Once found, she threw the items beside her father. But, with sad eyes and a stopping heart, she realized the futility of the journal's pages and the pen as both were useless without ink or a hand capable of writing the needed words.

"No, Ibna! I need not the pages. Go find me some—" The pain grew stronger, and Varus collapsed to the ground. "Find me—"

"Bark," Varelia said. "Of course," and she ran up the embankment and found a large oak tree with a piece of bark slightly peeling, because if they couldn't use paper, bark could serve just fine. She needed something to write on, and she'd routinely put ink on bark in the sewer to make pictures. Varelia grabbed it by both hands and pulled with all of her might. Hoisting herself up and pressing her feet against the tree, she hovered in the air for a moment trying to break it. All at once, a massive piece released, sending Varelia flying backward and onto the ground. She recovered quickly and sped toward her father as blood pooled around his mangled leg.

"Grab—" Varus said with a fading voice as his head drooped onto the grass next to the river. His eyes rolled back, and blood rushed from his body. "Quill," his voice struggled. "Blood."

Varelia shuddered at the words and pulled herself back for a quick moment. *If I don't, he dies. If I do, then what? It's blood...it's what killed Mom.*

Varelia wasted no time grabbing the quill, rushing to her father's side, and dipping the tip in his blood. Varelia grabbed hold of the bark and wrote the incantations her father said. The incantation—Varelia noticed—had failed her father and took all those years to produce nothing more than a stumbling mud dummy for a few short seconds. *What if it fails? These words haven't worked for my father, why would they work for me?"*

The blood-drenched words on the bark evaporated as Varus lay bleeding alongside the riverbed. But then, the hard skin of the tree, red and gray scales dripping with blood, carved into itself, words appearing and replacing the fading blood:

Bloody your lips and speak

Varelia saw the essence of life pass from her father as his breaths drifted further and further apart. She rushed to her baba and wet her fingers with his blood, painting her lips red. *What does it matter? The contracts he used never work! To Unda with it all. I'll beg the damn gods if I must!*

"Beliria!" Varelia shouted. "I beg you to give my father a body renewed. I call upon the words of Baylar to aid in my time of need. I will do anything—" She fell to the ground as her father heard her cries.

A final tear crested over Varus's eyes as he knew his daughter did not say the words the way she was taught. This recognition struck fear into him, not knowing how the Shackled Maiden, Beliria, would respond if she responded at all. In his last moments, Varus pondered why his daughter didn't listen to his teachings.

But then, mud gathered around the dying sculptor. A swarm of water, dirt, and wind formed a dizzying vortex around Varus. At that moment, Varelia heard her father writhing in great pain. The sounds lingered as indiscernible from anything more than screams and Varelia felt as though her father's bones were being snapped, one by one.

"I'm sorry, Father," Varelia shouted. "I didn't know what would happen. I didn't want to cause you more pain!"

Varelia's eyes flooded with despair and as she looked further up the embankment, the guards from the sewer now rushed down the hill with reinforcements behind.

"Father is dead and...and now me," she whispered and fell to the ground in grief.

At once, a spear launched from above and hurtled toward Varelia. Instantly, a blockade of mud shot up from the storm surrounding her father, blocking the spear, and simultaneously capturing it. The blockade seemed like a gigantic arm stretching from the earth, and within a short moment, the spear launched back at the guards by the earthen hand. It impaled one of them so viciously it stuck into the ground, pinning the dead soldier to the dirt.

The storm about her father's body quelled and Varelia rose from her collapsed position to see a monstrous golem standing before her.

"Get out of the way you pile of mud!" a voice yelled, her father's voice, and to Valeria's senses, the voice came from the golem. This fact wouldn't have caused too much confusion if another, entirely separate voice, didn't also come out of the same golem.

"Groff fight better. It's Groff's body," replied the other voice.

The beast slowly stepped forward, leaving dents in the earth with each step as the deep rumblings of its grunts overpowered the thrashing waterfall. Valeria's confusion became something immeasurable with a dropped jaw showing as much. *Are there two people, or… ?*

"Run!" one of the guards screamed at a high pitch, noticing his companion already fleeing the scene. "Oh, no."

A large mound of earth plowed into another guard, smashing him into the dirt, and killing him instantly. The other guard managed to escape up the hill to take cover. Now, the menacing golem turned to Varelia.

"Do not be scared, my Ibna," said the golem. "It's me."

"And Groff," the voice changed, but it still came from the golem.

"Yes, and Groff," replied Varus. "Who seems to have little care for manners or introductions."

Varelia chuckled for a second. "What is going on?" Her brow slanted to one side with a half-shut eye, staring at the golem. "How did this happen? Better yet, what is *this*?"

"Considering you weren't at the trial, I'd imagine everything seems to have happened quite fast for you out here," Varus's voice answered.

"Trial?" Varelia gave in, knowing it would take a while for her to be caught up.

"My life was weighed against the use of blood magic, against my crimes, and against the life I've caused you to live," her father answered. "Groff here, he is Beliria's bailiff."

"I don't understand how all of this happened. Why didn't you tell me and how could you have done this in the sewers?" Varelia's frustrations grew.

"Ibna, I understand this seems awfully confusing right now but"

"Groff watches silly sculptor and make sure he does what Shackled Maiden says," the golem interrupted.

"I'm so confused," Varelia cried, furious.

"The trial wasn't here, it was on another plane, and that's why it doesn't seem like I was gone. But I was, for weeks. The Lady of Summons gives me life so long as I make sure her desires are met."

"What are her desires?" Varelia asked, her eyes sinking and a stirring in her chest grabbing hold of her breath. *What happened to him?*

"That you stay safe, and you truly learn the gift of the voice you have," her father answered.

"What voice? I have no such gift!" Varelia's anger mustered, and she wanted to burst. *This is too much. No. I don't believe any of this. I messed up the summoning...*

"Maiden's voice," answered Groff. "Now, sit down, silly man. Groff want to walk around. Has been many centuries since Groff get to see your land."

The golem jumped with a joyous skip to the river and started splashing about. "Ohhhhh, Groff love water! Feels so good to wash off dirt!"

Varelia watched the golem's demeanor change entirely once it touched the water. Groff jumped as high as he could and shook the earth around him as he crashed into the riverbed, and Varus said not a single word as the golem lived in his moment.

He's almost childlike, Varelia thought, watching the golem play in the ripples of the river. "Odd that he can be so capable of violence, yet so innocent to the world."

A horn sounded from the peak of the hill in the distance above them, and an army started down the full of mercenaries, pickpockets, and all others seeking a rare bounty for their heads.

"They've sounded the alarm, Groff," Varus said. "We must go, but I promise we will find more water for you to play with."

"Groff hurt men who take water from Groff," he answered.

"I know you can," Varus assured. "But I cannot. So please, will you come with me to keep Varelia safe as Beliria wishes?"

Varelia noticed the change in her father's mannerisms, the way he spoke. It seemed almost like remembering a piece of her childhood. Her father was always so understanding, so patient, no matter the mistakes she made. That same patience was being given to this creature Groff now, though Varus was clearly and easily annoyed by the golem.

Groff stood erect and stoic in an instant and stepped from the river and ran over to Varelia, each step pummeling the ground with an immense stride. She couldn't help but notice the lasting chitter typically in Varus's voice had fallen away in the moments her father spoke.

"Groff, you have not run in many, many years," Varus spoke. "Allow me control for a short while and I will help lead us from this place. I would speak to my daughter and deliver the wishes of Beliria as we make our escape."

Groff grumbled and his voice faded. He subsided and gave up control over the body.

"Flee, quickly," Varus said. "I have control now!"

The golem's steps fell lighter, still quaking the ground with each passing stride, but not leaving a crater with each footfall. This small change—Varelia and her father hoped—would lessen the City Watch's capacity to follow. Varelia took notice of how the motion of the golem's body dramatically changed as they ran.

"How do you run faster than Groff?" Varelia asked with strained breath.

"Groff has only ever known this body whilst I still remember my own," her father answered. "Though, I fear with time, Groff and myself may become one and the same."

"What makes you say that?"

Each word saw them weaving southward through the forest, darting around trees and shrubbery—Varus led the way and it seemed intentional.

"Groff is many," the golem's voice took over once more though his movement stayed the same.

"What does that mean?" Varelia continued, breaths growing harder.

"I've still yet to figure it out myself," her father answered. "Though, I do know, Beliria has given me another chance at life, it is just not the chance I would have picked."

Varelia could no longer hear the City Watch and slowed her pace after noticing they had reached the edge of a cliff. She walked to peer over the ledge and saw they stood atop a great mountainside, likely hundreds of feet in the air. Below, a deep blue lake shimmering with sunlight ebbing and flowing like an ocean with a lush and vibrant forest surrounding it. *It's stunning...*

"What's that?" Varelia asked, pointing to the far East.

"A storm, it would seem, from a distance," Varus answered. "Though, it does not appear to be like any storm I've seen before."

"Go. Maiden say woman there. That is where we go," Groff interjected.

"Where is it, Groff?" Varelia asked.

"There is where childs are taken," Groff answered with a heavy sigh.

"Wait! Is that Runefall?" Varus's voice grew louder. "Why should we go there? They tried to steal my daughter!"

It was then Varelia understood. Her father didn't know anything. Not where they were going nor what they were expected to do beyond keeping her alive. He was along for the ride and simply running forward.

"Mmmm," Groff rumbled. "Yes, strength of Lady's voice. Groff keep daughter safe. We go to Runefall. Another childs was taken. She keep seal together."

"What seal?" Varus asked, flushed with worry.

"No words," Groff replied. "Groff no good at those. We go find childs. Maybe Lady explain later."

Groff appeared to take back control of his body and cradled Varelia in his muddy arms. The golem slowly walked to the edge of the cliff, Varelia looking up as the golem smiled down at her.

Varelia did not return the smile.

"We must escape dangers," the golem said.

And with that, the golem jumped from the peak of the cliff standing hundreds of feet above the forest. The air ran so fast by Varelia's ears it seemed to cut her soft flesh, the very winds squealing as the weight of the golem broke through the air. They crashed down onto a tree which the golem nearly split in two. Having held her tight to brace for the impact, Varelia felt nothing more than slight whiplash as Groff laid her on the forest floor. Though, even with a damaged neck, she turned around to see the mangled tree which softened their fall.

"You rest. Groff keep watch," the golem mumbled as he walked over to a log. Sadly, the log immediately broke under his weight, but they all shared a laugh.

"How about you take a rest for a little while, Groff?" Varus asked.

"Mmm, Groff no sleep for very long time. Don't need sleep, not like squishy man do."

"All the more reason you should. It's hard to enjoy something you need," Varus said. "If I didn't need sleep, I'd probably get more of it."

"Mmm," the golem sounded as if he were gurgling mud. "Yes, Groff try sleep."

Varelia yawned as she looked to the golem who gingerly lowered his head onto the broken log. Thankfully, the broken half of the log supported the massive weight of it. In less than a minute, the golem drifted into his first slumber in well over a millennium.

Varelia spoke to her father, hoping not to wake the golem. "Can you talk while he rests?"

"Odd to say," Varus answered. "But it's almost as if we have separate homes inside of here when we want to go away. He will only awaken and hear me if he chooses to do so. Though, I didn't consider whether or not I'd be able to move the body whilst he was away. Miscalculation on my part. It seems I'll be speaking from this sleeping position," he chuckled.

"You mentioned a trial, and Beliria, and I imagine a great deal of other happenings whilst you were...gone?" Varelia noticed sounds of many guards yelling from the top of the cliff clouding the air, but it was no threat any longer. They were unreachable now.

"Yes, I'm sure all of it seems quite confusing. Suffice to say, I would be greatly confused by the entire thing... had I not been there."

"What can you tell me? Are you sworn to some secrecy?" Varelia leaned toward her father's voice as if she needed to whisper. "I can keep your secrets, Baba."

Varus laughed. "No, my Ibna. No secrecy. I fear if any secrets are being held they are within the hands of the golem."

"What secrets?" she asked. *I want to know. This is all so...interesting.*

"Hardly a secret if I knew of it to tell, now isn't it?" Varus smiled.

"Are you safe? Are we safe?" Part of her wanted the answer to be no. The sewers lacked fun and adventure. Now, it seemed, they could have both.

"One thing I do know, the only reason I am alive is because Beliria said protecting you was of the utmost importance. So, not only are you safe, I dare say you are protected."

"And you?" Varelia's worry for her father increased by the passing seconds. His fate seemed entirely unknown, unpredictable.

Varus sighed, eyes wandering around the forest for a short moment as he lay on the log. "I have a use, for now. I hope that remains. My body is gone, and likely Groff will not hold me forever. I imagine I'll have to contend with that someday, but it is not now."

"He said that he is many...what did that mean?" Varelia continued leaning in close.

"Yes, I doubt I'll answer this to its fullness. However, Groff is the champion of Beliria. Like me, it seems, Groff has housed the minds of many others within his body. I imagine it serves a similar purpose each time."

"And what happens to those who take harbor within Groff?" Varelia's worry turned to curiosity as a grin climbed over her frown.

"I do not know. I know they are no longer with us, but Groff claims none of them are dead."

"How many lives has Groff shared with his body?" Varelia's fast questions revealed her father's slow knowledge.

"Oh, dear Ibna," Varus sighed. "Groff lost count many, many years ago."

"You also called him a bailiff?"

Varus laughed. "A joke, and one he hates. He loves Beliria and championing her is his sole purpose. During my trial, he was often cold and unkind. Not in a menacing way, of course, he's strong and forceful, and quite the beast when speaking in matters of loyalty. He'd toss me about as Beliria wished to move me around from my cell to the courtroom."

"How often were you moved? Or rather, how long was the trial?" she asked, not grasping how events transpired. *He came and went from the world for weeks, and it seemed like seconds. How?*

"In total, I think it took three weeks for Beliria to reach a verdict," Varus answered.

"How?" Varelia shouted. "How could you have gone so long in what felt like an instant?"

"Kaiya holds no regard to how we pass time, it seems. We are where the lords, or gods, or whatever they are, want us to be."

Varus's answer gave a deepening level of understanding about him to his daughter. A once pious sculptor desperately clinging to the hope of creation, claiming to follow the ancient Vigil of Life, now seemed to suggest he felt anger for the divine.

Varelia contemplated the information for a moment, growing flustered at her inability to answer a simple question. *How could three weeks change so much?*

For a short while, Varelia sat in silence and looked at the golem. After much contemplation, she perched up to ask another question. "What were you being tried for?"

Varus smiled and then let loose a heavy breath, as if releasing a weight heavier than Groff from his shoulders. "Incorrectly teaching you how to use summoning magic."

Varelia's forehead grew hot, and his jaw clenched. "What?"

"In all those years I spent writing those contracts in that cesspool of a sewer, I always had it wrong," he answered. "I took it all for granted. I held expectations over life. I claimed dominion."

"How?" Varelia asked, realizing they approached the crux of her father's ethereal journey.

"I commanded. I never should have commanded. I was taught wrong many years ago and it's why I was never successful. I drove myself mad trying to become a great summoner, trying to sculpt these majestic golems, and thinking I'd be strong enough to control them," he sighed. "I was never meant to control anything, least of all the creatures I tried to summon."

Varelia sat completely still, not even a lip quivered.

"That's why my heart broke when I heard you abandon the ways I'd taught you to summon," Varus continued. "I thought you'd surely fail as I had many times before. But you didn't demand it. You begged and cried out for help."

"We are supposed to beg the god of summons?"

"No, my Ibna," he responded. "We are to respect them and treat them as equals. They do not answer to us, they answer to a higher calling, a stronger voice."

"That of their master?" Varelia asked. Now things made sense, at least, more than they had. Her father's failed summonings came from his treatment toward the process, not the dwindling of the magic itself. Life could be recycled, as her father explained many times over the years. *I can do it. I can bring back a dragon.*

"Yes, that of their master," Varus said. "Which means there's much learning to be had," he laughed. "But perhaps, if we are lucky, you may get to make something fly like you've always talked about."

Varelia cooed before catching herself in the act. Many nights they spent conversing over the grand beasts of myth and how they could be brought back. She knew it was silly then, but was it silly now? "Was it her who spoke to me, then? Was it Beliria who wrote on the bark with the blood?"

The eyes of the golem bent inward and seemed different to Varelia.

"What did the words say?" Varus asked.

"I was told to speak with your blood painted upon my lips. I didn't get to write a contract as you taught me. The blood seemed to disappear from the bark altogether until it came back and told me to speak the words. That's when I cried for help."

The golem's eyes closed, and its body remained completely still.

"Now I understand," Varus replied after a short moment. "You do have the voice of Beliria, and you've already used it."

Varelia's hands went damp with nervousness. "What does that mean?"

"Only those with her voice can call upon a summons without a written contract. Only those whom the Shackled Maiden has deemed the strongest among us. At least, according to the old teachings from my childhood."

Varus remembered much of his teachings in Vari, and then thereafter in Larina's Veil where he met his would-be wife. They were so stern, so strict in the practices. It all seemed well until the elves captured their goddess. It was then things changed and summoning, its ways, changed with them. The world became different and soon after, Varus had to leave the city.

"How can I be the strongest among those who use summoning magic when I've never successfully summoned anything?" *How is this strength measured? Who decided this? His chittering is gone but he's cracked, this is nonsense.*

Varus sighed, though not long, and quickly tried to call it back. These were strange events, and he knew it. "You summoned Groff," Varus answered. "And strength is not entirely measured in the act itself. It comes in many forms. Yours was just harder to see."

Stunned, Varelia's eyes welled. She could not tell if it was sweat, tears, or both. But she saw the eyes of the golem, drooping and barely staying open. She thought it might be Groff who had laid his body down and the comfort had started to win her father over, but then she recalled the trial and what a tiring experience it must have been.

"I have one more question, and then I think I'd like to get some rest if that's alright with you?" Varelia asked.

"Certainly," the golem's mouth opened to yawn.

"Why do you call Beliria the Shackled Maiden?"

"Ahhh," Varus chuckled, realizing what little of the Kaiyan Lords he had taught his daughter. "Beliria is not the Lord of Summons, you know. Baylar, to whom she is betrothed, is the God of Summons."

"Yet, her voice gave me this power?" Varelia questioned.

"She stole it from him as he stole away her lover a long time ago."

"She was disloyal to him?" Varelia's investment in the story became a memorable thing to watch for her father as she dove in like a bedtime story from her Madar.

"He was disobedient to the will of the other lords," Varus answered.

"He was to be cast out from Kaiya for his ill-will toward all life he deemed lesser than his own kind, wishing to rebuild the world in his image and create a paradise of his own. For this, Krishalla plotted to cast him down from beyond. He was locked behind a cell in the clouds for a time, somewhere beyond our senses, but during that time, learned of his wife's newest affections. Baylar broke from his prison and beat the lover senseless after finding Raknar in bed with his wife, and covered Beliria in the blood of her affair, but somehow, she was able to take that which was most precious to him—his summoning voice."

A short pause caused a tense audience before Varus released a long breath. "Krishalla had somehow taken the gods under his own command, for they had not always served him, at least, not if I am to believe your Madar. She spoke of older entities, stronger ones, in a way taken by these weak things we call gods... I honestly do not know. What is known to me is they serve him, and it seems they may all have served another before Krishalla. Nonetheless, Baylar escaped with his voice, beat Raknar to a bloody mess, covered his wife in what was left of her lover, and then stole her away to some unknown place."

Varelia's eyes shone a pure and incorruptible white, swollen with intrigue. "So, Baylar imprisoned her? How did she escape?"

"Escape?" Varus repeated with inflection. "No, Ibna. She did not escape."

Varelia's breath slowed until one large release bellowed out. "The trial?" she asked.

"Ah, yes. I guess that would be quite confusing for you," Varus answered. "Beliria can speak through her summoned creatures. I've spent a great deal of my time conversing with Groff, even when I wasn't speaking to him," he laughed. "No one knows where Baylar or Beliria are, but I imagine you now have a role to play in that discovery."

The two agreed to get some rest, though Varelia found it very difficult to sleep, and decided to keep watch while the other two rested.

Eventually, the golem awoke while her father remained resting, and the grumbles from the golem soothed Varelia enough to allow her to fall into a deep slumber, even if it was only for a short while.

After waking, the group started their way through the forest. Days passed in the wilderness of Cravenswood—the woodland area outside of Nightfall—as the group made their way toward Runefall. Groff was the only one who really understood why they were going to Runefall, though the other two knew they were being commanded by the Shackled Maiden to do so.

"I know travelers fear the woods," Varelia said. "Is it for these never-bright woodlands with the absence of daylight even when the sun blazes across the sky?" The golem chittered for a moment, smacking its clay-like lips and looking at Varelia as if struggling to speak.

"Cravens fear the—" Varus's voice began.

"Blood," Groff's thick voice interrupted.

"Odd thing, to watch you both fight to use the same mouth," Varelia quipped as they strolled through the woods.

"Seems we both have an opinion on the matter," Varus snapped. "Go on, Groff. Speak your mind."

"Was told to Groff that Cravenswood is where lady's lovers' people are. The ones that like blood."

"Yes, I'm forced to agree with the rude pile of mud," Varus said. "Though, the lady's lover is a bit odd to think about. Her love is, was, Raknar the Blood Lord."

"We share mud," Groff turned to face Varelia.

"Try not to take everything to heart," Varus said. "That is, if we have a heart."

"Groff loves the Shackled Maiden. Groff has heart," the golem said, sincerely.

Varelia's demeanor seemed to grasp the golem's body—to Varus's eye—for a moment as a sigh of relief flowed from its cracked, clay chest.

"I know you do, Groff. We will find her, and I'm sorry for suggesting you don't have a heart," Varus said.

"If you two are done..." Varelia said.

"The lover he speaks of is Raknar," Varus continued. "He is the one Baylar cast his wrath upon, and he is said to lead two separate tribes—Exiles and Nomads. Both practice blood magic. Exiles were thrown out from their tribes for its use of blood magic and the nomads chose to follow him based on piety, a piety that is mostly unknown to the more civilized world as they are found far less frequently than the marauding exiles. They are also far less threatening and rarely practice blood magic."

Varelia stopped walking. "And... if we should come upon these Exiles, what might that mean for us?"

"It seems the craven is settling into you as we speak," Varus chuckled, followed by a thunderous outburst of laughter from the golem.

"Small man craven," Groff bellowed once again.

"I just–I just wanted to know," Varelia tried to explain.

"It's fine, Ibna. I understand. I've never encountered them myself, so I cannot speak with certainty, though I imagine it most assuredly means a fight."

The shadowed canopies seemed quite beautiful to Varelia with vines hanging down all the way to dense undergrowth and animal musk strong in the air. She contemplated the piety of the Nomads and why they would follow the Blood Lord with religiosity, but then, her thoughts shifted to the almost unnatural formation of the springs that seemed divinely crafted by hand, wrapping around small bodies of water. Some had geysers exploding from the ground that frightened her. *Beauty with ugliness, divinity with mortality. All beginnings must end, and all good turns dark.*

Every thought of darkness and blood seemed to be interrupted by the dark impressions of the forest. Varelia thought the forest flowed as constant as the sewer, but in such darkness, she felt a constant euphoric rush of comfort rather than the dank shrewdness of her sewer home. *The darkness brings me home. Shadows bring solace.*

"What a great shame it is that this forest remains hidden from most yet given to those who would commit violence on the rest of the world. It seems rather unfair," Varelia said as they approached a breach in the canopies which lit up with lightning in the broad daylight.

"A few more miles yet," Varus replied, ignoring the comment. Well, he didn't really ignore it. He knew his daughter was in her own place of thought, and his words would mean little.

It was in that moment the ground beneath the golem's feet glowed a sharp crimson. "What's happening?" Varus shuttered. "Groff, I cannot move our body!"

"Groff no stopping you. Groff cannot move either."

Six masked figures dressed in maroon garb fettered with ebony fraying dropped from the canopies above. Varelia guessed, based on their body shapes, two of them were small women. Hope stirred in her as the obvious Exiles of Raknar stood before them. *They won't want to challenge a golem, will they?*

"We're stopping you, Golem. Though it has been some time since we've encountered one of your kind," the man spoke with authority as he walked toward Varelia. "Don't do anything stupid, kid," he said with a hiss. "If we can stop that golem in his tracks with a trap, it's probably best you not try to be a hero."

"Who stops Groff?" he growled. "Groff make elf stew from you if you don't let him go. Stupid ears and bad skin," he barked.

"Groff, you say?" The authoritative Exile stepped toward the golem and removed his mask, revealing strange skin. It was a dark-hued silver which seemed to almost glow in the darkness. "Do you remember me, Groff?"

"Please, my daughter has done you no harm," Varus spoke up. "Let her go and let myself and the golem pay whatever price you seek."

"Ha," the silver-skinned Exile chuckled. "How glorious! You've taken another life then, Groff?"

"Groff no speak with shadow," the golem crossed his arms.

"Quite pouty today, aren't we, old friend?" the Exile quipped. "Perhaps your other friends here would like to know more about how we met, or possibly, just a little more about you?"

The golem stood silent. Groff felt a great many emotions, but the greatest of them, as Varus felt, was grief.

"Very well," the Exile said. "I'm hardly a storyteller myself. Perhaps he will become more forthcoming... if we let him live."

"How did you trap him?" Varelia asked.

"When blood taints the well, blood also seals the well." The Exile's yellow eyes stared at her. "The only thing that can fight blood magic is blood magic."

"What blood magic?" Varelia's hands fidgeted as she bit her lower lip. "We don't know how to use blood magic."

All six of the surrounding crimson marauders burst into laughter.

"Girl, all golems are blood magic. At least, all of the good ones," answered the Exile.

"What do you want?" Varus spoke with a loud grunt, fighting the golem to speak.

"At first, we just wanted to rob you, and possibly kill you for entering our woods," the Exile said. "But now, I think I'd much rather have Groff give me my brother back, and then quite possibly kill him. At the very least, I think I'd much enjoy seeing him crumble into dirt and dust."

Varelia turned and saw one of the smaller women holding a stance with touched palms and hands bent, as if in prayer. Blood dripped from her fingers.

"We've taken no prisoners," Varus replied. "How can we return that which we do not have?"

The Exile laughed. "Seek more deeply, friend. For my brother resides in the same place as you, a brother-in-arms, as it were."

Varus's thoughts came to a complete halt. Perhaps he would die or fade away and become part of Groff. For this was no outlandish tale or string of lies coming from the Exile. *The Exile's brother was another of Groff's champions... and he's gone.*

"Groff will open mind to silly sculptor so he can see. I have no silver shadow."

A flood of Groff's memories suddenly opened to Varus, and he saw a great struggle as if it were his own. Elves were capturing a woman, shouting her name—Larina—holding her prisoner and demanding immortality be given to them freely without sacrifice or worship. She screamed in wretched fear. The elves' skin shimmered like gold under the sunlight and their voices chilled the back of Varus's neck as he felt like a swift but calming breeze.

"Now, Grendalla!" one of the elves called for the Exile to demand Larina surrender her immortality to them. Then, Grendalla appeared, and spoke to the elf who demanded Larina surrender.

"Kill her, brother," said Grendalla, but his skin was gold, not silver. His voice remained the same as it was in the forest, but his eyes contained the ocean's tide. "Kill her and siphon the blood! If the blood of Harei can create immortality for mud, certainly Larina's can give it to us!"

The elf holding the blade to Larina's neck turned to the leader of the marauders, to his brother. "It's our time, Dremhirra rises."

Then, Varus's flashback of Groff's memory came to an end, his vision cleared, and he saw the leader of the Exiles standing before him—Grendalla—no longer with the golden skin he wore in the vision, but with skin of stained silver and eyes of red.

"You betrayed your Lady, stole her gift, and captured her long life for yourself," Varus said.

Grendalla grimaced.

"You belong to the eastern elves, the ones who turned to darkness. You did not know what you were stealing from Larina, did you?" Varus asked.

"We gained our immortality at the cost of her life," Grendalla answered. "Yes, we live forever, doomed with the process of death eating at our bodies and minds over time. Our life force wanes as our energy and fullness flee with it, leaving us with withering bodies forced to decay and renew in an endless process of rebirth and agony."

Varelia spoke aloud once more. "Would you do it again, knowing what it costs?"

Grendalla turned with a heavy frown. "I would not choose so rashly to discount the gods, no. We had long life, at the cost of worshiping a deity who forced us to be subordinate to men and dwarves. Immortality, but held to a lesser value than those who fade within the blink of an eye. It was disgraceful, but even that was better than this."

The Exile was quick when he wanted to take Varelia. He may as well have phased into shadow before her eyes with the speed of wind racing toward a mountain, and by the time she realized it, the silver-skinned outlaw was behind her, had her arms crossed and held together with one hand, while the other held a blade against her soft neck.

The Exile sighed, stretched his back. The weapon against her was a worn blade with callous depictions of dark shapes about it. "So, you've seen me, and you've seen my brother," Grendalla continued. "The other god, Beliria. She sent this one as penance," he continued, looking to Groff. "He blasted through my kind after our sin and as the last price to be paid, he took my brother with him." His attention turned fully to the golem. "Where is he?"

Grendalla's blade pricked Varelia's neck, and her blood dripped. She quickly reached to feel the cut and the Exile flinched at her movement. Once he saw she was just checking the wound, his eyes averted back to the golem.

"Where is Flaurin?" Grendalla yelled.

"Dead," Groff declared, without remorse.

Grendalla pulled the sword away from Varelia's neck and thrust it toward the golem, piercing his shoulder.

"AGH!" Varus screamed.

"I'm guessing the golem didn't tell you how you're his shield, did he?" Grendalla smiled, knowing he was right.

As soon as the sword left Varelia's neck, she ran her bloodied fingers across her lips and whispered, "I call on Lady Beliria to protect my father... your champion. I call upon—" the Exile's sword turned back toward Varelia as its hilt cracked her across the jaw, leaving her bloody on the forest floor.

"Say one more word, girl," Grendalla taunted. The Exile turned toward the golem once more. "I hope you're paying attention inside that golem! My brother was the last to share his body. Don't expect your fate to be any different!" He swung at Groff with full force and a withered weapon.

Following the attack, Varelia grabbed a rock and threw it as hard as she could at the woman whose bloody palms were still joined together. It bashed against her forehead and knocked her to the ground, thereby also releasing part of the spell's hold on Groff's body.

Grendalla's sword made contact from his assault, but the golem's body seemed to harden in an instant, breaking the blade.

"Stop the women!" Varelia yelled.

At once, the golem's arms grew many times their normal length allowing his limbs to chase down the Exiles. Both arms crashed against trees beneath the pressure of the golem's massive, outstretched force. The males of the Exiles scattered to the winds, all except Grendalla... who now held Varelia by the throat with his shattered blade against his own.

"This doesn't end well for you," Varus's voice said as the golem took one step forward.

The Exile leader jumped backward, cutting Varelia slightly by accident. At the sight of blood, the golem's clay-like fingers clenched together knocking off dirt and forming together like a boulder.

"Let her go. We let you go," Groff said.

"He threatened my daughter and cut her twice!" Varus shouted. "We aren't letting anything go!"

"Ansei lets go of girl. Groff won't squish Ansei," Groff warned.

"Ansei," Grendalla snickered. "We haven't been called that since we sacked the dwarves and slaughtered their people. They called us the Silver Shadow, if I remember. Is that to be our name? Or is it Ansei?"

"Your choice what you say," Groff answered. "Others say their choice. You silver. You shadow. The rest mean little. Now, let go of girl, or Groff squeeze shadow and silver out of you!"

The Ansei lowered his blade's broken hilt and darted off into the woods.

CHAPTER NINE

A DIVIDED COUNCIL

"I've tested it on my armor. All it takes is a little blood to start a real fire."
— Harigamun, *Thoughts of War*

T ir sat in a crypt beneath the largest temple in Runefall under the council chamber shrouded in a white cloak in front of Salaril's shrine . The gloom of the room accented a scarlet sheen clinging to the moist marble. The scribe's eyes, weightless and closed, drifted away into a conscious and deliberate sleep with legs crossed.

"Please, speak to me," she whispered.

Her eyes opened to find herself strapped to a chair in darkness. Light slowly rose around the scribe to reveal the shine of metal bars. Out of the darkness stepped a dark-skinned man with eyes ebbing and flowing within a navy stream. The stream—the small stream of his gaze she studied intently—ran through his eyes and split the surrounding white-gold within. The closer the man stepped, the more she realized his fine clothing, worn for a noticeably long time, revealed a threadbare state. She thought his shabby clothing took nothing away from his majesty as she admired his long, braided hair.

Tir's eyes though... sanguine, a dark-hued red in one, almost frightening to some, making them also unique. Could this likeness—nothing more than unique eyes—be some connection to him? She felt pulled to him, but the sense was primal, not ethereal.

"Stone could never do justice to you, Lord Salaril," she lowered her head.

The man came within arm's length of the scribe and placed his hands on top of hers as she sat completely still. "I am guessing you have never seen Salaril, at least not outside of the statues you harbor across your city?" he asked, tightening his grip on her shoulder, but not uncomfortably so. The squeeze from his hand comforted her, warmed her. "Such a pious scribe to your *Lord*. Tell me, since you are the only one he has spoken to. What has your *Lord* said of late?"

"My lord?" Tir raised her head and her nose crinkled as the man admired her eyes, each one having an individual revelry within them, capturing his gaze.

"Call me *Lord* if you wish," he answered as he let go of her shoulder and stepped back from her chair. "I am probably alone among them who never desired to ascend to lordliness, or godliness."

"Salaril commands recognition, my lord," she responded with a meager voice.

"Aye," he answered, "and I am not Salaril. Though, I did once call him brother."

"Ishmael," she guessed. "Lord of the Dreaming Haunts?"

"Yes, my lady. I am he," the Lord of Dreams answered, "and Ishmael serves me just fine, if it so pleases the scribe of the Kaiyan Lords." He bowed, but it was not meant in reverence. He peeked his head up with a seductive smile

"Why have we never spoken?" Tir asked. "It's been many years since your brother has spoken to me, and he always did so shielded from my sight. Why now, and why you? Where has my Lord gone?"

"My *Lord*," Ishamel mocked. "I was never needed, and nor did I ever need. I should have liked to continue where I began. Giving life to those beyond it through the guise of eternal dreams. But that bliss has been taken from me."

"By your brother?" Tir asked.

Ishmael walked to her slowly and placed his hands on top of hers, now resting on the arms of the chair. He put his lips close to her neck and he felt her quiver, but not recoil. He brushed a light breath onto her neck and then raised his lips to her ear, and whispered, "Very good, my lady. But can you tell me why?"

Ismael stepped backward from her.

A rising heat gathered in Tir's chest as sweat poured. The scribe placed no effort into escaping, nor could she if she wanted. She felt a tingle on her skin as she shifted her position. The ever-soft presence of comforting darkness of he—the Lord of Dreams—swooned her with an insatiable curiosity toward corruption.

"No, sir," she said with a polite innocence.

"Sir is it?" he laughed. "Do I control you?" Ishamel came closer once more. "Will you do my bidding, so long as I bid it? Do you cling to power so frightfully that subordination is your only comfort?"

A nervous sigh and a slight tremor escaped her body.

"My brother condemned me to the very prison you sit within," he said. "Now I hold you here. I wonder... what should I do to you?"

Suddenly, light surrounded the cell, and Tir watched as she somehow overlooked Runefall. The city burned and screams unending, she could see the end of things.

"Please, let me go!" she exclaimed. But in truth, she didn't entirely know she wanted to be let go. The fear, the unknown of the end, came all too much with pressure too fast. The city would burn, or could burn, and she didn't know which. She needed to act.

"This has not come to pass, my innocent scribe," he replied. "This is one path of many that lie ahead. I am forced to dream and watch events as they play out from my cell. I am cursed to knowledge without action."

"Why?" the scribe stretched her back, as if regaining comfort.

"I have always had the knowledge. It was only recently I lost the capacity for action," he said. "I prophesied the death of magic to the gods you bend your allegiance. My brother, he made horrendous plans against his own kind, seeking to claim a throne unknown to this world. The dominion of magic... through its death."

"How?" Tir's eyes grew tighter as she saw lament in his sullen look.

"All I could see was his desire for dominion," Ismael answered. "He knew I would see his plans, should he create any. So, he baited me. I called on him to present his case to the council, and by enhancing one of his spells with his blood, he briefly shielded his intentions and dreams from me. He did so just long enough to cast me in here. Now, my vision is clouded, and I cannot see beyond what I knew could happen before I was imprisoned, not with certainty."

"If you can see the dreams of others, and also prophesy... I must ask again. Why have you never come to me before, as your brother did?"

"It is against the will of Krishalla for us to interfere with mortal matters," Ishmael answered. "And indeed, it was beyond my own wishes to intervene as well. I simply wished to create dreams for those who deserve them."

Tir sat for a moment in contemplation and then spoke once more. "What do you seek from me?"

Ishmael grinned with satisfaction. "A great many things, my lady," he said, stepping forward and brushing his dark, tatted hand across her cheek. His hand touched softly, warmly, though his presence felt oddly cold. "Speak to whomever can deliver this message: The prophecy on the rune is false," he said, pulling his hand, and warmth, away from her.

Tir shuddered. "We sent the wrong child?"

"There was no child to send," he corrected.

Tir's body fought to rise from the chair and suddenly the bounds released as she jumped from its confines, as if she was never bound. "What do you mean?"

"You've been misled."

"Salaril wrote on the rune to send the strongest among us to the Stained Temple to fulfill the prophecy!" Tir's body quaked as her hands experienced slight, uncontrollable, tremors.

Ishmael stepped within reach of her again and stared into her eyes. "Who among you has been to the Stained Temple?"

"None of us," she answered without thought, but with anger. *Is he tricking me?*

"Why?" he asked, provoking harsh and anxious responses of immediacy.

She paused before answering. She didn't like where he was leading her, at least, where it appeared he was leading her.

"The stone calls it a sanctified place beyond the reach of all our kind," she said. "It is only to be traveled to during moments of conquest, moments when one is called upon by our greater Lords."

"*Greater Lords*," he scoffed. "Don't you see, Tir? You were never able to travel there, for you never even thought to do so. You assumed the Lord of Runes would guide you. Now, the deity requiring you to send your strongest Ragi to an unknown place is the very same god positioning Runefall's destruction."

Tir's legs trembled, and she collapsed, staring at the blazing city beneath the cell, though the screams silenced.

"He wanted the city to fall," Tir said, explaining the thought to herself more than him. "He made us cast out the strongest among us to ensure our folly. The Stained Temple did not exist, it never has."

"Oh, to the contrary, my fair scribe." Ishmael reached his hand out for her to grab, lifting her from the ground. He put his left hand on her side and waited... she, once again, did not recoil. He pulled her in close and brushed her hair over her ear. "The temple lies beneath Runefall."

Tir's vision faded to black. Ishamel's voice lingered as a shadow, a deafening ringing in her ears. As her sight returned, it was as if a newborn was opening its eyes for the first time. She struggled regaining her conscious understanding of where and when she was. She was alone and back inside the temple crypts, but then she heard heavy footsteps descending the stairs coming toward her.

"Barigund," she said as he approached her. "Not often I find you in the crypts." She collected herself, controlled her heavy breaths. She needed to be decent in front of him—controlled.

Barigund looked around for a short moment to study the crimson-hued shadows surrounding the lordly statue. The walls inexplicably cared for; the floors more pristine than those in the temple's nave—this place stayed well-kept.

"Would that I had your piety my lady," he smiled. "Would that the world deserved such a force. Your willingness is something lost to us now, the world no longer seeking to obey, to serve." The City Commander stared into the shadows for a moment. "Perhaps, such should be the way of things."

"Why have you come?" she asked, sharply.

"A second bolt struck the city, and the barrier will likely fall soon," he grumbled. "I'd rather not have the only Mystic in the city hiding in our temple's basement praying at that time."

"I don't know that my foresight has quite the value we once thought," she replied. "I was deceived or am being deceived now. Possibly both at once." She released a great weight from her chest. "Ishmael, the brother of Salaril, came to me in a vision."

Stoic, Barigund's frame did not move. His facial expression barely changed, all but for the crossing of his arms and his body's weight being shifted slightly, though it seemed more to Tir like the signs of a bad leg than a bad mood.

"Ishmael says the temple lies not to the far-east, but here, under the city of Runefall."

"The Lord of the Dreaming Haunts," he replied. "Ever silent until now."

Tir knew the hard truth of it, same as the Commander. The Lord of the Dreaming Haunts was barely more than a myth to the peoples of Kaiya for all of their lives, and likely far longer. The absence of her Lord—Salaril, Lord of Runes—and the surprise presence of his brother, appeared altogether unlikely to be unrelated.

"Salaril imprisoned him for seeking the destruction of all magic, save his own," she continued. "It seems that my Lord, allegedly, seeks dominion over the other Lord's—at least, as his brother tells it."

"Thus, he commanded our strongest to be cast out, thinking we would send our ablest of bodies with them," Barigund grieved. "He misjudged the council as we ruled not to send her at all. The Stained Temple is known to our lore. He had to speak of it in his prophecy as all others have foretold similarly regarding the story throughout the ages. But our lack of knowledge in ever seeing the structure, and our faith... "

"Yes," Tir picked up his trailing statement. "Faith," she lowered her head. "It seems faith will be my greatest crime, my hardest failing."

"So be it," Barigund unfolded his arms, and his voice grew stern. "Salaril means to send our best on a fool's errand, far from here. That means he is protecting the very thing Krishalla clearly means to destroy, or perhaps, they are in league. I can think of no other reason for his attack on our city and showing us to the world. I hear word that Arimeus has taken the girl himself and means to break past Harigamun's army. Her teacher found me on my way here. Had we known Krishalla would come down on us, perhaps the council might have voted differently."

"What shall we do, my Lord?" she asked, quietly, frightened.

Barigund took only a second to ponder. "First, we fight. I see no peace between us and Harigamun. Then, we find this temple for ourselves and what Salaril meant to hide."

"What would you have of me?" The scribe's voice gave way to a harsh judgment against herself.

"Damn those silver-skinned slags for slaying Larina!" Barigund slammed a fist against the temple walls. "She might have warned us, or provided a vessel to speak to Krishalla and see if we might be persuaded to join in his efforts. They killed her for immortality, and now her absence separates us from directly speaking to her kind. How funny it is that the death of a god defines our mortality. Clearly, Salaril thinks the sacking of this city would turn a blind eye to what lies beneath, keeping it safe. I would speak to Krishalla if the gods would allow."

Tir thought him right to condemn the Ansei for their crimes against their Lady—Larina. And perhaps, Tir may have been a vessel to connect Runefall to her, but that option was now long gone. Indeed, no one could speak to the will of the gods when they themselves stayed hidden.

"They will not," she answered.

"Have you still the power to bend minds to your will?"

"Weaker ones, yes," she answered. Tir, in her own thoughts, was not the strongest of many of the mystic arts. She mastered the art of communication over large stretches, using images and sometimes outright words with others to convey a needed message, but she possessed little gift for mind control. "If I must. Though, I would hardly consider myself battle-worthy in such regards."

"Harigamun is not weak," he said.

Her vision cleared as her chest clenched and she felt the sweat and wetness from her eyes dry up instantly. Wind fled from her lungs as sticky moisture clung to her. "Would you have me challenge the mind of Harigamun?"

"I would have you try," he answered. "Stay here if you must. Once the siege breaks, I will sound the alarm through the city. Then you will know it is time."

"He has an army of Mystics at his behest, and I am but one, old caster," she groaned, but then an idea came. "Which means he will be using them..." she paused. "The most sensible idea would be for him to create a connection of thought within his army. Someone will be bridging that connection."

"Do what you must, and I'll do what I can," Barigund said as a loud crash boomed overhead. "I must return to Gremanhas and ready the troops. Our people are depending on a less-than battle hardened army and fewer than 100 Runics to protect them."

"I will await the alarm," she said with a calm voice, standing completely still.

Barigund left the temple's lower chamber in a rush to find Gremanhas surrounded by four young adults which the Ansei had mentored over the years. They waited at the training grounds outside the city barracks.

The grounds spread across a large field with targets crafted from straw and dressed in leather. Some of them, which had not been recently replaced, were scorched. Liquid pooled in spots on the grass while other spots were made of dislodged dirt from the crust being ripped from the ground.

"How fare the youths?" Barigund asked.

"A rare thing," Gremanhas answered with his back still turned. "A visit from the Commander himself." He slowly turned to acknowledge the behemoth of a man. "To what do we owe the pleasure?"

"I appreciate you sending word regarding Arimeus. How are they?" the commander asked, looking upon each of the four students. All of them looked like children to Barigund's eyes, so small, even though they were each nineteen years of age.

"Asmodeus could temper even the greatest Pyrosi. Hirkar has only enough knowledge of the earth to be a nuisance to himself and others. Belia's affinity for the manipulation of water is less than your standard glassware is capable of..." Gremenhas trailed off.

"And Kirkard?" Barigund asked as he walked up to the young man.

"To him, the winds are sharper than any blade we can forge in this city," Gremanhas answered.

"And the army?" the Commander asked with anticipation in his eyes.

"Come now, my lord," Gremanhas chuckled. "You know my responsibilities almost as well as I. I'm nothing more than a caretaker. You'll have to find Master General Galantis to gain such knowledge." He smiled in a way the Commander could not help but laugh.

"Your constant mockery of the politics of this city can often be a great gift, my friend," Barigund said. "Though sometimes, I admit, your tongue has more use when it's hidden."

A flaming boulder crashed against the crackling lightning above the city and bolts darted across the sky.

"Four Runics," Gremanhas shouted, turning the Commander around with the sudden shout. "One for each of the students, and we will lead with the vanguard!"

"I'll give your words to Galantis, it is his decision to make," Barigund said before taking off.

With a hasty step, the City Commander made his way inside the barracks. Elaborate alabaster walls towered above the highest steeple of Runefall with marble columns etched into a pattern mirroring a busting foundation. Tributary chambers spiderwebbed from the main hall housing Runefall's army of eight thousand.

At the head of the chamber sat a throne of adamantite. The seat was crafted by dwarves from many years ago, before the city sacked villages in the night for trying to break stone away from the runes that fell from the sky. Barigund often thought of those ill deeds when he entered the chamber.

At full tilt, Barigund approached Galantis, who sat surrounded by three of his generals lurking at the foot of his throne.

"There is much you do not know and possibly even more that I do not," Barigund said, regaining his breath. "I have not the time to explain. Tell me, is the army ready?"

Galantis eyed each of his generals and repeated the question to them. "Tell Runefall's Commander what he wishes to know. Are your armies ready?"

"Dalias Lanis, sir, at your service. I'll command the vanguard and the offensive, leading with those few commanders well practiced enough in the arts of runic weaponry," said one of the generals.

Dahlias Lanis was young, eager. His family was the peak success of mercantile in the city, often braving the exit of Runefall for the sake of trade through its hidden routes—at the behest of the council. Dahlias, however, had no interest in trade. He'd made his name on the battleground and skirmishing with the dark beasts in the forests surrounding Runefall. Now, he meant to make his name as Runefall's most prestigious commander.

"Rocco Frapor, sir, at your service," he bowed. "I'll command the men on the walls and within the city. Blockades and defenses are where my strengths lie. We've had plenty of time to prepare these many years. Not only are we ready, we're waiting."

The Frapor house specialized more in weapons crafting. He knew nearly every soldier behind the wall, as his family adorned each of them with their armor and weapons.

Barigund turned to the last remaining general. A small man, whom he recognized. "Elias Harkor," said he. "I know of these other two, but to them I've rarely had the chance to speak. You, however. How long has it been?"

"Long enough to receive a promotion, my Lord," he said with a smirk. "I'll handle the uh...alterations of the battle, my lord. And should the need arise, the escape."

Barigund stared at General Harkor for a moment, recalling their days of training on the battlegrounds, but most of all, he recalled ill-favored tactics which always gave General Harkor the advantage.

"Perhaps your tricks will win you this day, as they have so many times before," Barigund grumbled, jokingly. "I am pleased to see your progress, though I doubt it was earned fairly."

Elias gave a coy smile to the City Commander and took a pronounced bow, further than the gesture required.

"Now, now," Elias replied. "No need to hold grudges, old friend."

Barigund didn't feel as though he held a grudge, nor did General Harkor truly believe the accusation. Having gone through training together and simultaneously rising of rank in separate directions, the two knew and respected one another. One fateful night gave them a lasting bond which resurfaced both their memories each time the other stepped foot into a room, the night of The Gathering.

Their bond withstood the chicanery of General Harkor, but not without grandstanding and small amounts of resentment from Barigund here and there. Still, the City Commander trusted General Harkor would always keep soldiers safe, he knew the General wouldn't ask his soldiers for permission to save them.

"How many Runics do we have?" Barigund asked.

"More than ever and never enough," the Master General replied. "A city of forty thousand kept safe by an army less than a fourth its size. Scarce among them are those who can read and even fewer who can grasp rune magic. The three among you serve as generals, and for every sixty feet of soldiers, we have one commander capable of wielding some level of magical skill. Thus, we number less than two hundred practitioners in total."

Barigund gave a deep exhale. Tired and worried, the City Commander's raging doubts grew harder to hide. Good reason guided the city's attempt to stay hidden. Now, the finding of Runefall and its sacking marked a bloody end for Kaiya, for he knew this battle marked something far beyond that of normal war. *The prophecy meant nothing. When Harigamun arrived, that was the most fatal of all portents. All that is left is doom.*

Galantis rose from his throne and approached the towering City Commander. "How many is Harigamun likely to have?"

"We were a smaller people, at least in number," Barigund said with a dissonant soft voice. "The tribes and outer colonies, they always had more numbers than us. Reading was scarcely available beyond our walls, and texts may as well not exist beyond them. We've the intelligence on our side, and more information than we know what to do with. Their generals are primitive in their practice, though we barely surpass them, it would now seem. We have advantage, but not the sort an army wants to hear."

"Salaril assured us this was because our path was more difficult, that few could manage our burden, the burden of power," the Master General replied.

"Yes," Barigund said. "Salaril said a great many things. If I were to guess, I'd say Harigamun outnumbers us ten to one. His conquests have garnered a fearsome beast of an army, but it does not mean they move as a single unit. We have the defenses, the walls—"

"And the stronger magic." Elias laughed, "We will be fine, I'm sure of it! Rocco already said they've been planning these defenses for quite some time. It would have been a great shame for it to have never been put to use, if you ask me."

"Where will you be, when it begins?" Galantis asked.

"It's been far too long since I've seen my brother," Barigund answered. "I'll be with the vanguard."

General Dalias Lanis turned in shock. He realized he might be fighting alongside the City Commander. If his Lanis Troop ever made it to the vanguard, or could even watch them from afar, General Lanis would consider that an immeasurable honor. None had seen the City Commander fight in so long that, if not for his size, many would likely doubt whether or not the giant of a man could fight. *If I die, let it be beside him.*

"The vanguard will be the better for it," Galantis said. "I will serve along the wall and keep close to my messengers to deliver what commands need to be dispersed. However, should you find yourself in need—"

Barigund interrupted him. "I'd expect nothing less from a Master General."

All at once, a reverberating sting broke through the halls of the barracks and the marble clamored with pulsating rings stabbing into their ears. All of them fell to the ground shrieking in pain.

"What was that?" Rocco yelled, but no one heard his voice. A short moment passed before sound returned to any of them.

Barigund rushed to the door of the barracks. He looked over and saw fire striking from a collapsed steeple. "They've broken through the barrier, and the Temple of Salaril has been sacked by flame." Suddenly the sanctified protection of the wall seemed so ignorant. *How? What evil has he done?*

"Earth coated in flame," Elias said. "There is but a forbidden path to such success." He turned to face the City Commander. "Your brother no longer acknowledges good, nor evil. Blood is his tool as fire is his weapon."

"Galantis, can you spare me four of the Runics from Dalias's legion?" Barigund asked, hastily.

"They are yours, my Lord," Dallias said as the few remaining Runics bolted from their barrack's quarters.

Barigund stopped some of the Runics bursting from their lodgings and commanded four of them from the unit to follow him. At that moment, he rushed with those he gathered and headed to the front gate where he found many waiting for the onslaught, including Gremanhas.

"Gremanhas," the towering commander said, "I've brought your Runics."

The mentor eyed Barigund up and down and listened to his heavy breath. "A messenger, or the Runics themselves, could have very well delivered that message, my lord." Gremenhas bowed, slightly.

The City Commander's eyes turned gold as Gremanhas sat in astonishment before saying, "I cannot have you do this, Lord."

"What good does it do for me to serve as City Commander if I cannot defend the city in its time of need? What shall I command if not my own life in the final moments of servitude? What—"

"It is not the fighting I contest," Gremanhas said. "It would be the manner of your fighting."

"Ten to one odds," the City Commander said. "The likelihood of us winning becomes less if I do not join this fight."

"Once more, it is not you joining the fight I contest. It is what we both know will come."

Barigund muttered to himself for a short moment as he spun around to see the vanguard gathering before him. He turned back to face his old friend.

"One life for this unit"? Barigund questioned. "For a legion? For an army? For the city? What must the cost be in order to weigh it against one's life? *My life*?"

"I cannot stop you," Gremanhas said. "But go to your death knowing it was not necessary, and likely did not make the difference you believed it would."

"If I do nothing, I will likely be captured, and then death will ultimately come," Barigund explained. "If I should die, then I'll do so under the guise of inspiration."

"Your brother is a conqueror, not a beast," Gremanhas said. "He would spare you at his feet."

"I'd rather fall from death than cower at another's feet."

Gremanhas turned from the City Commander at the sound of Runefall's gate drawing open as the Wall of Turmin revealed the enemy. Legions beyond counting which could not be held by the rolling hills in front of the city. Their numbers outstretched the land before them, hiding many beyond sight of the front lines, even those who perched on the walls.

Rocco, now atop the wall, counted six armies surrounding the city, each independent of the others. He took a final moment of embrace with the one whom he loved, who stood there on the precipice of a dark turning. It was a small embrace, but meaningful and long. They whispered shared words, their secret words before they would separate. "Death will be our last trick."

"Shall we?" Elias smirked, looking his lover in the eyes.

Rocco nodded. "Let loose the trebuchet!" Forty trebuchets lined the inner wall, twenty on the West side and twenty on the East of the front gate. "Light the left stone aflame and soak the right with the ocean's tide! Water for fire, the rest of the siege weaponry belongs to Sodsheim's Mounders,

An operator of one of the trebuchet's shouted. "And should they move? How do we know which army belongs to who?"

Rocco shot back, "Vibrant reds for Pyrosi, deep blues for the Aqualytes, a horrid brown for Mounders, a simple shade of indigo for the Mystics, orange for Wind Riders, and white for Summoners. Harigamun has made it very clear that each army is still seperate.

As attacks came crashing into the city from ballistas, trebuchets, and catapults with a plethora of differing munitions, much of Runefall's army stood front-loaded onto the walls or in the vanguard watching as their own siege weaponry return fire. Before the next round of trading blows loosened, Rocco shouted "Aim the fire toward the siege weapons!"

Rocco's burning stones crashed onto the siege weapons of the enemy, lighting the fields into a bright maelstrom of flame. Those manning Harigamun's siege weapons shouted, "They are scorching the Fields of Dagora!"

As fire burned the soil, the commanders screamed their orders. "We must reposition! The singed soil takes away the metal!"

Meanwhile, the water-imbued stones came wrecking into Pyrosi armaments, covering many of them beset with lighting the stones aflame. The stones then crashed into some of their trebuchets, and once the boulders stopped moving, the Pyrosi unexpectedly became devoured by a small tidal wave.

Those who avoided the massive wave—which seemed to be cast from one of Runefall's trebuchets—started to bicker with one another, "Where did they learn this sorcery?"

One of the Pyrosi commanders yelled, "Light the city!" Their casters loaded the remaining trebuchets with stone already crafted by Sodsheim's Earth Mites, but they could not conjure a flame.

Singher, the Pyrosi commander, cursed at his army. "Dry yourselves off, you river rats!" His commanders, the few untouched by the water-holding stones, launched their trebuchets once more.

"Quite the devious trick, Rocco," said Elias, looking over the panicking Pyrosi to their Eastern flank. "Have you any tricks for the Wind Riders, or maybe the Summoners, or Earth Mites? Oh no, I'm sure you've got something up your sleeve for the Mystics though."

Rocco glanced at his fellow commander, and partner, as sweat pooled above his eyelid. Out of the glimpse of his eye, he saw a monstrous ball of fire racing toward him.

Elias jumped to push his lover out of the way and drew a rune his partner did not recognize, on his hand with a small blade before the attack could land. General Harkor struck his hand forward with an open palm and an emerald gale grew in size in front of him. The scorched rubble launched from the Pyrosi catapult froze in mid-air, held by the emerald gale. The fire-touched stone sat for a moment as the emerald sheen pulsated above the heads of those who stood near them, and suddenly, the stone launched itself backward, as if returning to the very catapult it came from.

In the distance, Rocco watched as the stone shot back at the siege device which initially launched it, destroying the siege weapon and operators, and many others surrounding it.

Rocco turned to Elias with glistening white eyes. "What was that? What was that rune?" Then, he noticed his partner's veins under his eyes, and small wrinkles he had not noticed before.

"Hardly time to teach you new spells during a battle," the short, but stout commander said. "Though, I wouldn't count on that one again. I don't have that much time to give."

Rocco turned away from his partner to the battalions of archers behind him. "On my orders, cast a volley at will!" When they shot, the arrows fell like dark hail overhead the encroaching enemy. To soldiers on the ground, the attack of unison by those archers sounded like the ripping of wind as the end of their times swiftly came like a wharf of black breath.

Barigund heard the volley of arrows fly over the Wall of Turmin. It came as a swift breeze and a cold chill marking a hard day of dying. For a moment, that volley signaled a switch for Runefall—from victim to defender.

The City Commander looked back from the front gate where the vanguard awaited the enemy and saw Turmin, the architect of Runefall. The architect, fighting his way through legions invading via rune portals, meant to make his way to the front gate, hoping to find allies.

Upon slaying an invader who had rushed through a portal by taking on massive swing with his hammer right into the opponent's chest, Turmin watched as two rune portals simultaneously disappeared. The soldiers of Runefall—he saw—handled themselves well against the rune doors and...they stopped in an instant as if pulled away.

"I didn't expect to see you on the field today," Barigund said, "brother."

The tall and heavy man made his way over to Gremanhas and the young ones whom the teacher had prepared to fight, standing next to the four Runics the City Commander acquired.

"Fear not the opening of the gate, young ones," Turmin said. "Think of it as a window only we can see through. They cannot break through my craft." The large man gave a larger, bellowing laughter, slightly shocking the students. "Once something of remarkable magic has occurred, only remarkable magic can undo it."

Then, a harrowing horn howled across the battlefield and rang through the city's walls. The marble stones sang a horrendous tune all the way down to the crypts where many of the women and children hid.

Belias's legs started to quiver, and she looked up to Turmin. "Who is protecting the others? Is it here that we are truly needed, or with them?"

"The council of Runefall has led those who are not fit for fighting to the lower levels of the city," answered Barigund, who saw the fear in the young Agualyte student. "Furin, Premus, and Shalix will protect them little one."

The ground quaked. Tremors rumbled against the ground. "Is this some giant?" Barigund wracked his brain trying to determine what could cause such a tremendous shutter. That's when he looked up and saw something in the distance, something heading toward the Wall of Turmin.

"Battering ram!" voices started to shout from the top of the wall. "Golems!"

"No," Turmin whispered.

"Can they break through?" Barigund asked.

"To measure the strength of one magic and compare it to another is beyond me," Turmin answered. "I have hoped not."

Belias mustered the courage to ask another question. "How do you know the wall can withstand their magic? What gave you this hope?"

The footsteps of the golems rushing forth with a battering ram continued getting closer, louder, causing sharper tremors.

"Adamantite is the only stone resistant to magic, young one," Turmin answered.

Barigund twitched at the words, for a select few knew what the wall was made of.

"But only dwarves can craft adamantite," Hirkar, the Earth Mite student said. "I cannot even touch the dirt that lies beneath that stone."

"Aye, young one. That be true," the colossal architect said. "Only dwarves can work with that stone. Do you know why?" he chuckled. "Because we were made from it."

Gremanhas turned to see the architect's red face filled with pride. "How many know of this?" the teacher asked.

The crunching of the earth grew closer.

"Is this the time to discuss Turmin's ancestry?" Barigund lifted his fist into the air, pounded his chest, and released a menacing growl. His armor banged with each hit as he eyed each member of the vanguard. "You heard him! You stand by a man made of stone! You stand by the greatest sorcerers each tribe of magic has to offer! You stand by the greatest fighter the city has ever known!" He glimpsed toward the old mentor. "And now you will witness the greatest strength I have within me!"

A voice cried out from the top of the wall. "There's more than one!"

Gremanhas saw the City Commander's eyes turn to black for just a short moment, and then they ignited with a frightful flaxen explosion before Barigund cast himself to the ground.

The City Commander muttered to himself, and no one could speak to him or move him. Turmin reached to move him, and his body seemed as heavy as his adamantite walls, there would be no moving him. Something old awoke within his brother, and the architect knew it would be its last awakening.

The trembling of the earth came to a sudden halt as golems crashed into the open gate. Once the armies came closer, following behind the golems, Rocco's monstrous voice roared through the city once more. "Volley!"

Arrows darkened the midday battlefield once more and wailed upon the converging armies of the Warlord. Golems rose from the ground, realizing the invisible barrier between them and the city, and started battering the barrier with their ram.

First, the ram crashed against the forcefield with a large metal spike dripping with blood which–to Gremenhas and his students–had no effect. None of Runefall's fighters saw the blood dripping from the spike. Then, a second ram banged against the back of the first from behind. Then a third, and a fourth. "A line! They are creating a line of rams!" shouted dozens of soldiers.

"Turmin," Asmodeus, the Pyrosi student, shouted. "Can fire travel through?"

"It can come from within, but not from outside," Turmin said.

"Stand back," Asmodeus said as he gestured to the entire vanguard. Gifted in Pyrosi practices, but rash to feats of strength, the student worried his teacher often, as in this moment, by being quite overzealous.

Thus, most soldiers present watched in waiting for the might they knew could come from the student, all save for Gremanhas who instead felt worry over awe. The teacher's body let out small, unnoticeable quivers with teeth wanting to jump out of his mouth as he waited for the next moments.

But then, the line of rams joined as one and dozens of golems locked themselves in unison to create one immense siege weapon. With a great thrust, the rams thrashed against the barrier, and one such blow sent a crack throughout the city but did not break the barrier.

Asmodeus stepped to the barrier, meeting many golems eye-to-eye. He took a deep breath and the heat in his chest rose so high the golem at the front of the siege dropped the ram, causing many of the other golems to do the same. The Pyrosi student ripped off his shirt, showing his ribbed abdomen glowing a harsh red, his torso grew brighter while also growing darker. Shadows crept over him under the igniting flames. As he took one last deep inhale, the golems re-regained their hold on the gargantuan ram. At the exact moment of the golems thrusting the ram into the barrier, with the ram's blood-soaked blade, Asmodeus seemed like a dragon to those in the vanguard as a fiery explosion prepared itself in his throat.

However, no one else saw the blood on the tip of the ram, not even Gremanhas. If they had, especially if the teacher had—the act would have been stopped. Asmodeus, though, saw it too late, but all he understood was fire.

A fearsome fire escaped Asmodeus's gullet and seared many of the golems and the ram, killing a hoard of them...and a warrish sight of magnificence it was, but the barrier broke under the pressure of the fire. He fell to the ground coughing blood. The break, not large enough for an army, but one by one, golems forced their way through while the Pyrosi student died on the ground suffocating beneath his own blood with a charred throat.

"Blood touched the fire," Turmin said. "Damn that boy for not having the strength, nor the knowledge, to stop himself. I ought to have intervened if I knew they were using blood." But the oversized dwarf did not expect such a display of ignorance from the student in his own craft, as the boy had proven himself many times over. But few would have known that blood could break adamantite. In truth, Turmin had only told very few that information, for he didn't entirely know it was true. "The pride of being a hero," he grumbled, lifting an enormous sledgehammer from his waist belt. "I know it all too well."

The architect knocked his hammer lightly against Barigund—his brother—who still pressed his weapon against the ground murmuring to himself. His brother made no signs of movement.

Turmin, Grand Smith, and Architect of Runefall, heaved his hefty hammer onto his shoulder and smiled at a golem breaking through the barrier...and raced toward it. *One last fight.*

Chapter Ten

The Slaying of Gods

"I ponder eternity. It seems a curse, to me, to live eternally. I have done things, things within a mortal span which carry endless guilt. I need not carry such sorrow for eternity."
— Harigamun, *Thoughts of War*

K arabella threw her blade to the ground, its edge clanging against a stone. "When is it enough?" The widowed dwarf wanted desperately to thrust her steel into her King, just for a moment. *This is on you . . . it's all on you!*

The dwarven king turned to Barklo. Regaining his strength from eating the sour dwarf meat mere hours ago, Barklo hung his head low with drifting eyes, not giving his king—his closest friend—a signal of what to say. He shone with shame, embarrassed he'd so greedily taken food out of desperation and placed their people, his sister, in danger. Indeed, he felt responsible for the events in the absence of their King.

"We were attacked by Ograas in the South," Krabella continued. "You said we needed to escape to the North, and we followed. You said we need to go to the North because the elves to the East and the men to the West, since both still either fear us or want us dead...we listened! We listened and we died! Why the hell did you bring us to a place you didn't understand? Why did you so willingly lead with blindness?"

Krabella walked up to her King and pushed her palm against his chest, knocking him back a step, repeatedly. "The Ograas wanted us dead, the elves wanted us dead, the men wanted us dead, and you said come to the mountains!" Krabella turned to face the surrounding dwarven company, or what was left of them. "We died from Ograas before we escaped, we died to the Silver Shadow on the road, and now we die in these forgotten mountains of ice! And now, he," she said, gesturing to their King, "wishes us to contend against a god? Tell me," She looked to all those around her, "who among you is willing to die, as my husband did, as your brothers and fathers and sisters and mothers have; who among you shall die with him?"

The company stood silent until Barklo gained enough strength to speak. "I will."

"Of course you will, so willing to die for a friend," Krabella said, disgusted.

"I will," said Dhamri. Gasps filled the air as he shot a glance toward his Queen.

"I will," Saroria said, followed by her son.

Many of the few remaining dwarves stood in shock trying to understand why Dhamri would ally with the King. Their hatred of one another was well known and it was clear Dhamri held their leader responsible for his recent captivity and almost being cooked on a spit.

"I will not," Krabella spat at the King's feet. "Enjoy your deaths."

The widowed dwarf lifted her weapon from the ground and walked toward the entrance of the mountain. Krabella's intended destination stayed unknown to the remaining dwarves who numbered far less than twenty, but each stood wondering where she might go.

The King turned to Dhamri and saw a scowl where others frowned. *Fear is setting in. But why should Dhamri be willing to help me? Ah...he's not.*

"Let's not play guessing games," Dhamri said. "It's no secret I've no faith in you, and this has all but solidified my position. I go with you to stand between your failure and the deaths of those who will follow."

"Reasons aside," Grunffi said, truthfully. "Good to see you in company, regardless of how much either of us hate it."

Grunffi turned to face the group before him. His closest friend and son held a glow with a fierceness in them, bent to some task, awaiting orders.

Dhamri made no attempt to hide a devious malcontent, while the Queen's eyes seemed heavy and she looked worn to him. The remaining company exuded fear, and he wanted to admonish them for it.

"I've been wrong," Grunffi said, addressing the company. "Many times, even though I wish it wasn't so. I never asked to be your leader, your King, or whatever title you lay upon my head after such failings. All of my decisions were made for fear of losing your lives, and in many times, I have failed to stop such from happening." He stopped and let out a long lamentable sigh. "Mayhaps the cloud of death is inescapable, or in my attempted escape, I tumble into its grasp. Our kind grows thin, our trust narrow, and I would not see the dwarves cut out from this world even if the world seems bent on doing so," he paused. "This god demanded a flesh sacrifice, a dwarven flesh sacrifice. That will be answered for as long as I can wield an axe...!"

Grunffi stopped and started pounding his axe on his chest, grunting heavily and rhythmically. As the chanting grew more and more, the surrounding company joined in, and anger could be heard within each chanting note. Under the chorus of the rising chants, Grunffi shouted, "For the Dwarves!"

The dwarven company roused itself and a yearning for revenge struck each of their hearts as they each lifted their weapons into the air, chanting, "For the dwarves!"

"Let's put those myths of dwarves to the test," Grunffi said, regaining his breath. "I'm willing to bet this god never fought a dwarf! Not the ones he should be scared of, at least!"

The remaining company journeyed into the heart of the lava mountain and each member grew increasingly cautious as squalls, howls, and roaring littered the air, as if from small creatures be hunted, or devoured, while they proceeded down the long corridor of small stalking shadows.

Approaching an opening to another large chamber, the heat rose to unfathomable levels, beyond what any of the dwarves had ever endured. Sweat drenched their tattered armor as each step became a sticky strain. Sounds of death grew quiet and the darkness turned pitch-black. Darkness veiling the corridor faded as they felt they were being cooked. But then, a hollow voice spoke to them as lava ran through the walls without leaking out. Creatures of myth and small birth—dragon younglings, draguar infants, children of the Fowls, and others with hard eyes and mean cries erupted into a cacophony of pain and terror, striking the hearts of each dwarf as they could not recognize a single one of them, save one gigantic lizard wrapped around a throne... with someone sitting on it.

"Dragon," whispered Barklo.

"Yes," hissed the man seated upon the throne of bones. Small and long, they were clearly bones of beasts, or maybe other things. Grunffi did not know. "Yes, it is indeed a dragon, my dragon, reborn. Though, he is sadly much smaller than his ancestors." The man rose from his chair.

Grunffi thought the man's hissing sounded like a serpent, the very serpent surrounding his chair. It was a sharp and pointed form of speech, ugly to dwarven ears, and harsh with condescension.

Grunffi stretched his back and pushed out his chest, fighting off the fear running down his spine. "You've been eating dwarves," he said. "What kind of god eats his own creation?"

"Creation?" the man scoffed. "I am Baylar, Lord of Summons. I'm not to blame for your kind being carved from stone. Blame the Dreadsmith, Dwarahir. I give life where death has come. You are simply talking rocks."

Grunffi did not recognize the name, and he saw the confusion in his company which told him none of them did either. The grimly worn flesh-eating dwarves thought this man to be their god, their creator. *Why give up the lie now? Who is Dwarahir?*

Grunffi grunted. "Why eat dwarves? They were sickly, malnourished, and desperate for help. You twisted them into something horrible and unforgiving. You told them you were their god. Why?"

"Dragons need to eat," Baylar answered. "And gods need worship... at least, we thought we did."

The inner chamber of the mountain chilled and a flurry of snow clung to the edge of the cavern walls as a zephyr wafted a white gust trailing over to Baylar. A creature, a small crystalline bird perched atop his shoulder, staring at the oncoming vortex. For the dwarves, previously unbearable heat turned into a lust for warmth within seconds. A pale wind gathered beside the throne as the Grunffi watched the god twirl his hand, as if a child painting. The wind formed into a white cocoon, and suddenly, the beast from atop the mountain—Crytungr—was alive once more, and Kaida slithered all the more closely to Baylar.

But... Crytungr much smaller than on the mount?" Grunffi thought.

"Kaida," said Baylar. "Are you hungry?"

The dragon slithered around Baylar's throne as it uncoiled its slender form. Each scale glistened with indigo starlight and its elongated tongue forked in three directions. Its claws were pronounced like a panther's, and it sat so close to the ground it looked as if it were crawling. It was not the dragons of old the dwarves' heard stories of as children from their fathers, but it was most certainly the only dragon they had ever seen.

The serpent slithered across the dirt to sit in front of the dwarven company. It rose up, to the height of Baylar sitting on the throne, and its chest turned to a shadowy haze before releasing a blizzard up through its throat. The beast scowled and screeched as freezing light rose to its lips with its squalls growing unbearable.

"Hide!" Grunffi leaped to the cavern walls with all of his might, grabbing his son and wife, knocking them down.

Frost.

A blaze of clear blue tore through the cavern and sent freezing pain seeping down each of the dwarves' spines.

Grunffi rose from the ground and turned to see Barklo—his closest friend and brother-in-law—frozen, enveloped within dark ice painted like sapphire. The dwarven leader's brow dripped with sweat amid the lowering temperature of the cavern, his limbs revolting against the freezing cold as stress contorted his mind. His chest pinched and his heart grew heavy as a piece of ore sinking into the depths of his stomach. The King tried to move his mouth and couldn't; he just felt a sting across his gums as his teeth clamped down, holding back an inevitable scream trapped behind a prison of bone.

Without warning, Grunffi's fingers traveled to the hilt of his long axe as the god laughed. In a moment of divine self-indulgence, Grunffi's fingers wrapped around the hilt of the blade, spun it once around his head, and launched the piercing blade right into the skull of the dragon. Blood pooled as its slimy body collapsed. No bones were heard but an uncomfortable squelch stuck in the wind upon the creature's end.

"Kaida!" Baylar wailed. "How?"

A second blade, then a third, and a fourth launched toward the god as their new target. Grunffi watched as the blades cut the very air of the cavern and sliced the cold clean through, all the way, until sharpened edges buried themselves, one-by-one, into the cruel god. Alas, all but two of the blades fell from him as he healed from the wounds instantly. But the two blades which stuck wrenched away at his core and spilled his blood. But the god remained standing.

Baylar looked down at the blades and pulled them out slowly, inch-by-inch. He glared at the blades for a moment. "So, it is true then," he coughed blood. "You truly can fashion a blade from the stone.

Impressive, and annoying. Sadly, for me, that means you can cause me pain. Sadly, for you, you still can't kill me. A rock isn't enough to kill a god, nor is it worthy of calling it life when one can speak!"

Adamantite, Grunffi thought to himself. *We are made from it, and it hurts him.* He looked down at his hands.

The wounds of Baylar healed upon the removal of the blades, but his skin remained scarred from the cut.

Now, the rebirthed, but much smaller, Crytungr flapped its wings and rose to the cavern ceiling as a chilling gust strangled the hearts of all present, save Baylar, as each one of them trying to take cover.

"You're not so big this time," Grunffi mumbled to himself.

Then, the dwarven leader stepped out from hiding and rushed toward the bird in a flash of fury, leaping high enough in the air to grab ahold of Crytungr and smash it into the dirt. Grunffi took hold of its head and turned it to its side, pushing the large and protruding beak away from him.

In that moment, Saroria watched as one great weight from her husband's fist crashed down on the skull of the beast, shattering its bones so loudly each dwarf, and Baylar, heard the crunch.

"No," Baylar whispered. "All of the legends are true then..." he fell to his knees. *It is time for the slaying of the gods. Our time is over. The smith spoke true.*

Grunffi approached the feeble god without remorse. "What legends? Speak!"

In a last attempt, Baylar launched himself backward and motioned his hands as if to cast a spell. A burst of white appeared in front of the King, but nothing happened. The dwarf closed the gap between himself and Baylar. Then, the stout attacker grabbed the back of Baylar's neck and threw him to the ground like a disobedient animal.

Grunffi shouted once more, "What legends?"

"Dwarahir," Baylar said. "'I'll smithy the weapon for your ruin.'

That's what he told us...perhaps this is what we deserved."

Grunffi, standing still, awaited more answers. Remorse poured out of the pathetic god, and he muttered to himself while under the heel of a dwarven King. "You're little more than a worm. How empty divinity now seems."

"That's what he told us," Baylar's voice cracked. "The gods, the Kaiyar, whatever you'd like to call us! He threatened us with the weapon to bring our doom! He said he'd bring our end as we wrought it on ourselves and you are that ending, you are our death." His head hung with desperation. *What made you so weak?*

"And what a weapon we are." Grunffi said. "We are locked in a game with death. Forever the losing dealer."

"He did not tell us it was you, or your kind," Baylar continued, reaching for the dwarf's pant legs. "He disappeared from Kaiyara and not a word was heard from him again. But then we heard rumblings...rumors of a new breed roaming the earth—dwarves." The God of Summons took an exasperated breath. "End it. All I needed to see was a spell from my own hands fail. I don't want this anymore. I have no place in the mortal realm, and my death comes where immortals still hide. If I am to die, let it be here." He clutched the pants tightly. "Just, do it. Just..." he looked to the frozen dwarf, the King's friend, "avenge him. End me for allowing my beasts to eat your pathetic, abandoned kin. Pick a reason, just do it yourself."

"So, you're saying he made us...this, Dwarahir?" Grunffi asked, ignoring the begging. "Why would he not act as you and demand piety as your lot does? Why does he not call on us to worship him if he made us?"

"That is the very thing he meant to punish us for," Baylar said, feeling his power drain beneath a powerful grip bearing down on his neck. "Dominion over all the other races. It seemed so deserved for the rest of us, but not Dwarahir. He told us if we were meant to follow the path of dominion, he would craft a weapon ultimately leading to our death and he did it using the only thing that can hurt us."

"Adamantite?" Grunffi asked.

"Yes," Baylar answered. "That rock you hold so dear. The legends are true, it's obvious. You're resistant to magic, so the Crytungr I summoned here was not old enough to hold you back, though clearly your friend was not strong enough for Kaida." He laughed and then coughed.

"What is obvious?" Grunffi demanded, squeezing on his opponent's neck so vicious breathing became a chore.

"You're made from the stone, you dwarven ingrate." Baylar spat at his feet.

The dwarven King stared at Baylar for a moment before speaking. "Why have you not tried to run?" Grunffi asked. "Why do you sit here, answering my questions like a beaten child?"

"The blade," Baylar said. "I'm the God of Summons, not teleportation. But yes, I do know some simple spells that might've helped had you not stuck that rock blade inside of me. But it's pointless. My spells did nothing to you, and I know what waits for me outside, should the rest of them come…no, I'm done with this world, and all the others. Just. Kill. Me… please. I'll answer every question, just don't make me deal with any more gods."

Grunffi looked down at the blade once more.

"If you can't run, then why be so forthcoming when you clearly hate our kind?" Grunffi asked.

"I cannot run, which means I cannot live," said Baylar. "And, as they say, the enemy of my enemy will end the world."

"That doesn't explain why you would tell me all this," Grunffi growled. "What do you want?"

Baylar sighed and looked at the ground, revealing his neck. "Cut cleanly when you do," he said. "But when you kill the others, go slow. We all deserve it. I'm just begging for quick mercy."

"Answer the question, or you stay in bondage with a stone knife permanently gutting you, or I may yet still drag you out of this mountain and through the cold with the knife lodged within," Grunffi threatened. "If I find the others, then I'll make sure they find you."

Baylar looked up at Grunffi, tears pouring, strength faded, as if willingly given up.

"He was obviously right," Baylar said. "He told us we would pay at the hands of his weapon. He crafted your very being from that damn stone and now you are the only race who can forge it. That means you are the only thing that stands between gods and death. With time, I would be able to remove your blade. As I said, that alone would not kill me. Leaving me allows me to live. I deserve death, but I was escaping torture. I'll take my end, but I won't face endless suffering. I deserve this for what I've done."

"You volunteer this information...so that we might kill the other gods for you?" Grunffi scratched his head. "So that we will kill you?" He turned to the company. "We are dwarves! We are the god-killing weapon!" He turned back as the few remaining gave a weak cheer, while most stayed silent. "

"I have taken that peace of death from others, from creatures, from my companions," Baylar answered. "All magic comes at a cost when we give it to the world, even for us. I made my creatures pay. They do not know death, only servitude. You still have more to learn. All I have left to tell you is Dwarahir's Forge lies in the very mountains we find ourselves in now. I know not where. Do you think I'm hiding in the depths of a volcano and feeding my pets dwarven flesh because I am in good standing with the other gods? I tire of eternity and the politics of godliness. I tire of hiding and my reason for life was lost a very long time ago when the only thing that truly mattered to me was stolen. Now all I have are my pets," he looked around to the beasts, no more than babies each of them, knowing they could not fight, "and one by one you take them from me as well. I have waited for a quick death, away from those who hunt me."

"Pets," Grunffi said. "You keep these creatures as pets?"

"Surely," Baylar answered. "The beasts of old were always my closest friends for they did not know it was me who stopped them from resting. You know, I signed many contracts in my youth to call upon them before becoming Baylar." He winked.

"You chose to become a god?" Grunffi's confusion became apparent.

He wondered why he was listening anymore. The other dwarves grew impatient and were whispering to one another about what their King should be doing. Baylar obviously wanted to turn the dwarves against the gods for punishing him. But should the gods be punished? *Are they all as he is?*

"You have much, much to learn," Baylar answered, chuckling with blood dripping from his mouth. "I fell out of favor with Krishalla and the rest when I chased my wife down for laying with another. The dreadful, loathsome, evil Blood Lord! I ought to have made her bathe in his blood when I was finished, rather than just throwing her onto his beaten carcass like I did. But the others saw fit to condemn me, 'punish me for an eternity', they said."

All at once, Baylar flung himself from his knees and placed his hands on Grunffi's chest and started pushing him backward with each spoken word.

The god pushed Grunffi, far enough the god had time to grab the dwarf's blade and jump. Grunffi caught the shaft of the blade with one hand and felt the god's strength falling away the longer the God of Summons pushed.

"Kill the others," Baylar whispered to him. "Salaril seeks to bring about the return of Krishalla. He lives below the depths of Runefall, imprisoned. Break him free of bondage, and then kill him!"

"What has this god done to me?" Grunffi asked, turning to look at his dwarven company, not really struggling to hold the weapon, but rather, choosing to listen. This had played out for far too long, but Grunffi wanted to know. *Why now? What should this information come to me for in a time of failure and death?*

Saroria was taken by silence, Haffi by curiosity, Dhamri by anger, and Barklo by the frost. The few others remaining stood petrified at their lack of understanding of the world, as was Grunffi. The dwarven King just couldn't show it. It all seemed like a performance to the dwarven company, a flurry of information bombarding their heads with doubt, curiosity, and intrigue.

"I wasn't the worst one," Baylar rambled as he lost grip of the axe. "I never planned for your death. I just wished it would happen! Krishalla, however, intends to wipe all of you from the earth. Your piety failed and magic fades away! You are the weapon against magic, against the Kaiyar! Not just you, but every race. He wants to start over with a more pious population. A people who worships and one who can learn the old ways better than you, and it all starts with Runefall. Your grasp on magic is primitive on this continent and that city held as much knowledge as it could for itself. Your world has tried to centralize our magic and weaponize it. Krishalla means to correct that..."

Grunffi stepped back for a moment, taking a deep breath as he considered what Baylar said. *This cannot be true. He is desperate for death and will say anything—*

Then, Baylar jumped at Grunffi to try and strip the axe from his hands. The dwarf threw the god to the ground, but he rose again, and again, and again. Finally, the God of Summons grabbed a rock and tried smashing it against the dwarf's head and for the last time, the dwarven king cast him to the ground.

"Oh, and one last thing," Baylar said with a smile, looking back at Grunffi. "The stone blades are for the other dwarves who can't kill a god." Baylar smiled and looked over at the rest of the company. "You should just use your hands; they are the ones who need the rocks."

The god tried to attack once more but Grunffi grabbed his head and ripped it clean off his shoulders with a strength he'd never felt and suddenly the summoned creatures faded away into a blue dust and warmth returned to the chamber. They were all small and harmless creatures resembling beasts of old, nothing like Crytungr.

Grunffi turned and saw a look of bewilderment and fear across his wife's face, now being held by Dhamri, who gave a solemn look to his wife and son.

Dhamri turned to a frozen Barklo, and then back to the King, whom he clearly blamed.

Barklo's eyes sat buried beneath ice with a harsh longing for cover. His pupils screamed for help as Grunffi took note of how wide his eyeballs were spread. A tailored glance and a squinted eye let the King see his friend peering at a rock to his left. *He realized it too late*, the King thought.

"Are we at enough, then?" Dhamri asked. "Have enough fallen for your own pride for the rest of us to live?"

The King stood staring at Barklo in silence. He didn't hear the taunting words. All he heard was his dead friend's laughter. The day the King and Queen were married, Barklo had gotten his new brother-in-law very drunk on ale.

Saroria wasn't upset in the slightest on that day. They were the closest of friends for years upon years before Grunffi ever became King. As King, Grunffi relied on Barklo time and time again to be the softer touch of dwarven leadership. His kindness was well-known, and his temperament saved many from succumbing to their own fury. Grunffi became lost in memory staring at his friend, frozen outside of the live world, outside of friendship, outside of love and life.

"Ograas, elves, men, and now gods, it seems," Dhamri said. "Our list of enemies grows larger as you remain the head of our company."

Grunffi did not move, he could not because he did not hear. His wife had snuck near his backside, wanting to reach out and comfort him, though she stayed, unsure how to do so.

Dhamri turned to face the rest of the company. "His failure will continue to be the death of our kin! Stay with him if you must, but I will climb back to the entrance of this mountain, collect what remains of the supplies, and journey back to the South. It is time the dwarves reclaim what is owed to us!"

"You'll do no such thing." Haffi raised both of his spears close to his face. "You'll leave, aye. You can do that. But you'll touch nothing of the supplies at the entrance. In fact, I'll escort you myself to make sure you don't leave with too heavy a burden."

"Step out of the way, boy," Dhamri drew his blades. "There's been enough death at the lead of your family."

"Then you're saying yes to my escort and leaving the supplies?" Haffi smiled, ready for a long-awaited conflict.

"No, Haffi," Dhamri sighed. "Get out of my way."

Haffi's blades clashed, one spear crossing the other. He stepped back with one held above his head and one lined up to his knee. "Make your decision, Dhamri. We've other battles to fight and we'd be best not to be killing each other with what lies ahead."

Grunffi continued staring at his friend's frozen carcass. His wife slunk further into the shadows, covering her mouth, trying not to scream, and terrified of the next moments to come. Then, she reached down and found her axe, and she quivered at the thought of using it against Dhamri, but she would if a decision needed to be made between him and her son. *Don't make me kill you, Dhamri. Don't make me turn a blade against my own kind.*

Bolting toward her son, the tip of Dhamri's long axe thrust forward and nearly pierced the prince's abdomen. Defending the blow, the axe was knocked to the ground by a well-timed spear, as the prince spun with a sweeping kick to knock his opponent to the ground.

Grunffi, snapping out of his grief, turned to see the commotion and came to his senses. The King jumped to help his son, but before he could get there, Haffi had already launched a death-dealing blow against his opponent.

Haffi raised both of his spears above his chest and brought the blades crashing down toward the beaten dwarf's chest, but he stopped, seeing his father approaching. *It's enough to know I won. The skulking imbecile doesn't need to die.*

Saroria squirmed as a squelching sound filled the air and her son's limp body fell on top of his opponent with a short axe in his back. A cowardly dwarf shook behind her dead son, enraging the Queen, and sending her into a wailing storm of cries. Her knees broke the dirt, and she bellowed into the dank heat. "WHY?" She smashed her hands all across the floor, screaming out against the darkness.

"Why?" Dhamri's rage spilled and shot spittle flying toward the cowardly dwarf.

Grunffi's sight bent inward, and his vision crossed at the glimpse of his fallen son. No sooner than his opponent's rage quelled, and the spittle stopped raining on the dwarf who slew his son, the King walked without haste over to the long axe buried in the dead god, ripped it from him, and turned to the cowardly killer. Standing nearly twenty feet from one another as he approached the trembling dwarf, and with Saroria crying in fading light as the lava flowing through the walls had started to wane, the King spoke in a low and callous voice. "Say your last, Ikba."

"I only meant to escape this mountain and I thought that—," Ikba tried.

"Say your last," Grunffi repeated.

"I just wanted to escape this mountain and live and I thought that—"

"Your last," Dhamri interrupted, picking himself up from the ground.

Ikba, with a fearsome quivering in his legs, begged while his teeth chattered among the fiery heat returning in the chamber. Sweat ran into his eyes, and he felt a salty burn mixed with tears as snot came from his upper lip into the gap in his quivering mouth. "P-p-p-please Dhamri. I-I believed you would save us!"

"Say your last," Grunffi and Dhamri said, in unison.

Ikba fell to his knees as inane babble turned to frantic and indiscernible cries of desperation. No final words were heard, or rather, understood.

The King looked over at his shattered wife and held the axe. As she walked closer to grab the weapon, the coward's cries rang through the chamber like a scalded child in a small room. She grabbed the axe and sundered toward the cravenous dwarf with an intentional speed designed to prolong her steps. With each, Ikba's cries grew louder and more harrowing.

Saroria finally reached the craven and stood so close to him he felt a drop of her sweat fall onto his chin as he looked up at her. She stared into him for a moment and the weakling thought he saw her eyes turn black as her mouth formed an otherworldly scowl.

Saroria raised the blade upside down with both hands, the tip between both of the axe's blades pointing down toward his skull. "Open your mouth," she said.

Ikba sobbed and begged her to stop, to spare him, to forgive him.

She gave him a scorned mother's stare, anger born only from maternity. "Open your mouth and I use one motion to take your cowardly life from you. Continue begging, and I take each limb, one-by-one, then a tongue, then each little snippet of flesh I can cut until you die from the blood loss. But not before I sear each wound with the lava from this mountain, delaying your death as long as I can."

Ikba slowly opened his mouth, trembling, with each twitch between his lips as his cries and deep gurgles surfaced from swallowing his own spit and mucus. The Queen let him sit in that misery for just a moment and took in each second of suffering as debt owed to her.

When it dug into him, the axe ran through his throat and pierced his lower belly as the blade burrowed into the dirt. There, he sat, with the King's long axe holding his lifeless frame up like a crutch, the coward's blood soaking into the ground.

Then, the King turned to Dhamri.

"Run!" Saroria shouted as as the King paced his way toward his next target.

But Dhamri did not move.

"Not without a fight," Dhamri said in a calm voice. "Your boy struck the first blow, it was defense, not malice on my part."

"I've no need for further words," Grunffi said with a scowl.

Saroria looked ather husband and there lived dark hate of which she had never known, not from him.

"Please Grumpy," she pleaded with a soft voice he usually loved to hear. "Please, don't do this."

"Pick yourself up and regain your breath," Grunffi said, turning his back to his opponent, stretching his arms, and preparing for battle. He ripped his axe from Ikba's limp carcass.

Dhamri turned to his sobbing, rageful Queen. "Do name the little one after me. It would be a shame for a name like Dhamri to fade from this world."

Grunffi went stunned for a short moment. His spine forfeited against the rest of him as his hand opened, dropping his axe. Dirt tufted from the ground under the weight of the axe and his ire swelled. He turned to see his opponent facing him with a glaring smile, one that said he had already won.

Grunffi's gaze turned to his wife and all she saw reflected back at her was his pain. He raised one hand and outstretched one finger to point at her, first with a steady stance, and then his hand quaked with tremors as he continued to hold it in place. *How could you?*

The angered King's jaw clenched like his bones were about to snap.

All at once, he released the tension and a thundering boom escaped him and went throughout the mountain, scaring the few remaining dwarves of the company and sending them fleeing through the cavern's tunnels. But Dhamri stood still as the Queen howled in anguish.

A warrior of women in Grunffi's eyes. *Saroria is not the Queen, she is my Queen.* She led battle after battle but became weak in recent weeks from the lack of food. She constantly gave to others, ensuring they were taken care of. Now, he knew she was just eating enough to sustain life, but not her life. He had hoped once they made a home they would rebuild, mend their relationship which seemed all but lost this past year. Now, Grunffi realized just how lost their relationship truly was. *She was my Queen.*

Dhamri watched as his King's sight turned toward him and felt surprised as he watched his opponent raise fists in the air to fight, dropping his axe, rather than clinging to his weapon.

"You never deserved to lead, and you never deserved your family," Dhamri taunted. "A weak King is no King at all, least of all a dwarven one."

Grunffi did not move. His eyes did not shift. His arms did not shake.

Dhamri lifted his axe into the air and placed it on his shoulder. "I always liked Haffi, which is why I held back. It was my hope that, after defeat, he would simply tell me to leave in anger. Our battle will not go the same. You will not know mercy, for you cannot show it."

"Because you will not live to see what comes after," Grunffi said.

Dhamri lowered the axe and covered its grip, strangling the axe's throat. The toe of the blade was pointed directly at the King. When Dhamri took his first step toward his opponent, the Queen let out a yelp as if it came from a scared and beaten dog. "Grunffi, no! We've lost enough!"

Grunffi turned to her, furious. "I've lost everything." He turned back to the First Lieutenant of the Legion of Stone.

Dhamri's first strike brought a heavy, overhead cleave down toward his King, but the blow was caught by the haft of the axe. He quickly let loose his hands on the throat of the weapon and gripped the top of its shaft, pushing with all of his force, but his opponent did the same. In lockstep, the axe became symbolic of their will as neither of the dwarves showed willingness to let go or change maneuver, but then the Lieutenant raised a knee between his opponent's legs, sending him backward and coughing, but not before the returning pressure applied on the opposite end of the ax cleaved the Lieutenant's chin, leaving a large gash.

Dhamri checked his wound and the blood on his hand caused the dwarf's anger to boil. After a struggle, the King regained his stance, and at the same moment, the First Lieutenant launched a second attack which his opponent recognized as the same maneuver from mere moments ago.

Grunffi threw up his hand once more to catch the blade, and suddenly, Dhamri ducked and swung the axe around with both hands toward the King's feet. He caught the attempt at just the right moment, saving his feet by giving him time enough to jump over the blade and land a crushing blow to the Lieutenant's head, causing him to lose his grip on the axe, and providing the King enough time to kick his opponent's weapon away.

Dhamri rose from the ground, freely, as the King stepped back and allowed him to do so. Now, the unarmed dwarf raised his fists and spat out blood and one tooth.

Dhamri initiated another attack with a large and overcompensated, unarmed blow toward Grunffi, which the King caught with his own hand. But a second strike snuck in with the other hand concealing a small blade, previously hidden, digging into the King's abdomen and knocking him backward.

Grunffi ripped the blade from his stomach and threw it back at the Lieutenant, who managed to dodge it. At the same moment the King threw the dagger, he watched as Dhamri side-stepped, revealing the Queen standing behind him.

The small dagger pierced Saroria and penetrated her stomach. The King looked as though he turned to stone and the First Lieutenant's rage bled out of him like a freshly lit forge. "To take a life, that mere moments ago you didn't even know existed..."

Dhamri's strength swelled, and within moments, he was on top of his King with a viscous and unmatched fury, pummeling his face into the ground.

Saroria pulled out the dagger and struggled over as quickly as she could and started beating on Dhamri's back to get him off of Grunffi. The First Lieutenant turned and knocked her down which sent the King back into a fit of rage of his own. The King pushed the assaulter off him with a bloody and mangled face, and then ran shoulder-first toward his Lieutenant, lifting and slamming him into the ground.

Saroria's cries filled the mountain as each of Dhamri's teeth crunched under the pressure of the King's hands. Blood covered her husband's fists and the First Lieutenant eventually stopped moving, but the King did not stop beating his hollow carcass.

When Grunffi turned to face his wife, he looked upon her bloody stomach.

Saroria found it difficult to tell Dhamri's blood from Grunffi's, her lover's from her husband's, as both were splattered across his face. *I have given birth to death. Our life is gone.*

Chapter Eleven

Kyra's Burning

"Arimeus claims she can break Salaril's seal. I wonder, will he be remembered as the Traitor of Runefall? Victor or not, I'll not write this history. Though, I will seek the story in my next life, if for little more than curiosity."

— Harigamun, *Thoughts of War*

"A shifting of the waters brings a fair girl to my shore," Harigamun said. "And such a well-defined physique for the young man you are still yet, Sam."

Kyra looked at the Warlord before her and knew, without doubt, she stared down at the Warlord of Kaiya, and the tampering of the portals became an obvious betrayal. The tales of the Warlord and his armor of stone were told throughout the last few years as he conquered city after city, people after people, but she always thought the tales were larger than the man himself. Now, she found herself considering how small the myths actually were. *He was made for war.*

"Hardly a girl," said Arimeus. "Though, far beneath your conquered years."

Harigamun sank to one knee, still taller than she whom he meant to instill fear as her head rested level with the scruff of his neck. *I'll bend you like the rest. You will break the gods' damned seal.*

"Tell me, girl," his tone, mocking. "Has nature prepared you for a union with a man?" Harigamun smiled, her irritation stretched. He didn't expect her to answer.

Kyra's eyes seemed likely to burst and the urge to let loose a great pain from her chest consumed her as she wanted to uppercut the Warlord. Then, a flash of skin went past her peripheral and a large fist crashed into his jaw, but his face did not move. Instead, the Warlord smiled, and looked toward his attacker with admiration.

"A fine hit. I'd expect nothing less from my own son," the Warlord said.

Samiel pulled his fist from his target and stepped backward, falling to the ground and eyeing the giant of a man before him.

"Yes, my boy," said he. "I've not the time to explain how, nor can I mend the time that has been lost. We will talk of it soon but know that I mean the girl no harm and we will clear the air of your lineage once Kyra helps me break the seal."

Thoughts of Ishmael came flooding back. His dark demeanor and long dreads seemed like branches stretching out from the night to her, gleaming with a soft and comforting calling to security. *Who knows the truth?*

The young Ragi looked the Warlord in his eyes. "The seal?"

"Do you know of it?" He looked into her gaze; a look of curiosity, not confusion. "Ahh," he laughed. "So, he was able to steal you away for some time. Very well, then. So, you know we must break it?"

"I know little." Kyra answered.

"Yet you seek much, I can see," Harigamun replied.

Samiel flexed his chest and arms, standing next to her. "What would you make her do?"

"Make?" the Warlord questioned. "No, my son. I'll not make the girl do anything. She knows the cost should she not assist me in breaking the seal beneath the city."

Samiel turned to her. "What don't I know?"

"Much," she replied. "I fear you don't know as much as me. Much as I fear I don't know enough to act."

"What seal does he speak of?" Samiel asked. "How can I help you?" He meant the offering, and she could see it. The Litree's features gave way for a clinging desire to help.

"The one holding all of us back from truly accessing our abilities to use magic," Harigamun said. "We were not meant to be limited in our use. Divided into warring factions and elitist practitioners, this was never meant to be the way magic was practiced. If we break the seal, Salaril will be released from his Kaiyan prison, and we can kill him!"

Arimeus, awestruck and his breath shortened, barked back at the Warlord. "Kill him? We are simply breaking the barriers separating Kaiya from true magic and returning to the way things should be. You would kill the God of Runes?"

"I would kill any who partook in the stealing of my only son," said Harigamun. "That damnable god is the reason magic is only practiced by few and the reason we are limited in our access to it. He fears the strength of others and seeks to imprison our abilities to solidify his divine position. No more! Once we have access to the powers of Kaiya, I will bury that forsaken god! Divinity is nothing but ego immortalized under the protective shadow of power."

Arimeus's lip quivered, and his legs stilled to a clear and intentional halt. His movement calmed as he waited for peering eyes to move elsewhere.

Kyra's sight, however, became fixed on the Warlord. "How do I help you break the seal?"

"See, my son. I need not make the girl do anything," he said and looked from Samiel back to Kyra. "I need your body, girl."

Samiel's face tightened, his cheeks reddened with heat, an odd, and unfamiliar, heat boiled in him. He wanted to open his mouth and release a life-ending flame upon the Warlord—his father—for speaking to Kyra in such a way. *You have no right! She is better than you!*

"What use is my body, and how would it be used?"

Samiel jumped in front of his friend to separate her from the Warlord. "You have no right to claim her body as your own!"

"Step away, Sam," Kyra said. "I need to know how this works before I say yes."

Samiel backed away, sad, and scared. He felt powerless, like those years of training and focusing on strength meant nothing. How could all of that time have been wasted for him to be no use to her? *Why would she say yes to him, and not me?*

A gust of wind swirled around the tent and darkness covered Kyra's eyes. In a moment, she could no longer feel the presence of Samiel, the Warlord, or Arimeus. The darkness crept up her skin and a chill clenched her jaw. But then she saw movement in the darkness, like a tree emerging from the night. His face became so clear and her fears vanished in a moment.

"His mind and body are useless, your mind is all I need, and your body is what I will take," said the voice, before the darkness receded. "Your body belongs to no one," the voice continued in a low, hushed tone as. "Nobody except me," a diabolical laugh trailed.

The darkness fell away. Kyra was back in the tent, and no one noticed a thing.

"We are to join in body and mind," said Harigamun. "Our conjoined strength will allow us to break the seal and return this land to its former glory, ridding ourselves of these petulant gods!"

"Your body, my mind," Kyra said. "You'll not need my body." She stood confident, standing far below the Warlord, yet so close to him.

Neither Samiel, nor Arimeus, could have predicted the pride she would have in confronting this Warlord. And indeed, this did little more than excite Harigamun as she glowered at him.

"There is only one way man and woman can be joined in body and mind, girl," the Warlord winked. "You will give yourself to me," he grumbled and smiled, shooting a look over to his son.

With a coy and innocent look, Kyra stared into the Warlord, inching closer. She held eye contact while slowly removing both of her ragged cloth shoes. Once both were removed, she placed one of her hands on his chest plate as he let out a satisfied groan and went to place his hand on her shoulder.

Samiel wanted to puke.

But, with a quick movement, Kyra stomped her foot against a sharp rock, penetrating her skin. Following the abrupt stab, a crystalline structure with a blue sheen emitting a burning flame enveloped her. The sudden explosion launched the Warlord backward and scorched his hand. The tent also was blasted away, leaving the Arimeus and Samiel on the ground looking up to Kyra who was levitating and pulsating a shimmering flame.

"I'll say it once more," she commanded. "Your body, my mind. Defy that decision once more and I'll prove how unnecessary you truly are to the breaking of the seal!" Her voice, dissonant, beyond human, and menacing.

Samiel saw power, Harigamun felt heat, and Arimeus lost doubt.

Samiel had seen this spell once before, many years ago. A protective rune of her own making cut into her foot, but he never saw it empowered with her blood.

Harigamun rose from the dirt and looked around at his army who awaited his next order. "Quite a sight to see something so pretty and so soft, yet so strong! Very well, Kyra. Have it your way! Clearly you have the strength we need."

Kyra lowered herself to the ground, holding the cut foot slightly pointed downward, with her toes on the ground to lift the arch in the air.

Samiel rushed to grab her shoes and bring them over to her and threw her right arm over his shoulder as he tried to help. With a quick glance and a sharp pain, she let out an exhausted breath and squeezed him, signaling him to slow down and allow her to move at her own pace. She slipped both of her shoes back on and took stiff steps, showing those around her that she suffered immense pain.

Harigamun smiled as the Chief Runic—the Traitor of Runefall—hurried to help her.

"Come," Arimeus said, reaching a hand to her. "I know just the treatment."

The young Ragi recoiled at Arimeus's attempted touch, still feeling an unnerving sense of urgency, betrayal, and clouded intention from the scarred old man.

"Very well, then," Arimeus said. "Sam, please help her and follow me to the baths."

"Shall I join for a good bath, my lady?" Harigamun's gruff voice laughed.

With Kyra so close, so vulnerable, Samiel's anger was becoming unmanageable. *Why does he insist on pushing me so much, knowing Kyra will not give herself to him?*

"There is no water in this world, be it natural or formed by the Aqualytes, which can cleanse the world of you, Warlord," Samiel said, with contention. Samiel carried Kyra to the Warlord's bath in his intricate tent as the Chief Runic followed with her staff—Dreadfall—and other small belongings. The tent loomed like a spectacle of war, something grand and performative meant to stand out among the rest. Rooms upon rooms and different paintings lined the heavy cloth walls from each of his conquered civilizations. It became evident to all that the man seeking her company would stop at nothing to showcase his conquests to the world.

Within the tent was an area of ground where Harigamun previously ordered his men to dig a small water hole. In all things, his generals found the Warlord was always eccentric, especially in ways of comfort.

Kyra examined the pool. Lined with shimmering, crystal stones, it was. Small enough to throw, those little rocks, but she realized they were too heavy for her to lift once she reached to grab one. Translucent almost, and they housed blackness within. *How perplexing*, she thought, to stare into a dark stone and feel as though she could see the ground beneath it.

"Kyra," Arimeus said quickly as he moved to take off her shoes. "You shouldn't have used the blood, girl!"

"Funny for you to tell me what I should and should not be doing. You should have been keeping me far from this army, yet you took me right into its heart. Isn't that right?" She pulled her foot away from him and cocked it back as if to break her toes on his jaw. *Touch me and die!*

"I'll not pretend I didn't lie, Kyra. I'm aware of what I had to do, but it had to be done! Now, I need you to let me cauterize your wound and clean it. You've broken your skin for that show of strength and all your essence will drain so long as the blood continues to flow. Such is the price of unpracticed blood magic," he trailed off into his own thoughts at those last words. *Of course she would. All she knows is to seek power. Those who use blood magic are set against the world. Tyranny can be a cure for the self-absorbed.*

She looked down at the previous white linen shoe and saw it faded to a dark red and black from the short travel to the tent and then noticed she still bled, but felt little pain.

"How do you mean to cauterize it?"

"Snap your fingers, boy," Harigamun said as he entered the tent. "Catch a light and seal her wound."

"I'm neither Pyrosi nor am I a boy, Harigamun," said Arimeus. "Exit this tent so I might save the only one who can help you achieve your ends!"

"I wasn't speaking to you," the Warlord said as he turned to his son. "You think yourself the son of the greatest Pyrosi alive and you cannot fathom a flame?"

Samiel turned to the Chief Runic. "But Gremanhas said…"

"Gremanhas said what he was told to say, Sam," said Arimeus.

Samiel's knees gave in, and he fell, burying his hands in the dirt. "Why wouldn't anyone tell me? I was raised to believe I was less than the rest of them, that all I had was…my body!" *They were scared of me!*

"And now you know you have the greatest strength in their world, and ours," Harigamun said. "Your strength is hard, and your power is deep."

Kyra's head slumped and fell to the ground. Arimeus quickly lifted her head up with one hand and checked her pulse with the other. "Sam, can you do it?"

Anger and abandonment consumed Samiel's thoughts for a moment before he fixated on his friend lying on the floor. *Did she know?* The knowing of a fiery presence in him made all the difference. Samiel had been told for so long he didn't have the magical aptitude of his peers and never listened to the teachings Gremanhas gave to the other students regarding the use of magic. But now, knowing he could do it; he didn't even feel the need to be taught how to call forth a flame. *I just…needed to know? Why am I different?*

He lifted his hand in the air, glimpsed at Harigamun, and snapped his fingers. Suddenly Samiel's entire hand became coated in flame. For a moment, he stood silent and felt no pain from the fire, but then he rushed to Kyra, placing his hand across her wound.

She sprang back into consciousness with a great cry as her skin burned in the hands of her friend. Her tears broke him instantly and he let go of her and pushed himself backward, ashamed of the pain he caused her.

"You did well, Sam, Arimeus said, lifting her up. "Now, boil the water. Leave," he said to the Warlord. "As your son stated, you have no right to h er."

Harigamun did as he was bidden and the Chief Runic tried taking Kyra's clothes off. Without a thought, she brought both of her hands together with open palms and slammed into him, launching the old man back into the pool of water. Her final bit of strength dissolved, and she fell limp, but still conscious.

"He's not the only old man that won't be looking at my body today," she said glaring at Arimeus as he lay in the pool.

The old man lowered his head and lifted himself up from the shallow waters. "I apologize, Kyra. I only meant to help."

The old Runic turned to Samiel before exiting the tent. "Make sure to warm the pool and scrub the wound. It needs to be cleaned and she will likely not be able to push herself to do it. The pool will do the rest."

Once only Kyra and Samiel were left standing in the room, she took a deep breath, and said, "Come then, Sam. Help me into the pool."

All at once, Samiel felt a sweat covering his hands surpassing the warmth he felt moments ago when his hand was aflame. Air crashed against his lips, which felt chaste, struggling to open his mouth to answer.

Samiel panicked, though he hid it. *I've never seen her...naked.* But then, thoughts and curiosities ran rampant within the confines of his innermost desires, urges he never outwardly expressed toward her. Still, he did not feel compelled to act. Instead, he felt a gross feeling of fear and contempt toward the other men for placing him in the position. He knew he cared for her, but life seemed easier without mentioning it.

Kyra made a feeble effort to lift off her robes, but she could barely lift her hands.

"I know you don't think of me like that," Kyra said, struggling to keep her eyes open, and still recovering from the blood loss. But she wasn't sure of that at all. In fact, now she was wondering if she felt the same. "Can you heat the pool?"

Samiel turned toward the water and looked down at his hands, but before he could make a move, he felt a tug against his arm.

"Help me undress," Kyra said. "Lift me into the pool."

"I will," he said with a somber disposition, both craving the act and fearing the request.

Samiel turned back toward the pool and set both of his hands ablaze once more, easier than the first time. "How could it feel so natural when mere moments ago I was unaware I even had the skill," he said under his breath.

"Magic comes to those who know it," Kyra said with a meek voice.

Samiel buried both hands beneath the water and she watched as he released pulses of flame throughout, which quickly disappeared. The pulsating embers grew larger and cast steam into the air, surrounding the two of them while bubbles formed at the surface.

"That should be warm enough for you," Samiel said as he turned back to her.

Their eyes met as Samiel slowly walked toward her and she smiled at him.

"I trust you," she said, as he helped lift off her robe. "These springs, I've read about them in the library. It will heal me, but I cannot be clothed. It will change the outcome if I do, focusing the magic on something other than my skin."

Once he lifted the robe, Samiel's gaze turned toward her breast band. The tattered cloth looked to be tightly pressing her breasts, hiding her full image beneath the loose clothing she typically wore. He couldn't help but notice her form, studying her for the first time. She also couldn't help but notice his gaze.

"Women are more often viewed for what lies under the robe, than they are for the reasons for owning the robe," she said, looking into his stunned eyes.

"I'm sorry, Kyra," he said, lowering his head in embarrassment. "I've never seen you like this and it's just not something I'm used to."

"You're not used to it because you've never seen any woman like this, Sam. Not just me," she said, bluntly. *You're too sweet.*

His vision returned to Kyra for a moment in anger, but it was quickly abated by the smile on her. "I suppose you're right." *But I wish you weren't.*

"Help me undo the rest," she laughed, mostly at his innocence.

Samiel did as he was told, removed the breast band, and her undergarments. He looked intently at each smooth crevice of her and noted what he considered to be a nearly perfect frame. Her long, flaxen hair rested on the crests of her shoulders and pressed against soft skin which called out to him in a welcoming and comforting distraction. Her arms, lined and toned with musculature but bore little thickness, remained hidden like the rest of her physique beneath the robes she so often wore. Each removal of clothing brought a stroke against the warmth of her skin. He studied each reveal, learning more about her than he ever knew, but tried desperately not to let loose any sign of how much he noticed, how much he craved.

Kyra caught on, and while she felt no obligation to stop it, she also felt no inclination to reciprocate the appreciation. She'd gone through great troubles over the years to hide her physique and put little effort into catering toward her appearance as her affinity to runic magic gave her enough attention. Today was the first day in which she felt appreciated for beauty, even if the person appreciating this beauty was her closest friend, whom she knew—or thought—she would never be physically intimate with. She took great comfort in knowing that Samiel would do his best to never discuss this, as he would never do anything to intentionally cause her discomfort. However, she found contempt in knowing it meant she would need to be the one to start this conversation at a later time, if she ever wanted it to happen. *Sometimes I wish he'd just...*

Samiel lifted her into the water by cradling her in his arms and walking her over to the pool. Her skin against his felt like a thing he'd been waiting for, yet never knew he wanted. But, when he placed her down, she turned back to him and smiled, playfully. In that moment, he remembered who he had just held and became ashamed of himself for his thoughts. *She doesn't want me that way. Not her, and not like this.* With that, he shrugged off the intimate impulses toward her and regained his normal composure once she fell beneath the boiling water.

Kyra looked at him and could see his eyes had changed. "The reason Arimeus brought us to the pool was so the wound could be healed and cleaned. I see fragrances and other vials on the desk over there. Is there something we can use to clean the wound?"

Samiel turned and found a table behind him full of vials. "Lyte Water," he read aloud. "Liquid Consciousness," he muttered.

"Have you found anything for cleaning this wound?" She asked, feeling her strength return.

A plethora of vials containing oddly named liquids laid about, but a simple soap or alcohol…nowhere to be found. Then, Samiel checked below the desk and found oaken shelves. There he found an open bottle of alcohol and something with a scraggly label that looked to say, "Liquid Love." He pocketed the latter and brought the alcohol over.

"Here you go." He stretched out his hand offering her the bottle, considering if the vial of Liquid Love would make her want him. *Would I use it if it did? Would it be wrong?*

"I'm still very weak," she answered. "Could you hop in and clean the wound for me?"

Samiel felt taken aback once more. Should he get completely undressed as she had? What would she think of his body? Would she study him the same way he studied her? It felt altogether unnerving as he froze in front of her.

"I can close my eyes if you like," she laughed. "But I don't want to be the only one naked. Who knows, it might mess with the magic." She chuckled and splashed some water in his direction.

Then, feeling almost challenged to rise to the occasion, Samiel stripped off his clothing; from his leather cuirass with a dark hue, to his tattered undergarments, and his linen pants. There he stood, naked, staring at her.

"I suppose it's only fair you see me the way I saw you," he said, nervously.

"Get in the water, Sam," she lightly splashed more water in his direction. "It's warm."

He did as he was told and stepped into the steaming pool, positioning himself in front of her. He lowered himself into the water and grabbed hold of her burned foot. He lifted it in the air above the pool long enough to pour the alcohol onto the wound. She winced, but only lightly as she'd already felt the pool's warmth. Afterward, he lowered her foot back into the healing waters and lightly rubbed it, removing the burnt skin which she seemed not to contain feeling even though she could enjoy the massage. It was pleasure exempt from pain.

They sat there in silence for a short time looking at one another before Kyra spoke to him with a smile, an unnaturally large smile.

"We can't exactly go back from this now, can we?" she asked.

"What do you mean?"

"Well," Kyra said. "I saw the way you looked at me. You've never looked at me like that before. It feels as though something may have changed between us."

Samiel stopped massaging her for a moment and thought about what he would say. "Change will come if you want it to come. Otherwise, I believe we have more pressing matters at the moment."

Kyra nodded in agreement and grinned. She thought for a time as he returned to massaging her, and then he changed to the other foot, now clearly set toward her pleasure. She considered what it might be like to be with him in that way, momentarily, but Samiel was right. *I need to focus on war.*

"A Warlord wants to bed me," Kyra laughed as the color returned to her face amid the steaming pool. "I go years without an advance of any kind, from any man. The first to do so is a Warlord looking to kill a god."

"And he's apparently my father," Samiel said, causing both of them to erupt into laughter.

The two continued to joke and laugh in the water as Kyra's strength returned. Once her full grip was restored, she offered to pay back his kindness with a massage, and asked him to turn his back toward her, placing himself between her legs so she could grab his shoulders. She sat much lower in the water than he, his tall physique allowing his upper body to sit above the small waves. In comparison, her small stature and short arms slightly struggled to reach the tops of his shoulders. Her eyes closed for a moment while he faced the opposite direction as relief and tension, simultaneously, took hold of separate pieces of her. *I can have him when I want. I don't need it now.*

After only a short while of reaching for his bulging shoulders, Kyra wrapped both of her arms around him and squeezed his upper abdomen tightly while pressing against him.

"It isn't that I'm not attracted to you, you know," she whispered as the warmth of the bubbling pool splashed against them. "I can't say I've thought about you in this way often, but I also wouldn't say I never have."

Samiel's disbelief and shock kept him stunned and silent as her hands ran against the outline of his lower stomach.

"Perhaps we can talk about this, you know, once we're done with the battle," she said, as crashing could be heard way off in the distance. The battle was far from over though, and they knew it.

"It's odd," Samiel said. "Our city is being attacked, and here we sit, in the attacking camp, bathing in a pool."

"Well," Kyra answered, squeezing him tight and pushing her chest against his back. "We just got here, and I made a mess of myself immediately. We can stop this fight, but I need strength to do it."

Samiel's hand stretched back behind him as he gripped her leg under the fading warmth of the pool. His grip tightened; he pulled her closer as she let out a surprised sound of shock and happiness.

"The water is getting cold," she said, now seated on his lap under the water, looking him in the eyes.

At that moment, Kyra looked down at his hand wrapped around her thighs. He removed one and placed it in the water. Then, a flame erupted from his fingers and shot through the pool causing her to jump in an effort to avoid being burned once more. But he held her down and just said, "You're safe," which gave her respite. "I've got you."

The flame left no marks nor feeling of burn. All she felt was warmth from his hands. *I like him telling me what to do. I do feel safe.*

"But, when it was my foot," she gasped, trying to reclaim calmness.

"The flame listens to me," he answered. "I've more control over it than I initially realized. I can feel it bending to me at all times now. I feel embers trickling through my nerves and flame embedded into my blood," he said, pulling her closer and placing hands on her hips, tightly. "All my years I've felt an extreme sense of burning under my skin and the only rest I would feel was under immense physical struggle. It caused me to work the way I did, and the anger I bore for being less than those around us who were gifted with magic just drove my rage even further, pushing me to my utmost limits. All this time, it was the fire trying to get out, and I didn't know."

Kyra wrapped her legs around his defined hips and looked into him, seeing a shaking, reflective light dancing where his pupils laid, but the dancer grew ever so dim. She'd never seen his eyes this way and thus pulled herself closer. Then, she felt him, below the water. She knew he wanted her. *I want it...I don't want to wait.*

Kyra reached to his neck, and with a light touch, pulled his face closer to hers and gave him a restrained, but long, kiss. "After the battle, let's find a quiet room...for both of us."

Samiel smiled and rose from the pool with her still wrapped around him and stepped out to place her on a bench to help her get dressed.

"How is your foot?" he asked.

"Honestly, I can't even feel the pain anymore."

After grabbing her clothes, Samiel walked over to her and bent down on one knee. He looked at where the burn was to find the wound had completely healed, all except the rune she carved into her skin years ago.

"It's healed," Samiel said with confusion.

"I guess we know why Arimeus brought us to the pool," Kyra said. "It was one of the Agualyte healing springs I've read about."

The two got dressed and, as Samiel laced his boots, the Chief Runic's voice could be heard from the entrance of the tent. "How goes the healing?"

"You may enter," Samiel answered, continuing his lacing.

"I take it you also decided to take a swim?" Arimeus asked.

"What lies next?" Samiel pointedly asked, somewhat surprising the Chief Runic with his tone and ignoring the rhetorical question.

Kyra noticed the way he spoke, specifically to the old man, had changed. *What's gotten into Sam? I think I like this version of him...*

"Are you ready to face your friends?" Arimeus asked.

"Our friends, you mean?" she corrected. She looked at the old man with dread written in her eyes. *I... we might not have to fight them. We can't fight them. I won't fight them! Oh! We might not need to.*

Samiel's movement froze, locked in a stare toward her, awaiting a response.

"The temple lies beneath Runefall," the old Runic continued, reading the look on her face for what it was. "You did not think they would let us walk in without a fight, now did you?"

"How could you plot knowing you'd be betraying friends and those whom you've claimed to love?" she asked with a solemn voice.

"Ishmael said you needed to break the seal, and Harigamun told you where the seal was," Arimeus explained. "You've known we had to enter the city, so let's not pretend you didn't know this was coming!"

"You used a portal to get us here and mine was tampered with to take me to the Dreaming Haunts to hear from Ishmael," she retorted. "Why can't a portal be made once more to take us into the heart of the city where we might break the seal? Is your magic only good for betrayal?" Kyra's frustration with the old man grew more by the passing moment as she tightened her fists at her last words. "There's a way that doesn't involve killing my friends!" she screamed. "And *you* are going to figure it out or *you* have no value in this fight!"

"The portals are an old magic from Ishmael himself," said a gruff voice from outside the tent.

Harigamun threw open the draping of the tent as his heavy stone boots broke the ground beneath him.

"Portals that are the only ones that remain, and only Ishmael has the power to manipulate them," the Warlord answered. "There is but one way to the center of the city, and that is through its people."

"Let me speak to them!" Kyra begged. "I can convince the leaders and its army to stay their hands, they will listen to me if they understand the price!"

Harigamun answered, "Do you understand the price if they do not do as you ask?"

"There is no other option," she said with a distraught look. Her eyes darted to the flames pummeling the city against the cracking of thunder as lightning struck Runefall. "They must hear me."

Kyra realized something just then, standing with the Warlord. The prophecy called for the seal to be broken to save Kaiya. The Warlord wanted to break the seal to kill the rune god. But Salaril was the god who made the prophecy to start with. *Why would Salaril willingly put himself in a position to die?*

"Very well then," the Warlord said. "You will ride out under a white flag and seek a parlay with the Council of Runefall. Should negotiations fail, my retaliation against the city will be unrelenting."

Kyra's face drowned in an anxious, foreboding uneasiness as she glared into his pure hatred. His ferocity seemed a stoic pigment of intentional design crafted by the hands of some talented artist. A carving of frustration spread across his face as if his devotion to devastation and conquest were innate to him, like a part of some beautiful and menacing sculpture of stone. She awaited the Warlord's call for parlay for a few hours, contemplating what she would say to the ruling council.

During the wait, Kyra and Samiel stayed in the Warlord's tent, given to them as they awaited the gathering of the generals who would come to an agreement regarding her proposed intervention.

Samiel exercised in the corner as she sat reading a journal she'd found behind a desk. It was the personal journal of the Warlord, and she found it quite surprising he'd not gone through more trouble to maintain its secrecy by placing it in a more difficult place to find, or rather, to even carry it on his person. The journal was titled *Thoughts of War*.

These are the regrets of war. I never wanted any of it. I never wanted to replace Harigamun; my father, he was far better at ruling than I. All of the surrounding tribes, those far from us, all feared him. Blood Ravagers, elemental clans, the Mystics, and any other who dared to defy him found themselves circulating on a spike, roasting on a fire.

He knew how to squash a rebellion, as he'd done before. But no... I was not tasked with the calming of a storm. I was to bring the storm."

– Harigamun, *Thoughts of War.*

Harigamun watched in the distance as the crashing of metal and flame against the city stopped and quiet fell across the war camp. Amid the silence, heavy footsteps approached the tent as Samiel finished his exercises, pushing himself from the ground.

Kyra sat staring at the entrance of the tent with the journal open in her hands. The journal was an un-chaptered cacophony of zeal and regret, like littered quotes from a disgraced philosopher. The Warlord entered the tent and looked at both of them before shifting his gaze purely to her, seeing his journal in her hands.

"I hope tonight will not become another entry in that journal," the Warlord said. "At least, not one of the regrets."

"Why do you not hide this?" she asked, genuinely.

"It seems you are the only one in this camp who has no concern for the consequences of reading it," he answered. "I need not hide a thing people are too frightened to touch."

"We're not afraid of you," said Samiel.

"No," Harigamun laughed. "I see that she most certainly is not. It may yet take some time to come to a decision regarding you though, my son."

"I'm not your son!" he rebutted. "Not in any sort of way that matters."

Harigamun released a deep, heavy sigh and his eyes lowered to the floor. "No, I suppose not. Though that was not of my own devising."

"It matters not," Samiel responded.

"What must we do?" Kyra turned to the Warlord and awaited his reply.

"We have gathered a small party," Harigamun said. "You will join this party and ride to the main gates of the city, where likely Turmin or Barigund will be awaiting you from behind the wall's entry. Once the parlay has been set, in or outside of the doors, you are to broker peace granting us entry into that damnable temple at the heart of the city where we will break the seal."

"And why should we say we are doing this?" Kyra asked.

"Because, otherwise, your friends will die," he answered.

"No," she corrected. "What shall we tell the Council is the reason for our necessary visit to the city's temple? They will not be supportive toward the killing of their god and likely have no idea what Salaril has done against them."

"Do you now support my killing of the god, Kyra?" he asked.

"It means nothing to me," she answered. "I am here to break the seal, as Ishmael told me it must be done. We cannot continue in the state of war and hiding such as we have, and we must restore magic to how it was meant to be experienced, not this elitism we have now. We do not need to have the same end goal, because for now we require the same means."

Samiel's gaze shifted over to her as he tried to understand what she was feeling. *Does she really care so little for the life of the god which gives her power? Is she trying to manipulate him?* If so, he found it hard to understand her plan because he had clearly not been made part of it. *Why won't she tell me? Or is there simply nothing to tell?* He felt lost as Kyra continued her conversation with his supposed father and it became more evident, she had started playing her own game. Samiel thought it gave him reason enough to start playing his own game as well.

"Gather at the hilltop and prepare yourself, Kyra," Harigamun said. "You do not know what is to come, and should any moves be made against you, my coming will be swift."

Samiel found the Warlord's ferocity toward her to be insincere, as he knew very little of her, including whether or not she was actually on the Warlord's side. Following, the Warlord turned his back and left the tent, leaving them alone once more.

"Whose side are you on?" Samiel asked.

"Our side, Sam," she answered. "He will do what he can to burn this city to the ground and kill Salaril. I mean to prevent both."

"How?" he asked, frightened of what could happen, scared for her.

"Gremanhas holds the heart of Galantis, who holds the ear of the army," she explained. "I know where a portal is to take Runefall's army right to Harigamun."

Chapter Twelve

The Golem's March

"When we march...it is often to our death, and for the purpose of others. Even now, my anger guides me, but I did not determine this path. These deaths are the requirement of consequence, consequences wrought by them who chose to hide and take power. No more. I march...to die."
— Harigamun, *Thoughts of War*

"Does Flaurin live?" Varus's voice suggested doubt, or an uneasiness lingering in the air as he awaited an answer.

"Groff not know," replied the golem. He shifted from left to right as control of the mouth switched between them.

"How can you not know what happens to the lives of those sharing the same body as you?" Varus asked. "How—h—," his speech fractured. "You have to know."

"Groff do as Beliria tells Groff. The Shackled Maiden knows."

"You're not being honest with us Groff," Varelia said, contemptuously.

Groff, maintaining control, collapsed onto an oversized log wrapped with moss, which bled a violet fungus, and split the log with his weight.

"Groff keep friends as long as possible." The golem's eyes lowered, finding a puddle below his feet. In the puddle's reflection, Groff and Varus restarted their dialogue.

"I am your friend, Groff," Varus said. "I would like to be your friend for quite some time. Is this something we are not allowed to do?"

"Eventually, all of Groff's friends go away. They no speak to Groff anymore," he said with heavy sadness. "Groff never told why they leave, or when. Friends just leave."

"I don't think we are going to get anywhere with this conversation, Baba," Varelia said. "Perhaps it's best we continue moving forward, and we may yet learn of Groff through some other means."

The mouth of the golem chittered nonsense and gurgled indiscernible sounds, unclear whether it came from a nervous Groff or a mentally degrading Varus.

"Fine! You speak then!" Varus's voice boomed.

The golem rose into the air with a quick, upward thrust and Groff's angered voice quaked the leaves that had been privy to their bickering.

"Groff must kill!" the golem shouted, landing back on the ground.

"What?" Varelia, struck with confusion, watched as the golem bolted through the woods.

Varelia found herself chasing sounds—threats to kill someone—as she tried to follow the golem through the forest while her father shouted questions as to who they were going to kill, and why. The golem's speed increased by the minute as Varelia found it harder to keep up with each step and each threat spouted.

At a moment of complete exhaustion, when Varelia's body could no longer continue the chase, she released a howling command. "Stop, Golem! Return to me."

The stampeding sounds of the forest cracking beneath the golem's feet came to a silent halt as Varelia heard slow steps, with equally heavy footing, coming back toward her. It didn't take long before she saw the golem once more feral foliage, downed trees and blinding canopy, and raced to catch up to it.

The closer Varelia got to the golem, the more she saw he shook with each step, unnaturally, in a backward direction. It looked as though his muddy legs were trying to step forward, but it was forced to move backward away from her.

Groff's voice strained and grunted as if lifting a horrifically heavy object, and the tension was simultaneously felt by the champion he carried within.

Varelia realized something was turning the golem's body against its will. It fought to move backward, but the command from her seemed to cause Groff to retrace his steps and return to her. She started to think maybe it was true... *I do have the voice.*

As Varelia watched the golem finish its last step backward, locking it in place, the forest felt as though it were beginning to shatter and split in two as the ground quaked with tremors fit for catastrophe. Trees cracked in the distance and huge outpourings of water could be heard nearby, like a dam breaking through its restraints. Birds rushed away from whatever was coming and the songs of the insects came to utter silence as life was choked out in little more than an instant. The sky turned black, and a white sheen striking down from the sky surrounded them, illuminating nothing more than what sat immediately in front of them. Out of a small puddle, chains rattled as the form of a woman in white ascended from an otherwise ethereal realm, bound and shackled.

"My lady," Groff said as he started to sob, "Has been much long."

"Indeed, it has, my dear friend." Her voice, lovely and fragile to Varelia's ears. Something worth protecting.

In a single moment, under brief words, Varelia understood the golem's desire to protect her. It was an odd connection she did not understand. She quickly turned to the golem to address her father.

"You saw her merely days ago, for the trial. Isn't that so?" she asked, pointedly.

"Beliria oversaw the trial, this is true," her father answered. "But she was never there, my Ibna. She spoke through Groff."

Varelia turned to Beliria, a long-haired, shadowy maiden with deep eyes piercing through her long hair, hiding obvious beauty.

"Why have you given me this voice, and who does Groff mean to kill?" Varelia asked.

"Ahh," she smiled and raised both hands to her mouth as she chuckled. "I like impatience."

"Then please, answer my question." Varelia looked questioningly at Groff who glared at her with disdain. "My lady."

The last part made Groff smile.

"My husband is dead," she answered. "Groff seeks his killer."

"Why would you send Groff to kill your husband's killer?" Varelia asked, clearly confused. "He mistreated you, hunted your lover, and condemned you to a life of bondage and secrecy away from others. We know not even where to find you because of what your husband, what *Baylar*, has done to you."

"You speak as one who believes to truly know his tales," she answered.

"Then please," Varelia said, "tell me where I am wrong."

"Right or wrong does not matter, Varelia," the Shackled Maiden said. "What is lost, is lost in the details, and details serve you little purpose for what is to come. For now, know that I have not commissioned Groff to pursue my husband's killer. That is the work of Baylar himself. Indeed, if it is not that, then it is some other foul play made by the same hand."

"How, if he is dead?" Varelia asked.

Beliria stared deep into Valeria's watery eyes as stress mounted upon her crinkled brow.

"The voice you possess is not my own, but something stolen from Baylar," Beliria said. "Long ago, he spoke a command to the summoners of Kaiyara, and below to Kaiya, to pursue, until the end of time, any who might take the life of my... late husband."

"And who is the killer?" Varelia continued.

"Ask not that of me, for I am not the one being called to avenge him," she answered. "Ask that of the one called to slay in his name."

Both Beliria and Varelia's gaze turned toward the golem.

"Tell me, Groff. Who killed my husband? I have much to thank them for."

"Rune god. Runefall," Groff said.

"Salaril," Beliria laughed. "Now that is an odd thing to hear. Even more so when you tell me he currently hides away in Runefall."

"Why is it surprising that Salaril is in Runefall?" Varelia asked.

The forest erupted into a sudden scream as the ground trembled with Beliria's frustration. "I've not the time," she said. "My husband's control will guide Groff to vengeance. Once the god has died, Groff will be set free from Baylar's voice. Should you seek to free him sooner, and save the god who slew my husband, you'll need to—"

With a flash of light and a shattering scream into the pitch-black darkness surrounding them, Beliria faded away into a silent and dull mist as light returned and sounds began anew.

"Why should we care whether or not the god is to be saved?" Varelia asked.

The golem trembled once more as Varelia's command weakened. Then, the creature returned to her side. The hardened, muddy figure stepped forward, clearly heading toward Runefall once more, but at a more contained pace, a pace which allowed her to keep up.

"It is likely any who would oppose Baylar could be an ally for us," Varus said. "Baylar was cast out long ago by the other Lords of Kaiyar and hid himself and Beliria from the rest of the world. If opposing Baylar means supporting Beliria, this could be a friend in need."

"Groff body want to kill stupid god."

"We know Groff, but what do you want to do?" Varelia placed her hand on the golem's back, walking beside him at the same pace, though it had quickened.

"Groff want to save Shackled Maiden."

"Don't you think if this god was able to kill Baylar, then he might be able to help us save Beliria?" Varelia asked.

The golem's head jerked to the side but maintained its pacing. "You think rune god can find her?"

"I think he's the only one who might have an idea where we *can* find her, Groff," Varelia explained. "If we kill him, we may never find her."

Groff suddenly fell to the ground, weeping tears of clay and mud which dried instantly upon contact with the leaf-laden floor of the wood. His wailing trembled the surrounding trees as their trunks shook with ferocity, the Cravenwood struggling to contain his uncontrollable sobbing. His forward steps came to an instantaneous halt and the golem's sorrow shattered the hearts of the forest as its creatures became deafeningly silent.

As Varelia's heart ached for Groff, she could not help but notice the golem's immense pain at the thought of never retrieving his lost maiden. He had managed to take back control of his body if only for a short time.

"Groff!" Varus said. "You've taken over your body once more! You're not marching toward Runefall."

Groff's sobbing stopped for a short moment and instantly his body rose from the ground and with one foot in front of the other, he marched toward the city once more.

"*Extreme emotional states allow him to take back control of the body,*" Varus thought to himself.

"Groff not emotional. Sad man without body is emotional, not Groff."

"I forget you can hear my thoughts," Varus said, "but in your heightened state of sadness, or rage, you were able to take back control of yourself, Groff. Don't you understand what that means?"

Groff released a heavy grunt and tried not to answer the question as he did not know what the answer was.

"It means you have power over Baylar's voice, Groff!" Varelia nearly yelled.

She stopped walking beside the golem for a short moment and brought her hand to her shoulder-length hair, running it through like the mane of a thin-haired mount. Her brow was beading with sweat and the wetness dampened her hair, causing a portion of it to stick to her neck and face.

"It's that simple. He just needs to want it," Varelia said with a light breath, light enough the other two could no longer hear her as the golem's march did not slow.

"I wonder what that means for—" Varelia heard her father's voice echo beyond a cluttering of trees now separating her from the golem. He was in danger.

Varelia quickened her step but remained as silent as she could, passing through the shrubbery, and avoiding any branches or sticks that might snap and give away her position. She approached the staggering tree line of Grand Pines which stood so high their canopy could not be seen from below the trees, however, by looking into such vastness, she saw rope structures of some sort—bridge-like connectors and small platforms overhead—hanging high above the ground.

She peeked from behind the veil of moss which fell like drapery over the forest, hiding her in his frothy embrace, and saw something—Grendalla had returned, but this time with far more numbers than before, and a great jungle cat by his side.

"Headed to Runefall for the god, Golem?" Grendalla perched above them on a large boulder with the jungle cat purring at his side and a host of maroon-clad marauders at the foot of his view.

"How do you know about the god?" Varus asked.

"Sheiba, my own summoning from ages ago," he placed his hand on the jungle cat. "She's a complex one, you know. She felt the same pull you do now."

Varelia, enamored with the cat, wanted to ask so many questions she knew would go unanswered. She noticed the same spell, the one which had trapped the golem in place before, had appeared as a shining sigil growing beneath Groff's feet. Though, now significantly larger than the last.

"So, your cat speaks to you?" Varus laughed. "How lonely must one need to be to converse with a cat...though it does beg the question; how have you restrained her?"

Grendalla scoffed at the question and jumped from a stone peak. His strut condensed as the Ansei placed his hand on the golem's chin, grasping it, and pulling the creature's face closer to his own. The spell kept the golem from physically rebutting Grendalla's encroachment, though the welling of spit and quaking jaw let the elf know he had successfully angered both the golem and his champion.

Varelia remained hidden beneath the mossy canopy and tattered across thick trunks of Great Pines. Counting the assaulters, Varelia spotted ten adversaries, more than twice as many as in their previous confrontation, which required the full force of Groff and a breaking of the spell. Moreover, this time, she counted five mages holding the spell together, when last it was only two. It was hard enough to break the concentration of them previously, but now she faced more foes, and they would expect the same tactics, even if they did not expect her.

"Where is the other one who was with you?" Grendalla asked. "Where is the girl? Is she hiding about waiting to ambush us, thinking she can turn the tide with a stone once more?"

Varelia let loose a heavy sigh realizing the only hope, the hope of surprise, was also expected. *What should I do? I'm one against ten, and a weak one at that.*

"Tell me where the little one is and she might just live," Grendalla said to the golem. "We have many good uses for such a small girl," he smirked.

"We had not the control over Groff you have with Sheiba," Varus answered. "The golem outpaced her, and she likely lingers somewhere back in the Cravenwood. You have us to contend with, and that's more than enough!"

Varus knew his daughter was nearby, and he hoped she had room—and sense—to escape and leave her father and Groff to face the consequences Grendalla appeared so clearly determined to inflict. But then, a whistle broke across the air of the forest and a murmuring flowed through the winds. Varus listened intently and focused on slowing his breath to make out the words, but all he could hear was the last word spoken from somewhere in the distance, behind a cropping of moss-covered trees.

"Beliria."

Instantly Sheiba disappeared into the wilderness, sprinting far, far away. A hissing gathered above the peak of stone Grendalla had jumped down from. It grew louder and unsettling to... to everyone.

"What trick is this?" Grendalla demanded. But he received no answer as the hissing continued, forming a thick mist of fear.

"Hold the spell!" The Ansei stepped behind the golem and tried, best he could, to peek above the stone and see what lay behind, but he could not make out any shapes, only a growing hiss.

"Agh!" one of the spellcasters shrieked and ran with an unmatched quickness. "Draguar!"

"No," Grendalla said under his breath before backing away from the golem. "How have you brought them back?"

"We did not," Varus answered. "But let us go and we can help fight!"

Then, three of the great beasts crested over the stone peak and Grendalla trembled with a fear he had not known since the downfall of the Ansei. He stared into deep and bright yellow eyes crusted with black shimmering eye lids. Their skin, made of a thick scale, sharper than blade and hard as steel, but so too did it move as fluid as the breeze, a dance of flesh following each breath of the four-legged monsters.

Varus noted they stood larger than the tales of the dead dire wolves who once roamed the North, reaching upward of ten and twelve feet high, if spotted upright. The beasts slowly opened their mouths as the hissing stopped, and long, split tongues curled from their mouths as boiling spittle dripped from their jaws onto as cloven claws cut into the stone beneath them.

"Run!" Another of the blood mages broke rank and sped toward the trees, making for the structures hidden above.

All at once, the remaining blood mages abandoned the spell, setting the golem's body free. Grendalla stood glaring at the beasts on the stone and his eyes locked in on the one who crept around the rock and had frightened the first mage to flee. And then, he saw the worst of them. An alpha Draguar, twice, if not three times, the size of the other two, growled heavily as its claws gripped the stone, tearing it apart from the rest of the gigantic rock. The beast took a deep, bellowing breath and released a hail of fire onto the stone, scorching it with flame and causing it to glow a bright red. The alpha lifted onto its hind legs and cast a rock at one of the fleeing mages. The stone split through the mage's head like a blade through paper.

Groff's arms grew in length as they had before, but Varus stopped him for a short moment.

"Wait," he said. "These beasts were lost long ago; they were the descendants of the High Wyvern. Only one remains who can control the Voice of Baylar. Beliria has sent them."

Groff halted all movement. "My lady," he whispered.

"At long last," Grendalla said, turning to the golem after hearing Beliria's name. "Larina's debt comes due."

The Ansei started walking, oddly relaxed, toward the alpha Draguar. He shed his weapons and removed his cuirass, leaving nothing but linen trousers and a tattered long-shirt made of cotton. Lifting his arms as if to greet a long-lost friend, Grendalla approached the pack of Draguar. "Now that it comes to it, I am glad it was by your hand, Beliria."

The alpha leaped from the stone, landing on all fours beside

Grendalla. It circled its prey, hissing and spewing its tainted saliva.

"My sister," the beast hissed. "You thought you could claim her, an immortal soul, for the price of my Larina?"

"I have many regrets, Beliria," Grendalla lamented to the Shackled Maiden's voice within her beast. "The rebellion of my kind against Larina stands as the highest among them. But I expect no forgiveness, I want none. I simply want this endless cycle of life and death to truly reach the end. Blades have failed to take me; what can you say of these fangs you wear?" She smiled a final smile.

"The fangs of a dragon are one of the few things that can kill a god," the beast hissed.

"I am no god," she answered.

"No, but you live by the blood of one!" The Draguar rose to its hind legs once more, reached out one of its scaled arms, and wrapped its hands around the Ansei's throat.

"May Larina find you in death." The Draguar stuck its tongue out, wrapping it around the Ansei's quivering head before devouring his skull in a single bite. Then, the beast turned to face the golem while the remaining Draguar watched like stoic hounds waiting for a meal, the other Exiles long gone, and faint growls coming from other predators off in the distance of the deep woods.

"His pet escaped!" Varus said. "The jungle cat."

"Did it now?" Beliria questioned. Fur rubbed against the hand of the golem as they noticed the jungle cat, startling Varus and Groff at once. "You can come out now, Varelia."

She emerged from the trees in what seemed to be a drunken stupor to Varus. While she stumbled toward them, her father noticed a tinge of blood dried beneath her nose. It had left a trail to her lips.

"How did you summon the Draguar?" Varus asked. "They were lost many ages ago following the extinction of dragons."

"You are right, she cast a summons," Beliria said from the mouth of the alpha Draguar. "But you have not yet guessed what she summoned."

"Girl summoned Shackled Maiden!" Groff smiled and reached to grab ahold of Varelia. "Good job, little one! You free my lady!" He jumped with unparalleled joy.

"Not quite, my dearest friend," Beliria interjected. "She has summoned me as she did before. This time was with a greater strength allowing me to lend my own powers to you for a time. I brought the Draguar back from the crypts of time, but I have not much time left with you."

Varus felt frustrated at the explanation. *How? What determines this strength? How does she refine it? No one speaks on anything!*

Sheiba's purring grew as she strutted to Varelia. She knocked her to the ground and tried to nuzzle her aggressively. Then, the cat dropped her body, softly, on top of Varelia.

Beliria watched as the jungle cat burrowed into its new friend and realized her time was fading. She needed to speak before she fell away from time, back to her confinement, to make sure Varelia knew what would be necessary to save Groff.

"Varelia!" Beliria shouted, breaking her attention away from the playful jungle cat. Valeria looked confused as the cat continued purring beside her, as if it were awaiting permission to play. "The only way to make a spell more potent than at the time it was cast is to imbue the spell in blood. Baylar cast a spell long ago to bend each summoned beast to his will to avenge him, should he be killed." Beliria explained. "However, his death means the spell only has a certain reach, which now I see can be undone by blood. That's how Grendalla was able to set Sheiba free. They likely captured her and recast her summoning, and they did so with a blood contract."

"So, if I summon Groff again through the use of blood magic and your voi—"

"Baylar's voice," Beliria interrupted.

Varelia swallowed a pain in her chest, recognizing there was still some emotion to Baylar the Shackled Maiden felt, which was unclear.

"Mixing the voice with blood will allow me to summon Groff anew?" Varelia finished.

"Groff's summonings are beyond count," she continued. "The years have molded into the lifetimes he has been by my side, even when he was not."

"How many times has he been summoned? Was he not summoned by blood when you asked me to cover my lips with my father's?" Varelia asked.

The Shackled Maiden turned to Groff. "You did not summon him that day. I did, on your behalf. I just wanted to make sure you would listen to me when I spoke. As far as how many times Groff has been summoned? I do not know, and I fear what may be lost in doing it once more. Take Sheiba, for instance. She is not a jungle cat by nature. She is a Shade, a conjurer of the dark elven tribes to the far east. They can shift their form if they wish, but Sheiba was the only one ever to achieve a connected soul to her chosen body, similar to the connection Mystics make with their own. But the soul Sheiba connected with was lost in battle many years ago. In their dark arts, the elves sought to bring her back and wield power over death. Grendalla likely thought he could save the lost soul, but once he summoned Sheiba again with blood magic, she had forgotten her true form, lost the soul Grendalla chased, and now remains a jaguar."

Sheiba stared with painful depth into Beliria's eyes as the Shackled Maiden stepped closer. Then, the alpha Draguar fell on all four of its legs and took a long moment to speak. "I'm fading, and the Draguar will fade with me. I do not know what will happen to Groff once the spell is redone. My hope is that his death will undo Baylar's hold, but even so, I know he will head toward Runefall when I depart. Thus, there is little choice. My presence has stayed his march, but the longer he is left to walk, the harder it will be to stop him."

"What of Sheiba?" Varelia asked.

"She is free, though she does not know who she is. I cannot say what would happen if she were to remember that life. For now, her path is up to her."

The Draguar's armor-like scales started evaporating as Beliria's voice diminished against the coming wind and the rest of the Draguar brood also fell away from existence, returning to their tombs of time.

The golem's march started once more, and Groff began nervously asking questions.

"Will Groff remember his name? Will Groff remember Shackled Maiden?" Groff asked, terrified.

Varus could not be heard as Groff continued asking questions clearly showing how fearful he was of existence after being summoned again. He wanted to make sure he would know who he was, but he mostly wanted to make sure he could remember Beliria. He asked a hundred different ways, fearing what was to come. He'd been summoned likely hundreds of times, but never banished back to where he came from. To be summoned and released, according to the teachings Varus received in his younger days in Vari, would be different than being banished. One allowed a creature memory, the other—was a punishment—a means of resetting a bad summoning.

"Groff cannot protect one he does not know!" Groff yelled.

Varelia and Sheiba paced next to the golem when Varus spoke again.

"Grendalla was a novice at his craft," Varus growled. "You hold the voice of Baylar, which means your words will be both wise and full. We will lose nothing in doing this. In fact, Groff may yet become stronger so he can help protect the maiden even more so than he can now."

"Stronger?" Groff contemplated what more strength could mean for the formidable force he already knew himself to be.

"Groff could be god of golems," he said.

"Calm down, Groff. Don't get ahead of yourself," Varus said, causing the golem to lower his head in frustration.

"Groff could be god," Groff mumbled.

"I think you'd be a great god," Varelia said with a coy smile.

"Then Groff could be with Shackled Maiden," Groff said, discomforting the other two, though they tried hiding it.

Varelia walked beside the golem as they silently strode through the forest, picking up their speed with each hour passing. Small bits of conversation were started by Groff to break the silence while the other two contemplated what was next.

Varelia considered that, in order to summon Groff again, the golem must first be dead... which caused a sorrowful dread. How could she summon something that was standing in front of her? The method, or the means by which she needed to do it, was simple. As, earlier that morning beyond the Great Pines, she simply needed to prick her skin and rub the blood on her lips. Thus, the voice of Baylar would meet her bloodied lips and carry her orders for Groff unto... well, wherever summonings came from. *Where will he go? Can I follow him?*

But then she thought, could some horrible thing happen to Groff if Varelia were to recast her summons? And, if it were absolutely necessary for Groff to be dead before he could be brought back, then how must he be killed? *What happens to Baba?*

Varelia thought to her days in the sewer with her father, when a plague ravaged through the lands of Nightfall and the dead were burned, and the sick were discarded.

"A parasite cannot live without its host," her father had said.

Is Baba the parasite? She drifted off into thought. Could her father no longer survive without Groff, or would he also come back if the golem was resummoned?

It all became too much and Varelia's contentious thoughts drove her to grind her teeth with a clamped jaw. Within her furious thoughts,

Varelia released a relaxed and elongated breath of air once she felt the golem's hand slightly pat her on the back, followed by her father's voice.

"We're going to be alright, Ibna," Varus said.

A feeling of absolution washed over her for just a short moment, until Varus decided to speak once more.

"Groff," he said.

"Yes," the golem answered.

"Have you always been a golem?"

Groff scratched the top of his head as they continued walking toward the edge of the forest where a piercing and pulsating crash of light thrashed against the dimming evening sky.

"Have you always been a golem, Groff?" Varus asked a second time.

"Groff has always been Groff. Never remember be nothing else."

"Were you ever a human?" Varus asked.

Varelia's eyes flashed at the two as they went back and forth, and she tried to figure out what her father was trying to discover.

"Groff never human. Always Groff." The golem's head turned toward Varelia.

"If Groff has never been human, and has always been a golem, this golem," Varus confidently explained, "then it is likely he will be summoned once more as a golem."

"What else would he have been?" Varelia's curiosity spiked.

"Human," Varus answered. "And if he were, then we would have been beyond the aid of your voice."

"Why?" she asked.

"Because a golem, or really any magical vessel, is the only thing capable of holding more than one being within it. Me and Groff, we couldn't have shared a single human body. One of us would have withered, and if I were to bet, it would have been the one of us most unfamiliar with the biological aptitude experienced by humanity."

"Groff makes better human than crazy sculptor," the golem muttered.

"Be that as it may," Varus quipped, "I'm suited better to adapt to a human body. I've known it more than you. You've only ever held human consciousness."

Groff groaned. "Groff no agree."

"You don't have to," Varus answered before the golem's sight turned back to his daughter. "Ibna, do you remember all those times I tried to summon a golem?"

"How could I forget... the madness and tantrums," Varelia trailed off, wanting to say more.

"LOOK AT—" Varus stopped himself, and the golem's face smiled.

Varelia thought the mudded beast would blush if it had skin, or blood.

"It's been a moment since those failures haunted me," Varus said, "but look at where we are now. All those failures and now I've become the golem. Perhaps it was madness that drove me. Even still, do you remember what I did with each of those failures?"

"You panicked," Varelia said. "At least, it seemed like you did. It felt like the chanting and scribblings you'd made to create the golems were then done in reverse, or that they worked backward."

"That's right! You see, one can kill a summoning—" Varus was interrupted.

"No one kill Groff!" the golem yelled.

Groff's foot stopped mid-march and his champion's voice rang through the hollow trees surrounding them. "No one is trying to kill Groff! Just shut up and listen!" The golem's pace quickened again, and he fell silent.

"I never killed any of those failed summonings," Varus said. "I just banished them."

"To where?" Varelia asked.

"Roki's Garden."

Varelia paused in confusion. Her father named the place like a common landmark, something she should know, but she didn't. They'd never spoken of it, though. It fell off his tongue as common as a greeting to a stranger, and yet, the name was entirely foreign to her.

"Where is that?" Varelia asked, curious as to why she had never been told of this place.

"We don't have time for all that now, Ibna. Now, in order to banish a summoning, its original spell, or contract, must be made backward. But, considering how old Groff is," the golem grunted, showing his lack of appreciation for the comment, "we will have to approach this in a different way."

"How?"

"You hold the voice of Baylar, and that likely means Groff will simply listen to the command, especially if imbued in blood," Varus continued.

"What if it doesn't work?"

"It will," he answered. "Once the golem is lifeless, because with Groff gone, I will also not be here, it is up to you to summon him by name."

"Groff?" Varelia asked.

"Not quite," Varus replied. "Groff, tell my Ibna your name so she may call you back from Roki's Garden."

The golem grumbled once more, and his pace stopped. Vibrations emitted from him as the leaves above fell to the ground, splashing with droplets of water that sprung from little puddles. A deep moaning climbed from Groff's throat as his trembling voice—his real voice—was heard for the first time in ages.

"I am Groffrick Heilimdower, Champion of Beliria, Steward of Unhoused Souls and The First and Final Golem!"

Varelia's eyes glinted with the night's shade as a single tear crested her cheek whilst hearing the splendor of the golem's voice.

"Are you ready, Ibna?"

Varelia nodded her head as her voice cracked under the surmounting pressure of what was to come. She unsheathed her blade and slit her finger, rubbing blood on her lips.

Then, she shouted, hoping she would not regret the words. "Groff, I banish you to the lands of Roki's Garden!"

Chapter Thirteen

The Call for Giants

*"I wish for the piety and ignorance of my brothers. Perhaps things would
have been different. Perhaps, I would still have brothers. It's a shame our
blood should be shed by one another, though, it is by their shame it must
happen."*

— Harigamun, Thoughts of War

Turmin's heavy hammer sat cradled in the bulging arms of the
architect as one golem among the many broke through the gate's
barriers which had been left bare following Asmodeus's fatal mistake.

Barigund stood beside Turmin who remained higher than Runefall's
City Commander. However, Barigund's spear and adamantite helm
sprung just slightly over the half-dwarf's height. The sight of the two
towering figures brought shade to the gathering forces behind them
and lit a spark of unrelenting confidence in the face of death to the
inexperienced army of the city as battalions cheered.

Meanwhile, the barrage of fire and metal continued breaking and
shattering against the defenses of the city. Siege munitions blasted
through the layers of protective magic, lighting the city aflame one
building at a time. Water from broken pipes burst hidden orifices
uncovered by war-torn brigades. Fear clutched the minds of every soldier,
cowering as they united behind their giants.

"Let me play with the rocks," Turmin said. "You have your brother to contend with."

"*Our* brother," Barigund corrected with a grin.

"Hardly," Turmin scoffed. "Mother was drunk and your father was adventurous. Only one of us has dwarven blood so gimme the damned rocks!"

Barigund's jaw nearly fell from his skull as his brother's hammer was pulled from its cradle. The heavy stone slab of the weapon's head buried into the dirt beneath the cobblestone streets with an immense weight. The half-dwarf's wide body and heavy feet stomped slowly toward the golem, his enemy now moving at full speed in a hasty pursuit.

With one swift swoop, Turmin grabbed hold of the golem's neck, standing nearly two feet taller than himself, lifted it into the air, and slammed it onto its back. In almost as quick a motion, he tore the head from the golem's shoulders with both hands and launched its hardened clay skull toward the break in the main gate. The dead golem's head pummeled into another of its kind about to break the gate's threshold, launching the encroacher backward, and sending it flying into the swarm of golems nearby.

Turmin started toward the break in Runefall's barrier which still held the mass of golems as another started to force its way through. The soldiers behind this gigantic builder watched as the dried clay of the dead golem—the one whose head the half-dwarf had just thrown—once hard as armor whilst the golem lived, crumbled into little mounds of dirt.

"The golems can be killed," whispered one of the soldiers. "We have a chance!"

"Hold yourselves steady," Barigund's voice roared across the front lines. "Golems are summoned by magic, and dwarves are largely unaffected by such a weapon. Turmin, being half-dwarf, is a unique tool against a purely magical enemy."

The commander gripped his spear with a tight and strained hold as he watched his brother rip creature after creature apart as they squeezed through the unseen crevice.

"Do you grow tired, brother?" the Commander yelled as he stomped the head of one into mud.

"Dwarves nary grow quite as weary as you folk," he answered. "Perhaps you'll be the one needing a nap once we see your brother."

"*Our* brother," Barigund burst with deep laughter. "But you're only half dwarf. So perhaps you're only half-tired?"

Barigund's face grew grim as the smile he held only moments ago now became difficult to keep under the thought of his other brother—Harigamun—breaking down the city gates. *How did it come to this?* His thoughts drifted for only seconds to the days of their childhood, days of wrestling and playing along a riverbed. Those memories felt lost to a bygone age as he stared down the army of golems trying to force their way into his city.

As the Commander snapped back into the moment, tremors and clambering from the soldiers behind him grew so loud he could not discern the words being yelled back and forth. Then, one of the soldiers split from the ranks, quartered behind Barigund, and launched forward at a full sprint toward Turmin.

The builder fell to the ground beneath four golems overpowering him, his hammer lodged at his feet. Realizing Turmin's life was in danger, the City Commander tossed his towering spear into one hand and grabbed the hilt of Turmin's hammer with his other as he pounced onto the golems like a wild animal, roaring from the depths of his fearsome soul as Turmin cried for aid.

The hammer thrashed against the great skull of one of the largest golems, sending a cloud of dust into the air. The deteriorating golem vanished within moments and Barigund tossed a glance toward his new weapon for a moment, not recognizing the strength he wielded. Quickly, he turned to another with its foot on Turmin's chest, bearing down on the half-dwarf and halting his breath. Barigund let loose his spear into the head of the beast, but it only pressed further down on the half-dwarf. The spear only angered the beast as the golem ripped the spear from its head, launched it back toward one of the many soldiers still cowering behind the City Commander, piercing through like a soft slit of parchment.

A soldier breaking rank jumped onto a golem who was crushing Turmin's ribs and drove her sword deep in its gullet. However, the golem remained unphased, grabbed the soldier by her neck and held her out in the air above Turmin who fought for his last moments of breath. As the golem snapped the neck of the soldier with little more than a twitch of its wrist, the City Commander launched forward once more in a second strike, but this time he wielded his brother's hammer.

The head of the hammer broke through the golem's chest as three others held down the half-dwarf by his limbs. The other beasts of clay cowered, watching the golem—who was previously towering over Turmin—disintegrate into a pile of mud. Breath came rushing back into the architect's lungs as he immediately shouted to his brother.

"The hammer is adamantite! Kill them all!"

Violent swings from Barigund scattered dried dirt across the battlefield like blood as he tore through the remaining forces breaking through the gate. A boulder came crashing overhead, ripping a building next to them down to its foundation and bringing a fiery chasm onto the soldiers still hiding behind their giants—Turmin and Barigund.

Few of the troops remained, and those who did scrambled and screamed amid the death, realizing they could not turn backward without passing through the chasm, which, at this point, each soldier recognized would be the choice of cowardice.

Drum beating grew from beyond the blocked sight of golems as chants of war rhythmically railed against the ears of petrified soldiers standing in front of the fire-stricken building. Barigund and Turmin both raised their heads, peering slightly around those blocking the gate as another one tried squeezing its way through.

"Some new beast comes," Barigund said.

"If it be magic," Turmin said, "it be dead." The oversized half-dwarf cracked his knuckles against his great hammer's hilt and grinned.

"No," said Barigund, "It's our brother."

As the breaching of the golems continued the battering of the main gate, Dalias Lanis, commander of Runic Vanguard, readied his troops to bore through the trenches of their enemies under the protection of fellow commanders, Rocco Drapor and Elias Harkor, who stood atop of the Runewall.

"What is he doing?" Elias shouted.

Lanis shot through a passageway made of runes which allowed the general and his army to pass through the deep walls of the city, unseen and unheard. The shocking act of reckless showmanship appeared as nothing more than avarice for glory to the two generals sitting atop the wall, but even still, they understood.

"He's meeting them head-on," Rocco said. "Give him cover!"

General Harkor gazed upon the battlefield, noting the jarring distance between Lanis's legions and the siege weaponry of the Warlord's armies. Before the troops could breach the wall, General Harkor cast a bag with a rune engraved onto it in front of the threshold where Lanis's soldiers would need to pass. The bag seemed to fade away as General Harkor whispered an incantation Rocco could not understand.

Then, as Rocco watched Captain Lanis and his thousands rush from beyond the wall, he saw them vanish before ever passing its stony facade.

"Have you trapped them?" Rocco asked.

"No, Rocco. I've only given them what they need to make it across the field."

"What? How?" Rocco's confusion was ignored as General Harkor, his lover, didn't have time to explain every spell. "Speak to me, dammit!"

"Think of it as a veil. They pass through, and suddenly they are invisible."

"For how long?" Rocco asked.

"Hopefully, long enough," General Harkor answered with a strained voice.

A smoldering boulder came crashing toward the two partners once more, but it looked to overshoot them. Upon realizing its destination, General Harkor understood the futility of intercepting the impact.

"Elias!" Rocco yelled, terrified and unsure of what to do. The boulder was aimed right at the ranged units behind the two generals. The boulder came down behind where a troop of archers awaiting their commands stood securely behind the wall. The entirety of them died under the emblazoned strike, and those who were spared an instant death wreathed in flame with cries to their leaders.

"Could you not stop it, El?" Rocco shouted at General Harkor who remained uninterested and fixated on the Lanis battalions. "Do the lives of soldiers mean so little to you?" Rocco's frustration grew and he turned to the remaining archers and siege operators upon the wall.

"Rally!" he echoed across the city's walls. "Rally my good men and women of Runefall. The defenses will be held! Gather weapons and songs, gather your brothers and sisters in arms and in love! Gather your courage and the heart you bear for this city! If your soul fails on this day, then this city was never worth the fight! Stay strong and hold true to what matters to you and make this day your own! Fire and blood make for a red day, but when the sun rises tomorrow, it will do so on the bloody battlefield surrounding the splendor of Runefall and its people as they bring in a victorious song and celebrate our legends of death! Hail and welcome your glory! Hail and welcome your death! Ere the world's breaking! Ere the end begins! Claim your honor!"

Elias continued murmuring under his breath, staring out toward the Lanis troop who were now visible on the battlefield. Siege weapons from the Pyrosi turned toward them as they approached their total assault against the war machines due East. To the North, at the main gate, Rocco saw the sickening sight of many golems approaching and the Warlord's wide cavalry behind them.

"The mounted troops won't be able to reach Lanis in time," Rocco said as General Harkor continued whispering incantations. "What are you doing?"

The air fell silent and the siege weapons to the East, their operators, and the cries of the Lanis troop could no longer be heard. However, fire and battering commenced at the main gate and its sound overtook the battlefield. Rocco watched as Lanis and his legions swept through the trenches East of the city, though he could hear nothing. No screams, no sign of the engagement whatsoever. Then, he realized what General Harkor had done.

Rocco quickly signaled to half of the troops located there on the Eastern wall, and a secondary archer troop nestled behind which had not been crushed under the previous attack. "Gather at the main gate. Help Dragario take out the cavalry!"

Rocco turned to General Harko who stared out into the field watching Lanis rip through the Eastern front. "Do you need me here?" he asked.

"Go!" Elias answered without turning to him. "Take the rest of the troops with you."

"What if they break through the Eastern wall?"

"They won't," Elias answered. "I see Barigund and Turmin. The Warlord's army stares down on our giants. Please, get to the Northern gate as quickly as you can and make sure that cavalry is dealt with, otherwise, Lanis is in trouble."

Rocco wondered how General Harkor could see the city's commander and architect. Both of them were at the Northern gate and he stared East. Still, he did as his partner commanded, and motioned for the remaining troops to rally at the Northern gate.

As Rocco arrived at his new post, running along the wall with his troops following from below and on the wall itself, he looked and saw many golems bearing down on Barigund and Turmin.

At that moment, Rocco's eyes averted from both of them long enough to see the cavalry, made up of non-magic-wielding soldiers from each tribe, dispatching from the siege of the front gate and speeding toward the Pyrosi on the Eastern front of the city where the Lanis troop was turning the tide.

Rocco realized not only was he not in place to fight the golems breaking through as many buildings had fallen under the flame of the siege which blocked his battalions from assisting; a massive shield wall still protected the army marching at the main gate. Shields were being erected overhead, a barrier to prevent arrows from raining down upon them, and the wall of troops seemed to stretch all the way back to the tents beyond the Northern front of the city.

Rocco's beating heart went cold in an instant as he realized the depth of Runefall's outnumbering. The Warlord's army had reached a vastness in which it managed to create a shield tunnel from its camp to the main gate of the city.

From above the main gate Rocco could see Master General Galantis with a battalion of archers drenching the encroaching assault with arrows, the vicious cries from Harigamun's impaled soldiers spilled into the void empowered by the Wind Riders who realized their inability to injure the golems surrounding the gate, let alone pierce the tunnel of shields.

"Master General!" Rocco shouted. "They ride toward Lanis!"

Galantis turned his gaze outward and away from the insurmountable force to see the cavalry less than a quarter of its way toward the Lanis troop. He looked back toward the uncountable foes below and then back to Lanis who tore through the Pyrosi trenches.

"They are breaking away!" Galantis shouted back, seeing soldiers from the shield wall breaking off in pursuit. "Their armies are grouping!"

Rocco thought to himself, seeking his own answers under the howls of war. *How? Elias silenced the battlefield; how could the armies still be speaking to one another?*

"Sir," Singher, General of the Pyrosi army psionically said to his Warlord. *"They've come through the walls and driven us into the dirt of our own trenches!"*

Harigamun saw through the eyes of his generals—his gift from Halorin. The Warlord, immersed in the senses and bodies of others, felt power. *I will end this. This... is too much, even for me—especially for me.*

"Whaleback," Harigamun said. "Move faster! Get your cavalry over there and wipe through Runefall's mistaken general!"

Whaleback motioned for his cavalry, far beyond the reach of Runefall's archers, to rush toward the head of the Lanis troop. The Agualyte general rode upon a stout mount, more akin to a donkey than a horse, as it needed to be stronger to hold the obscenely large man. His remaining cavalry rode on SeaHorses trained to tread water using the powers of the Agually. Thus, the cavalry, to the surprise of their enemy, increased its speed to outrun Lanis as a great many of the Acolytes of the Deep wrought a howling witchery to the battlefield and called for a storm. It started to rain and suddenly the Seahorses picked up pace.

The Lanis troop couldn't outrun them now.

"Tell the archers to break from under the shields and soak the city's walls in arrows," Harigamun said to Airwei, Master of Winds.

"They will fly true, my liege," Airwei answered.

The Master of Winds signaled for his archers beneath the shielded tunnel to step out from their protection, and all at once, the shields split open revealing a terrifying amount of them who let loose their fletchings in unison.

The arrows caught Master General Galantis and his soldiers off guard. The sight of Harigamun's army, and the inability to break the shield wall, caused soldiers to lower their weapons for a second... seeking hope. That second was long enough for the Wind Riders to cast their arrows into the sky, piercing the hearts of most of the Galantis troop.

The Master General's men ran in their final moments, following the volley of arrows, and many died feeling chased by broadheads as if life was given to their shafts and legs to their arrows. Following the quick and fatal assault, the Wind Riders returned to catch their breath, under the shield wall.

Galantis fell, reaching to the dead surrounding him on the wall as he cried over the death surrounding him, "Rocco, get to Lanis!" Forlornness and want to abandon his post seeped into his tear-soaked pores.

Far back to the Eastern wall where he originally stood with General Harkor, Rocco saw his partner casting another spell as he stood alone on the wall. Rocco took off as fast as he could, shouting a final command to his battalion, "Move! By the orders of Galantis!"

While the number of troops Rocco left was many, the devastation the city would endure at the loss of the Lanis troop would be unsustainable. Sprinting across the wall back toward his partner, Rocco questioned whether or not he was fit to be the general of the ground troops. He'd never fought, and he considered it likely that... *They promoted me because of Elias, because I wouldn't let him do anything alone.* Even now, Rocco was abandoning his troops to his love, but he also knew General Harkor might be one of the only ones left who could save them all.

"Focus!" Rocco said, running across the wall and closing the distance between himself and Elias. "We need him!"

Rocco considered the age of Lanis a mere twenty-two years compared to his own twenty-six. As the gap between him and Elias shrank, he thought of the militaristic upbringing the three of them had, imagining the shining smile of Elias when he'd cheaply won a game.

"Focus," he repeated. But his mind continued to wander back to his younger days of military education. He stopped for a second as he looked out toward the Eastern front, watching the Agualyte cavalry lead the Warlord's grander cavalry... and they were about to trample Lanis.

They only attacked from two directions, and we only defended two walls. Rocco shook off the thought and regained his initial speed towards his lover and quickly closed the remaining gap. "Elias!"

Reaching his destination, Rocco extended his arm toward Elias, grabbing his forearm. As he touched the skin of his partner, he felt a surging vibration—a fearsome trembling gripping his bones—and witnessed the wall beneath Elias's feet glow a dark emerald, a mean light carving into the stone. At the last moment of Elias's chanting, the two of them vanished from the wall and found themselves standing with the Lanis troop at the Eastern front.

"Rocco!" Elias yelled. "Why? You saw me and clearly had no idea what spell I was casting! Why would you grab ahold of me?"

"I knew you were doing the right thing for Lanis which meant it was the right thing to do," Rocco said. "And I never let you do anything alone." He always believed Elias did the right thing, even when others doubted him. He loved him, and Elias knew that... everyone knew.

Secretly, Elias was glad his partner found and joined him. But he was terrified too. *Please, Salaril. Keep him safe. Let me fall if one of us must.*

Flames blew through the air in front of them, like the ocean's water blowing from a whale, and caused both the generals to quiet instantly and rush toward the blaze. Arriving at the source, they found Lanis circling Singher—the Warlord's second-in-command of the Pyrosi army—about to fight. Rocco noticed Elias starving himself of strength as his lover's walk had become feeble.

"Awful young to be leading all of these fine folks to their death," Singher said.

"Years of proving myself on the battleground—" Lanis replied.

"Training ground," Singher interrupted. "You've never known a battle like the rest of your so-called generals. All except Barigund and

Turmin, your supposed giants." He laughed.

Lanis tried to hide his fury at the comment. Not only was his worth as a general being challenged in front of his army, but Singher was right. Lanis, Rocco, and Elias; they all came from the same class, each of them stolen in the night from one of the other tribes of magic. They were told their strength would protect all of Kaiya from war as long as they united under the banner of Runefall—and Lanis remembered hearing those words. But then, each of them watched Runefall do it again and again. It never became easier. As long as Runefall stood resolute, the lands of Kaiya would keep war at bay, at least that is what the Ruling Council always told its people. But now, war had come, and Lanis couldn't help but wonder if the city, the council, had brought war to its own gates.

"Our seclusion and strength are what has kept the lands of Kaiya from falling into disorder and chaos," Lanis said, not entirely believing himself.

"What war do you fool yourself into thinking you've stopped? Harigamun waged war on all the tribes of magic, uniting us under one banner so we could turn our sights on you. So, tell me, *general*, how did Runefall prevent war? It seems to the rest of the world... Runefall is the reason for the bloodshed that plagues today's soil." Singher had two fingers pressed to his chin at the end, smiling.

Lanis, staring down the Pyrosi general, was at a complete loss for words. Singher was right, again. Runefall taking the strongest and most elite of each tribe did nothing but cause anger and distrust. Hiding and stealing children didn't prevent Kaiya from going to war, it only prevented Runefall from participating in the fighting—until now.

"Then let us work together to stop this fight, here and now," Lanis said. "Put down the blades and take our fighters to the main gate. We can right the wrong that was done to each tribe. We can reunify."

"This is beyond you and me, boy," Singher answered. "Harigamun not only seeks to break your gates, but your god too."

"Salaril means nothing to me," said Lanis. "Does he lie within the city? Is this why the city must be sacked?"

"Your god lies at the heart of your city. And lie he does," Singher replied.

"Then let us bring this battle to heel and negotiate, Pyrosi! I was taken from the Mystics and my home long ago. I would see those people once more and the lands of Kaiya reach peace."

Singher lowered his weapons and took a long gaze into Lanis's eyes, trying to decide whether or not he could trust the young general. The Mystics were capable of many things, and their ability to manipulate the minds of others was well known. All of Harigamun's generals knew each of Runefall's and who they were taken from.

"Perhaps the deaths of many are unnecessary," the Pyrosi general answered, disheartened. "You'll go to the gates of Runefall with me and we will council at the feet of Harigamun. You'll have to live in your hope he will see peace as we do."

"Thank yo—," Lanis stopped speaking as he watched Singher's body contort as he writhed in pain.

Singher screamed, "The flames boil me from within!"

"You'll do it for the good of Kaiya and you'll do it for the death of Runefall. But mostly, you'll do it because I say so," Harigamun said to Singher, through their psionic connection.

"No. No, I won't!" Singher wailed in panic in front of Lanis who could not understand why the Pyrosi general seemed to be overcome with a psychotic fit of rage. "You can't make me!"

"You'll do it, Singher," the Warlord said. *"You don't get a choice. No one will ever know it was me who made you do it, so there's no sense in screaming!"*

Singher's lips tightened, and his face cringed as he tried to scream, "Harigamun!"

The Pyrosi general's mouth sealed shut and his screams became frustrated mumbles covered with the tears of a man contending with death, which he knew was unstoppable. He fell to the soiled earth of the battlefield crawled toward Lanis, reaching out as his arms burned a hot and deep flame. The fires, Singher knew, were searching for an orifice, a release of some kind. He accepted his fate knowing he was nothing more than a warlord's tool.

"You thought you could convince me to give up my pursuit?" Harigamun's voice continued tormenting him as he pleaded for help. *"You think I would conquer these peoples, storm the gates of a hidden city in revenge of a false god, and then merely turn away because you don't want to fight? Because you have the heart of a child?"*

Singher knew his time was ending. Harigamun would kill him for being disobedient and hoping to end the bloodshed. The Pyrosi's memory fled back to the day Harigamun invaded his village, Pyra. The flaming festivals and the crisp food. It all came to a dismal end when the Warlord brought his treacherous group against his own people and the city to its knees within what felt like minutes. It was then Singher realized Harigamun was his death, he'd just mistaken the timing, and worst of all, he had decided to serve him out of fear.

"Oh, it's not just you who's going to die, Singher," Harigamun said, torturing his general.

Singher's eyes blasted open as he realized what was happening and suddenly, he started viciously waving and pointing, gesturing to Lanis to get far away from him.

"That's all it takes for you to betray your own kind, is it?" Harigamun asked.

Lanis, Elias, and Rocco all watched in confusion as the cavalry headed straight toward them and stopped in the middle of the wide field. They were watching and waiting. The cavalry knew something Rocco and Elias did not.

"RUN!" Elias turned, grabbing his partner by the hand as

the two rushed toward a siege trench before a massive explosion disintegrated everything surrounding Singher. His body became a flurry of pyrotechnics, cracks and whips breaking across the battlefield.

The blast seared Rocco and Elias, leaving them dead in the trenches along with the surrounding Lanis troop and the casters manning the siege weapons. All of the Pyrosi and other casters on the Eastern front melted away.

Rocco and Elias, who never separated, were scorched in a trench, their arms wrapped around one another. In the days that would follow, when their bones would be found by the first surveyors from Vari, they would be memorialized as the Burned Lovers; but that day was not today.

On the battlefield, Whaleback sat with his cavalry and stared at the emblazoned field screaming with fire in shock of what he, and others, had heard.

"You forced him to kill himself?" Whaleback said to Harigamun, still psionically linked.

Harigamun was stunned. *How does he know?*

"Who of us are safe from your rage against this city?" Airwei, commander of the Windago people, chimed in.

"Halorin, and now Singher. Who could be next?" Sodsheim of the Mounders asked.

"Of all the contracts I've made," Varin, Lord of the Summoners said, *"joining you seems to have been the worst of them."*

Harigamun found himself confused and afraid all at once. He was in control of the connection—or he thought he was. How was it possible that his commanders watched him sacrifice Singher to destroy the Lanis troop? How could they all see through Singher's eyes as Harigamun had, and hear their commander forcing his general to do such a thing?

Harigamun felt his eyes recede into the back of his head and his vision become a dull, white void, pulling him into the cells of his own mind. His skull fell fractured, as if it pounded upon itself as the feeling in his limbs became a dry and faded memory.

"Where am I?" the Pyrosi Warlord cried in the emptiness in front of him. "Where am I?"

The white emptiness contorted into a vibrant black shadow as water covered the ground beneath him. Ripples broke across the stream, shimmering under a small light far off in the distance, barely illuminating Harigamun—which he could now see was tied to a chair with nails driven into his palms and feet.

"Your connection is broken," a deep voice came from the darkness. "Well, broken isn't quite true. It's just not yours to control anymore."

"Who are you?" Harigamun cried out.

"I am he that is seen when one dreams to be seen," the dark voice answered.

"Ishmael," Harigamun snarled. "Brother to ilk, and seemingly, bringer of my doom."

"Aye," Ishmael answered. "Few are fond of my brother. You least of all."

"He will die once I return. I have a battle to fight." Harigamun's spit spewed into the dark circles of water rippling under his bloody feet. "The battle you set me toward."

"You're not the only one who has a vendetta against Salaril, you know," Ishmael said with condescension. "And I'm not talking about myself."

The Warlord squinted his eyes, studying his opponent. "What would you have me do against your brother?"

"My brother is of little consequence," Ishmael said, "but taking what matters to him means everything. Others will do the rest of the work for me, much like yourself, much like you already have."

"And how do I do that?" Harigamun leaned forward.

"By breaking the beast," he answered, "beneath the city of Runefall—"

"The seal," Harigamun interrupted.

"The beast," Ishmael repeated in correction. "The beast guards the seal it seems. It can be ignored, and the seal broken loose. However, should you leave the beast, you leave Salaril's power. Should you leave the seal, but kill the beast, then you open your world to ours."

"Salaril is in your world?" Harigamun asked.

"He remains a prisoner, yes," Ishmael answered. "If you set him free with his power, you will surely lose."

"Why tell me this?" Harigamun grew hot. "You're one of them!"

"Even dreams need their sleep," Ishmael said. "Salaril imprisoned me long before his own imprisonment. Now, I live only in dreams and visions. Where you seek revenge, I seek peace. Where you need blood, I need freedom."

"So, kill the beast, and then break the seal?" Harigamun confirmed.

"Yes."

"One more thing," Tir said, shocking the Warlord as the Scribe of Runefall stepped into the small light.

"Tir," Harigamun said. "Such a sad thing to see you taken from your homes still fight the battles of Salaril."

"The only fight I see outside is between life and death," she answered. "This is not the bidding of a god, but of a man lost to rage."

"It was you, then?" Harigamun asked. "You broke my connection and brought me here to speak with Ishmael. But why turn on your own god?"

"I serve where the truth is spoken," Tir answered.

"Then, what will you have of me, my lady?" Harigamun dug, staring into her distorted eyes, and impressed his desire for her with a smug lick of his lips and a grunt.

"Protect the girl, Kyra. And should you lay a finger on her," Ishmael walked right up to the Pyrosi warlord and ran a hand up Harigamun's inner thigh. "I'll take something precious from you, before your life comes to an unfailing painful end," Ishmael grabbed his crotch and squeezed tightly while licking his lips as the Warlord had done to Tir. "I wouldn't think of putting a finger on any of *my* women if you care to continue life as you know it."

Tir quivered at being referred to as *his*. It was odd, but not... well, she didn't know, honestly. She grew more frustrated at her lack of disgust than anything.

Harigamun gulped a light breath. "I'll see the girl remains safe."

"Beast first," Ishamel said, "seal after."

"What happens next?" Tir asked.

"The end," Ishmael said.

Harigamun's consciousness left the Dreaming Haunts, abandoning Tir, though he had no say in the matter. She found herself instantly back inside her temple, and Harigamun found himself surrounded by Whaleback, Airwei, and Lord Varin as if time had stopped.

The Warlord's anxiety rose as he felt the warmth of hatred piling onto him from his remaining generals. Whaleback sat atop his oversized steed which brayed as Airwei whisked a mild hurricane to barricade the entrance of the main gate, motioning Sodsheim and Varin to retreat their army of golems and siege weapons from the city. The warpath of the remaining generals, to the eyes of Harigamun, was redirected back to him as the slicing winds held the city trapped behind its walls; though, Airwei himself looked to grow sick, almost like breathing had become difficult.

"You would end the lives of each of us and our people if it meant your revenge on that damnable god," Whaleback said, spitting down at the Warlord.

"We all bowed before the great *Warlord of Kaiya*," Airwei said, weakly. "We all feared you and yet we all still followed out of our own anger. Our own hope for revenge. But what cost is this to you? Runefall stole from us; our people, our sons and daughters, just like they did you, and just like they did everyone else. How many sons and daughters would you see gone from this world just to break a god?"

Harigamun stood silent on the battlefield, watching as Whaleback's Agualyte troops surrounded him. The Wind Rider's archers pointed their tips toward him while Sodsheim's battalion of golems, commanded by Varin, circled around. The connection Harigamun once thought belonged to him had now completely cut him out. His generals were in charge and talking to one another—the army had turned away from Runefall.

"I cannot make you unsee what I have done," the Warlord said. "Neither would I want to take away my actions from your sight. What you say of me is true. I would make every sacrifice necessary to get to that god and put his head on a spike."

The Agualytes raised their spears to the Warlord's neck and Airwei held a signal for his archers to launch a volley of arrows at his feet.

Harigamun shuttered at the sight and put thought into his next words as he stared at the few remaining golems of Sodsheim.

"I would lay myself at a bloody altar without regret and without thought if it meant preventing the deaths of you all, and that's exactly what I mean to stop," Harigamun said.

The army whispered amongst itself, and indiscernible fear covered the battlefield.

"What death do you speak of?" Whaleback asked. "What further lies do you tell?"

"He spoke to me," Harigamun said in a low whisper, moving his eyes around the surrounding crowd of soldiers. "Ishmael, the Lord of the Dreaming Haunts, and brother of Salaril. His brother means to end all life on Kaiya and start anew. He thinks we've wasted magic, wasted our resources, and wasted the land! I mean to show him the only thing that was ever wasted on Kaiya was worship to him and the other gods!"

"He speaks the truth," Tir's voice whispered to the generals, taking advantage of the connection she and Ishmael had stolen from the

Warlord. "Salaril will take you all!"

Airwei, now joined by Sodsheim and Varin, turned to Whaleback seeking guidance. "What should we do? We cannot trust him."

Whaleback took a moment, staring at Harigamun. The colossal warlord that had taken down the mighty families of Aqualyte, Pyrosi, Mounder, Summoner, and the Mystic tribes was now at the hands of Whaleback. His folded brow, battered in sweat and stench, held the power to collapse an army onto the Warlord, and Whaleback felt as though he would have deserved it. He deserved to have the army he forced together to turn him on.

Whaleback thought of breaking his stone armor in front of him if only he knew how to break it. He wanted all the power held by Harigamun to be lost in an instant, but now he had some unknown voice in his head telling him the enemy of his current moment was not lying and that some unseen god meant to cleanse the world of him and his people. A weight fell on Whaleback. As he took a deep breath, about to deliver his final condemning order against the Warlord, darkness veiled the battlefield.

As darkness swept the land, Kyra and Sam housed in a wagon with Arimeus far behind, watched the shadows fall. On the top of Runefall's gate, Kyra saw a small shadow of a figure who looked to be bent over.

The shadow smothered Galantis as he lamented over his arrow-filled soldiers both beside him and below as the clouding smoked his vision. Galantis, Turmin, and Barigund walked outside the shattered forcefield of the front gate through the small crack and peered into the growing blackness. Every person from both sides of the battle watched, surrounded by flames or death, as a hidden figure crested upon a sharp horizon in the night's veil, now floating high in the sky. Its head seemed as large as the burning sun, but its illumination could only be matched by a bright and fearsome nocturnal moon.

Kyra recognized the face.

"A giant's blood and a giant's blade," Ishamel, Lord of the Dreaming

Haunts spoke in a deep, heavy voice to all those present on the battlefield. "They stand at the gate."

Instantly, an entire army shifted its gaze toward Barigund and Turmin, standing vigil outside the main gate of Runefall. The two looked at each other and smiled.

"With one dead you accomplish our end. With none you accomplish Harigamun's end. With both dead, you put an end to the destruction of your world. Storm the Cistern of Runefall, claim its temple as your own, and lay waste to its offerings of false and priestly gods. Bring down the halls of worship and the need for worshiping will come crashing down, ushering in a new era of Kaiya. The era without gods!"

The limbs of Barigund and Turmin shook with small adrenal tremors, but the two could not help but rejoice in what was to come.

"How long has it been, brother?" Barigund asked.

"I've been long enough for this world," Turmin answered. "But it's always been too long since a fight, brother."

The two hoisted their weapons high and bored their deep voices into the air. Their war drumming of shouts blasted louder than the entire army of Harigamun, rallying the whole garrison behind Runefall's walls to stream from the now opening gate. The army would fight beside their giants without the protection of the wall.

Chapter Fourteen

Dwarahir's Burden

"Were I to have my pick in this world, I would lean heavily on dwarven smiths. Now, without the help from the highest of smiths from their lowest of places, I face brothers who may yet wield their secrets. I hope, if they can, they realize it too late."

— Harigamun, *Thoughts of War*

G runffi sat on the cavern floor riddled with Dhamri's blood as his wife's tears had finally started to wane.

Barklo's frozen body tormented the former dwarven King as he glared at his friend's glistening eyes, hardened by ice in the depths of a burning volcano which had no effect on Barklo's crystalline state.

Blood leaked from Saroria's wound, though, not nearly enough to be life-threatening; still, the pain in her abdomen could not match the splintering of her heart as she grieved what felt like the loss of her husband, and possibly her unborn child, even as she saw Grunffi sitting idly stoic in front of her.

"Would you have this be our end?" Saroria asked.

"It seems our end was not for me to decide," Grunffi answered, aching in pain for his lost friend.

"You would mourn your friend, and my brother, before you would mourn the loss of the mother of your child?"

"I would mourn those who were loyal," Grunffi sighed. "I would mourn the loss of the woman I loved, if only she stood in this chamber with me now. Whomever you may be, you are most certainly not dying today, least not of that weak wound." He went and pulled his thrice-bladed axe from Ikba's body. "Barklo's death is near and sudden. Yours, it seems, happened some time ago. By what should I call you, if not Saroria, my wife?" His glare penetrated her as her throat clenched and her eyes fell into an ocean of their own making.

She shuttered a short breath with a hidden squeal and tried to hold back tears as her hands covered her mouth. A singular tear grazed from the top of her lips to her hands as she swept it away.

"It seems I am to be the most tragic of dwarves. I was doomed by the loss of love, of fatherhood, of kingship, and people. I never wanted to rule. Why did that lack of want condemn me to a life of loss? Why would a dwarf be forced into a kingship he never wanted... be forced to sacrifice his time with those whom he truly loved? Is it some damned curse on our kind, on me? Or is it something more revolting? Something unplanned, some unfamiliar happenstance staging tragic events like an unstoppable whirlwind of downward pressure meant to grind the very stone from which I am made? Perhaps I am made for death. That is what Baylar said. We are made as a forged weapon meant to bring death to those that Dwarahir loathes. Perhaps it was in his loathing that my doom was foretold."

Saroria stared at Grunffi with regret, wishing she had never betrayed him. He was right, he never wanted to lead their people, never wanted to leave their home, and he certainly never wanted to leave the mines. He stepped out into the light of the world and continuously made every decision based on what he'd thought was for the good of his people, but it wasn't enough. It was never enough for her because with every movement made for his people it took her love farther from her. Saroria didn't blame Grunffi for stepping away... at first.

Saroria's mind turned to darker times as she stared at his fury, remembering the moments of frustration on the long nights when he would cast her away. She would try to sway his opinion; not to take the Eastern path, not to flee North but to head West. She would try to comfort him on those long nights, and he would shed away her kindness to be locked in the depths of his own mind. She felt unnoticed, unloved, and unworthy at the same time. How long was she to endure the constant coldness and absence of adoration, going without even a hint of being noticed? Why must she subject herself to a life without liveliness in order to satiate the self-loathing of a resentful husband and absentee father? No, she had not made the right decision in choosing disloyalty to her husband, but she felt she had also not made the wrong decision in pursuit of her own happiness.

"You did not deserve the pain I have lain on you, my love. You did not deserve the hurt of seeing another allowed into my heart," she sniffled.

Grunffi shot a look of pure hatred toward her. It was more than just a child. Grunffi didn't realize the depth of loss until now. It was not merely her attention and her desire Dhamri had taken, it was her love as well.

"But I did not deserve what I was given these past many years," Saroria said, broken. "I have given you my life, and I was there in support when most others would have failed or chosen to leave. The long, sleepless, cold nights without a touch! The days without a word! All to lead to one moment of fury where you'd lash out against me with your words. Never did you place a hand on me, but the scars you left were, and are, beyond the repair of any smith."

Saroria checked her abdomen once more and noticed the bleeding had stopped. She still felt pain but could move without fear of continued blood loss under the wrapping she'd thrown around the wound.

"What happens now, my King?" she asked, disappointedly.

Grunffi lowered his head, staring at the cavern floor as his fingers trilled and tapped the ice of Barklo once more.

"I have lost my purpose as a husband. I have lost my purpose as a father. I have lost my purpose as a King. So, now, I seek to fulfill that purpose which is the only one I have left."

Saroria's tears dried, and her skin became moistureless in the heat. "What purpose would that be?"

"I will become the weapon of prophecy! The Hammer of Dwarahir. I will bring an end to these foul gods and the games they play! Were it not for these gods, I'd have my family, I'd have my peace, I'd have my life. But no! They seek to play their own games and rule over the lives of many. I say no more! I will travel to the city of Runefall in the West, and I will strike down the first of these gods. I will wield this power given to our people all the way until I reach Dwarahir himself, and I will grind him down to the hilt for daring to place such a tragic end on me!"

"And what would you have of me?" Saroria asked, fearfully.

"I would have nothing more of you. Return yourself to the South, the East, the West, or wherever you think you may find peace in your loss. I do not deny I have caused you hurt. But I have never betrayed you nor wished against you and I will not start today. Find yourself a home, and perhaps one day I will find you there. On that day, perhaps, I will have more to say should you still want to speak."

Grunffi walked back up the cavern path and toward the entrance of the volcano after those final words. Saroria stayed in the warm depths of the cavern as he made his way to the top and found Krabella—the widow—standing just outside the entrance, far enough away from any heat, frozen solid in a prayer stance. She had stripped off her clothes and given herself to the frost. As he stayed there, gawking at the willingness to give up, he realized something—*for her, life without Skolgrim wasn't worth continuing.*

Grunffi stared at her, admiring the depth of her loss and the love she clearly bore for her husband. He wondered if his wife had that much love, that need for him, at any point. Did he possess that love for her? In a way, he was abandoning his life, and he knew that. He wanted nothing to do with his dwarven people anymore, nothing to do with leadership, nothing to do with *Saroria*. But would his guilt return for the worse down the road? Would he find himself shedding his clothing in the cold, just as Krabella had done?

"Here marks The Path of Tears, a trail of dwarves lost by their own making," Grunffi said, forcing his way through the snow and down the mountain. As he turned back with a last glance at the mouth of the mountain, he saw a shadow standing next to the frozen Krabella. He knew it was Saroria, but he didn't know how true of a goodbye he'd said in that cavern, or if he wanted it to be goodbye.

Weeks went by as Grunffi wandered the wilderness heading West. The dwarven King knew he was heading West, toward Runefall, but how far he was from the city and where he was exactly was unknown to him. As he had ventured off the mountain and down from the tragedies that befell him, he often relented and harkened back to moments spent with Saroria.

"I cannot have it again," he would mutter as she came to his mind. "I cannot know peace. I cannot feel warmth, or comfort. I must live in the discomfort of my own making."

Grunffi would recite those words each time Haffi or Saroria or his people came to his thoughts. He became fixated on the idea of being a living and walking weapon, convincing himself of his own loss of mortality, morality, and responsibility to anyone beyond death-dealing.

"I am the weapon crafted to destroy my maker," he would say. "I am the Hammer of Dwarahir, and my smithy too will fall."

Grunffi's words became incantations as he descended from the snow-struck mountain tops and explored the deep, cavernous valleys below. He knew, because of his father's journeys, the ravine located at the foot of the mountain led to an indescribable depth in Kaiya, far below what any had recorded before. Rumors of the great beasts of old claiming its depths prevented most from wanting to travel there, even though traveling through the valley would allow a significantly shorter path into the West.

Many years ago, Grunffi, in traveling with his father as they descended to the Southern reaches of Kaiya, was told of this barren land. Its haunting scenery immediately gripped the heart of anyone peering into the canyon as the snow from the mountaintops unnaturally stopped at the edge of the ravine. A desert-like barren waste of rock painted with reddish hues splattered like thick pooling blood had become covered with dust and sat inches away from the snow-covered wasteland of the Northern mountains.

"Here the dragons lie," Grunffi said as he looked down into the canyon depths. Stories, stories from his people, told weary travelers of how the fire of dragons buried here long ago still kept the snow at bay. Thus, the fear of dragons and other beasts, in addition to the fear of not being able to sustain life such as this barren land offered, kept most from ever daring to enter, at least, that is what most assumed, including Grunffi.

"Weapons do not know fear," the dwarf said as he plunged into the canyon deeps of Dragon's Spine. He could not help but appreciate the name of the canyon as he continuously stepped on jagged rock protruding upward like an arrowhead. The farther down into the depths he went, the closer he came to seeing the beauty of Dragon's Spine. He watched in awe as rock that looked to be bone staggered across the top of the canyon above him in an odd, and seemingly intentional design, befitting the spine of the great beasts of old.

The spine sprawled out like a labyrinth of broken bones. Caved in passageways, former passageways, lay beneath collapsed mounds of rock which looked to hide away secrets of a forgotten age with old shapes of claws framing the outlines. Over and over, the former dwarven King struggled to find his way through the basin of the canyon deeps, often turning and returning time and time again, losing his breath and feeling the dry scarceness of the region.

Then, Grunffi came upon a frail and tattered nest, something someone would call home if only for a night. As he approached the nest, he came to find it lacked the stench of rodents usually paired with such a structure. It was oddly clean. Furthermore, he found an opening which allowed him to peek inside, and there was nothing in it. No hoarding of any sort, no sickening blackness of mold nor collected garbage or food. It was simply a roof made from... well, he could not tell what it was made from. Even still, he couldn't help but notice he could have lived, or at least slept, in this little canopy earlier in his life when he still held the small stature of a mine dwarf, or maybe he would need to be a bit smaller than that.

Moreover, Grunffi had reached another dead end, and there was only the nest before him as night came.

So many rumors from travelers who never set foot in the canyon deeps. I might have known. It seems most would have been lucky to even find their way out of this maze, let alone find their way through.

Grunffi took a moment to sit down, to think. He crossed his legs and closed his eyes and began to hum a deep and continuous note which shot vibrations into the stone as pebbles from the dirt bounced and danced about him. The thrumming of his vocals struck against the cavern walls and spoke to him.

I miss Stone Song. I long for the Stoney Widows and their songs, for my own tune is a harsh failure of memory. Haffi's lady... she knew it well, before the fall.

The spine of the canyon only spoke one thing back to the dwarf, as his skill in the art was nil and nearly absent—neither being enough to truly speak to mountains nor use it to craft adamantite.

"Hollow," the Dragon's Spine sang.

If I'm not meant to find my way around the rock and bone, then I'll just make a new way through.

The dwarf raised his battle axe in an instant following the Stone Song and tore down the nest. The structure splintered like bone and cracked just the same. Amid the rubble, Grunffi saw a small hole bored into the wall. It was nowhere near big enough for him to crawl through. He turned, facing the cavern wall, and shot off a great kick like that of a mule. His stone-plated boot smashed into the wall, and he watched as the hole grew in size. The dwarf lowered himself to the ground, reaching both calloused hands into the hole after setting down his blade, and ripped the stone from the mountain. He tore the skin from his fingers, leaving blood on his knuckles, as he tossed away pieces of the mountain. Then, he opened the crevice enough to fit through.

Just in through the entryway a few berries were strewn about the ground. Grunffi thought perhaps the berries were in the structure, in the valleys of Dragon's Spine, and he'd just missed them. In any case, he decided to eat the berries as it had been days since he'd had a snack. Dwarves were notoriously good at storing food, sometimes going weeks without needing food if the proper amount of gluttonous consumption prior to the long period of waiting was had, and he had most certainly reached the point of needing replenishment.

Stepping into the underbelly of Dragon's Spine, Grunffi became overtaken with a sense of beguiling curiosity and child-like desire to grasp the unknown sights in front of him. What should have been a cavernous ceiling with stalactites stabbing to the lower reaches of the underbelly was instead a night sky. Stars littered a void of darkness, or what seemed to be stars. Some bright but timid illumination beat down from the starlike structures enabling him to see the path that lay ahead. A large ravine, akin to an empty lake, stretched from one end of the cavern to the next with a winding path downward. He tried to measure the distance from where he stood at the far, opposite end of the cavern but the illumination from the starry lanterns above only stretched so far, dimming his ability to see the full stretch of the basin.

Looking to the depths equal to fathoms underneath the small cliff Grunffi stood on, he saw embers trickling away in the distant darkness below.

Travelers. Or have I intruded on some unwelcoming home?

Putting his hands out against the wall, running his fingers down the stone as he descended into the depths of the Dragon's Belly, Grunffi's hands tightly gripped onto the wall, and it felt like an alluring familiarity—the stone was adamantite.

"Have I come from you, or you from me?" he whispered to the stone. "To think my carving, the carving of my people; it was nothing more than forging."

A membrane of fungi wrapped itself to the cavern walls and covered much of the surrounding rock, save the adamantite Grunffi found, which became more prevalent the further he descended into the underbelly. The fungi, in tandem with a soft and wetted moss, covered the stone like bone wrapped on marrow.

The hardened rock bore the scrapings of bone against stone, or a thing of historical strength clawing into ore. The design felt all too natural and simultaneously hand-crafted. The further Grunffi descended, the more he started to recognize he was in a mine. But even still, the constant caressing of structures mirroring the inside of a great beast was hard to ignore. The dwarf started asking himself myriads of questions regarding his surroundings. Could this truly have been a dragon? Or are there many dragons? Is this even bone, or some uncommon material hidden from us by the fear of this place? What matter of fungi is present here, and are the elves privy to its effects?

Most importantly, Grunffi found himself asking the most immediate question in front of him: *Who chose to live here, hidden beneath the stone?*

The closer he came to the bottom of the winding and narrow stairs, the thicker the beating of drums from the darkness became. It became clear that not only was someone living here, but it was also an entire people, a people unknown to the seeing world above.

How long? And why?

Approaching the bottom of the trench, Grunffi jumped behind a large stalagmite protruding from the ground, fettered in a luminescent fungus very similar to the marrow-like fungi draping the cavern walls. The dwarf noticed small voices tiptoeing through the air as if the voices were aware they needed not to be heard. Their whispers concerned him, and after a few minutes, he decided to take rest and sat on the ground. Vegetation broke through tiny cracks of the cavern, and deep in the crags where the wall met the floor, he found more berries by following the line of vegetation tucked under the stone. There was a moist dryness near the berry stones.

The whispers fell away from the air and moments turned into minutes, and many of them passed as Grunffi snacked away at the berries. He didn't keep track of the amount of berries he ate, he only minded how good they tasted. It had been so long since he'd had such a sweet taste, and the crispness of the berry cracking against his teeth with a slightly cold chill sent tingles down his body and became almost euphoric. Additionally, it could be quite some time before he had the opportunity to eat again; thus, like any good dwarf, his gluttony became a tool for his survival.

Grunffi's gluttonous and depraved gorging of berries quickly resulted in the dwarf nodding off into a much-needed slumber. His head cocked to his shoulder and his hand dropped the remaining berries to the ground as his snoring made his presence known, if it wasn't already—he heard whispers as his eyes closed.

Hours passed and Grunffi found himself on a cot, by a fire, and near singing.

"It's ok that you took my berries," said a low and tapered voice. "You're quite big. It's understandable you would need so much food."

Grunffi turned to see a child, or man, a small man, standing beside the fire. He looked like a dwarf, but he was smaller than any dwarf he had ever shared mine or mountain with.

"Have a drink too," the small man, or dwarf, or something else, said as he placed a goblet in Grunffi's hand. The cup was quite miniature in the former dwarven King's overgrown grip.

Grunffi scanned the lower reaches of the Dragon's Spine, or where he assumed was still the Dragon's Spine, so long as his newfound acquaintance had not moved him to some other location. He found many small, dwarf-like men and women running around with cheery attitudes, most carrying stone or some other craftsman material.

"For what do you and your people build?' Grunffi asked as he took a sip from the cup, but not before wafting in the aroma of the sweet nectar within it. He recalled the scent of the berries he'd eaten earlier. Oh, how he wished he had more of those berries.

"Not even a name between us and you would ask our ways, Ogre?" The small person giggled a chittering laugh.

"What makes you call me an Ogre?"

"To start, the berries did not kill you. Thus, you must be a dwarf," the small man answered.

Grunffi finished the drink given to him in one gulp and dropped the goblet to the ground upon hearing the answer.

"And that also quite confirms you are in fact a dwarf," said the small man. "The juice is a concentrated cocktail of the berries, plus a little of our own dousing of Ada's Song."

"Ada's Song?" Grunffi questioned, still weak.

"Oh, yes," the little person said. Grunffi thought he must be a dwarf after what he'd just learned about the berries. "How beautiful a lady. How beautiful a song."

"Who is Ada?" Grunffi asked.

"Who is Ada, asks the Ogre?" The small, dwarf–person, man laughed.

"I am no Ogre." Grunffi rose from the cot, standing substantially higher than his squirrely counterpart, though his balance was notably off. "I am a dwarf!"

"Of course you are," his counterpart answered. "All Ogres are dwarves. But not all dwarves are Ogres. You must know this."

"Perhaps if I knew what it is to be an Ogre, I might better tell you if I were one or not," Grunffi said, growing frustrated.

"You do not know Ada. You do not know of Ogres, even though you are one. What do you know?" he asked.

"I know I am growing tired of questions," Grunffi said. "My people have often called me Ogre, but it means nothing more than growing larger than the other dwarves, like others who also lived under the sun."

"I see," the small one answered. Hammering against stone and smithing rings tolled through the mountain air. "It seems much of your people's story has gone to myth, then."

"My people? Are we not one people? Are you not dwarven?" Grunffi was getting angry, confused. *He toys with me in the darkness of a forgotten place!*

The small, possible dwarf started cackling and holding his belly as it swayed back and forth. It was a large belly on such a small body. As Grunffi looked around, he noticed most of them were of the same description. Their hair mirrored many dwarven styles from long ago. Most dwarves had taken to a shaving of the sides of their heads with intimate designs and braids. Often those cuts would go many days, weeks, and sometimes months without a washing in the mines. But these smaller folk, they had long, flat, thick, and coarse hair. It seemed quite long and rather unkempt, but also surprising for a people shrouded in darkness, as their hair seemed to shimmer with health. In fact, as Grunffi watched, what he was now convinced was a dwarf in front of him bellowing in laughter, he could not help but notice pureness of skin and shining eyes. Grunffi never thought one's appearance could be described as looking happy, but here these people stood.

"Dwarven? Ha! I am Melro of the Petty Dwarves! But we have not known ourselves as dwarves for quite some time. Our stature, our being, our pleasantries. No, sir. We are the Gnomes of Dragon's Deep! But quite petty we still can be!"

"What of your people seems so unbecoming you would call yourselves petty?" Grunffi's eyes pinched. The rumbling and tilting of his inner bowels caused him to grip his stomach and sides. The pain began to swell and traveled from the bottom of his stomach to the underbelly of his chest.

Melro kicked a bucket over to Grunffi with a sly and devious smile.

Within moments of conversation, the former dwarven King clung to the bucket as his retching stopped all the clattering of hammers and carrying of stone. Everyone turned to hear the Ogre vomiting and crying out with his voice ringing against the bronze of the bucket. Almost fifteen minutes passed with Grunffi struggling to breathe and reclaim his sight from the tears rushing down his face. Once he finally recovered himself, he turned to face Melro.

"To start, one thing about a petty dwarf, or gnome, as we prefer to be called," Melro said, "you probably shouldn't eat someone else's berries, least of all a gnome's."

Grunffi spat vomit toward Melro, "You've poisoned me!"

"I've taught you manners," Melro laughed. "It seems I'll be teaching you many things this day."

Grunffi finished spitting up his innards, or so it felt, and gripped onto the cavern wall to lift himself from his collapsed stance with a loud grunt and turned toward the Petty Gnome. First, he looked at him with anger and violence, but all the gnome did was look at him and smile.

It was clear Melro didn't feel as though he was in danger, and why would he? He was surrounded by his own people in the depths of a forgotten wasteland, and Grunffi was a lone dwarf.

"I'll be sure to only eat what is offered to me," Grunffi said. "Though it may be some time before I trust a gifted drink in your halls."

First Melro, and then Grunffi in a lighter fare, burst into a jolly laughter.

"You truly know nothing of Ada, nor of Ogres?" Melro asked.

Grunffi's face crinkled with curiosity and engagement as he awaited the gnome's explanation.

"Ada was the wife of Dwarahir," said Melro.

"Was?" the recovering dwarf asked.

Melro cleared his throat and clapped his hands together with an exciting amount of force as a hefty smile hanging from each of his ears slowly showed.

"Yes," Melro said. "They lived happily together in matrimony under the stars of Kaiyara, along with the other Kaiyans. That is, until Dwarahir was cast from the heavens with such a force he crashed into the lands of Kaiya under a magnitude that cracked the earth and he lay buried beneath it. Until then, no such thing as a mine was ever heard of, let alone used for craftsmanship. It was not until the first of us, Dwarahir, was cast down from the night sky."

"And what happened to Ada then? Did she remain?" Grunffi asked, highly interested.

Melro sighed and a horrible weight seemed to be thrust onto his shoulders. "Dwarahir's wife," Melro began, "she fell too. Or rather, she was thrown."

"By whom?"

"It is not known.," Melro said. "There are no writings recounting this. Many believe it was the Bloodlord, Raknar, who corrupted her against the Kaiyan lords' wishes. Others claim it was Krishalla who banished Ada from Kaiyara for resisting the spread of magic to the lands of Kaiya. She foretold war and calamity with help from the prying eyes of Ishmael, Lord of the Dreaming Haunts, who delivered to her the prophecy of destruction. The prophecy that called for the end of all magic"

"She was thrown down from the heavens because she thought magic would bring war to our world?"

"Yes," Melro said. "She was the first voice to resist the magic of Kaiyara. Whether it was Ishmael or Raknar, it is of little relevance. Both were either cast down or imprisoned long ago, so the stories say."

"What of Dwarahir?" Grunffi continued, wanting to know more of his creator.

"He plummeted with her," Melro answered. "Amid the fall, Ada used her magic to make Dwarahir unbreakable. That is why he became so lodged into the earth he created the first mines, here, at Dragon Spine. It is said that Dwarahir, being so hard and rough like no stone of Kaiya, broke the back of Kaiya's largest dragon ever known when he fell—Bancala the Scaled, named for the fierce and unyielding armor made from his supposed remains."

"What were his scales made from?" Grunffi leaned in with a clearly noticeable amount of curiosity.

Melro laughed. "What a good question, Ogre. The answer—adamantite."

"From what we are forged?" Grunffi grew excited and concerned.

"Ah, so you do know some." Melro laughed once more.

"I know some." Grunffi nodded.

"Having only been able to cast the unbreakable magic on Dwarahir, Ada fell to her death, cursing Dwarahir to an immortal life without her.

The lady gnomes say that she did this because the thought of immortality alone was too much for her, so she instead chose to save her lover."

"Where are they now?" Grunffi asked, remembering his wife, thinking over his decision to leave.

"Who? Dwarahir and Ada?" Melro asked.

"Yes," Grunffi said. "Where may I pay my respects to Lady Ada? And where might I find Dwarahir?"

"Dwarahir sits with Ada who is encased in adamantite in a brilliant design of smith work constantly carved by her husband. He dragged the armor of the great and mighty Bancala to the depths of the earth where Ada lay dead to forge weapons from it in the hopes of setting her free. He is wrapped in the stone and forges a terrible and beautiful weapon out the adamantite from the hottest cores of the world. The heat down there surpasses any found in the lava mountains. There is his forge. It is there where he made all dwarves and gnomes in his and Ada's image... so the stories say," Melro smirked.

"Do you believe those stories?" Grunffi asked.

"What is belief? Whispers of something you hope to be true?"

"Do you hope the stories are true?" Grunffi pressed.

"I do not need to hope, Ogre."

"Why do you still call me Ogre? Have I offended you further, beyond the eating of your berries?"

"I call you but the thing that you are," Melro answered. "I would never call an elf a dwarf, as I would never refer to you other than an Ogre."

"But," Grunffi said, "what is it that makes me an Ogre? What separates me from being a dwarf, a petty dwarf, or even a gnome? Save my size."

Melro chuckled. "To think you have lived this long never knowing it, never using it."

"Using what?" Grunffi's impatience grew with such an immensity he tightened the skin of his hands.

"You too," Melro said. "It is not only Dwarahir who became

unbreakable through the fall of Ada. Your skin will change to that of cracked stone, and your movements slightly more stiff, though from what Dwarahir has said, it does little to impede your movement."

"I can turn into stone?" Grunffi looked at his hands as if he'd grown new limbs.

"Ogres can become living stones," Melro said. "Well, I suppose we all, dwarves and gnomes, each of us are living stones. You can just do it better than the lot of us."

"And Dwarahir says this? When? Where?" Grunffi's mind turned frantic.

"Here. Now. Below us, in the depths of the Dragon's Deep, where the fires of Bancala still run hot—Dwarahir's Forge."

"Will Dwarahir speak with me?" Grunffi asked, tensely.

"I would hope so," Melro answered. "It would be quite rude of him not to. He's been waiting for you for quite some time"

Grunffi's face took on a puzzling look. He had so many questions to ask but if he was to meet his god, then he would ask the questions to that god. "Will you take me?"

"Tell me what you want to speak with him for, and perhaps," Melro cackled, lightly.

"I wish to know a great many things, though you have shared a great many with me already, Melro. But, most importantly, I need to know what I was forged for. Am I to truly be a weapon? Was I always cursed to lose that which I loved? If so, there must be a reckoning for any who would consign me to such a fate."

Melro's smile fell to a slight grimace before letting out a long sigh, though it sounded as if the gnome felt relief in the gesture.

"If you were to find Dwarahir responsible for your tragedies, what then?" Melro asked, seriously.

"As I've said, Melro. If it comes to pass that Dwarahir intended for me to suffer thus, if my creation was only as a means for death, then there shall come a reckoning."

"That's what I was hoping you would say," Melro said. "Follow me."

They left after gathering supplies. Grunffi followed Melro for what felt like days down the winding corridors of Dragon's Deep, down toward the core of the underbelly. With each day that passed, Grunffi began to recognize Melro's earlier comments regarding the heat of the core being far beyond that of the lava mountains. After the second day, or what felt like the second day of traveling, Grunffi recounted his moments in Baylar's cavern and the heat he felt then. It was a protrusive and moist heat of vile discomfort. The heat rising from the underbelly of Dragon's Spine was not the same. It was intense, it was fierce and heart-piercing, but it always had a feeling of survivability to accompany it. As he felt the sweat swell inside his legs, his forehead collected a fine shine that could be recognized in the most dimly lit places of the world. Still, Grunffi knew he could survive.

Berries and uncorrupted nectar from the berries, which Grunffi distrusted at first, sustained the two as they made their way down to Dwarahir's Forge. On Grunffi's reckoning of their third day of travel, his skin started peeling under the pressure of the immense heat. He turned to the Petty Gnome once he realized what was happening to him and found his companion perfectly content with the environment. In fact, he took offense once he realized the gnome was still not breaking a sweat.

"What odd adaptation do you gnomes have that protects you from this heat?" Grunffi asked.

Melro broke a short laugh but immediately recalled it. The smile and features receded from the gnome's face after recognizing Grunffi's pain.

"This is for a few reasons, my dear Ogre," Melro chuckled again. "First, we gnomes have called Dragon's Spine and its wasteland our home for many an age. Following the forging of the first dwarves, the gnomes came to be. Thus, we have a certain affinity to the climate. However, as we descend further into the depths of the underbelly, the heat is obviously more concentrated than what you felt in Dwirehall, where we first met. Much like you as an Ogre, Dwarahir imbued the gnomes with the adamantite from Bancala. Being that we were the first of dwarven kind to be made, the heat from Bancala's scales still lives inside of us today. See, we both are made from adamantite. The difference is that I and my people were made from the adamantite of Bancala, before it was ever known as adamantite. You were made from the adamantite still growing from the body of Ada, from whom the stone is named."

"How can Ada have been made of adamantite as well, if it came from Bancala?" Grunffi asked.

"Scales were brought back to the depths of the underbelly for Dwarahir to break Ada from her tomb. In mining this adamantite tomb of sorts, the stories say a song could be heard rising from the greatest depths of the world, weeping for the death of Ada as Dwarihir weeps for her."

"Stone Song," Grunffi whispered.

"Yes. Stone Song allowed Dwarahir to mold the unbreakable adamantite how he wished, which in turn allowed him to create gnomes. However, as I mentioned, he made us from adamantite from Bancala which he pulled from the dragon's body. The line of Ogres was made from the adamantite molded from Ada's tomb through Stone Song. It is said that Ogres possess unbreakable skin because Stone Song created a connection between the stone and Ada. In a way, Ada lives through the line of Ogres."

"So, all of my people were Ogres?" Grunffi asked.

Melro gave another small laugh. "No, friend. A direct lineage between you and your forefathers are the only Ogres who were or will ever be."

"Why did Dwarahir not make more of them? The other dwarves crafted from the same stone as me, how are they different?" Grunffi was learning about his people for the first time, and he felt ashamed for it. *I've known nothing... and was a King.*

"The Song of Dwarahir was said to only have been heard once by Ada. He sings to this day, still trying to commune with her one last time. He chisels away at her adamantite tomb, gathering ever more resources to mold the creation of dwarves and gnomes if he so chooses. Something, some deeper and misunderstood magic brings back more of the stone each time. He is cursed to forever dig at the tomb of his lover. However, at one time, he had some tool, or something that allowed him to craft a different kind of dwarf—an Ogre. In truth, I do not know why he stopped."

"But that stone which he gathers is not the adamantite empowered by her unbreakable magic? Her magic no longer flows through the ever-expanding tomb of adamantite and now Dwarahir refuses to use whatever tool he had to craft Ogres? If the adamantite no longer holds Ada's magic, it is likely that even with the tool he would still not be able to make more Ogres."

"Now you understand," said Melro. "Come, we have another day of travel yet."

The conversation distracted Grunffi from the overwhelming heat for a short while, but he was immediately reminded of the treacherous dryness climbing up and down his limbs as they proceeded further into the bowels of Dragon's Deep. Sweat ran like a pouring drain emptying its reservoir onto his clothing at a constant and excruciating rate. Grunffi attempted to cough but only a dry puff escaped his lungs as he desperately reached for the berry juice. After three days and immeasurable heat, a moment of recognition glossed over the dwarf as he recognized the juice maintained its temperature. It was neither too cold to give shock amid the unhinged levels of heat, nor was it boiling from the ruthless air.

"How is this berry juice unaffected by the heat?" Gunffi asked.

"Evolution is a pretty thing," the gnome answered. "We are here."

Grunffi and Melro both stopped, looking upon a slab of stone larger than any Gruffi had seen before. The slab covered the entirety of the cavern, from floor to ceiling. Its vast scale quickly became immeasurable once it surpassed their line of vision and Grunffi, for only a short moment, thought they'd reached a dead end.

In that moment of reconsideration, Grunffi heard a deep rumbling gather in Melro's throat. At first, the sound raised like a grand horn in the night, bringing awareness to those who might be taken advantage of in their sleep. The hollow fullness of his voice carried the sense of safety one would feel behind the lines of many practiced warriors ready to bring revolution down on the world.

Words were not spoken, and sounds were barely discernible, but the veracity and bellowing nature of the Petty Gnome's voice rang through the cavern like a magic of its own in a way which Grunffi had never experienced in all his years of hearing Stone Song. In fact, the former King could no longer recognize what his people used to craft adamantite as Stone Song, not in comparison to the pounding beauty and harmonious tremors exploding from Melro.

As the gigantic slab of adamantite blocking the entrance to Dwarahir's Forge opened, a fierce ray of light, as red as the sun, broke through the tiniest crevice and blasted Grunffi's eyes with a pulsating heat. The dwarf winced backward and cupped both of his hands trying to regain sight. As he continuously tried to blink, he could only shut the eye which was not stricken by the light.

"Melro, what has happened to my eye?"

The dwarf removed his cupped hands for his gnome companion to examine, and out of his working eye, Grunffi watched a sly smile grow onto the Petty Gnome's face once more.

"So, it is true then. The fires of Dwarahir call for the Ogre within."

Melro gazed upon his friend with awe, studying a scarlet orange that seemed to breathe within Grunffi's eye. Where the dwarf once had white, he now had the light of the sun with roots of black shooting from the pupil to the outermost regions of his eye. There was a darkness in tune with the heroic light simultaneously molding together. The soft whiteness of his left eye had now been hardened into an unmovable stone. Even the skin of his eyelids grew callous and dense like a cracked quarry. But he could still see.

"What do you see now?" Melro's curiosity piqued as though he'd been waiting for this moment for quite some time.

"Heat," Grunffi answered. "I see the traveling heat. I see a large white structure moving from place to place, smashing downward onto some structure that radiates a lighter form of that same whiteness. I see blackness surrounding the flames and the pits of lava spouting from beyond this door. Under the blanket of darkness, I see the glowing fires of warmth in all things."

"This is but a taste of the magic that is owed to you," Melro said.

Owed to me?

Perhaps Grunffi was owed something for the tragedies placed upon him. Was Dwarahir the cause of this tragedy or was he something else entirely? All the dwarf knew was he needed to speak to the dwarven god, and he needed to understand the purpose of his pain.

"Will I survive the heat of the forge?" Grunffi asked.

"No," he answered. "You will evolve."

Chapter Fifteen

The Lost Garden

"Legends say the great dragon lay here—Dagora's Veil—the fields now surrounding Runefall. Those legends tell of the great dragon living on two plains. I will bring forth the beast and bring back the Talon of the Titans to end the false eternity of all gods—starting with Salaril."
— Harigamun, *Thoughts of War*

Varus awoke to find himself surrounded by unfamiliar flowers and plants with a color palette that spoke a boldness louder than the sight of any rainbow. He recalled dark and dreary nights tucked into the sewers of Nightfall, hiding from the authorities in the damp cold of the city's underbelly. As he gazed at the open fields surrounding him, he realized he was in the antithesis of where he and Varelia had lived those past ten years. This vibrant garden housed flora stretching from one end of the breaking horizon to the next under a breeze which felt like a lover's hair brushing across him after a kiss.

"Not to be petulant," a wry voice said, "but I don't know whether you're supposed to be here."

"Petulant or not, it'd be hard for me to disagree with you," Varus said before realizing he was speaking with his hands, the hands of his old body. "H-ha-have I died th-then? Is this where the souls of Kaiya go after their death?" His chittering returned; his heart rate rose. Sweat poured. "I can't leave yet!"

"Souls and death," the wry voice said once more, emerging from beyond the flora. "Big words for such a small place."

Varus looked at the man who was quite small in stature. His hair seemed almost black but held the shine of thickness in the right light glaring a burnt chestnut color. His eyes showed small to him, but they matched the spring sage of the surrounding weeds with stripes of white flickering through them, almost like dandelions parading in the very field they stood in. His skin was soft and unaged, but the way he spoke seemed to carry a learned wisdom. He was a child.

"Your t-t--tongue tells me you're certainly no child," Varus said, "but it s-seems your shape would tell me something entirely different. Tell me, young sir, if you please," Varus said with an almost mocking level of courtesy. "Who might you be, and what have I gotten myself into?" *Calm yourself, dammit. Ibna needs you. Breathe.*

"For the mad man who relentlessly pursued the summoning of a golem—even after the loss of your wife—after the loss of your home, and the loss of your freedom; do you now fear what you've stumbled upon?" the boy asked.

"Fear and madness," Varus smirked. "Big words for such a small man..."

"Point taken," the boy said, returning the smirk. He crossed his arms. "I am Roki, Reaper of the Lost Garden."

"Roki the Reaper?" Varus asked. "Perhaps I should be afraid."

Roki's grimace broke and relaxation dripped from his face. "I do not reap souls, Varus. I gather the remnants of those who were summoned and repurpose them."

"To what purpose?"

"To *the* purpose. The purpose of life. What else?"

"And what is the purpose of life?" Varus asked.

"To be needed," Roki answered. "In some rare moments, a portion of those whom I find here in the garden may be called back to serve a former, or new, master. In most cases, they are lost, abandoned, and often unfitting for this realm."

"What realm? The Garden?"

"Yes, Varus," Roki said, unbothered. "The Lost Garden is a harbor for tranquility and beauty. It is a place in which life can flourish without conflict."

"How do the creatures who find themselves in the garden find it hard to fit in with such a place?"

Roki breathed deeply and cast a shadowy glance toward the horizon, revealing a previously unseen temple.

"Most creatures who find themselves in the Garden were summoned for a particular purpose," Roki said, hanging his head low.

"War," Varus answered.

"Yes," said the Reaper. "It's a pitiful thing how rarely something is summoned for love."

"How do you help these creatures find their purpose once they arrive, and what if they should choose to return?" Varus asked.

"You are worried about your friend," Roki said. "Groff is also my friend, and he has certainly supplied the garden with many hands."

"What do you mean?" Varus became worried instantly. Had Groff killed other creatures who were summoned and banished to the garden, or was Roki speaking of something else? Thinking on it, Varus considered it highly unlikely that, with all the time Groff had lived, there wasn't a single other summoned creature he might have harmed.

"I'm sure you've been wondering where all of the other champions housed within Groff had gone," Roki grinned. "You've been living in his mind for some time now, and you've heard no other voices in there, other than your own and his."

Varus's eyes shot open at the revelation. "The champions within Groff suffer the same fate as any other summoning. We will go to the Lost Garden?"

"Is it really such a punishment?" Roki asked.

"Whether it is a punishment or not is irrelevant to the timing. Should Groff be able to return, will I also be able to return with him? Where is the golem?"

"You misunderstand, Varus," Roki said. "Groff has already returned, he is with your daughter, and he no longer holds the memories of who he once was in his prior time. He is simply a beast at the behest of a girl. Your girl."

"Why should he be allowed to return but I could not?" Varus ground his teeth. "You know me, my pain, my life, my daughter! You know so much of me, so why would you hold me back from helping my Ibna?"

"Purpose," Roki answered.

"What purpose would I serve the Garden, or you?" Varus's breathing became violent and fell out of tempo with the rest of his body. His squeezing fist and the veins of his arms rose to the edge of his skin and frightened the Reaper, though the boy did little to show his shock.

"I can teach you, you know," Roki said, reaching out to place his hand on Varus's shoulder as he approached with caution. "I could teach you, so you never fail a summons again."

Varus flinched backward away from Roki's hand and the ill-tempered father shifted into a tight stance. The blood in his face rose with a ferocious boiling and Roki sensed the man was about to jump on him. Varus didn't have time to learn, he needed to get back to his daughter. *I'll find you, Ibna. No god nor reaper is stopping me!*

"Wait!" Roki said, holding both of his hands out in front of him. "You have learned the ways to treat a summons from The Shackled Maiden. The champions here with us in the garden are long past their years of combat or knowledge, whereas you've communed with the goddess herself."

"And? How does this mean I should be kept from my daughter?"

"Because if you choose not to help me, then there won't be a world for you to go back to, and your daughter along with Groff and the rest of Kaiya, will likely fall to the hands of Salaril." Roki's eyes slimmed, focusing on Varus. His demeanor, his stance, his tone changed in an instant. Roki was serious. Would the world really end? Was Varus even in the world anymore? Would this garden also fall?

"What has the rune god to do with any of this?" Varus asked.

Roki's eyes fell and his breath drifted as his unmoving features looked toward the solitary temple to the Eastern reaches of the garden. As Roki's slow air escaped his lungs, a dreary plain of desolation seemed to consume the glory of the garden near the temple, slowly consuming it inch-by-inch with a hateful blackness.

"What is happening here?" Varus asked with a withered gasp.

"A trick," Roki answered. "A dastardly and great trick bending the will of Kaiya back onto itself."

"What do you mean?" Roki's eyes flickered with wet shimmers as if there were a tear to be shaken. "Come with me."

Reluctantly, Varus followed the young protector of the garden hoping to receive further answers on why he'd been forced to stay, but also on what Roki had referred to by the "great trick". Who had the power to trick Kaiya to fall back onto itself, and what did that mean? Would he be able to get back to his daughter in time, and was Varelia safe with a version of Groff who'd lost track of who he was, or who his memories made him?

Then, Varus's thoughts went completely tangential and sent him spiraling into a depressed state. Did Varelia and himself know Groff, or was Groff someone else without his memories? If he was different, would that mean the only thing making anyone who they are is simply the experiences they've made, or is there a more natural occurrence to a creature's behavior? *Something innate and ineffable, perhaps?*

The thought of Groff becoming a rage-driven golem hell bent on servitude frightened Varus, not only for the safety of his daughter, but of what conjuring an anger might do to change her. However, if Groff's changing due to his memories being lost could influence Varelia, then perhaps it was only experience that made someone who they were. Could neither be true, or could both be true?

"Varus!" Roki yelled, pulling Varus out of his stupor. "Meet Toak."

"That'll be General Toak to you," the creature said with a long and drowned voice.

Toak was a hor—no he was a—, Varus's thoughts were interrupted.

"Yes, I imagine it is quite hard for you to discern my being," Toak said. "Would you like to try?"

Varus studied the creature in front of him. It spoke with an aged reverence and command only fitting to one of militaristic stature, but his body was something only found to oral legends and supposed lost texts.

"No," Varus said. "This cannot be. You were a children's story, a fable."

"As a man with the lower-body of a steed, the chest of a—"

"A bear," Varus said. "Or an ox. Some great unfathomable strength of the forest lay upon your chest."

Varus looked at Toak's waving hands and noticed his fingernails outstretched as protruding talons, clearly capable of ripping flesh without effort. "How does a being like you come to be?"

"You've already said it yourself, Master Varus," Toak said. "I was the story you told your children."

What could he mean?

Varus recounted the many tales he'd told his daughter of Toak. The Forest's General, leader of the Woodland Army, Protector Among the Trees; the Centaurian commanded the military prowess of the forest and kept the woods safe from the evil blood rogues and nomads. He kept the creatures of the forest safe from intruders looking to tear down their homes. He was a fable to teach children, to take care of the wildlife and the forests, and to care for the world around them.

"You're saying we made you by telling stories of your kind?" Varus prodded.

Toak laughed with a hearty and bellow drumming of his jaw. "If it were so simple to create something such as myself, I think Kaiya and even the Kaiyan gods themselves would have bigger issues at hand than controlling the use of magic."

"Then how?" Varus became eager and displeased simultaneously trying to understand Toak's existence.

"There is a matter of storytelling of which you do not know, and sadly, we do not have the time," Toak answered. "In due time. For now, I would like you to join me and the remaining Thorns as we march on the Stained Cathedral."

Varus continued finding himself confused more with each word Toak spoke. "Thorns? Stained Cathedral?"

Varus understood himself reverting to the frustrations he felt back in the sewer, when he'd failed to give true life to that golem which felt so long ago. His strong back bent forward as his neck cracked from one side and then the other; a shaking of his jaw seemed to be gnawing at itself and his anger spilled over like a boiling stew.

"GET ME BACK TO MY IBNA!" Varus descended into a slew of low-volume rambles and chittering, oddly close to his emotional state when he broke the table in the sewers trying to get his quill back. "I can't—stupid gods and damned—hmph. WHY ME?"

"He truly is a mad man," Toak said to Roki.

"His madness is all that can connect you," Roki said. "It is his madness and immeasurable love for his daughter which will drive him to the ends of Kaiya to reclaim her. It is madness that led him to the Shackled Maiden. It is within the instability of madness where our only chance lies. No other has bonded with a summoning in the way he has for a very long time, and you need his vessel!"

"I'll show you the meaning of madness." Varus leaped from his hunched position, flying toward Roki with a right hook ready to break open the reaper's skull. However, he found himself phasing through Roki's body and crashing into the dirt.

"I am not here," Roki said. "I am in the temple, trapped by Salaril... with Salaril."

"I don't understand," Varus said, rising from the ground.

"That much is clear," Toak said. "The Thorns are the garden's army, those loyal to Roki and the life he seeks to protect. I am their General. Together, as Champion and Summoning, you will join with me as you did Groff, and we will break down the barriers of the temple and kill the god before he is set free."

"Why must I join you?" Varus asked.

"Salaril's runes prevent a summoned creature from breaching its gates. However, whilst we are one, my body will recognize you as the one in control, not me."

Now it all made sense to Varus. "You need me to get in."

"And you need me to fight," Toak said.

"And you need me to get back to your Ibna," Roki said.

"Very well then," Varus said with an unpleasant disposition. "Gather your Thorns, General."

And pray I don't need to burn down your garden to get to my Ibna.

Toak and Varus headed toward the western provinces of the Garden. Varus studied the beast beside him for so long, but didn't realize he was staring at the Commander of the Forests. Toak noticed but didn't care enough to show it.

Toak's existence and the surprise dealt to those who would meet him was not lost on the General. He knew he was a child's story, something to give children hope for a bright and joyous future for the forests and the woodland creatures within. He also knew there was a sunny disposition associated with his character which Toak did not possess in actuality. In fact, Toak found it rather difficult to maintain any amount of cheer. The weight of his being was a crushing experience.

If only they knew what creation meant.

"How was Roki captured?" Varus asked as the two of them broke over a hill revealing an enormous structure carved into the ground. "Where are we?"

Toak laughed. "Which should I answer first?"

"Roki," Varus answered. "But I certainly must know what this place is."

"A battle," Toak said.

"A battle with Salaril?" Varus asked.

Toak nodded his head in agreement.

"How did Roki end up fighting Salaril? Did he receive no help?"

Gazing to the bustling town below them, silver archways and fetterings of fauna sprawled across cobblestone paths. There were no markets, and fewer houses. It was a home for the glorious creatures living there. Some emerged from small holes in the ground, others left the comfort of their caverns, and some many golems stood looking out into the horizon.

The creatures were still so far away Varus couldn't make out what he was looking at, but he knew one thing for certain: he was looking at creatures thought lost to time many ages ago.

"Roki serves the Temple of Beliria—" Toak was interrupted.

"The Stained Temple, you called it?"

"Yes," Toak said. "Salaril has stained the once great Temple of Beliria, otherwise known as the House of Summons. When a creature summoned for the bidding of others passed, they were reborn there, in the House of Summons. Roki made sure that each of them were tended for, no matter how great and terrible the beast, and the temple always remained standing."

"Why did Salaril attack?" Varus asked

Toak let out a long drag of breath, showing a slight level of either irritation of sadness, Varus could not tell. "He did not attack. He escaped."

"Salaril was held prisoner in the Temple of Beliria?"

"Yes," Toak said. "But more on that later. For now, I welcome you to the Court of Flowers."

The two of them continued walking and amid the conversation, Varus lost track of his immediate surroundings through his fixation on Toak. The glory of the garden became immense and immediately understood. The scent of eucalyptus and the taste of earth sweetened by the pleasantries of the Court slid across Varus's tongue as a deep, cold, and refreshing breeze rushed down his throat into the core of his stomach. The cobblestone streets shimmered with the silver linings from above, seeming like pearls woven into a walking path.

Overhead, a monstrous beast with fearsome scales thrashed about its large wings, and Varus knew he was staring at a dragon from the lost stories. The beast's claws on all four of its limbs showed a terrifying grip as the serpent grabbed ahold of the top of a nearby mountain and debris fell from it. As the beast caught its footing, a larger wyvern rose from behind the mountain with a menacing and piercing scream.

"How did I not hear these great beasts until now?"

"Roki protects the Court of Flowers even still. You cannot see nor enter the Court unless brought in by one who knows of its being. All else is hidden until one is truly welcome."

Varus hid his blushing and the warmth he felt for being welcomed so quickly. Toak knew almost nothing of him, and he'd only just met Roki. But the Reaper did seem to know a lot about Varus and his daughter, so maybe they knew him better than he thought.

Varus watched as golems, Draguars, fire drakes, and a plethora of other beasts he could not name, claimed the Court of Flowers as their home—men too, dwarves and such, champions of old.

"Will they all help us?" Varus asked.

"Of course," Toak answered Varus. "This is our home."

"Why does Salaril want to take it from you? What has Roki done to anger the rune god?"

"What has anyone done to anger these so-called gods?" Toak's anger swelled. "It was not Roki's decision to imprison the bastard in the temple. That damned Baylar offered him the safety of the Stained Temple, under the protection of the Lost Garden. From here, none can hear him, none can see him. He would have been removed. The two damnable gods plotted with one another. Salaril helped Baylar escape, gods know where, and Baylar gave him access to the hidden depths of the temple. Baylar could not hide himself there because the other Kaiyan's would come looking as the garden was made by his wife Beliria. But once Baylar was in hiding, and he could no longer have access to the Garden, well Salaril couldn't let an entire realm of great beasts go to waste now, could he?"

"Baylar enslaved all of the beasts in the Lost Garden? How?" Varus continued his line of questions, wrapped up in the entirely new realm.

Varus looked around the Court of Flowers recounting the myriad wild beasts he couldn't even describe. Horns, claws, and beauty untold in the flashing eyes of some and fearsome debilitating stares from others. Fur, scales, flesh, and clay molded some while bone, hair, and what seemed to be organs externalized made the bodies of more. Great winged beasts from old songs and tales, such as dragons and wyverns, littered the air. Gargantuan birds mirroring the monstrous lost hawks from the East crossed paths with slender serpents which possessed no great limbs, only feathered appendages carrying a colossal and majestic reptile. Mixes of different hybrid beasts, much like Toak, wandered the courtyard with the lower body of many strong, four-legged beasts with the upper bodies of fighting creatures.

Toak saw Varus studying the many hybrid creatures and laughed as he caught the man darting his eyes back and forth, between Toak and the other creatures he was trying to understand.

"We are all the same, yet different," Toak said. "Some creatures you see are from fables. Oddly constructed creatures of childish nights. Others belonged to your world. And yes, for a time, Salaril did bend the creatures of this world to his will."

"How?" Varus's curiosity was ever-expanding in that moment. He knew Toak had to be getting sick of his questions, but this world, the events surrounding him, it was all too grand.

"I imagine that 'how' is referencing many things in this moment; however, I'll try to stick to the thing relevant to us now. Salaril claimed the minds of each of the beasts you see here, and many more, by conquering the greatest one."

"One of the dragons?" Varus asked with a pain in his chest, fearing what a dragon turned to evil bidding might be capable of.

"Ha!" Toak laughed. "Never has it been so clear how much the world has lost from its story. No, Varus. Salaril did not conquer a simple dragon." The centaur pointed toward the Stained Temple. "There, not only will we find Salaril encased, but also the Titan which he conquered."

"Titan?" Varus recalled no stories of Titans.

"Titans were the first beasts ever created and bent to the voice of Baylar. They are beyond the scale of any normal woodland creature, and each of them so unique in appearance and abilities there is little more description that can be used for them."

Varus squirmed for a moment, recognizing not only there were beasts lost to an age now walking and flying around him that could take his life with ease, but something far more terrifying being controlled by a god.

"Do we know which of the Titans he captured? Do we know how to beat it?"

"Beat it?" Toak asked, intentionally showing his frustration at the suggestion. "We will not 'beat' Dagora... we will free him."

Varus fell back into himself for a moment beneath the immobilizing shadow of General Toak. He'd suggested attacking a friend of the General's without knowing it. There was a deeper relationship he did not consider in his desire to return to Varelia.

"I'm sorry," Varus said. "I did not realize. Tell me, can you describe Dagora to me? How might we set him free?"

Toak gathered his anger and brought calm to himself with a long breath as two rather unique centaur hybrids, which seemed to be a mix of bull and ape, walked past the general.

"We set him free the same way each of us are set free," one of the centaurs said. "Death."

Toak turned to the two hybrids and cast a look of doubt, which he quickly dispelled with a grin, as he noticed the coy smile hanging from their furry lips.

"Death indeed will free Dagora," Toak said. "The death of Salaril. However, it will be up to us to break the seal carved into Dagora's head, severing his connection to the other beasts of the Garden. Before the seal is broken, Dagora will likely take many lives at the behest of Salaril before we free him, and I do not envy the shame Dagora will carry the rest of his days once he must come to terms with the actions of his body. Just as I will have to come to terms with how I must break such a barrier."

"How will you break it?" Varus asked with a nervous and shaking disposition, staring at the two menacing centaurs winking at him.

"The God Quill," Toak answered, looking toward the Stained Temple.

"What?" Varus asked.

"An item," Toak began. "A quill, really. It would appear much like a long-headed scythe with a feathered handle, standing taller than most men. The blade is straight, unlike the bent scythes used by Raknar's Nomads. The Titans are carved from Kaiya itself; their skin is stone and dirt, their hearts are the hot irons beneath the surface, their limbs grander and more hearty in stature than Grand Pines. The God Quill is the only item known to carve runes into Titans. Its origin and creator are unknown, but Baylar took it long ago for his own use and captured Dagora and other Titans with its power. With it, I can break the runes carved into Dagora by Salaril and set him free."

"Where is this God Quill?" Varus asked, stiffening his back and puffing out his chest with a tight-lipped face, staring at the hybrids as he tried to show confidence.

"The God Quill sleeps with Salaril," Toak answered. "Once the barrier is broken, he will awaken Dagora. We must survive Dagora if we are to kill Salaril."

"When do we march on the Stained Temple?" Varus asked, walking toward Toak, and stomping his feet onto the cobblestone walkway.

"They won't touch you," Toak said. "And they won't hurt you, so please stop." The two Centaurians burst into laughter.

Varus, in his constant measuring of the two hybrids toying with him over the past few moments, had failed to realize the gathering army of beasts surrounding him.

"This is going to hurt," Toak said.

Before Varus could ask what would hurt, Toak lifted him high into the air and brought the madman crashing down onto the General's knee, shattering his neck and spine in one fatal swoop, killing him.

A light humming fell upon the air and the brushing of flowers on top of one another as the scent of a thousand gardens crashed into one magnificent breath, as if words were whispering from a far-off mountain bringing down the scent of rain and hearth. Toak's eyes closed for a moment, only a short moment, before reopening. Suddenly, the General's body convulsed into an exasperated attempt to reclaim a lost life and Varus started speaking through General Toak's mouth.

"You killed me!" Varus yelled.

"Roki has brought you back," Toak replied, pointing the centaur's eyes forward as a fading body of Roki sat in the air... smiling.

"How many times must I die and be placed into another's body?"

"As many as it takes," said Roki. "Now, Toak. He will soon awaken."

Varus stood watching as Toak commanded a fearsome horde of creatures, both known and unknown to the people of Kaiya. The winged-beasts perched along the glittering floral mountaintops of the Lost Garden as monstrous horned-beasts and hybrid centaurs marched alongside a select few humans, dwarves and elves, which Varus took to be previous Champions of Groff and possibly others, though he did not have time to learn. The sounds accompanying the rallying of the ragtag band of mythological and lost creatures echoed the cries of a dark poetry seeking to strip comfort from hearts and replace peace with calamity. Varus thought if he were to ever hear the impending march of the army and its screeching cries from the skies, he might very well freeze at that place in time, terrified to utter even the smallest breath. However, he was on the side of this army, and he resided within its General. Varus and Toak marched with the ferocity of an impending lost age against a beast forgotten to legend, and now Varus found himself fearing what a Titan might truly be if it required such a host to contend with.

"Can we win?" Varus asked, being sure not to express his caution to the surrounding horde.

"If we do not," Toak said with a long pause, leaving him awaiting an answer in the dark recesses of Toad's memories. "Then all will be lost."

"You've had a long life," Varus said.

"Not one quite so long as the story that is still to be told," Toak added. "I'd caution rummaging around in the crypts of my memory. In some you'd find truth, in others you'd find stories. In all, you'd find fear."

Varus refocused his attention to the marching horde and fixed his gaze toward the Stained Temple, which now had a growing blackness with a light, and bright dim purple haze breaking through the clouds. A rumbling and thunderous clapping grew with each step as they approached.

The flowering plants and shrubs brimmed nearly as high as the clouds, as the vegetation rolled upward, heading toward the hill the Stained Temple sat atop. Trees with berry brussels fed into the makings of a forest which shot off on either side of the hill, surrounding the temple with Grand Pines reaching for the deepest depths of the heavens. Red cedar, pine oak, then the eucalyptus came back to smack Toak and Varus's nostrils with berry hints and lingering lemon balm. The smells swelled into new concoctions of immeasurable quality and the horde marched with a gallant pride, many of the creatures sweeping their limbs to touch the magnificence of the garden.

Climbing the hill to the Stained Temple's courtyard, the garden shook with unmistakable violence. An earth-shattering tremor broke from the opening's threshold leading all the way down to the army. It was a small crack, a surface warning, and a telling sign of what was coming, but it created little more than a crack in a wall. However, its effect brought many of the horde to a feeble and striking halt.

Roki's whispers surrounded Varus and Toak though he could not be seen. "You won't have long. Salaril's tomb is in the middle of the cathedral hall as soon as you enter. It's a wide structure with him placed dead in the center. The tomb is the only thing keeping him locked to the garden, which means he will be able to run if he chooses. We need to kill him before he can run back to Runefall,"

"How do we break the tomb?" Varus asked.

"Once inside the temple, you won't have to. Toak has the strength necessary to lift the top slab of adamantite off the crypt. You will merely need to take the God Quill from his hands before his strength recovers and kill him," Roki explained.

"Seems easy enough," Varus said.

"Well," Toak sighed "Once the barrier of the tomb is broken and Salaril can grab hold of the God Quill, Dagora will immediately awaken and raze the temple to ashes."

"The Titan sleeps below the Stained Temple?" Varus asked with a gulping sound in his throat.

"Besides," Toak answered. "But close enough. He will destroy any structure standing in between him and... his master."

"And should Salaril escape?" Varus asked.

Neither Roki nor Toak answered. Toak simply lowered his head, stiffened his shoulders, and leaned pressure onto his hind legs readying to take off toward the temple. "We're out of time, Varus! Take control of the body and lead us into the temple!"

He felt a force against Toak's body vanish in an instant. There was a weight the General held over his physiological self which surpassed the physical will of Groff. Varus didn't know there was a contention between champion and the physical body of the host until he felt the complete control given to him by Toak. The body was fully surrendered at will, something Groff had never done. *What reason could Groff have for not giving me the freedom of physical form?* Could it be that Groff was too concerned with the power of the host body being given to Varus, or was it a problem of trust? Perhaps Toak simply had no other choice, thus forcing himself into giving Varus autonomy over his body.

How odd it must feel. Absolute physical surrender within the prison of your own being.

"It is an uncomfortable thing," Toak said, causing Varus to remember it was not just the body that was shared between them.

Varus launched Toak's body forward, hurtling toward the gates of the Stained Temple at a speed never felt by men. Hundreds of yards were closed within seconds and with only a short distance to go, Toak whispered, "I go into darkness, the mind also belongs to you."

Silence covered Varus's thoughts as his mind bridged a connection with the physicality of Toak and Varus's thoughts became his own for the first time since his initial death. A wash of euphoria and liveliness stretched out into each of the Forest General's former limbs; all four hooved-legs and his two thick, hairy arms.

Varus recalled the feeling of his own body and counted it immeasurable to the experience of driving the ferocious vehicle of what he now controlled. There was strength and power and a desire to cause wanton mayhem for the recent pains brought down onto him. He held complete physical prowess to a level unknown to his world, and likely, Varus thought, to any other creature or race in Kaiya. He knew this strength was the most dangerous thing he'd ever encountered, and it made him want to become the worst threat ever encountered in order to get back to Varelia.

In a final leap, Varus launched through the air and brought all four of his legs down onto the thick oaken door shielding the Stained Chapel's threshold. Each hoof connected simultaneously, and Varus kicked, sending himself flipping backward, splintering the wooden door. Varus landed on Toak's feet and saw a chapel room with a cylinder container to the far back with a large tomb at its center. Without pause, he bolted inward and brought his gnarled fist crashing down onto the adamantite stone slab, amazed to see it shatter under his thrashing. The rabble flew into the air and time seemed to slow as Varus realized the tomb was empty.

"He's gone," Varus said. "And I see no quill."

He turned to the cylindrical container behind him and wondered if that's where Roki was being held. Roki could help him find Salaril. At once, the centaur bashed into the container with his skull in an outrage, screaming, "Where is he, Roki?"

Blood dripped from the remnants of horns ripped from the centaur's head long ago and mixed with the water leaking from the damaged container. Varus grabbed hold of the small break in the cylinder's metal with both hands and ripped it apart, slowly tearing it, and his skin, further bloodying the growing pool of water beneath his feet.

"Roki! Are you in there?" Varus shouted.

"He never was," Toak answered, surprising Varus by retaking control over his body.

"Where is he then?"

"Here," Toak answered, pointing toward the floor's open room within the chapel and the battered tomb at its center.

"What do you mean?" Varus became frustrated with the lack of answers. There was no Salaril, no Roki.

Why did we come here?

"Roki is the Lost Garden, Varus," Toak answered. "His soul manifests to speak to those of us who dwell in the garden, but only when he is needed."

"Then why was it said he was being held captive inside the Stained Temple?"

"Because Salaril's very being in the Lost Garden is imprisonment for Roki," Toak said. "Salaril's dominion over the Titan has assured segregation of the garden from all the realms of Kaiya. We are alone so long as that beast, and Roki, remain captive to him."

"Has Roki ever been real?" Varus asked with a glint of shine in his eyes, signifying a disappointment Toak did not expect.

Toak hung his centaur head low. "Roki is seen as a child because he was a child himself when he was summoned. He was the first creature to ever be summoned, which makes him the most powerful, wise, and patient of all who reside in the Garden."

"If he is more powerful than you, then why were it up to us to fight Salaril?" Frustration welled in his eyes as the glint faded.

"Because more than he is the most powerful, as I said; he is the most wise, and patient."

Clearly Roki knew something neither Varus nor Toak did. At least, that's what Varus immediately convinced himself of. How else could the most powerful being in all the garden be reliant on a summoner who couldn't manage to give life to a basic golem and a centaur?

"Your thoughts are not your own Varus. Doubt yourself if you must, but do not doubt me."

"Sorry," Varus said. "I just don't understand what's happening. Where is Salaril then? What must we d—"

The temple became flooded with convulsions and a quaking of the earth split the temple down its middle in the shape of a small hairline fracture. The immense shaking of the ground grew exponentially within seconds and the structure started to crumble with Toak and Varus inside. Dodging the rubble, the centaur managed to evade each fatal blow with his incredible speed and agility in such a way Varus couldn't keep up with. He lost sight in a dazed dance of survival as Toak reclaimed the entirety of the body, leaving Varus a bystander to watch as Toak drove their escape.

As they ran, of body and two minds, they stared at the falling temple admiring the numerous stained windows and unique painting of its marble architecture as each part broke away. It shone like daybreak across a bleak night with a harsh hue of scarlet embedded into its rocky foundations. In moments, a masterpiece of architecture, built long before either Toak or Varus could breathe, vanished from existence, as if it were for nothing as far as Varus was concerned.

"Why the vat of water?"

"I don't know if it was water," Toak said. "Whatever it is, I imagine it was built by Roki long ago to sustain Dagora in his sleep."

"Have I destroyed what kept Dagora alive?"

The ground beside the fallen temple split open as if a mountain had sprung from the depths of the earth.

"I think Dagora is doing just fine," said Toak.

"Groff is back. He is better, but I miss Baba. I hope I don't need to hurt anyone to find him ... but I will if I must."

— Varelia, *A Mad Journal*

CHAPTER SIXTEEN

BREAKING THE SEAL

"Titans, war dogs against relentless gods, they were the last force used against a race of defiant beings bold enough to claim themselves divine. Tonight, I will call upon the dogs of war, my Divine Hounds."
— Harigamun, *Thoughts of War*

SeaHorses—the steeds of the Agualytes—drove the carriage of a war wagon down the disproportionate slopes of the battlefield surrounding Runefall with the Warlord's army gathering just beyond the city's front gate.

Kyra, Samiel, and Arimeus sat in the carriage as a blinding darkness swept over the battlefield and the howls of war stopped. Kyra leaped from her seat in the wagon, still unsure of her position in this war, finding the Lord of the Dreaming Haunts enveloping the sky in his unique form of sanguine and emerald darkness. Ominous laughter with a deep ring of Ishmael's voice blotted the ears of everyone on the battlefield and within the city. The laughter grew to a hearty bellow of mockery as fear gripped the minds of everyone who could hear, including Harigamun.

"Whilst you toil away with your primitive weapons of war, you stand to create a field of bones," Ishmael said, still cackling. "But what of the bones that are already here? For here, there be dragons... and those who lay with them!" The Lord of the Dreaming Haunts faded away as his laughter diminished.

"No," Arimeus said, leaping from the war wagon. "I must reach Varin!"

"Varin?" Kyra asked. "Why? What is happening?"

"Dremhirra," he answered. "Many do not know, in fact, most don't. Runefall was relocated to this particular field long ago at the behest of Salaril. He said it was to protect the world from Dremhirra's return. He is a titan of old, one I do not have the time to explain. But if he comes back... "

"Where is Varin?" Samiel asked.

"Likely near Harigamun," Arimeus answered. "Come with me!"

The three of them darted off toward the center gathering around Harigamun. They found the Warlord encircled by his generals.

All at once, Harigamun commanded each of his generals, save Varin, to their knees. Surrounding troops hoping to take positions of leadership themselves acted on the command. Harigamun's sights set on Whaleback while the other commanders sat on their knees watching. The Warlord took small and slow steps toward the Agualyte general, knowingly crushing Whaleback's spirit with each brush in the general's direction.

Whaleback screamed in excruciating pain as Harigamun bore down into his eyes with malice and fire, fire which spat from the Warlord's own gaze, and burrowed into the bloated man's skull. The Warlord let loose a plug of spittle in the Agualyte's face and placed fingers in both of his eye sockets as he cried for aid. The Warlord released a horrid laughter, terrifying all close enough to hear as his fingers grew hotter. Whaleback's trembling squalls broke the hearts of his surrounding soldiers as the flame of Harigamun seeped into his body, burning his insides as his eyes melted. The smell of the obese man burning rotted the nostrils of many as the Warlord threw him onto the ground, still steaming.

"Go on then," the Warlord yelled across the battlefield. "Who else would turn on me, such as Whaleback? You think I do not know the oppressed will have their day? Do you think I did not know I was on borrowed time? People do not want to unite! People do not want to fight! We want to live in strife and famine to justify our daily war and allow the aging process to take its toll. It is easier to hide behind the small problems of the day rather than face the threat of a generation. Nay! Of an age! I have no desire to hold the title of your *Warlord*, of King, or of any other lordly title. I mean to put an end to the taking of children from their families, an end to the abusive systems of magic! Help me save this land, our children, our livelihood, and separate ourselves from these childish gods! Help me do this and I will relinquish all power that has been taken on my behalf!"

The crowd of soldiers stood silent. The fiery hail of destruction collapsing the city of Runefall had long stopped since the advancement of the Lanis troop failed. A quiet befell the field of war and each soldier mulled over the words still ringing in their ears.

Can the Warlord be trusted? Will he relinquish the power? Who else will he turn on to meet his ends? More importantly, who would assume the mantle to challenge him? The army could turn on him, but who would make the decision? *Who is brave enough?* And even if someone could be brave, was that what was needed? Each soldier experienced conflicting emotions and questioning moments watching their generals in bondage while Whaleback was mutilated at the hands of a Warlord. While none spoke, it became clear the lack of action signaled agreement. They would follow the Warlord to the end, and hopefully the end would be soon.

Harigamun's sharp gaze swung toward Varin. "You, I trust. You understand. Now, tell me. Can you raise him? Is he truly here?"

"I've felt a great pull from the ground, a desire to rise beneath this dirt of Near Hearth," Varin said. "The titan is here. But what could you possibly want with his return?"

"Remind me," the Warlord said. "Why did the gods, Salaril in particular, decide to kill the Titans?"

"Survival," Varin answered with a sour look.

"Shall you ask me once more why we should raise Dremhirra from the dead?"

Varin chose not to respond. There was no convincing the Warlord of folly in regard to bringing the great beast back to life. "This is no easy task. Call all my remaining summoners to this point. He lay at rest below, as does his father, Dagora. It will take all of us. It will take unmitigated concentration, and it will take death."

"Dagora? Death?" Harigamun snarled.

"If you want life, you must take it from somewhere else," Varin explained. "Someone else. And yes, though, Dagora simultaneously exists in this realm and the realm of summons."

"Who would suffice?" Harigamun asked.

"There are no beings of equal stature," Varin said. "There are no Titans whose life carries the value of Dremhirra that we can sacrifice, none save his father—Dagora."

"Do other Titans live?" Harigamun asked.

"The only known remaining Titan is Dagora," Varin continued. "He is held prisoner in the Lost Garden, a land of summons by Salaril himself. The Titan is connected to this Field of Bones. Their betrayal happened long ago, as is said, and Salaril supposedly cursed Dagora; he trapped the Titan under the very dirt covering his son but separated them by realms."

"How do you know this?" Harigamun asked. "You said Dagora is here, with Dremhirra? How is this more than a story?"

"Communion with Baylar, prior to his disappearance," the Lord of Summons said. "However, bringing Dagora here from the Lost Garden will be difficult."

"Where is the Lost Garden?" the Warlord asked.

"Here," Varin answered. "In order to sacrifice Dagora we will have to sever his ties from Salaril. Once his life is traded for Dremhirra—his son—the dragon Titan will be mine to command."

Harigamun raised his eyebrow.

"Yours to command, my lord," Varin bowed nervously. "Through the mind melding from the Mystics, you will be able to issue commands to the Titan through me."

Tir's grasp on Harigamun's psionic connection to his generals had faded, but the Warlord wondered if relying on the bridge once more could prove disastrous. Regardless, it seemed leaving control of the Titan Dremhirra to Varin might be equally disastrous. As the Warlord considered the risks, he turned and looked over the heads of those surrounding him. He saw Kyra and wondered why she'd left her carriage before she was told.

Kyra, Arimeus, and Samiel trudged through the battered field under the beating of heavily armored soldiers stomping the earth. Pools of slush and mud formed as the sky broke into darkness, but not the haunting darkness of Ishmael. This was a morose shadow blanketing the field of battle coupled with a rising rumble from the West. A heavy and foul thunder with frustrated lightning tore through the falling blackness, and a dark figure hid beyond the clouds.

"Oh no," Arimeus said, quivering at the foreboding sight beyond the darkened sky.

"What is it?" Kyra asked, following the Chief Runic who guided the three of them.

Arimeus struggled with his throat for a moment as trying to let something escape but terrified of what the words might cause. "I don't—" he stopped. "I can't—"

"You can't what?" Kyra asked, anxiously.

Arimeus stopped and crouched beneath the horde of soldiers surrounding them. Those soldiers fell into a cacophonous chant.

"Dremhirra! Dremhirra! Dremhirra!" The soldiers beat their chests and stomped their feet under the pouring rain and tremendous rumblings of a growing storm. "Dremhirra! Glauring! Dremhirra!"

Arimeus placed one hand on each of their shoulders—Kyra and Samiel—beneath the canopy of soaked soldiers chanting for a power they did not understand. "Know whatever comes next... I only ever meant to rid Kaiya of magic. I feel as though I was wrong and have a hefty price ahead of me to pay."

Kyra looked into the old man's scarred eye as rain drenched him, his hair becoming thin and thick altogether, revealing the true markings of his burns from all those years ago. Under the weight of the rain, she could see tears. It was plain to her they were tears, even amid the heavy rainfall. He was hurting, or scared, or remorseful, or some mixture therein. Her empathy grew as his fear gathered upon her witnessing a heightened regret taking over. He quivered as if cold, but it was not from a lack of heat. It was something else entirely bringing him to a complete and constant tremor—this she knew.

"It is likely I will not survive," Arimeus said. "No, it is necessary I do not. For if this is true, then I couldn't live with myself any further."

Arimeus removed his hand from the shoulder of Samiel who watched intently with unimaginable confusion. The old man grabbed Kyra with both hands and pulled her in close. "When you must pay a price, let it be me," he said with a gruff and unforgiving tone.

Kyra glanced back at the storm rolling in, and with a brief flash of lightning, she saw the dark figure beyond the pale clouds. She wondered who hid beyond the dark veil and why they brought this fear to the Chief Runic. Moreover, why would the sight of this figure bring Arimeus to his knees with regret?

Who are you?

"There are many forces at work for entirely opposite and misunderstood goals on this battlefield, Kyra," Arimeus said. "I was among them. I thought I was bringing an end to the cruelty of magic, and instead, I fear I have brought on a far darker end. Come! We must stop Varin before he completes the summoning ritual!"

"Dremhirra! Gluaring! Dremhirra!" The horde's chanting continued to fester into a wild and frenzied war calling.

Arimeus darted into the crowd with the other two following as they pushed their way through rows of endless soldiers. The vastly different arrangements of shining armor and cloth standing side-by-side created a moment of comfort for Arimeus, though it was short lived. There was unification of separate peoples, but for all of the wrong reasons.

The three companions broke to the front of the line and the Chief Runic stopped at the sight of Varin.

The Lord of Summons was suspended in air and coated in an emerald aura as his acolytes surrounded him with the Warlord standing off to the side, staring. The acolytes were linked by an unseen chain branching each syllable of their speech, connecting their limbs as they moved as one entwined body. Their movements were convulsive and sporadic, resembling a psychotic painter wielding a brush for the first time in years, mimicking the lost and forgotten quill of an eager writer. In each random movement there was an undeniable unison bending each of the acolytes to its will. Individual form faded away into an unconscious experience of life being called forth, calling to the bones beneath Near Hearth.

"Harigamun!" Arimeus shouted. "You do not know the destruction that follows Dremhirra! You do not know the age in which you are about to usher! This is not the end of magic. This is the end of Near Hearth and all of its people!"

Harigamun stood unphased with his unimaginable army crying and clamoring war chants and rain clapping against his adamantite armor.

Arimeus bolted forward in an attempt to attack Varin, but he was launched backward, some great force smashing against his chest. The pain was great, but he tried once more. This time, the knock sent him even further, landing him on top of a soldier who immediately pushed the old man off and then kicked him in the flank with some indiscernible slur as the soldier spat on him.

"Go," Arimeus said with a strained voice crawling back toward his companions who were struggling to understand his words. "Tell the Warlord he brings about a greater threat than Salaril if he continues."

Kyra turned her gaze toward Harigamun but before taking off to stop him, every soldier and citizen of Runefall felt a rising quake splitting through the core of Near Hearth. The impending doom felt with each spine-shattering tremor broke the confidence of all the soldiers on the battlefield—except Harigamun.

No, the Warlord was not scared of what was to come; he was eager, and impatient to the surmounting end. He was calling forth the end of magic, the end of Runefall, the end of gods.

"The splintering of the god's whip is nigh," Harigamun said under his breath, where only he could hear. "The oppressed become the oppressor in order to defeat our own. Such is the cycle of liberation."

Beyond the Northern veil of rolling hillsides, now covered with mud from the trotting footfall of battle, the cracking of Near Hearth sang as Harigamun continued speaking to himself as though he were taking notes in his journal while the world opened to rebirth a Titan.

"At my final culmination, when the curtain falls and Kaiya stands as a free world, no gods, no magic, no otherworldly oppressor, I will diminish. Be it by death or surrender, I will have no further place in the world. I can only hope to bury this age of cataclysm so deep its markings and scars will dissuade any from returning to the blindness of piety and the ludicrousness of religiosity." Harigamun stared at everyone who could see him, daring them to challenge him.

Kyra watched in stunned fear as dirt rose to the heights of the night sky and shifted her stare from the Warlord to the rising Titan of old who stood from the darkest reaches beneath Near Hearth. There was no stopping the fearsome power. There was no telling what would come next. And there was no knowing how to stop it from happening.

Harigamun eyed the rising Titan from afar, anxious but ready. "A dragon rises from the ashes of a divine war! It wields the power of godly destruction and places the god's whip into the hands of man, mine own hands! As the world crumbles beneath this Titan's feet, the bane of the gods, Dremhirra, will serve my calling and lay waste to a broken city! Give rest to a broken magic and save a broken world," the Warlord rallied, staring at the unburied behemoth's flashing red eyes peering through a tornado of dirt and dust.

Kyra saw the Warlord's creeping smile taking over and she came to understand there was no stopping him. No warning could have swayed him from the decision. The Warlord had decided long ago... the end of magic and the destruction of Runefall was worth any price.

"Bury me beneath the sands of my forefathers," Harigamun whispered. "Hold me beneath the Scorched Desert. Lay me under the hot sands once I have fulfilled my oath and returned Kaiya, Near Hearth, to its people!"

The Warlord stretched his arms outward as if he was enjoying a cool breeze and a peaceful smile struck him while a violent gale of dust swirled around his entire army with a screeching howl, terrifying to hear.

"Give me the old power of Titans," Harigamun said to Varin, using their reformed connection. "Let me bring fire down on this city!"

"He needs time, Lord," Varin answered. "He has been dead for a lost count of ages, for none truly knows when the gods laid the Titans to rest. Dremhirra's part in this war still has a moment to wait. For now, it seems the army of Runefall is preparing a full assault!"

Kyra watched the Warlord turn toward the front gate and the two of them noticed the same thing. An emerging army rippled out from the city gates readying themselves to march on the Warlord's army which clearly outnumbered that of their assaulters.

"Let them try," Harigamun scoffed. "They've neither the numbers nor the skill. This is my brother trying to keep his honor, and I shall give it to him."

The Warlord spat on the ground as Kyra still struggled to make out his words. However, whether she could hear the words or not, it had become clear there was no stopping the incoming battle. Nor could she likely prevent the end of the army of Runefall—her home.

Why? Why would they willingly walk into death?

Harigamun stepped forward, seeing the looming giants that were his brothers—Barigund and Turmin—leading the vanguard.

Barigund turned away from the mountainous Titan emerging from the depths of the battlefield and looked at Turmin before they both turned to the foreboding force of Harigamun.

"You're sure?" Barigund asked.

"There is but one way to slay the beast as there was but one way to slay him the first time the dragon fell," Turmin said.

"The first time the gods had a weapon which allowed them to kill a Titan," Barigund added. "You've heard the stories same as me."

"Yes," the half-dwarven builder said. "The God's Quill. But now we are forced to use a different method. The God's Quill is lost to us, but Dremhirra's life is not as it once was. He was once a being of natural occurrence, a life form which did not defy the natural order. The God's Quill weaponized the art of creation. In its capacity to create, it could also destroy. Thus, the one who held Dremhirra's creation, or the weapon which enabled his creation, also held Dremhirra's destruction."

"That's why this plan will work?" Barigund asked.

"That's why it has to," Turmin answered. "He who is Dremhirra's creation is also his destruction. We must kill the summoner before it is too late."

Horns rang from the top of the Runewall and called forth a united forward stance from its army. The army became a single unit. The war calling of horns under the chants of ferocious and fearful soldiers triumphed over the calamity beyond the Northern reaches of the battlefield, even surpassing the whirling defiance of Dremhirra's coming. A glistening army, one battalion linked to another in a shining, marble-like garb, cracked against the rising sun as rain continued to pour.

Harigamun's army waited in the downpour and watched as the water glided off the Runeguard. Under the maelstrom of Dremhirra and gathering deluge, the Warlord idly stood as his army continuously wiped their eyes and fixed their vision on their opponents. In that moment, the army of the Warlord felt a fear facing the menacing vanguard of soldiers unaffected by the weather, nor by their clear disadvantage. This realization made many of Harigamun's forces question whether or not Runefall truly did face a disadvantage, or if their bravery showed confidence.

"Kyra," Arimeus said, limping over toward her after being kicked and spat on. "We cannot break the forcefield protecting Varin. If we do not have a chance in stopping the coming of Dremhirra, we must stop Salaril's."

"How? Why? How do you even know that's the right thing to do?" Samiel's patience waned and his silence broke under the growing threats. "You blindly followed Harigamun and only recently realized something may have gone wrong and have yet to share what that something is! You think offering yourself as a sacrifice to something we don't even yet know is necessary somehow absolves you from your fault in this? You lied to us and brought us to the enemy's camp who now seeks to destroy everything we've ever known. Now you say the answer is to stop Salaril. Shall we stop Salaril, Harigamun, or the dark figure beyond the skies? Who is the real threat and how can we trust you actually know what the answer is?"

Kyra's shock became a shattering chill stretching toward her fingers. Samiel rarely had moments of outburst, but he was right. There was so much confusion and there was little to no way of knowing who the true

enemy was. The only player on the field whose intentions were clear...
was Harigamun.

"Tell us why the answer is to defeat Salaril," Kyra said with a divisive
anger.

The surrounding army rushed forward, screaming under the
staggering torrent against the rising sun's breaking horizon. Soldier after
soldier brushed and pushed against the three companions as they fought
to hear one another and realized the battle was starting, at least, the end
of the battle was starting.

At once, Arimeus yelled over the thundering herd of soldiers to his
companions, "Grab me!"

Kyra and Samiel did as he instructed under the commotion of
clamoring soldiers launching themselves into war, and within seconds
of touching Arimeus, Kyra and Samiel found themselves twisting into
a vortex of a strange, pale blue light with streaks of bleached white. The
odd sight lasted only seconds, but it felt much longer to them before all
three were spat onto the ground.

As Kyra regained her vision and stability, she rose to find herself back
inside the temple's training room where she had left Gremenhas and
gathered her garbs from the closet... before following Arimeus.

"Why have we come here?" Kyra shouted as she searched the room for
the Chief Runic.

She found him bleeding out behind her with Samiel rushing toward
the old man. The battle-hardened runic had lost his left hand. It was cut
off entirely in what looked to be a singular, clean slice from a sharp blade.
Quickly, Samiel's blood flared and his temperature rose calling forth the
flames resting within, and his hand became a glimmering torch in the
dimly lit temple. Samiel grabbed Arimeus's stub, searing the wound, and
causing the old runic to scream in great pain, knocking him unconscious
for a moment.

Kyra, unforgiving in the moment, rushed toward the unconscious elder of Runefall and smacked him in the face as hard as she could, waking him from his pain-riddled rest.

"What happened to your hand?" she asked him.

"You know there is a cost to magic to the rest of us," Arimeus answered. "Not everything could come, something had to be left behind."

Kyra considered he may really have intended to sacrifice himself. She wondered if the old man now wanted to die. Was the pain of what he thought might come too terrifying to face? Would this desperate plea to regain whatever honor he had thought he lost be enough for him to die with pride? She couldn't tell if he wanted to die, or if he was seeking redemption at any cost. She found it likely an unnecessary designation so long as the Chief Runic was willing to sacrifice himself to win, it was all she needed. However, she still had no clue how to win, or who the greater threat was.

"How do we stop him, and will we save Runefall?" Kyra asked.

"It is likely this is the end of Runefall, no matter the outcome," Arimeus answered. "But if we can stop Salaril from entering Near Hearth, we can focus all our efforts on the Lord of Summons who holds command of Dremhirra."

"How do we stop a god?" Kyra's shout made it clear she was no longer asking. The young runic had become impatient and scared, causing Samiel to reach out and wrap her up in his arms as tears broke from her eyes.

"Salaril is held captive in another realm," Arimeus explained. "So long as his captivity remains, if you break the seal connecting our realm to his, we can kill him. We can use the connection for ourselves and kill him within his prison."

"How do you know?" Samiel asked.

"Tir has told me," Arimeus returned. "Much like Tir has told me a great many things. She has only meant to protect Runefall as we do now."

"And what will we use to kill him?" Samiel asked with ferocity.

"A weapon on his person, a quill." said Arimeus. "A very large quill, resembling more of a scythe."

"How do I break the seal?" Kyra asked.

Arimeus pointed behind Kyra toward the great adamantite statue of Salaril.

"I must break the Shrine of Salaril? I must destroy adamantite?"

"You must break the unbreakable," he confirmed. "The more potent the blood, the more potent the amplification of the spell." Arimeus reached his arm toward her with his palms facing the ceiling. "Mine is quite potent."

"Do it," Samiel said. "We don't have time to quibble over the morals of such an ask. There's an army of soldiers on both ends losing their lives to an unnecessary battle. Take his blood and break the seal. We can end Salaril, and hopefully use the weapon to either defeat Dremhirra, Varin, or both."

"There is likely a battle to come after," Arimeus interjected. "One that goes beyond Kaiya's use of magic, and beyond the sins of Runefall. Do me one favor, Kyra?"

She looked at him with a questioning and doubtful gaze, still unsure of anyone's intentions, except Samiel. She saw the remorse draped over the Chief Runic's face and his eyes fell with heavy failure, though it still could not guarantee he led her in the right direction. By his own admission, Arimeus had led her incorrectly, and falsely.

"What would you ask?" Kyra's voice became a wide disparity between empathy and distrust.

"Have me remembered as one who meant to rid the world of the cruelty, one who hoped to end the senseless kidnappings, one who hoped for a world without the pressures of forces greater than we can truly know."

"You really thought you could end magic without destroying

Runefall?" Samiel asked.

"I knew the risk was worth the reward. I knew the only way for us to truly exist in our own peace in Kaiya was to separate ourselves from the world of magic. I've done wrong and I know this. I seek to do right. Break the seal with my blood, and ready yourselves for what is to come."

"How much do I need to use?" Kyra asked.

Arimeus's eyes broke a tear as his lips quivered in an almost unnoticeable fashion, the fear and knowing of imminent death creeping into his heart for the first time.

"Goodbye, friends," Arimeus said, whipping a dagger from a sheath and slitting his remaining wrist.

The blood of the old runic ran down his wrist as light faded from his eyes and darkness wrapped around him like a comforting serpent. A smile washed over him as he felt a final release from his ageless responsibilities, as though his remorseful heart drained into a feeling of contentment... which he had never known.

Arimeus watched in his final moments of life as his companions both panicked at the shocking sight. Kyra's cries demanded more information from him, and Samiel's rage burned within his heart. In his final fleeting moment of sight, Arimeus smiled as the two demanded answers to questions that did not need to be answered, at least, not in that moment.

After battling panic and shock for a short bout of time, Kyra became enraged at the Chief Runic's decision. She didn't even know what spell to use to break the seal. Why would he leave both of them without answers they clearly needed in order to stop Salaril?

He didn't know.

At once Kyra whirled onto the floor with one leg spinning outward, placed her palm onto Arimeus's draining blood, whipped out a dagger of her own, and stabbed her hand, combining her blood with the old, dying runic's. Then she stabbed her other hand causing it to drip.

"Grab my hand!" she shouted to Samiel. "Burn me!"

Samiel reached out and rallied his inner flames to his palms, scorching Kyra's other hand covered in blood.

"BURN ME!"

Samiel's fire became absorbed into Kyra as she seemed to take hold of his devastating flames and Arimeus's blood looked to be doing the same.

What the—Samiel started to think but then something unexpected happened.

Fire broke from Kyra's mouth and her whole body went shining red as her eyes became filled with a fearsome and bright flurry of fire.

Kyra lifted her hand from the now drained trail of blood leading to the old runic and stripped her other hand away from Samiel's flames. She turned toward the adamantite statue of Salaril, grabbed Dreadfall, with a precise aim at the statue, and covered it in a treacherous and unforgiving flame, shattering the stone into seared pebbles.

Samiel shot a glaring and seeking gaze through the smoldering adamantite mist filling the air. He looked for Kyra as menacing laughter rose from beneath the ashes darkening the temple. Quickly, Samiel rushed to the somehow still breathing Arimeus and scorched his wound, stopping the bleeding. He was alive, but barely.

As the smoke cleared, a figure stood resembling the statue of Salaril. The figure was as large as the statue had once been, towering with a stretched smile. They stood clad in a heavy white-cloth robe with streaks of the ocean running down its sides and a pointed priestly headdress with long raiment flowing down his cheeks. The figure's hands were strong and wide. It gripped onto a scythe-like weapon clearly forged from something golden and sturdy. The blade shimmered like untouched and finely welded steel. At the top of the shaft sat a pointed edge of a pen. It was as if this great and fearful weapon could simultaneously be used for ... *writing?*

Samiel's eyes found Kyra beaten and bloody on the floor beside her staff, Dreadfall, with a flame-touched hand under the light of this figure's rising maelstrom.

She knew it was Salaril, and a storm was forming in this small chamber.

CHAPTER SEVENTEEN

THE CLAY DRAGON

"In truth, I regret this war. Were I given the chance, I'd repair the relationship with my brothers. I fear their piety will never allow it. I fear my anger will never allow it. I fear my actions will never allow it."
— Harigamun, *Thoughts of War*

A thundering clash burst the ear drums shared between Varus and General Toak as a striking emerald glow ripped open the sky overhead, dulling the senses of all standing in the Lost Garden. As the two came back to heightened senses, they felt a difference in the breeze, and a foul stench to the air. Varus recognized the scent of the thickening fear, a force of adrenaline in the air while Toak recalled the iron of blood.

An upward gaze at a broken city alerted Varus of where he stood; the long and fabled city of Runefall amid its downfall stood as a raptured and desecrated portrait of its former grand architecture. His thoughts wandered to his daughter—Varelia—and whether or not they'd made it to the city. He hoped for her safety, but quickly had his attention pulled back.

Toak's tenured ears for the hardness of war called him to the sundering screams of the battlefield far beyond their sight, hidden by the enormous and tumbling city blocking his gaze. The armies of Harigamun and Runefall would lay beyond that burning city. The General turned behind him and saw the Lost Garden, though he now saw it through a tear in the wind, some gaping portal to what now seemed to be an entirely separate world. In that broken veil between worlds, he saw the cowering fear of many magical creatures awaiting a command, the command of their General. Toak approached the connection between his garden and the crying field of battle but turned his head to a frigid and contemptuous rumbling of the earth. Beyond the burnt marble of the falling city, Toak saw a horrid evil rise, and crumbling earth climbed high into the air like a newborn mountain delivered in front of his eyes. In that moment, Toak saw the red eyes of one he thought to be long dead. He turned back towards the doorway to his garden and let out a ferocious roar.

"The Garden is no longer separate from the primal world of magic and men!" the General said. "The God of Runes and his confounded weapon have connected our worlds so that he may be free of us! And now this world has called forth the Demon of Titans, the Divine Talon, Dagora!"

Unnatural cries erupted from each and every creature on the garden's side of the broken veil. Through the connection between both worlds, Dagora could be seen raising the Lost Garden from its deepest roots as the Titan emerged from its deep slumber beside the Stained Temple.

Toak called to his army—the Thorns of Lost Garden. "Come, my friends! Come not as one summoned for the bidding of others as you have so many times before! Come not for the endless calls of war! Come not for the gods, whose love has shown to be anything but divine! Nay, I say! Come for the love of the Maiden who stood against Salaril! Come for the heart of she who would have set us free from the voice of captivity! Come and claim the head that shackled our fair Maiden and take the world back from the clutches of those who have claimed dominion over you and yours since the knowing of time!"

At once, the army of the Lost Garden emerged from its secluded realm through broken doorways, portals; a multitude of them springing open and scattered across the battlefield connecting Near Hearth to the Lost Garden.

"How has this happened?" Varus asked.

"It seems in Salaril's need to break free, he bridged a connection between Kaiya and Lost Garden to call Dagora forth. His tomb in this world was his seal."

"And that seal has broken," Toak said.

The two watched as a figure broke from beneath the depths of the city, launching itself into the air. From so high into the burning sky of the setting sun, the shining white of the figure stunned the glares of many that day with a fierce and unforgiving glimmer. General Toak made out a sharp blade in the figure's right hand and he knew without question it was Salaril holding the God's Quill.

Salaril turned downward to the city, casting a spell which looked as though he were writing through the air, like a piece of parchment. With a signaling dash of the blade, the God of Runes stabbed the scythe as if to break the earth, shaking the city with tremors.mThe buildings cracked and the streets split as the ground beneath Runefall gave way.

"Come, Gayllen," Salaril's voice echoed. "Your redemption awaits!"

"No!" Toak shouted, calling his army of creatures to his side as he launched forward, galloping toward the front of the city.

"Who is Gayllen?" Varus asked. The two—Varus and Toak—raced amid the stampeding steps and thundering flaps of an uncountable number of mystical and terrifying creatures.

"The Final Son!" Toak yelled.

Varus receded into his thoughts, recalling old fables as he lost complete control of the body to Toak. Through the Forest General's eyes, Varus watched as a great number of commanders and soldiers hacking and slaying one another under the shadow of a rising Dremhirra. His thoughts bent to the insanity of it all as he tried to grasp an understanding of why this was all happening, and then he realized what battle was truly beginning.

The Final Son was a legend Varus recalled being told to him by his father. The legend of The Last Son of a forgotten race of divine creatures of creation preceding the known gods. The Final Son was the last of those divine creatures, the last of their offspring, as the rest were hunted by the gods who used Titans as nothing more than attack dogs against the divinity of creation. Gayllen was the last remnant of divine making brought back to life by Salaril to fight the Titans, who took the lives of those responsible for the creation of everything.

"Salaril means to hold the power of creation and claim real divinity for himself," Varus said, with a disheartened voice that slowed their speed. "He's wielding the last known weapon to kill not only the Titan he faces, but the only thing capable of killing divinity and creation itself."

"And he faces the demon of them all, the one who brought down the mightiest of the divine so long ago," Toak said.

"Dremhirra rises here and Dagora there," whispered Varus.

"Not two separated," Toak explained. "Two combined. Look!"

Toak pointed back toward the largest portal connecting the Lost Garden to Near Hearth and watched as Dagora evaporated into a gas of shadow. The shadowy essence escaped from the portal with a squalling screech across the battlefield as it enveloped Dremhirra.

Dagora, the Father of Titans and King of Dragons, became one with the deadliest of them all. The father of Dremhirra—Dagora—now took control of his son's form, making Dremhirra nothing more than a titanic vessel.

Standing larger than the highest peaks of Kaiya, Gayllen crushed the city of Runefall with each step as he approached Dagora whose surrounding maelstrom was a calamitous tumor on the land. Salaril hovered over the dying city and thrust the God's Quill toward Dagora as Gayllen picked up speed in pursuit of the Demon of TItans.

Meanwhile, Toak's centaur being housing both Varus and the General led an unthinkable army of forgotten creatures from Lost Garden to the scene of battle at the Northern gates.

The Warlord of Kaiya—by Varin's psionic connection—saw through the eyes of Dagora and considered if the feeling was the power one felt as a god. "Wasted. They wasted divinity."

Harigamun felt the sting of ancient wisdom and an unquenchable thirst for vengeful destruction. Not hatred toward any one particular being, or even race, but for the death of the world and all its magic.

The cruelty ran too deep. Each of Dagora's wings spanned a city, and his talons breached skin like razors peeling scales. The burning redness of Dagora's eyes stung as a searing pain brought from a boiling liquid slowly poured into Harigamun's sockets, giving him a sense of heat and movement paired with an unimaginable agony which was now inescapable. Harigamun's mind had linked to Dagora's and Dremhirra's through the bridge offered by Varin, and now the warlord felt as powerful as he ever thought possible... while also being trapped in a most terrifying prison.

Harigamun's movements felt like a juxtaposed physical impairment with perfection and impeccable form. Within the same second, he would feel in complete control and utterly powerless; graceful and incorruptible with each step whilst clumsy and willfully ignorant of his true movements—he was a dragon, but not an adept one.

The Warlord watched as Gayllen pummeled the city gate, shattering the adamantite walls. "A fortress of unthinkable force broken by the footsteps of true power," said Harigamun.

Through the eyes of the demon, Dagora, Harigamun watched the remaining troops within the city of Runefall and those housed within the walls lose their lives in a screeching moment of fear beneath the shadow of The Final Son. Those who had gathered outside the city gate ran toward Varin and Harigamun's troops. There was no longer an assault, it was an army fleeing the terror of a colossal shadow being forced to run right into another army.

"They cannot kill me," the Warlord said, forming the words out of the dragon's mouth which roared across the battlefield.

In that moment, whether it was Dagora or Harigamun, for he could not know; the dragon's belly furnaced a flame deep into its gullet and released a cataclysmic blow of heat in the shape of a boulder, launching it toward the incoming force from Runefall.

The ball of fire rolled over half of Runefall's forces like wet weeds beneath a stone, scorching and flaying skin from bone. The heat of the boulder alone melted raiment to skin if the soldiers were within a few feet of the unbearable atrocity.

Witnessing the incomparable desolation of Dagora, Barigund's sight locked onto Turmin as they both continued sprinting toward the summoning. The circle shielding Varin. Now vastly outnumbered by Harigamun's forces, Runefall's army stood in earshot of the Warlord's. Neither army wanted to move as they watched in terror of the Titans.

"We are outnumbered, Barigund!" Turmin shouted as the two of them closed the gap to the summoning circle. "The city has fallen. Shalix, Premus, and the rest with the women and children... the crypts have surely fallen. We are all that is left under the shadow of Titans and gods!"

"No," the Commander answered back with his deep, calming voice. "It is three armies against a god and his pet. Dagora is with us, so long as Harigamun is with us. Above all, he seeks the death of Salaril.

Overhead, the winged creatures of ancient tales and forgotten stories swarmed Dagora as a helmet the size of a lake crashed against the Demon Titan's skull. Gayllen had thrown his helmet at the dragon and now sprinted toward his enemy at full speed, leaving a quaking and scarred ground beneath each step.

Harigamun's forces scurried about and huddled together, afraid of what was to come as Barigund and Turmin's armies stepped within fighting reach of Harigamun's forces.

"We are no longer the enemies of this battle," Barigund said, addressing both Harigamun's Generals surrounding the summoning circle, and Runefall's own forces which dwindled.

Barigund watched as Gayllen and Dagora pummeled one another like two mountains fighting for dominance over an entire range. The clanging of Gayllen's blade against the scales of Dremhirra's body under Dagora's control rang against one another like an orchestra of metal. Its symphony clashed louder than the banging of a thousand gongs.

As Barigund and Turmin watched, the two Titans squared off against one another in a battle of ferocious revenge.

However, Kyra, Sam, and Arimeus gathered themselves beneath the temple which had fallen around them following the rise of Gayllen. Kyra's protection rune shielded the three of them from the collapsing temple and she was able to cast the debris away. However, the three of them found themselves trapped beneath a shattered temple... and Kyra was exhausted.

"What do we do?" Samiel asked with panic. "Can you teleport out of here like you did to get us in here?"

Arimeus looked down at his singed stump where a hand used to be and sighed. "I likely can," he answered with an exhausted voice.

"Even if you get us out of here, what do we do? How do we stop whatever shook the city?" Kyra asked.

"It was another Titan, I think," Arimeus said. "I don't know who he would have summoned, but it can't be good."

"Then what do we do?" Kyra groaned. "We can't talk about this forever!"Arimeus sat for a moment in thought and looked toward his other hand, which was still in good shape. The old runic's pointer fingertip glowed a strange blue as he drew a rune carving which Kyra had never seen.

"Can you remember this?" Arimeus asked.

"Yes," Kyra said. "What does it do?"

"We don't have time. Once I get us back to the battle, I need you to carve this rune into my back and utter the phrase 'From life to death and death to life.' Can you do that for me?"

"Yes," Kyra said. "If I must." She wanted to ask questions, but there was no point, no time. She didn't even know if this plan would work, or what lack of a plan there was. But it was all she had, and she couldn't fight Arimeus on his right to die.

"Once you cast this spell, look toward Salaril and his weapon. Put all your focus onto that weapon, you'll need a good view of it, and cast the spell with your staff. Can you do this, Kyra?"

"Yes," she mumbled, tears running down her face. Samiel tried to grab her hand and comfort her, but she pulled away.

With a shining hue lighting his finger once more, Arimeus drew a rune on the floor before gripping onto his dagger. The old runic's eyes welled as he recognized Samiel cast him a look of farewell, though the Litree did not speak a word. Arimeus's hand felt the sting of tiny needles loosening his grip on the blade, realizing he'd held it too tight for too long in a dissociated moment of contemplation while dealing with the fear of what would come. The Chief Runic lessened the grip for a short moment, long enough for blood to return strength to his grasp, and quickly slit his wrist. Arimeus held his draining wrist over another porting rune and watched his blood stain the temple floor one last time. He smashed his bleeding wrist down onto the rune, and with a loud burst of pain, Arimeus teleported all three of them to the battlefield directly under Salaril who now commanded the colossal Gayllen—the Final Son—in battle with the long-dead Dagora, now in control of Dremhirra's menacing body.

Kyra's eyes shot upward to the rune god and then back to Arimeus. The old runic's blood spat from a second dismembered limb as he wailed on the ground with a bloody stub. It deafened the shrieking fear of both armies as they set against one another in the face of two Titans.

Samiel's fire burned hot in his core as he readied to singe another of Arimeus's wounds but the old runic stopped him.

"There's no sense, Sam! Kyra needs to cast the spell!"

Kyra readied the spell by drawing the rune onto Arimeus's back with Dreadfall and turned the old man around to see his eyes were beaten with the weight of unthinkable sorrow. The old runic's consciousness dwindled with the outpouring of blood. His head dangled while he leaned back onto his elbows, laying on the ground. Kyra grabbed him by his tunic, pulled him in close, and said "Goodbye, Arimeus," as he smiled at her in return.

Without remorse, Kyra grabbed Arimeus's bloody body and threw him onto her back. She immediately turned to Salaril and his weapon before uttering: "From life to death and death to life," with Dreadfall aimed directly at the God Quill.

The quill vanished and Salaril quickly switched his focus to Kyra, rushing to the ground at an immense and terrifying speed. Looking to where Arimeus's body lay, or should have been laying, Kyra saw a petrified mound of dirt and a patch of scorched grass with a rune burned into it.

"Arimeus is dead," she said, looking now toward Samiel.

"The rune is fading," Samiel said, just before Salaril landed on the ground beside them, leaving small dents in the earth.

Kyra stepped over the fading remnants of the rune used against the God's Quill before Salaril started berating her with questions, screaming at her so loudly spittle flew onto her face. "What have you done with the Gods' Quill? Who are you to tamper with the will of gods? Do you know the unrighteousness of which you fight for? You insignificant parasite!"

The towering god lifted Kyra by her throat, causing Samiel to light his fists and launch himself at the opponent, pummeling Salaril's backside with a flurry of scorched strikes. But the God of Runes remained unphased and continued choking the life from Kyra.

At once, an immediate distraction came as Gayllen's enormous sword was knocked from the Titan's hand and flung across the battlefield. The sword's incomparable size plunged deep into Runefall, eroding any sign of life left within, and causing a quaking of the earth, interrupting the standoff with Kyra's companions and the god.

Still yet, Kyra's breath returned as Salaril's grip loosened when the god looked to Gayllen and found, without the God's Quill, his attempt to command Dagora failed. Salaril lifted himself into the air, tossing Kyra away like a plaything, and flew like a winged beast blasting toward Gayllen.

The First Son, turning toward the incoming God of Runes, swung a mighty and heavy blow with a closed fist, perfectly timed to bring his adversary crashing back onto the ground.

Dagora, taking advantage of Gayllen's turned attention, heaved an incinerating breath of fire onto the Final Son's back, searing his ceremonial armor from a lost age.

As the Final Son fell to his knees, shaking the earth, the thundering footfall of an army of magical beasts hurdled itself onto Dagora with screams of desperation. The beasts, led by commander Toak, climbed and flew onto Dagora, biting, clawing, and scratching their way across the mountainous Talon of the Titans. Some beasts spat fire or venom, others brought fire and ice, and some cracked against the devil with the weight of forgotten history bringing marks of pain indescribable. In this deep droughting of suffrage, a grand and oral epic would later be told of this day and its magnitude of pain—History's Lost Screams: The Final Days—by an unlikely source then present for the battle, though now unnamed.

"Bring down the devil!" Toak echoed across the battlefield as he leaped onto the shoulders of Dagora.

"Where is my daughter?" Varus yelled as he and Toak traversed the scales of the beast, making their way to his head. As the two of them approached Dagora's seal, Varus saw a large creature making its way from the Western side of the forest. The creature sprinted toward Dagora but still had some distance to close, but he couldn't make out its shape.

Dremhirra's body—with Dagora's soul—lifted from the ground, nearly shaking off Toak and Varus. Dozens of other creatures were knocked from the devilish Titan, but the General held strong with relentless footing. Before the beast could shake the centaur off of his head, Toak lifted his two-handed blade and brought it down hard with all of his force into the eye of the Titan, digging a wound to the center of its brain, and sending Dagora into a thrashing, resulting in Toak and Varus being thrown from the top. Toak's strike broke the Seal of Dagora atop Dremhirra's skull. As Toak and Varus plummeted toward the ground, the spirit of Dagora faded back into a gaseous form and fled for the sanctity of The Lost Garden, returning to the soil near the stained temple in search of the Titan's own body.

As Varus and Toak looked to the East, falling from Dagora, Varus could see the silhouette of the large creature closing its distance. Far off in the field toward the Eastern line of the forest—Varus could now see—Varelia and Groff were rushing toward the dragon. Though, they stopped mid sprint as they saw a small silhouette breaking against the setting sun and falling from the top of the Titan.

"Them magic creatures," Groff said as the two of them closed the distance separating them and Dremhirra.

"Where are they coming from?" Varelia asked.

"Garden," said Groff. "Where Groff was before coming back."

"The same place my father was sent, then?"

"Mmmm. Yes. Groff think he was in garden too if you say he was with Groff."

"How have they escaped?" Varelia asked, approaching Dagora.

"The garden no place for being escaped," Groff laughed. "Garden is where magic things want to go. There we safe. No one control us till they call name."

"Until they summon you?"

"Yes," Groff answered. "He may bring army of magic beasts with him, if he here."

As Groff and Varelia grew closer, deep cries erupted from the combined armies of Runefall and Harigamun surrounding the summoning circle, which sat hidden behind the cover of soldiers. Being preoccupied with a fixation on Dremhirra, Varelia and the golem increased their speed toward the Titan even though their curiosity and anxiety rose with the armies' growing cries. As they approached, Groff, being tall enough to see a small glimpse of the summoning circle over the heads of the remaining soldiers, noticed something odd happening as an emerald burst knocked soldiers backward.

Within the summoning circle protecting Varin and Harigamun, the Warlord fell to the ground shrieking in pain, followed by the Lord of Summons, coinciding with the burst of energy. As they both dropped to the ground screeching and covering their left eyes, the acolytes powering the circle broke concentration and the barrier fell as Harigamun's army backed away.

Though Varelia didn't know it, the pain of the Warlord and Varin was felt at the same moment Dagora's seal was broken, right after Toak stabbed the beast.

"Break the connection, Varin!" Harigamun's cries boomed throughout the battlefield.

"Gayllen is of his own free will, and now you would set Dremhirra to his own as well?" asked Barigund, now free to confront his brother.

Varin, obeying the commands of his Warlord, severed the connection bridging the Titan Dremhirra with Harigamun. The Warlord and Varin's eyesight returned and their pain—from the stabbing of the Titan—vanished instantly.

Even still, with the Warlord's returned sight and focused mind, he turned toward the chest-beating taunts of Barigund and Turmin—his brothers—now standing before him. His army stepped farther and farther away as the Warlord approached his opponents, his family.

"Two Titans fight freely on our plane due to your negligence, and your army falls away from you, deciding at the last moment to cast you aside," Barigund said, shoving his gigantic blade into the dirt. "Remove that armor, dear brother. I'm sure we need not cast stones to settle the blood between us."

Barigund took off his helmet, casting it to the side. The thought of hand-to-hand combat with his brother both frightened and excited Harigamun, causing him to remove his adamantite cuirass, leggings, pads, and helmet, and dropping them onto the field. Each piece of his dropped armor dug into the ground beneath the weight of the adamantite.

"You took the wrong children, brother," Harigamun said, approaching his brother. "You took my son, and you knew what war it would bring."

"I knew what I was told to know, *Warlord*," Barigund spat the title as an insult. "We were protecting the world from the outbreak of war by housing the strongest magic users in the city of Runefall. That power could not be dispersed among the tribal cities of Kaiya, it was too risky, too likely to cause war across all of Near Hearth."

"But you never got all of the strongest of us, did you?" Harigamun's hands lit with bright flames.

"I followed a false god," Barigund said. "I took from those who didn't deserve the taking and I followed one who did not deserve to be followed. But I did not bring war to our world, brother. That mistake lies on your shoulders."

As Harigamun struck with a fierce and menacing blow, cracking against Barigund's jaw, Turmin herded the armies of both generals. Turmin's great shoulders and broad width, paired with the same form found on his brothers, kept all who considered attempting to intervene at bay.

The Warlord's first strike critically claimed its mark, sending his brother to the ground. Barigund was able to recover as the Warlord celebrated. The City Commander rose, launching an uppercut to the ball of his opponent's chin, and the strike caused the Warlord to bite down onto his tongue, severing it.

Harigamun stepped away and shot a glance toward Turmin. With a waterfall of blood dripping from his lips, the Warlord condemned the Architect of Runefall. Though Turmin could not discern the words coming from his brother's bloodied mouth, he knew it was a condemnation of the loss of brotherhood they once shared.

Turmin stood listening, recalling the final day of separation between the three of them. He recalled the piety of Barigund and the concrete solidification of beliefs; the need to take magic away from the general population and to hold its power behind the concentrated walls of Runefall for *"the betterment of Kaiya"*. On that day, Turmin, along with his brothers, bore witness to one of the most vile acts of magic, and within that recognition, he could not help but side with Barigund. The world needed to be protected from the strength of magic. But now, decades after that decision, war and strife had come in full force, and the architect wondered if the events were far worse than what might have come had he just made a different decision. *We were doomed to this failure. There is no greater good when power is present.*

A splitting cut tore through Barigund's upper brow from Harigamun's hard strike, whose speech now seemed like vomit preceding the end of life and drenched with a crimson river. Blood slowly ran into the Commander's eyes as he watched his brother's broken condemnations against all those who surrounded him. Then, the Warlord's curses turned toward the sky. Barigund only assumed it was an assault against Salaril.

"We don't need to do this, brother," Barigund said. "There are healers, and there is a way back from this. It doesn't need to end with one of us bloody and done!"

Harigamun stayed the choking of his blood and spat upon the ground, clearly aiming for his brother. The Warlord wiped his chin with his leather bracer, now stained with the blood of its wearer. The tongue-slit warrior bore his weight onto his toes, hunched over, readying himself to launch forward, and showing Barigund the City Commander of Runefall was wrong—there was no turning back, no healer to stave these wounds.

Barigund stiffened his stance and lowered himself to stop the rushing of his brother. Before his attack, Harigamun spat one last time with what the Warlord meant to be his final words, and though Barigund could no longer understand his brother's speech, one word was clearly understood.

"Sam."

The Warlord rushed, leaping into the air with a flying kick, and caused his brother to raise his guard in an attempt to catch the incoming blow, trying to throw the Warlord to the ground. Alas, the kick distracted the City Commander as a crushing blow from the Warlord's right fist came thundering down toward his skull. The Warlord's landed hit brought his opponent to the ground, though this time the Commander struggled to regain his footing under a dazed concussion.

In his desperation, Barigund initiated a sweeping kick, luckily knocking the Warlord to the ground, and snapping his brother's leg. The Warlord's screams further terrified the onlooking armies as blood continued leaking from of his mouth while he latched onto his shattered bone, wrenching in pain.

Barigund, now slowly recovering from his dazed stance, jumped onto his blood lusting brother, and viciously assaulted him, smashing his face with crushing blows. Blood covered his fists and his brother's bone cracked and split under each concussive blow, however, the Warlord only smiled, as if he could not feel the pain.

Shocked at his brother's response, Barigund leaned back slightly to look at the damage.

In that delay, Harigamun spat blood into his brother's eyes and pushed the City Commander of Runefall from his straddle position. Barigund blindly attempted rising from the ground, weakened by the loss of sight from the sting of his brother's blood welling in his eyes, and the feeling of a destabilizing kick across the chin. Once again dazed, the City Commander tried finding his footing only to be knocked down by a furious kick—from Harigamun's working leg—to Barigund's flank. The kick was followed by another, and then another, until Barigund spat out more blood than Harigamun.

"No," Turmin said, looking down at his brother crawling on the battlefield. Raising his voice, Turmin yelled, "Don't make me watch this!"

Barigund spat a lump of blood, teeth, and flesh, crawling away, "I—" he coughed. "I chose this path. Do—" he tried once more. "Do your best to make a new one."

Friends and enemies watched as Barigund's bones cracked under fatal blows. Blood drenched the dry field and Turmin felt the death of two brothers at once as the thrashing of the Titans Gayllen and Dagora raged in the distance.

"You shouldn't have sided with him, Turmin," said one of the soldiers.

"With your strength there wouldn't have been a single tribe, not a single strand of fight to go against us," said another soldier.

"But no, you *chose* Barigund. You chose to steal children away in the dead of night because you thought you knew better," spoke another soldier.

Turmin looked toward Harigamun, now rising from the ground with a deadening stare, and leaned on one leg while the other seemed to hang...

"Like my new trick?" the first soldier asked. "I don't even need my own tongue anymore."

Harigamun's let out a wild and terrifying cackle. The Warlord held his stare with Turmin as he picked up his adamantite reignment and readied himself for a final battle.

"You won't enjoy this end, brother," Turmin said as his brother approached.

"Salaril has no Titan, and neither do we. Runefall has fallen and so too will this *god*. I need live no longer, for the only deed left to me is to take the life of those who decided to take my child away and send this land into a decaying war! Your council has fallen, your generals are dead, and your city is rubble. Tell me, brother. To what end do you fight? What keeps your heart angry?"

Turmin's increasing speed formed into a full sprint as he picked up a spear and launched it. However, the Warlord dodged the spear with ease, catching it by the hil—mid air—and tossing it to the ground.

Harigamun's rage intensified as he readied a chaotic punch aimed directly at his brother's jaw, but the half-dwarf easily side-stepped the assault, catching the swing inside his palm as the two met face-to-face.

"Is this the end you choose, Harigamun?" Turmin asked.

The Warlord smiled with blood-stained teeth and excitement. Turmin pushed his brother backward, kicking the shattered leg. As the Warlord fell to the ground, Turmin readied his hammer—Stone's End. With a single swing, the architect of Runefall shattered Harigamun's adamantite armor as his brother lay on the ground. The Architect of Runefall looked down on his brother and asked, "Any last words, brother?"

"Such a pity our mother would lie with a dwarf," Harigamun said through the voice of another soldier. "But the greater pity is knowing you never wielded your strength until it was too late... and for a lost cause."

Turmin watched as his brother readied his final words, and he was given the opportunity to say them. For, in Turmin's heart, he did not truly believe his brother's actions were malicious. *Were it me who had a son, were it my love stricken down by you... I too would crack the foundations of this land.*

"You knew," the mouth of a soldier spoke. "You knew when my wife was taken from me because of magic that I would burn this world! But then you came back and took my son... you see, that's when I knew fire wasn't enough. It wasn't enough for this world to burn! This world—your world, your precious magic—it all needed to be forgotten. By all the piety given to those who would call themselves gods, or creators; I will end your world, and theirs. Be it in this life, or what comes ne xt!"

Harigamun's head smashed like fruit on rock under Turmin's single crushing blow and the Warlord's army gasped in disbelief as the sounds of Dremhirra and Gayllen struck fear into the heart of a leaderless army.

Turmin, finally recognizing the threat of the titans—Dremhirra and Gayllen, The Final Son, and the Devil of Titans—after the fall of his brothers, were preparing crushing blows toward one another. Thus, the architect turned to see Dremhirra clamping his jaws against the shoulder of Gayllen as fire rose from the gullet of a forgotten beast to scorch The Final Son.

"Go," Turmin yelled to those remaining from both armies. "Bring down Gayllen!" He grabbed hold of Airwei, Lord of Winds, and chased o n.

Turmin raced toward the Final Son, shocking all who could see.

The soldiers whispered to themselves, "Dremhirra is the Devil of Titans... how could Turmin want us to help against such a devil?"

Sam and Kyra closed the distance separating them from the Titans and divided armies of Runefall while Salaril battled with both Dremhirra, and an army of winged mythical beasts.

"Kyra!" Turmin yelled, approaching the foot of the Talon of Titans. "We must bring down Gayllen!"

"Gayllen?" Samiel asked. "Do we think he is the greater danger? There's a pretty big dragon..."

"I don't know," Kyra answered. "But Turmin knows things we don't. Even if he is wrong, I don't see how things can get worse."

"Come Kyra," shouted Turmin. "This is Airwei, Lord of Winds."

Airwei bowed as a dagger of momentous size unsheathed from a hilt on Gayllen's hip. The dagger's sharp and otherworldly blade pierced the unbreakable scales of Dremhirra, knocking the Devil of Titans to its knees with shrieking winds howling beneath the beast's great wings.

"What can kill The Final Son?" Kyra asked, gesturing to a need for quickness.

"God's Quill," Turmin answered.

Kyra's head hung low before revealing that a spell cast earlier sent the weapon tumbling into an unknowable void, thereby removing the only weapon capable of killing Gayllen from their grasp.

A blazing and surprising fire melted the battlefield within seconds, searing and killing many of the soldiers now standing at the foot of the behemoths, a mere hundred meters or so from the Titans. The remaining troops of soldiers spasmed into instant panic with many of those who remained fleeing to the Eastern tree line of the forest while those who stayed ran as fast as they could to escape the burning field.

"Airwei," Kyra said. "Can you get me to Gayllen's head?"

"What are you doing?" Samiel asked.

"Yes," the Lord of Winds said. "Just you, my lady?"

"No," she answered before turning to face all those who remained. "Who would sacrifice themselves so we might kill The Final Son?"

With silence pouring over the trembling crowd, each individual soldier took to cowering behind the one in front of them, including many soldiers who went as far as to take many steps backward.

"I will," said Samiel.

"No," she trembled. "No! Stop!"

"It only worked last time because it was Arimeus," Samiel said. "It likely requires a strong source of magic to embolden the spell. Everything has a cost."

"No," Kyra repeated with tears fathering around her eyes. "Not you! I need magic but not you!"

Samiel growled. "And what happens when the spell doesn't work? What happens when you've sacrificed a life without cause and Gayllen survives? What happens when it is too late because you thought you should decide who lives and who dies?"

A flash of light and a crushing blow against Turmin knocked the half-dwarf to the ground as Salaril appeared, interrupting Samiel's condemnation.

"Are you alright?" Samiel asked, rushing to the fallen half-dwarf's side.

"If he was going to attack any of us, be thankful it was me," Turmin answered.

The rune god floated overhead and glowed with a fiery aura resembling the last crackle of a fanned ember, but the glow kept growing, igniting the sky with a dark and blazoned horizon that spread fear across the battlefield. The darkness grew deeper, and the deep and hollow laugh of Ishmael returned before the Lord of the Dreaming Haunts' face appeared under the dark horizon.

"Run, brother! They cannot escape if you are still alive," said Ishmael, laughing and looking down at all those below him who cowered as Titans continued to roar.

"Begone with you and your dreams," Salaril said, snapping his fingers as if to seal Ishmael away, causing the Lord of the Dreaming Haunts to disperse into nothingness and silence beneath a flaxen aura.

"If he lives, we cannot escape," Samiel said, looking at Turmin and Kyra. "You heard him! He can see all! He has visited too many times with too much knowledge. He sees how this ends! We need to kill Salaril, otherwise we face our own death!"

Kyra shot a terrifying glance to Turmin, hoping for guidance.

"Bring him down to me," Turmin said, pulling himself upright and shaking off his wounds. "He's the one there will be no escape for."

Within seconds of Turmin's uttered words, Kyra drew a rune on the ground with her hands in the blood from a quick slice of an unsheathed dagger.

"What are you doing?" Samiel yelled. "You don't need to use your blood!"

"You don't know what we need," she answered, readying herself to bring the god to the ground. At the same moment she started casting her spell, a torrid scream broke out from Dremhirra, the Devil of Titans. Everyone who could see turned to see the dragon, not being killed or wounded by The Final Son, but being consumed by some unknown gray matter consuming its body. The Titan's scream shattered the ears of many, causing some to bleed.

Gayllen even fell to his knees causing a rush of force and knocking nearly everyone to the ground. The Final Son started retching and writhing—from his own blows—as he watched Dremhirra become swallowed whole.

Silence struck the field and now Dremhirra stood as though he were a dragon made of clay.

"You're a dragon and a golem, Groff," said Varelia, with a light chuckle. "A dragolem."

A smile brimmed across the dark jaw of the dragolem as Groff replied, "Groff kill big man and floaty man?"

"Yes, Groff," Varelia said. "Let's save everyone and find my dad!"

Varelia's eyes rolled to the back of her head, revealing the whites of snowy translucent emptiness. As Varelia pulled back her fist, the limb of the dragolem also winded back as together Varelia and Groff sent one massive blow to the head of The Final Son. The blow extended beyond Dremhirra's original reach as Groff's muddy form gave further length to the former dragon. As the mighty strike broke against Gayllen's head it looked as if the limb of the dragon dripped and ran like a river, an unstoppable current, pummeling the Titan into submission, and then death. The Final Son's enormous body lay broken and empty for only a short moment before decaying into a powdery dusty mirroring flakes of burnt gold.

"Where is my father?" The mouths of Varelia and the dragolem moved in unison as the broken-hearted youth readied herself to fight a god, if necessary.

The dragolem stepped forward, meeting eye-to-eye with Salaril, who floated in the air.

"You don't have the power, child," Salaril said. "You don't even know how to keep true control over the power you do have." The God of Runes turned to the battlefield. "None of you understand anything that is happening! Each of you has tested a power greater than you can wield! I am not your enemy!"

Salaril shot downward, launching his body toward Varelia's fixed and empty stare, but the arm of the clay dragon moved faster, catching the god in a tight hold. Varelia started squeezing with all the strength shared between herself and Groff, but to no avail.

Varelia shuttered. *Salaril cannot be killed, but I can contain him.*

A shock, like glass against a shrieking, sharp wind being stripped of its power, wisped through the gaps in Groff's grasp, instantly setting the god free. At once, the dragolem and God of Runes became locked in battle. The dragolem breathed a molten lava form of clay at its foe with wild and furious strikes from talon, wing, and limb. As bile spilled across the battlefield, Turmin, Kyra, and Samiel watched the devastating fight from below.

"Burn me," Turmin said to Samiel.

"What?" Sam asked, terrified.

"Set me on fire with every ounce of your power," the half-dwarf answered. "There is only one way left to kill this god … "

Chapter Eighteen

Smelting the Ogre

"Only men. I failed at conquering the dwarves and elves. Were I successful in bringing that damn dwarf King to heel, perhaps I would be as unstoppable as they claim me to be. I wish I'd known the legends before my assault."
— *Harigamun, Thoughts of War*

As an obelisk of adamantite moved from blocking Grunffi and Melro's sight, the two of them became the first in known history to set eyes on the Forge of Dwarahir. The petty dwarves, or gnomes, usually led by Melro, had always found piles of adamantite waiting for them outside the forge, never stepping in.

Lava bubbled within a flowing river of volcanic rock and song carrying nearly indestructible adamantite through the deep cavern tranches of the forge. A lone strand of rock connected the farthest reaches of the cavern walls to the center of the burning chamber, far off to the side.

Within the center of the forge, Dwarahir stood swinging his hammer.

Melro explained to Grunffi the hammer was older than all living dwarves. The dwarven god's beating of steel and stone captivated the former King's attention. Each swing laid upon his craft was faster and more precise than the last. It was as if Dwarahir were bent against time for the completion of the weapon, or tool. The god's forging rose to something unmistakably faster, broader, and more precise than any ever known by dwarven culture.

Upon sight of the purposeful dedication to craftsmanship, Grunffi fell to his knees, understanding the true depth by which dwarves had failed to become the craftsmen their maker clearly intended them to be.

"Why is he racing against time?" Grunffi asked.

"Time has been Dwarahir's opponent for longer than we have lived, Grunffi. He races to break free his wife, his love, his meaning for craft."

"How can he set her free? The adamantite grows with each mined stone stripped from this forge. He cannot outpace the magic of his wife."

"Yes," Melro said. "There is a cruelty in knowing the greatest tool of the dwarves, and the reason for which we are known, is only available to us due to the endless toiling of he who created us. Thus, we are truly made in his image, and likeness."

"What do you mean?" Grunffi asked.

"As Dwarahir forever forges and forever mines to reclaim the love he once had, we too endlessly forge and endlessly mine seeking a love we never had," Melro said, taking a short moment to lower his head. "The world has never truly been kind to dwarves, or gnomes. We have always scraped and squalled under the rocks of others. We have all, at some time, been forced from our homes or treated with fear, contempt, or both."

"Why has this burden been laid upon us?"

"Only Dwarahir knows," Melro answered. "But I suspect knowing the answer does not give the possibility of a solution, for if that were so, I cannot imagine a god who has spent many lifetimes digging for his own love would hold it away from his own creation."

"How have you come to know what you know, Melro?"

"From time to time, Dwarahir leaves the solitude of his forge and comes to us. Sometimes he seeks conversation, most often with me. Sometimes he just needs to empty the never-ending stream of adamantite blocking him from further mining. And sometimes... I suspect even a god needs to breathe."

The rising heat became nearly unbearable for Melro, who took a moment to study his companion. Grunffi seemed unphased by it, which confused the gnome as he saw the former King profusely sweating on their way down. *Has he adapted so fast?*

"Is the heat becoming too much?" Melro asked.

"Actually," Grunffi said. "I'd quite forgotten the heat for a moment."

Grunffi looked down at his hands and saw them slowly cracking. The lines breaking against his skin split like a fissure in the earth, a break against sturdy stone. He saw his hands hardening but his flexibility suffered nothing as his fingers and grip strength stayed intact. In fact, he noticed his hands feeling stronger.

"I feel as though I am peeling," Grunffi said.

Melro laughed at his new friend. "You are," the Petty Gnome said.

They started walking around the edges of the forge as lava continued bubbling to the walkway. The long bridge to the center of the forge leading to Dwarahir, being on the opposite side from the entrance to the chamber, meant the two needed to take a rather treacherous path.

Indeed, one part of the path tightened against the wall, leaving little room for dwarves of a thick build to squeeze around its ledge. Upon seeing the ledge, however, Grunffi turned to his friend, whose eyes seemed somewhat glazed, with a heavy panting breath. The clanging of Dwarahir continued.

Then, Grunffi asked, "Can you make it?"

Melro took a deep breath, and with a weighted and planned step, he stretched an arm out to the rigid wall looking for a grip and turned back.

"Grab my hand," Melro said.

Without thought, Grunffi did exactly as he was asked, grabbing the hand to follow behind him as they inched across the volcanic ravine. Halfway around the bend, the Petty Gnome's hand tried to grip the stone, instantly searing it, and causing the gnome to pull backward.

Then, Melro stumbled, and the destabilizing fright jolted his attention too fast for him to grab ahold of the wall once more, sending him tumbling down the trench.

Thankfully, Grunffi, having held the gnome's hand, pulled him up, but he did not place his companion back on the ledge. Instead, the Petty Gnome looked like the bright-eyed dwarf grabbed hold of the same spot on the wall which had previously scolded Melro, though it bore no effect.

Holding his friend in the air with one hand, Grunffi scaled a small and treacherous path brimming against the walls of the burning cavern. The sight seemed an afterthought of no concern to the gnome's eyes as they kept moving forward.

"Stop there," Melro said, pointing to the approaching ledge. It was large enough for the gnome to rest. "I cannot continue."

"What is it—" Grunffi started to ask, but then saw Melro's face. The gnome's eyes were swelling shut and the skin of his face drooped almost like age had taken hold of his features within an instant, but the sagging skin was beyond normal aging.

"I—the heat," Melro stuttered. "I can't. The heat, the forge. It's too much. It's killing me, Grunffi. I cannot."

"I'll take you—"

"No!" Melro shouted, pulling himself backward and regaining his breath. "We do not have the blessing of time in this place. Dwarahir told me of the events to follow your arrival. You must go. I will be fine so long as you rest me here. Grab me as you return to the surface. I obviously—" Melro spat a dry heaving breath. "I cannot go as far as you."

Grunffi grunted at his friend in agreement, turning to face the remaining path toward Dwarahir. Flames and lava spat and spattered like a thick paint to a rigid canvas. The volcanic bubbling rose to a contentious and frightening level as his skin seemed to burn away as liquid fire etched into his skin leaving a barren and muddied rot of hardened stone in its place.

The clanging of hammer against adamantite grew louder and more impressive with each step to the center of the forge as Dwarahir mined, digging for his lost wife. Each battering moment of clambering bent Grunffi's ears like a sharpened point against worn glass, dragging torment out from moments of creation to and forging them into eternal wailing.

"Why am I here? Why have you brought me here?" Grunffi asked.

Dwarahir turned, revealing the god's brimming teeth and harboring a silver glean.

"You are here for the same reason all dwarves are where they are," Dwarahir answered with a low, groaning voice.

Now standing directly in front of his maker, only inches from one another, heavy profuse breaths escaping him, the dwarf found himself desperately trying to refrain from attacking. With each splash of flame against his skin, though he no longer felt the pain of fire, Grunffi's rage grew as his skin diminished.

"For the sake of the craft," Dwarahir said, still smiling.

Grunffi stared into the laughing god's eyes. "I'm a tool, then?"

"Aren't we all?"

"Bent to what purpose?" Grunffi demanded.

"The only true purpose. The one of worth. The one of meaning. My own purpose."

"And your purpose is the only one of true worth, of true value, of true meaning? Why? Because you are a god? Because your need to create and then dominate trumps the survival instincts of your lesser creations?"

"Because my purpose is the one that seeks to put that lesser creation in charge of their own lives," Dwarahir said, growing more stern. "You are a craft, one of ancient making. One made long ago, and one mostly lost long ago. Your lineage remains as some of the last standing Ogres of my making from many years ago."

"Why not make more? Why not seek us out over these long years? What is the strength or reason or need of an Ogre?"

Dwarahir took a deep breath, forgetting the burden of knowledge he carried. "I can no longer create living beings, Grunffi. That tool which could be used to make life and take it from those most difficult to kill was lost to me long ago. In being cast down from my home, I eventually found myself at odds with Salaril, that malcontent god of ego. By some magic unknown to me still, he vanished that tool within a second."

"Then why not come looking for us? Why not tell us of your plan?"

"My leaving this place risked placing me under the sight of Salaril, or his damnable brother. I chose to spend my years here, digging. I thought if I could free Ada then maybe we could take on those forsaken gods."

"Were you not forsaken, like them?" Grunffi asked.

Dwarahir bowed his head and placed his hand on his sweating brow. "I suppose I was, but not for the treason of him. Not for the treason against this world. I was cast down for my love of this world, whilst Salaril was cast down for his will to dominate it."

"Then the other gods forsake us? If you were cast down for your love, and Salaril for his need to rule, that means those left seek something worse."

"Far worse," said Dwarahir.

"Ogres are meant to be your weapons against the gods?"

"Aye," the dwarven god said.

"Will you stand with your weapon, then?"

"The fight is not mine just yet. I cannot risk discovery and I stay protected by the lacing of adamantite throughout this cavern."

Grunffi did not notice upon entering, but now, gazing atop the ceiling of the forge, he saw the glimmering of unbreakable rock, adamantite, lining the cavern.

"Have the Ogre fight your battle, then? Let me solve your problem as though I have not been solving problem after problem since my making?"

"I leave you with the smallest of the problems yet," Dwarahir said.

"When my time comes to join the fight, you will see why I did not ascend at the same time as you."

"How do I fight them?"

"By becoming an Ogre," said Dwarahir.

"I thought I was an Ogre?"

"Not yet," the god said laughing as he grabbed Grunffi against his will, casting him into the lava pits and raging fires of the forge. "But you will be soon."

CHAPTER NINETEEN

A NEW AGE

"Of all the things a Warlord can hope for, this one only hopes his death brings about the end of the cruelty of magic."
— Harigamun, *Thoughts of War*

Flames swirled within Samiel's belly as he placed one foot behind the other, forming a brace, readying to smother Turmin beneath an unrelenting fire.

"Do not stop until I say so," Turmin said.

Kyra rushed to Samiel's side as heat swelled within him, burning herself as she tried to place her hand on his arm.

"There is always a cost!" Kyra yelled, as the inferno grew. "You may be the son of one the greatest Pyrosi, but even you have limits! You don't know what you're doing! You haven't had such power long enough! This isn't one of the stories we were told growing up, dammit! You're not ready!"

Samiel looked down at her, and for the first time in years, he spoke to her with an almost condescending tone. "We don't have the luxury of weighing the cost, Kyra. Step back."

Kyra's eyes caved beneath her tears, knowing he would go further than he needed to. "You don't have to prove yourself. You were always as good as the rest of us!" Her screams went unheard as Samiel was beyond her pleas.

At this point, the flames inside of Samiel took over him, and a dancing ember swayed in his pupils like a determined spark. The half-dwarf shot a winking glance at Samiel, giving small comfort to him, but Kyra missed the gesture entirely.

"The boy will be fine, Kyra. Step aside and let him show his power," Turmin said.

With remorse, Kyra stepped backward as a growing smile crept over Samiel's face. As the son of Harigamun prepared to unleash every ounce of hidden flame held within him, she watched as the dragolem overhead faced off against the God of Runes in combat with spell after spell being flung as mythical beasts of all kinds bore their talons against divinity. With each battered groan from the dragolem, Kyra accepted it would not be able to take on the god, no matter how many beasts of legend aided it.

"I will scream," said Turmin, warning Samiel. "But do not stop."

Samiel's fire coursed through every crevice, and at the moment of uncontainable force, he poured a river of flames, breathing a gust of destruction equal to that shared throughout stories of the old dragons. The blow knocked Turmin back, but the half-dwarf held his ground as fire melted his skin, sending the architect of Runefall into a painful mess of screams terrifying all who heard.

Samiel watched through the fire, seeing the architect's skin melt away as his screams grew louder, but Samiel had started to feel his own skin burning asunder. A gale of menacing embers surrounded him, separating himself from Kyra and anyone else, and suddenly Turmin's scorching agony became a shared experience between the two of them. Each of them shrieked louder than the other in a back-and-forth frustrated melting of their bodies.

Kyra attempted to help, casting every protective rune she knew. Alas, no spell could shield her from the ferocious fire enough for her to get close. She felt Samiel's flame as she approached him through each spell, one failing after another. She became forced to watch as her friend, and one of the strongest guardians known to Runefall, vaporized under an unforgiving and blazing maelstrom.

Within the vortex of fire, Samiel let out one final heart-wrenching cry under his own destruction, causing Kyra to collapse as her closest friend, and recently found love, vanished in a pile of crisp embers.

Kyra turned to the half-dwarf who stood like a gargantuan made of scorched clay. The architect lifted his axe onto his shoulder and shot a glance toward the crying woman before him, revealing a single dim-lit eye of blazing orange.

Turmin's gaze rose to the fighting dragolem and its opponent—Salaril. A great roar let out a torrential outpour of mud as Groff spat at the god, covering the field below in a thick clay as its spit missed. One of the dragolem's monstrous claws came swinging toward the god, who managed to dodge the secondary strike with a quick phasing where it had seemed to vanish from one point and appear in another. To Groff's surprise, the God of Runes bent his hands inward in such a way they seemed to be collapsing on one another before launching a seismic blast, knocking the dragolem on its backside.

As the gigantic beast came crashing to the dirt, Turmin leaped onto the dragolem and rushed up its limbs, digging his axe into its body to keep his balance as he traversed the otherworldliness of the beast's new form.

Before Groff could reclaim his stature and rise, the Architect of Runefall made it to one of the dragolem's palms and shouted into the ears of the beast.

"Cast me onto the god! I will smite him to ashes!"

Hearing the thundering roar of Turmin, Kyra rose from her feeble and crying position, cleaning her hands of the ashes of her lost... Sam. She looked upward to the god, knowing he would likely dodge the dragolem's next strike, she unsheathed her dagger and carved into the ground. She slit her palm and released blood into her freshly drawn rune. Once more, she took the blade and reopened the wound belonging to the protective rune located on her foot. It wouldn't have helped her with Samiel's flames, but it would help with what was to come.

Locking herself in place as blood drained from both wounds, Kyra pointed Dreadfall into the air toward the god and suddenly neither her, nor the god, could move; though the excruciating pain of the spell and continued blood loss for Kyra would not allow it to hold for long. *I'll die making sure you don't move a single step!*

Within those short moments of Kyra's preparation, the dragolem rose to its feet once more and Turmin, who stood in the palm of the beast, glared into the eyes of his enemy. Without much more than a moment of thought, Groff and Varelia rose a claw of the great dragolem high into the air and brought it crashing down onto the god, sending him barreling toward the earth beneath immeasurable force.

"Stupid god," said Groff.

The force of the blow crippled Salaril causing the rune god to rise slowly, but he noticed his powers fading. As he attempted to lift himself back into the air, he found he could no longer levitate and was locked in the dirt. *Fine, then. Be your own demise. He was right.*

Salaril realized his power was greatly diminished and watched as a dark and growing shadow blotted out the sun above. Kyra held the god in her grasp as she clenched and blood dripped from her nose; a growing shadow from above formed into the half-dwarf Turmin, whose charred body came crashing onto the god.

A burst of dust flooded over the battlefield like a dirty fog beneath the immense weight of Turmin and, as the dust settled, Kyra's grip on the god broke as she fell.

All who could see watched as Salaril held the blade of Turmin's axe between his hands, inches away from splitting the god's skull.

"I don't need magic, half-breed," the god spat.

Salaril pushed Turmin off him with a single attempt, knocking the Architect of Runefall back a few meters. Instantly, Turmin launched forward, rushing back to attack with another blow, but Salaril sidestepped the attempt, knocking Turmin down. In a counteroffensive, the god quickly appeared above the half-dwarf and struck his opponent with speed and fury. Those watching simply saw blurs where the god's striking fists should be. The weight and ferocity of the attack on Turmin seemed to be at a loss for the half-dwarf, but suddenly a burst of laughter erupted from beneath the continued beating.

At once, and seeming to be without effort, Turmin latched onto the god's speedy fists and held him still.

"Can a half-weapon kill a half-man?" Turmin asked.

Salaril's eyes bulged and his features shrunk to a surprised and belittled frozen frown.

"Look at me you insect of a god, and tell me, what am I?" Turmin's body hardened, his skin formed to stone, cracking in front of the god.

The flickering of the architect's eye turned a solid gold and Salaril, for the first time, felt the lost strength of an Ogre Dwarf, though a half-dwarf he was. The god sat, staring at the half-dwarf while being held in place, struggling to move.

"What am I?" Turmin shouted, spitting in the god's face.

Salaril leered at the stone-like skin, the burning blaze of gold bleeding from the architect's eye, his single orange eye, and realized what depth of despair he truly faced in the hands of this foe.

So, the weapon was made. The Price of Dwar has come.

"A half-ogre," Salaril said with a breaking and battered voice.

"Too bad there is no such thing as a half-death for your kind," Turmin cursed.

"What comes next is worse, half-breed. If you kill me, I'm all that stands between you and your true subordination to the gods above. And we both know you can't sustain this. Tell me, do your friends know what is about to happen to you?"

Kyra heard the words and tried speaking out but she couldn't even put a voice to the words she mumbled beneath the gurgling of her blood. Her body was collapsing, the spell she used against Salaril too much.

"It was a lie," Kyra wanted to tell him. "The seal was never meant to be broken." But now, Kyra would watch as the prophecy she was called to do, the false prophecy to lead her away from the defense of Runefall, was meant to do nothing more than distract her from what Salaril truly meant to happen.

Ishmael led her astray, though Kyra could not understand why. It was all becoming obvious, and terrifying for her. Tir's initial vision must have been planted by the Lord of the Dreaming Haunts who would further lead Kyra into a state of confusion when she would later meet the Lord of Dreams in his cell. The seal was never meant to be broken, not the real seal. Ishmael and his brother—Salaril—ever planned to do was lead the strongest of mages away from the city so he might be set free and the rune god could claim dominance of the land of Kaiya, and that's assuming the God of Runes had anything to do with the plan. Now, after all of the deceit, after the death of Arimeus who foresaw the coming end, she would have to watch it all happen the way it was planned. Kyra would have to watch as the last thing separating the world of Kaiya from destructive gods vanished with the death of a power hungry and insatiable god, and there was nothing she could do to stop it, not even a word she could speak. If she let loose her hold on Salaril, there was no guarantee in her weakened state she could grab ahold of him again.

Turmin gave a wry smirk before snapping back the wrists of the god. The half-dwarf peeled the god's skin from his arms like a fruit, slowly growing with excitement as torment grew with each passing scream. He cast the god onto the ground and looked to see a broken and bloody Kyra, reaching out with one single arm... drenched in tears.

"I can save you girl," he said, before turning back to the god who begged on the ground with bloody stumps and broken bones folded out toward Turmin.

Then, the half-dwarf stuck each of his hardened thumbs into the mouth of the god and slowly pulled outward, stretching his jaw. The architect plunged his fingers deeper into his throat as the god's screaming became muffled and hard. Once he felt satisfied with the pain given, the half-dwarf ripped the god's head open, wiping his hands of the blood when he'd finished.

Immediately following Salaril's death, the sky exploded in a pale-yellow burst of light and beams of white rays shot from the heavens.

Kyra knew what it was, and she could say nothing. *So, divinity falls, and mortality creeps closer to an end.*

The generals of Runefall were dead, the half-dwarf Turmin was scorched as a half-ogre, Kyra laid broken on the battlefield coughing up her own blood and unable to speak, and the once great city of Runefall—home to all written history and magic—was hidden beneath rubble.

Varelia peered across the battlefield for her father, releasing her shared connection to the dragolem once she found the body of the four-legged creature who fell from the top of Dagora.

Groff returned to his normal form, frightening all who watched the monstrous dragolem shrink to the size of a large golem. Groff and Varelia both took off toward General Toak, thinking the General of the Forest shared Varus as a champion within his body, as Groff did before.

Groff told Varelia of her father's would-be companion upon his return from the Lost Garden, as the golem was made aware of the Garden's plans to lay siege to the Stained Cathedral. Even still, neither Groff nor Varelia imagined this was what would come to pass as a result of the planned attack.

"Baba!" Varelia shouted as they reached the General's body. "Baba!" Varelia shook the carcass of Toak, but alas, the General of the Forest lay dead. No movement, not even a twitch of a muscle. The long fabled General Toak of children's tales passed from life in the Garden to death on Kaiya.

"What happens to him?" Varelia asked.

"Toak, or... " the golem sighed.

"Both! What happens to the General and my father? Are not their outcomes intertwined in this moment? Does the death of one not mean the death of another? They chose to leave the Garden of their own free will and there are portals between the two realms closing by the second!"

Varelia pointed toward the tears between worlds which connected the Lost Garden to Kaiya as a myriad of magical beasts rushed through the doorway back into their world. "It cannot be as simple now as the two worlds were joined at their death," Varelia explained. "They cannot die here and simply appear there on the other side of a doorway... can they?"

"Groff can't choose to leave and die," the golem said. "If Groff choose to leave garden and die, Groff doesn't know where Groff goes."

Varelia delved into a lashing of madness, shouting at Beliria, the Shackled Maiden, begging her to bring back her father to life, and the General, but it made no difference. The Shackled Maiden gave no answer and Groff also shed a tear, not only for the losses of Varus and the General, but also for the absence of his Maiden.

While Varelia wailed and the golem lamented, the architect rushed to

Kyra's aid who laid broken and bloody on the battlefield.

"Come with me," Turmin said, lifting her onto his shoulders as she let out a piercing cry. "The pain you feel is temporary. The pain we will deliver will be remembered."

Kyra's crippling affliction kept her from speaking, but light muscle spasms and the ferocious twitching as she struggled to point down to the ashes of Samiel made it clear to the half-dwarf what she wanted. The Architect of Runefall brought her to the ashes to lay her down next to Samiel's remains.

With strained breaths and immense suffering, Kyra moved from one elbow to the next, crawling a short but hurtful distance and stretched out her hands to Samiel's ashes. They still burned with an unforgiving heat singeing the tip of her finger and a few of her knuckles. With a calloused hand, she drew a rune into the ashes, and the half-dwarf watched as she lowered her lips to the remains. The half-dwarf could not make out the words uttered to the remains, but he recognized the rune from his time building the wall of Runefall long ago. It was a rune not seen for a long time due to its inconsistency and unpredictability—the rune of Elemental Life.

With the drawing of the rune and the collapsing of Kyra's last moment of physical strength, the architect rushed off with the girl taking her to the only place he thought might help—a healing spring but hidden in a cave years ago in case the city was found.

With the last generals of Runefall dead, Turmin took her as the stone rubble of the fallen city of Runefall burned. The city's homeless and leaderless army scattered to the far reaches of the forest.

However, beneath the smoldering remnants of the shattered city, under the broken foundations of an abandoned temple, Tir lay crushed beneath the unfathomable weight of her place of worship. As she lay there, fighting for breath and unable to move, Ishmael came to her in her final moments of life.

"Thank you, Tir," Ismael said, appearing as an apparition.

Tir knew she wasn't really there, but he was. He was touching her, grabbing her forearm, and squeezing it. She felt safe as life faded. The former prophet of Runefall cried with the ache of pillars crushing her limbs, but also from the knowing she caused its downfall.

"Why would you trick me like this? Why would you trick all of us? Was my part even necessary? Did the Runics need to leave for all of this to happen? Would you not have set Salaril free regardless? The girl didn't even need to leave!"

Tir had watched Kyra blast the temple from behind the shrine of Salaril. She heard their cries and conversations in her hidden room where she used to convene with the God of Runes. She couldn't interfere because Kyra was fulfilling what the prophecy—Tir—had communicated. How was Runefall's Scribe to know she was delivering a false message?

"The use of all was simply to show you the pawns that you are," Ishmael laughed with a horrid grimace. "Some of what happened was needed, and some was not. But all of it was what we wanted and what we made happen, or, what I made happen. You do well to remember that."

"Not all," Tir smiled and spat out blood.

"Yes," Ishamael groaned. "I suppose that the death of my brother would seem like a setback in your eyes. These last events were not the making of Salaril, they were the makings of dreams. I have plotted to dethrone Salaril's dominion over Kaiya and to break the barrier he held against the other gods from this realm. Though, it is quite prophetic you would bring this doom upon yourselves, rather than having to do it myself."

"I don't feel his presence anymore. There is nothing left for him to speak. Thus, Salaril is dead, and the wrath of your kind follows," Tir said with regret. "Why would you break the barrier? Kill your own brother? You claim to be different from them, so why welcome them to this world, to your realm?"

Tir's eyes started fading into unconsciousness and shortly death to follow, but before she could pass, Ishmael uttered one last condemnation; a final prophetic warning she could not stop.

"We would have simply made you our subjects," Ishmael laughed. "There are no gods falling to your world, those came before. They have an old enemy to contend with. Now, your world, and those false gods, will truly understand the cruelty of gods."

Tir's breath dimmed and she fell into silence. Her pain faded, and her last moment was spent wondering if Salaril ever spoke to her.

"I've seen through the eyes of a dragon and killed a Titan. How, with all of this power, can I not speak to my Baba one last time?"

— Varelia, *A Mad Journal*

CHAPTER TWENTY

MY FINAL THOUGHTS OF WAR

I t begins with lies and fire, and will end with my will to die.

Have you ever been woken in the night by the screams of one whom you love? Not empty screams, the ones following hard dreams in the night where your mind plays cruel tricks. No. Real screams. Painful screams... I should have been in bed with her.

It's been weeks now, since her death, and his taking. For the world cared so much it found me deserving of the worst attention. Be not it enough for a man to have his wife taken and killed under deceitful darkness, no, surely not. Then they took my son, my Sam.

I am starting this... *journal*, so that I may process my way out of a bad thing—many bad things. It is my hope in writing all this hate down, in expressing my living sorrow, that I will come to recognize the futility of what my heart calls me to do.

Indeed, herein there will be pages of war, of plotted bloodshed, of taking kingdoms and severing the heads of leaders across all of this land. More so, I will detail those plots. I will write down each plan, each betrayal, kinship, forced marriage, and taking of all that is good in this world—it will all be written here.

As I have to hope for justice, however, it does become determined. In my writing here is my confession. I have done and will do this thing.

If eyes are reading this, then I have failed. My press has come up short, and my wanton need to make the world burn has been stifled. I am yet unbalanced in my considerations of this possibility, for I may still accomplish it. I may bend an entire land to its knees. In all honesty, I likely will.

Therefore, should I conquer the land, and should I kill gods, end magic, and slay the divine, then I will spend my final days in a cell—if I should live. I'll have nothing worth being free for then. I have nothing worth being free for now, nothing but death.

It will start here, in my home. I will strike against my father first. He deserves it, though that is not of much importance. I will make it public, visible and loud. A pike shall do. And I'll bring Pyra to its knees. I have fought long enough and for more than enough to have more than a battalion or two at my call. It will be a rampage of a night, full of glorious celebration and hard drinking.

I'll make sure there's drinking. I'll make sure it's fun for them. For what will come after, well, they will never forgive me, not in the end.

I will spread like wildfire to the city of Vari. They won't see it coming. It will be a taking of the Mystic Eye unlike they've ever known. I'll burn their tree. That'll make them squirm.

Then the Wind Riders will fall, and Mounders thereafter. Each city, each closing triumph will be one step closer to that damn city.

And it will all mean nothing.

I do not care if the world ends when I go. I do not care if the world is held together by the very magic I mean to destroy, nor do I care if the world falls to endless war in the thereafter. I simply... do not care.

I mean for the price of my rage to be seen in the greatest burning, the harshest punishment to ever be wrought upon a deserving world. As I have ever known and will die knowing, they do utterly, completely, deserve.

I will conquer courts first. Befriend the dark ones of high places, those who move shadows like furniture. I shall commend their mischief, reward their dastardly efforts, and empower the worst of people. I will ruin that which is touched, for how else should a man treat a world that takes what is his?

The answer for cruelty is singular, a unanimous, unilateral thing which can be the only answer. It is not cruelty in return, nor is it death, nor punishment, nor pain. That which is cruel must be rewritten, wiped out—ended.

The cruelty of magic shall be retold, again, and again, and again, until the final coming of selfless beings. The world's repeated ending is the only path forward, and I will start with a lie, a small lie, and it's not even of my own making.

For, as Ishmael has told me in a recent dream:

"In a world led by dogma, full of those eager to be pious, all you need to start a war is prophecy. And it doesn't even need to be true."

About the Author

Shawn Amick is a high fantasy author, founder of the Between the Pages author community, and by day works as the director of a wireless franchise.

The escape he felt from the world of Tolkien inspired him to create his own story, full of rich lore and legend, hoping he might provide the same escape to one who sits in the corner, among the silence, hoping for a world full of splendor...much as he still does.

9 781962 739252